THE NEXT PRESIDENT IS GOING TO BE A WOMAN...

Catherine Young, the Vice President and newly-selected Democratic nominee, is surging in the polls. The race is on against GOP candidate Jerusha Hutchins, a former stewardess and blonde beauty, who is the darling of the far-right Liberty Party. But Catherine has the brilliant political strategist Zane Zarillo running her campaign, and she's looking like a winner.

Suddenly a medical emergency puts the President in the hospital and forces Catherine to act in his place... which provides the perfect opportunity for her to show her Oval Office stuff. Just as the White House is within her grasp, Catherine's romantic entanglement from decades ago comes to light. Someone is blackmailing the Vice President.

Will the American public accept a woman with a past?

#2 in Bestsellers - Kindle Political Fiction, 12/26/11

More than 50,000 copies downloaded

Praise for *Running*

5.5 out of 5 Stars – Top Pick

--Underground Book Reviews

Running exposes the fascinating high stakes world of the politician, laying bare some of their most craven desires. With a fast-paced plot and an unerring feel for the cinematic, Fitzgerald creates a thriller that will resonate not just with political junkies like myself, but the suspense-thriller reader as well. I recommend this book highly.

--J. Carson Black, best-selling author of
The Laura Cardinal Novels

When her past comes back to haunt one of the first two women who are running for President, is the election already over before it can begin? This riveting debut novel raises all sorts of questions and keeps you thinking even as you're being entertained.

--Anne Kelleher, author of *How David Met Sarah* and the
acclaimed *Shadowlands Trilogy*

Mark my words. Patrice Fitzgerald has a bestseller in the making! I read the whole novel in one sitting, it was that good. The characters were fun, the plot line fresh, and the pace of the story right on target. I look forward to reading more of Fitzgerald.

--Traci Hohenstein, best-selling author of *Burn Out*

Fitzgerald is a gifted storyteller who fully understands the value of offering a little something for everyone — action, suspense, domestic drama, romantic intrigue.... She may be seeking your vote but she's already got mine!

--John Valeri, Hartford Book Examiner

What readers are saying about *Running*

… I picked up *Running* on Saturday evening and put it down on Sunday at 8:15pm… what a ride! From the strong female lead to the charmer turned villain, the political intrigue and the romantic longing for what might have been, I was riveted to my Kindle. Trying to concentrate on some gardening I found my mind returning to the book and gave up on the roses to head back to the wonderfully rich world that Ms. Fitzgerald has created. (My boys had to make their own dinner but the dog and cat did get fed!)

… *Running* had me up till the wee hours of the morning! And, when I was not reading it, I was thinking about the characters. This book is at times funny, heartbreaking, and suspenseful.

… writing, pace, and storyline were so good that I found myself putting off other things so I could keep reading.

… it grabbed me and didn't let go. With a fast-paced plot and an unerring feel for the cinematic, Fitzgerald creates a thriller that will resonate not just with political junkies like myself, but the suspense-thriller reader as well.

… Fitzgerald did a superb job with the different points of view. The voices were powerful and distinct. Catherine grew as a woman, a mother, a candidate and an individual, and the blackmailer (I don't want to give too much away) rapidly spiraled, causing the reader to both hate and pity him while looking upon him with absolute disgust.

… Several times, all I could do was shake my head at the truth behind the scenes.

… This story is crying out for a movie adaptation, you'll mentally be casting it as you read! It breezily moves along the way to a thrilling conclusion, with never a dull moment.

… This is a great piece of writing that belongs on every bestseller list in the country.

… Can't believe this is a first novel.

… I loved this book from the very beginning!

… Just when you thought you knew where the story was going it surprised you.

… Terrific plot - I had to keep turning the pages (metaphorically speaking). The characters were intriguing and I had no idea how it would end - always a good thing when you're reading for escape! Looking forward to the next one.

… A stunning suspense novel.

… You will not be sorry to purchase this -- it's a great read.

… This book was extremely quick moving and engaging.

… My interest was sparked in the first chapter and I just got more involved in the story and characters as I read.

… This was a great read. Catherine is an immensely likeable character - somewhat reminiscent of the Geena Davis president there was a few years ago on television - very intelligent, savvy and warm.

… I absolutely LOVED this book. I picked it up for the train ride home from work and ended up staying up late into the night because I couldn't put it down. There was everything in the book you could ask for - politics, heart-felt emotion, a riveting story.

To Serene —
In praise of powerful
women!

♡ Patrice
2/15/17

Running

Patrice Fitzgerald

Cover art and design by Christopher Steininger
eFitzgerald Publishing colophon design by Ian Leslie

eFitzgerald Publishing
ISBN: 1478216263
ISBN-13: 978-1478216261

To women who are born leaders, including my daughters Kathleen and Laurie.

1

"ARE YOU READY?" The man with the headset turned to Catherine and gestured toward the stage. "It's just about your time."

"Yes. I'm ready," she said.

"Um... Mom?" Lily, standing beside her looking uncharacteristically formal in navy and pearls, was making a face. "You've got a smear of lipstick on your front teeth."

Catherine reached up and ran her index finger across her teeth. "Better?"

"Much," Lily said.

"Thank you, honey," Catherine said. She waited in the wings, feeling breathless, sensing the energy from the crowd as it sizzled around her. She couldn't see the thousands out there, but she could feel them, and she knew many more were watching live.

Her throat was dry, but she knew she would be okay. She wanted this.

The Senator from New York thrust his arm stage left and the crowd roared to its feet, making a sea of blue signs bob in tune to the applause. "Ladies and gentlemen, I give you the next President of the United States!"

"Young! Young! Young!" the people spread across the huge convention floor chanted, echoing the name on the signs. The collective force of rising bodies and breath created a human wave of excitement.

Vice President Young moved across the stage to the oak podium, striding against the current. The television lights were so bright that it was difficult to see through the shimmering circles they formed. The heat was intense. A trickle of sweat started down the Vice President's back, under the tailored jacket, sliding from hairline to collar to bra strap.

Stand up tall. Smile. Look presidential.

Whatever happened, the next President of the United States was going to be a woman.

Catherine gripped the lectern at the D.C. Convention Center and thrilled in the sensations as thousands of clapping, stomping delegates rocked the stage floor. She had been to hundreds of rallies; made hundreds of speeches. But this was the big one – the Democratic National Convention.

She was now just one election away from the White House. So close she could taste it.

And her feet were killing her.

Catherine raised her arms for quiet. She smiled and nodded, mouthing thank you's over the din. Gradually, the applause slowed and then stopped.

"Mr. Chairman, my fellow Democrats, and my fellow Americans: I thank you for honoring me with this nomination, and I humbly – and proudly – accept."

Cheers and brief applause flowed through the crowd. The people in the hall smiled back at her. Round ladies sporting crocheted vests with donkey designs, gray-haired men in straw boaters. Buttons, flags, red, white, and blue bunting. A picture of political America having a party. A party for her.

"I accept the nomination of the Democratic Party, and I look forward to charting the course for America during the next four years." Pause. Beat. Smile. "I'm glad you agree that sometimes the best man for the job is a woman."

Whoops of approval. Applause. Stamping of feet.

"Today, with this great country only now recovering from difficulties on many fronts… with our economy at last showing robust improvement… with domestic issues from health care to immigration reform revealing dramatic rifts in our national will… and with the ongoing threat of terrorism never far from our minds… we are at a turning point in our history." Catherine watched the teleprompter as the speech she had carefully honed flowed by, the words feeling familiar and right on her tongue. Her voice rose and fell in the practiced cadence of a master politician.

The rhythm of her speech moved like a current through the audience in the hall. Shoulders hunched and bodies leaned forward, rocking in agreement. Catherine's voice rang into the microphone.

"You are my brothers. You are my sisters. As your president, I will seek equality for all people – black, white, male, female, able-bodied and challenged, young and old, straight and gay."

The crowd roared its approval. The people were on their feet, nodding, clapping, cheering. She was preaching to the choir. Catherine spotted her campaign manager Zane Zarillo sitting in the third row, a smile lighting up his handsome face. A political wunderkind in his early 30's, Zane had masterminded the strategy that put her over the top. His people smarts, combined with her years of government service and the power of the incumbent president, had catapulted her onto this stage.

She gathered her voice for the big finish.

"And so it is time...for America to move forward from the greatness in our past...to the greatness in our future!"

Waves of applause washed over Catherine, and she felt the adrenalin of relief flow through her body. Her face was hot. She made herself smile despite the cotton in her mouth.

She was dying to wipe her upper lip, but the cameras were still rolling, and her children were walking onstage to stand beside her. She put her arms around Lily and her tall son Mike. Catherine felt a quick pain at the thought of how proud Paul would have been – had her husband lived to see this moment. But perhaps, somehow, he knew.

The audience was on its feet. "Happy Days Are Here Again" boomed from the speakers. Balloons drifted out of nets on the ceiling in red, white, and blue flocks. People clutched each other and swayed. Her face was blown up to a hundred times life-size on the multilevel screen behind her.

§

In the middle of the crowd, a woman looked on with a pounding heart. She had waited years for this moment. She had saved, and planned, and arranged her life so that it would happen.

And now the moment had arrived. Soon, she would be face to face with the woman she had come to see.

The Vice President of the United States.

Her palms were slick, and the pulse in her neck fluttered like a wild bird desperate to be freed.

§

Catherine Maguire Young personified the ideal presidential candidate – female pioneer category. She was tall enough, at five feet ten inches, to look powerful even when standing in the middle of a dozen dark-suited men. Her hair was a graying chestnut, and her eyes were copper. She was attractive, but not so attractive as to invite the dismissal which unusual beauty often warrants. Her clothes were impeccable. Today she wore a royal blue suit that had been custom-made to accentuate her shape without being the least bit seductive.

She was in the right place at the right time – ten years a respected member of Congress with a record as a fiscal moderate and social liberal, now a well-liked Vice President under a popular Democrat who had presided over eight fairly tumultuous years which had ended in prosperity. A 56-year-old widow with two grown children, Catherine was coming to political maturity at a watershed moment when the country was ready to accept a woman in the top spot.

Catherine made her way slowly through the tight clusters of people eager to shake her hand after the acceptance speech. She kept moving, smiling, clasping the reaching hands.

Keeping a close eye on the hand shakers were the ever-present Secret Service agents, who stayed directly behind her shoulders. She could hear their quiet reports as they whispered her position into the tiny microphones hidden at their wrists. "Firebird is in the hall. Dense crowd conditions." Firebird was her code name, which made her smile.

Finally she and the agents reached Zane in the middle of the smaller room where they were having a reception for invited guests. She put her arms around his tall frame and gave him a hug. Usually she was cautious about physical demonstrations. As a woman running for a job that had so far been filled only by men, she watched every public move. But tonight was so full of the sweet taste of victory that she didn't care.

"Zane. We did it." Up this close, she could smell his cologne, and feel the richness of the fabric in his suit.

"You were brilliant, Madam Vice President," he said. If he was surprised by the hug, he didn't show it.

"I couldn't have done it without your help, Zane," she said.

"It's been a pleasure and an honor. And it will be a particular thrill to be able to say I worked for the first woman to claim the Oval Office as her own."

Catherine grinned. "That would be one fine day, wouldn't it?"

"It will be one fine day," Zane said, his voice thick.

A small group of campaign staffers had gathered around them. Zane gazed down at the device in his hand and spoke in the just-between-us tone of teammates huddling in the middle of a game. "Our poll numbers are in good shape. You're twelve points ahead of Jerusha Hutchins, and that's after the Republicans got their convention bump."

Catherine turned to him, shaking her head. "Zane, were you watching the numbers on your iPhone the whole time I was making the speech?"

"Of course not... I waited until the balloons dropped." He smiled like a man who knew his smile was irresistible.

Camilla Jamestone, who helped with logistics for the campaign throughout the country, pushed a strand of long red hair behind her shoulder as she leaned over to see the screen. "Governor Hutchins's numbers keep moving, I see."

"Every day," Zane answered. "Their convention got wall-to-wall coverage in the political blogs, and the video of Hutchins's nomination speech has gone viral. Over ten million hits, as of this morning. You know how they love to cover her – the more provocative the better."

Catherine nodded. "How does she find time to do all that Facebooking… that Twittering?"

"Oh, she doesn't do it all herself," Zane said. "She has professionals to do it."

"There are professional Twitterers…?" Catherine smiled. "Does that make them twits?"

Zane laughed, and Camilla leaned in for privacy.

"Last I saw, her positives were high but her negatives were higher," said Camilla. "Too many people find her not sufficiently serious to consider as presidential material. And I think they're in the majority."

"Exactly. She went up, but now she's down again," Zane said, keeping his voice low. "Hutchins's numbers are tracking at 36 percent among those likely to vote. She's entertaining – but not much else. If she weren't married to Quigley Hutchins, with his evangelical power base, she wouldn't be the governor of Georgia."

Camilla shook her head. "I don't know how she finds the time. My lord, the woman has eight children. One would think she has her hands full without taking on a presidential campaign." She reached for a glass of champagne as it floated by on a tray. "Word is that Reverend Hutchins is the mastermind behind her candidacy – which I can believe, because this kind of strategy is clearly not coming from a political neophyte like Jerusha."

Zane nodded. "Quigley's planning to be the power behind the throne. With Jerusha as the new face of the GOP, the Republicans figure they've reinvigorated their base and aligned themselves with the Liberty Party folks at the same time."

Catherine smiled. "And a very pretty face it is. Although, if Quigley Hutchins thought he could get elected, he'd probably be running himself."

"You've got that right. He's a good ol' boy from way back." Zane gave one more glance at the iPhone and tucked it into his pocket, then nodded toward the harsh brightness of the news lights at the side of the room. A reporter was speaking into a mobile camera with the crowd as backdrop. "Your acceptance speech tonight will lead the evening news, and be the main topic online," Zane said. "Based on past years, we can count on a post-Convention bump of at least five percentage points."

A young woman with long black hair stepped out of the crowd to stand beside Zane. Her skin was mocha-colored and her eyes were an arresting gold. She wore a black dress that skimmed her tall, youthful body with perfectly respectable but utterly alluring understatement.

"Ah...here you are," Zane said. "Madam Vice President, may I present my friend Maria Flores-Jenkins. She's been looking forward to meeting you. Maria, this is the Vice President."

"It is an honor to make your acquaintance," Maria said. She had a melodious voice with a gentle accent and spoke in precise but cautious English.

Catherine held out her hand. There was a painful vulnerability about the young woman, who gazed at her with unusual golden eyes for a long moment before looking away.

"Maria's from Brazil," Zane said. "She's the assistant to the Cultural Attache at the Brazilian Embassy."

He tucked the exotic beauty's arm under his own, making it clear that she was more than simply a friend. Catherine hadn't missed the fact that women found Zane attractive – it was easy to see why – but he seemed to cycle through companions rather quickly. And he had rarely invited a woman along to one of her political events. There must be something special about this one.

"I'm pleased to meet you, Maria. Have you been in this country long?"

"For three months only," Maria said.

"And have you been enjoying Washington?" Catherine asked.

"She has been since she met me last month," Zane said, grinning at his beautiful companion.

§

Zane beeped the lock on his silver Porsche Panamera, opened the door, and slid in. Leaning back and loosening his tie, he glanced in the rearview mirror and jumped when he saw a familiar face. "Jesus, Devon, what the hell are you doing here? I just about – "

"Zane. How lovely to see you again."

Zane felt fear ping at the top of his skull. Devon, wearing his usual elegant clothes and perfectly lightened hair, was covering his right hand with his jacket and the bulge underneath it looked dangerous.

"The boss says it's time for you to pay up, Zane dear." Despite the fluorescent smile, the voice was cold and the eyes were even colder. "I regret to say that you are overdue."

"What? Now?"

"Indeed. Now."

"Devon, I can pay with no problem after the election. My job prospects with the new administration – "

"The boss is not concerned about your job prospects. It's due now, as you well know. A hundred thousand bucks. I am informed that you will be granted one more week."

"A week? You're joking. I can't raise that in a week."

"Actually, Zane darling, no. I don't joke." A flat laugh. "But – "

"You'll find it somewhere, I am quite sure. An intelligent, educated man like you."

"Where am I going to get a hundred thou in a week?"

"That is a challenge, I agree. But you'd better get right on it. Otherwise, you won't be around to see who wins the election." A saccharine grin preceded the click of the door opening, and Devon was gone.

Zane felt his stomach start to do sit-ups. What the hell was he going to do? A hundred thousand dollars? It couldn't be that much.

He had borrowed a little petty cash from Catherine's ad budget a while his credit card was temporarily maxed out. It had added up so fast. He would pay it back, of course. Zane wasn't a thief. It was tough to cover the damn lease payments on the Porsche. And then he spent a bit on coke, not much really – just enough to keep the edge off while he was working 24/7. He would quit just as soon as the campaign was over…he'd kicked it before, and he could do it again. But suddenly a few thousand dollars had become twenty, and twenty had turned into fifty plus.

The man Devon worked for, a lobbyist who was definitely a fan of Catherine's, had offered him cash, discreet and quick. Zane knew he could pay it off, once the campaign was won. Just not yet! Not now.

The voice in his head that was always mocking him spoke up again.

You're a fraud. They think you're smart, but you know the truth. Every step higher you go, you just make the fall harder. And this time, when they catch on to you....

Zane put his hands over his ears to stop the voice. He needed some coke. But not here. The Secret Service was all over the place. He had to be very careful. They weren't stupid. He had to play the part just right.

Man, he was tired. Up every night till 3:00 a.m. Meetings, strategy, ads, press releases. He shoved the car into gear and straightened his tie. Play the part, Zane.

Zane Zarillo, part of the first generation of Zarillo's to be born in this country, the first to graduate from Harvard Business School and certainly the first to work on a presidential campaign, was a symbol of success for his family and for his community. He was counting on a plum spot after Catherine was elected. And after that, the rest of his life should flow in predictably wealthy and prestigious directions. This campaign was his ticket to the big time.

He was damned if a stupid thing like the loan was going to wreck his future.

It was just his luck. He was the kind of guy who always did things for other people – it was Catherine he was protecting when he borrowed the money from these sleazoids – so that no one would point any fingers when her war chest was missing funds. Well, he wasn't going to be the fall guy.

His stomach lurched, and he looked for a spot to pull off the road. Bile washed his throat and tasted like fear.

Zane jerked the wheel toward the shoulder and shoved the car door open just in time to lose the Democrats' fine pre-speech supper into the dirt beside the road.

2

CATHERINE FLOPPED DOWN on the worn leather couch in a very unpresidential way, flinging her sensible navy pumps into the air one by one. She lifted her hips off the cushion to shimmy out of her pantyhose, wondering if the new code of bare legs was ever going to make it all the way up the food chain to the executive branch.

Wiggling her toes, she gave a sigh and punched the remote. The large blonde hair of Jerusha Hutchins filled the TV screen and her perky voice filled the room.

"It's more of the same, isn't it? We've had the Democrat Party...yes...eight years now. Where are we? I ask y'all. Taxing and spending, the usual. Folks barely making it. Me and my family...the ten of us...beautiful children... so many...and we are proud! Being fruitful and multiplying. Celebrating the culture of life. The country – y'all know it – going in the wrong direction!" The crowd cheered, and Jerusha nodded vigorously, her arms spread.

"Going away from what our forefathers – the God-fearing founders of this nation – fought for. The American people – the good people, the Americans from way back – have had enough. We have the memento...the momento... it's our moment now! And we're takin' the country back! Am I right, y'all?"

The phone rang, and Catherine hit the mute button on the television.

"Catherine? Are you still up?"

"Nancy. Yes, I'm still up. Winding down from the convention. I wanted to veg out in front of the TV, but guess who's on sharing her latest wisdom?"

"From your tone of voice, I'm going to go with Jerusha Hutchins."

"Correct." Catherine punched the power button and the television went dark.

"Listen, I wouldn't waste your energy worrying about her," Nancy said. "She's not in your league in terms of political experience."

"Unfortunately, a lot of people seem to like that lack of experience these days."

"Well, a lot of people are fools. She's only governor because her husband wanted a puppet so that he could pull the strings. I mean, come on Catherine – the woman doesn't even seem to think clearly – she sure can't string a coherent sentence together. How could she run the country?"

"Well, I don't think she could. And that's what I'm worried about. I don't want to be any part of giving her that chance."

"By the way, you were brilliant tonight, you know."

"Thank you, Nancy. It felt good." Catherine reached down and massaged her sore feet. "It was pretty cool being up there."

"Well, get used to it. You've got a lot of campaigning ahead of you."

Catherine groaned. "Don't remind me. Ten straight weeks of talking and smiling and shaking hands before Election Day. I'm off to California tomorrow – L.A., San Fran, and then…another stop somewhere. Nevada? I don't know." She laughed and switched the phone to her other ear, removing an earring as she did so. "And somehow I still have to find time for my day job."

"Hey – I don't want to hear you complain…you get to travel around in a private jet. Not like us little people who have to wait in endless lines."

"It's not as glamorous as it seems, Nance, believe me."

"Oh yeah, I pity you, surrounded by all those hot young Secret Service guys…."

"Good night, Nancy. You'll have to keep your Secret Service agent fantasies to yourself. I have to work with them!"

§

Zane roared his Porsche down the narrow Georgetown streets and pulled up tight against the curb, startling a couple strolling arm in arm on the warm August evening. He led Maria to the door and took out his key, pushing it in and turning the lock with an angry shove.

The Federalist entrance way and ornate balustrades of his historic row house normally gave him a rush of pride – knowing that he lived in a building with which his ancestors would have been awed – but tonight he felt nothing but anxiety. "I'll be in the bathroom," he said.

He looked at himself in the mirror over the sink and noted with a grimace that there was a spot on the $180 Hermes tie bought new for tonight's speech. At least the tie – a perfect reminder of where the damn cash had gone – had been unsullied when he gave his comments on the candidate to reporters from CNN and NBC. He untied it and tossed it in the wastebasket, then turned back to the mirror and gave himself a wide smile, inspecting his teeth for food.

Zane was a handsome man, and he knew it. He looked as good in nothing but a smile as he did in a thousand dollar suit. His body was tall and lithe, and he carried himself in a way that took a little something from both Exeter and the seamier side of New Jersey.

His face featured dark, amused eyes, generous lips, and a smile that flashed across a room straight to any desired target. Zane had no trouble finding companionship when he wanted it.

He opened the medicine cabinet and took out his emergency stash of cocaine. He knew Maria didn't approve, so he didn't bother asking her to join him. He set up a small private snort. If he had ever needed it, tonight was the night. That surprise visit from Devon had jangled his nerves.

Whoosh. Cleared his head right up.

Zane splashed cold water on his face and dried it off with a towel. He felt pretty damn good. Pushing the bathroom door open, he saw Maria sitting in the living room.

"Maria." He walked over to her. His stomach muscles ached from their earlier vomitous spasms. "I hope you've forgiven me for sending you home from the reception on your own. I had something to attend to. I'm really sorry. But I'll make it up to you."

"It is okay." She turned to him with the shimmering eyes that had first bewitched him at an Embassy Row party six weeks ago. Tonight, though, there was something hidden in them.

"You pissed at me for some reason?" he asked.

"No. Why?"

"You've been so quiet since we left the convention."

"I am just...thinking," she said, pushing her curly dark hair behind her shoulder.

"Are you thinking about me?" His libido had kicked into high gear and he was eager for the pleasures in store.

"Perhaps," Maria answered. She looked at him with a coy smile that was at the same time tentative. Maria's politically-connected family in Brazil had kept her carefully sheltered, and sometimes it was easy to see that her youth had been spent in convent schools. From what she said, he didn't think he was her first man, but he figured he was on a very short list.

She was a sweetheart; an innocent. Sometimes Zane thought she might be, finally, the woman he could fall hard for. But not right now – not in the middle of a campaign, and with everything else that was going on in his life. He knew he owed Maria more of his time and attention. He also knew she would have to wait until after the election to get more of anything from him.

They walked together into the bedroom. The elaborate green and gold swags over the windows matched the linens on the unmade king-size bed, whose tasseled pillows lay in disarray on the floor. Expensive clothes were draped over every available surface. Papers and books were piled against the wall.

Zane peeled Maria's clothes off slowly while kissing her warm brown neck. She had a magnificent body, well-matched in height to his, and the combination of the coke and her nakedness had an instant effect on him. He dropped his pants to the floor and pulled her down on the bed, devouring her mouth with kisses. Her hair was so long that its curly blackness covered her breasts, and Zane pushed long strands aside to find her nipples. He lapped at them hungrily, feeling his hardness against the soft skin of her leg.

"God, I want you," he said, his right hand running down the length of her smoothly undulating hip.

He swung his body over Maria's and slid into her, feeling her sweetness wrap around him. Her honey skin had a warm fragrance and the sensation of her hips moving under his drove him to an exquisite and torturous pleasure.

Zane gave a final push. "Oh Jesus," he said, almost a moan. "Oh yes."

He rolled off Maria. "Thanks, baby. You're incredible."

§

Maria lay beside Zane as he slept, her eyes wide open, hugging the sheet across her breasts.

Her thoughts were a wild tangle of wishes, dreams, disappointment, anger. She had stood directly in front of the Vice President – Catherine – and looked into the older woman's eyes. And she had seen...what?

Nothing.

Nothing beyond polite interest. A bright smile, genuine but preoccupied. A direct look that could have passed for sincere, but was the same look bestowed on every potential voter. Catherine had shown her, in short, her politician's face.

And what had she expected?

A small sob escaped her. Zane turned his head on the pillow, looking groggy and surprised.

"What. What is it?" he asked.

"Nothing. It is nothing." She was crying now, rivulets running down beside her eyes, which were squeezed closed to no avail.

"Nothing? What's going on?"

"I...I am sorry."

"Maria. What the hell is going on? Was it the coke?"

"What coke? No. No. This has nothing to do with you."

"Well, either tell me, or let me go to sleep. I've had a hell of a day."

More sobs escaped her. She felt foolish, but she couldn't stop. Great gulps of air alternated with yearning pain that came out as cries. Briefly, she thought of ways to end the pain. A speeding car. A bullet. A razor.

It was too much. All the planning. All the waiting. All the hope, building up slowly over the last four years.

Everything leading up to meeting Catherine. And now this. This feeling of...nothingness.

"I can't help you, Maria, if you don't tell me what's wrong."

Should she tell Zane? Could she trust him?

Of course she could trust him. He loved her. A man who would introduce her to his colleagues and to the Vice President of the United States, making it very clear that they were a couple – surely even in America this meant something.

He would ask her to marry him, at some appropriate point. When things slowed down for him with his whirlwind job. It was only a matter of time.

Zane passed her a box of Kleenex and she soaked up some of the tears. With difficulty, she choked off the sobs that still pounded deep in her rib cage.

He sat up. "Come here." He got another tissue and wiped the tears. He took her in his arms. The warmth of his embrace squeezed more tears out.

"Sugar – what is this?" he asked. "This isn't like you...you're my hot Brazilian babe. The most beautiful girl at every party. I've never seen you cry."

"That is because you do not really know me. You do not know me at all." She covered her face with her hands.

"Okay, then. Tell me. What don't I know about you that would make you cry?" Zane kissed her neck. "Tell me, baby."

"No, I…it is nothing. I just…do you love me?"

Zane pulled away for a moment and looked at her, sleepy but smiling. "Do I love you, Maria? Baby, don't I love you over and over?" He ran his hand down her neck and lowered the sheets to expose her breasts. "Let me show you just how much I love you."

3

CATHERINE WATCHED THE clouds go by the windows as the jet rose with a powerful roar. Nancy was right about one thing – travel on a private plane with door-to-door service and personal security was a lot easier than flying commercial. Not to mention the convenience of being able to take off on her own schedule.

Outside of the private flying office she had created for herself sat the press entourage that came along for the ride. There was also Zane, Camilla, and a couple of other folks who travelled with her regularly. Now that the nominating convention was behind them, the campaign was in full swing, and her first big speeches would all be on the West Coast.

Looking down at the draft on the laptop in front of her, she thought about the challenge of saying something both true and interesting – one of the reasons the Liberty Party got so much attention was simply that it was something new. New and rowdy and out of control much of the time. But one couldn't deny that it was better fodder for the pundits than talking about the same old speeches being given by the Democrats and the Republicans. And now that the Liberty Party had thrown its support behind Governor Jerusha Hutchins, they were in the bigtime.

Catherine flipped her browser over to the front page of the Buffington Beast. There she was, smiling on the stage of the Convention Center with Lily and Mike on either side of her as hundreds of balloons rained down around them.

Not a bad photo, she thought. Thanks to the talents of her stylist, Chloe, who managed to cover up a multitude of middle-aged lines and shadows with some kind of cosmetic magic. But her skirt was wrinkled – it was fine behind the podium, and not so fine once she got out into the middle of the stage.

Catherine skimmed the article about the reaction from the GOP and the Liberty Party to the Democratic convention. Senator Everard Lutfisk of Minnesota, one of the most supremely boring men in America, had said that the Democrat message was "liberal big government politics as usual – tax and spend."

Jerusha Hutchins was in fine form. She was just off a national book tour for her populist tome, "The Christian Roots of American Freedom." She was quoted as saying that, "the real people are waking up…as they wake up to what is really going on here. And as my wise husband, the Reverend Hutchins, often says, the American government is through the people, by the people, and with…of the people of America."

Catherine wondered for a moment if Hutchins knew that the statement – or the correct version of it, anyway – wasn't original with her husband.

One of the BuffBeast columnists remarked on the same thing, musing about whether the self-titled "Georgia Peach Pickers" who followed Jerusha had ever read the Gettysburg Address.

Catherine looked up as she heard a knock. "Come on in."

It was Camilla. "Madam Vice President, I wanted to talk to you about the schedule…" she trailed off and her eyes focused on the windows beside Catherine.

"Oh my God," Catherine said, following Camilla's gaze and gasping as she saw the military jet flying close beside them. "I hope that's some kind of exercise…"

Suddenly they could feel their jet take a wide swing around. Camilla grabbed the wall to steady herself, and the laptop slid toward Catherine.

She turned to her right and hit the intercom button beside her that connected with the cockpit. "This is the Vice President. What's going on?"

"We've been ordered to turn the plane around, Madam Vice President. I apologize for the sudden movement –"

Catherine heard a quick knock and then Zane appeared at the door, "The President has been rushed to the hospital —"

The phone rang and Catherine picked it up. "Madam Vice President, it's Jeffrey."

She recognized the voice of the President's Chief of Staff, Jeffrey Silverstein. "What's happening, Jeffrey?"

"President Drummond is going into emergency surgery at the Naval Medical Center. It looks like his appendix may have burst. He's about to be sedated. We're not sure how long he'll be on the table or how serious it is, but he may be under for a while."

Catherine looked at the faces around her on the plane, which now included Zane, Camilla, and several other staff members. In the hall she could see a gaggle of reporters craning their necks to look through the open door. She made a quick decision and punched the speaker button on the phone so that everyone could hear what was going on.

"There will be a temporary transfer of executive powers on an emergency basis while the President is being operated on," Silverstein's voice continued over the speaker. Catherine could hear the Chief of Staff take a careful breath.

"Madam Vice President, you are now the Acting President of the United States."

4

"THANK YOU, JEFFREY," Catherine said as she looked up at the people around her. She put down the phone. After a collective intake of breath, there was a quick retreat of the press in the hallway, as phones, laptops and notebooks were all suddenly put into service.

"So we're turning around," Catherine said, almost to herself. "Obviously," she continued, gesturing toward the jet outside the window, and noting that the sun was now streaming into this side of the plane.

Zane spoke up. "Madam Vice President – should I send in Chloe for hair and makeup?"

Catherine looked up at him and spoke sharply. "Would that be the first question you'd ask if I were Mr. Vice President instead of Madam?"

"Um…no, probably not." Zane looked more annoyed than abashed.

"I think we have more important things to worry about than my hair. Like how long I'll be acting president – and whether I might have to make some real decisions while the President is unable to attend to his duties."

For a moment Catherine let herself feel the full weight of the responsibility she suddenly held. From long habit she took the time to examine her reactions. Fear. Excitement. Surprise. Curiosity. And pride.

Then she brushed it off. This was mostly a formality. The President might well be awake and recuperating by the time she got back to her desk. Which she certainly hoped he was, she thought to herself, quickly editing any internal thrill. For Catherine to really have the power of the presidency, she would have to keep campaigning and make her own opportunities.

She realized that Zane and Camilla were still looking at her. "Sorry, Zane. I know I snapped at you..." Catherine sighed. "Having established that there are more important things for the Acting President to worry about than her hair, please do have Chloe come in. She can fluff it up a bit. Oh, and Camilla, will you check the weather in D.C.? If it's still windy, I'll let her spray it."

Shaking her head, she continued, "Other than that, I'm just going to put on some fresh lipstick. Now, if you'll excuse me..."

She headed for the small bathroom as Camilla and Zane left, and after she shut the door and latched it, she leaned against the chilly metal wall for just a moment. She hadn't expected this. Suddenly it occurred to her that the President could actually be in danger. She remembered from Paul's medical training, years ago, that a burst appendix was a serious matter. During his residency, he had seen an otherwise healthy young man die fast as toxins entered his body.

Catherine said a quick prayer for her friend, the President. It was important for the whole country, not just her, that he recuperate quickly.

As she looked at herself in the bathroom mirror, she realized she didn't even have a lipstick with her. Like the Queen of England, high-level women politicians carried neither cash nor cosmetics, leaving that to handlers or artfully placed pockets. It would never do to be photographed carrying around a big old purse like everyone's grandmother...or like the Queen.

But Catherine definitely needed lipstick. She needed more than lipstick. There would be a gazillion reporters on the tarmac when she landed as the first woman to be the chief executive of the United States — even temporarily.

She opened the door and saw Camilla and Chloe standing there. "Why does Jerusha Hutchins have to be so damn beautiful?" she asked to no one in particular.

"Well, she was a stewardess – excuse me, a flight attendant – before she got married," answered Chloe.

Catherine glanced down at her laptop, still open to the BuffBeast. A glaring new headline, all in red, met her eyes: "Emergency Surgery for Drummond. Catherine Young, Acting President, First Woman Ever."

The Twitter feed below the headline revealed tweets both elated – "Girls are in charge for a change!" and snarky – "I bet this is all a set-up to make her look more presidential."

Camilla looked down at the screen. Jerry Rash, the right-wing provacateur, had proclaimed, "This is the first step toward martial law. Nazi-time ahead!"

"My lord, but he's a nitwit, isn't he?"

In Camilla's British accent the comment sounded like something out of Monty Python, and Catherine found herself laughing. "This is going to be a circus, I'm afraid," she said, "and it's only just beginning."

She sat down and Chloe started on her hair, adding hot rollers and then setting out her makeup case.

"Madam Vice President, you do realize that your arrival in D.C. will be carried worldwide," Camilla said.

Catherine nodded. "How long before we land again?"

"About an hour, I think."

Catherine leaned over to the intercom and pushed a button. "Zane, can you ask Sarah to bring me my red suit, please?"

A moment later Sarah, her personal assistant, walked in carrying a garment bag. "Red? Really?" she asked.

"If I'm going to be on TV screens all over the world as the first woman 'acting' president of the United States, I want to come out of this plane blazing. Power and confidence. The mantle of leadership and all of that. I certainly don't want to look timid – or scared. After all, I'm asking the country to give me this job permanently."

"Red it is, Madam Vice President. Or Madam Acting President. A bold choice."

Catherine pushed the intercom again. "Zane, could you come in here? I'm going to have to come up with some words. We need to discuss the appropriate demeanor."

She reached up for a moment to run her fingers through her hair, and then realized that there were rollers in her way. Chloe was trying to put on some blush, but Catherine waved her away for a moment as Zane appeared in the doorway carrying his laptop, and then closed the door on the reporters outside.

"So what's our basic message here, Madam Vice President?" Zane settled into a seat across from her and opened the laptop.

"The first point to make is about our concern for the health and well-being of the President. And of course I need to sound suitably gracious about the honor of serving in this temporary position. But I also have to grab the chance to look like I'm ready, willing, and able to be president of the United States in my own right."

Catherine smiled at Zane as he started typing.

"Because I am."

§

Maria walked down the hallway of the Brazilian Embassy, the plush red carpet softening the impact of her tall heels. As she passed a door to her right, she heard excited voices raised and saw five of her colleagues gathered around a screen.

She stepped into the room.

"What is going on?"

Her friend Ester turned around and gestured her over to the laptop. "The American president is in the hospital. He handed over the government to the Vice President."

"Temporarily," said Rodrigo, one of the interns. "It's not like a long-term thing. Just until he's out of the hospital."

"Unless he dies," said Ester. "His appendix burst, that's pretty serious, no?"

Maria looked at the photo of the Vice President on the screen and the headline underneath it: "Catherine Young, First Woman Acting President of the United States."

The hair on the back of her neck rose and she felt a tingling along her spine.

§

Catherine stood at the top of the flight stairs for just a moment before descending from the plane. It was important to get her bearings. Surrounding the aircraft was a phalanx of reporters, television cameras, and satellite vans.

She resisted the automatic urge to smile. This wasn't a campaign stop. This was a serious moment for the country.

Carefully maneuvering down the steps, she stopped at the bank of microphones and makeshift podium that had been set up on the tarmac. Though the sun was still high in the sky, at 6:00 on a late summer evening, bright lights were pointed at her face so that the cameras could see every detail. For a moment she thought about the Nixon-Kennedy debates, her first political memory, and worried that she would sweat.

Well, what if she did? It was a moment for sweating. The President was in surgery, and it was her job to reassure the country.

She tried to swallow before speaking, and for an instant, she couldn't. If she won the election, would she feel like this? A little tongue-tied, a little petrified, knowing how much of the world was listening?

She swallowed.

"I want to send a message to the people of the United States, and to the world." She could hear that her words were going into the microphones, but there was no resonance in the outside air, as there would have been indoors. Catherine wondered if she could be heard. For just a moment, she had the surreal sensation that this was a dream about being President of the United States. A dream from which she would awaken any moment, her alarm buzzing beside her bed, her young children, tousle-haired, climbing in beside her.

Then she blinked, and it was all real again. Real but nearly unbelievable.

She opened her mouth and continued speaking the words that she and Zane had prepared. "The operations of the United States government are undisturbed and are completely secure, and will remain so until President Drummond is able to resume his duties, which I am certain will be very soon.

"He is getting the best of care at the National Naval Medical Center in Bethesda, and is likely to be recuperating comfortably as early as tomorrow. As is provided in Amendment 25 to our Constitution, the President has empowered me – an assignment which I accept as a great honor and with considerable humility – to act in his stead should the need arise during the brief time that he is incapacitated.

"I know that all Americans join me tonight in wishing President Drummond a speedy recovery and a quick return to his duties as chief executive."

As planned, Catherine turned away from the microphones swiftly just as the expected barrage of questions arose from the assembled reporters. She had taken only two steps when she heard a male voice shouting out, "Vice President Young, what do you think of Jerry Rash's claim that you and President Drummond cooked up this scheme to enhance your chances of being elected?"

A visceral shot of anger made Catherine turn back. Her calmer side said to ignore him, but some instinct wouldn't let it go.

Stepping back up to the microphones, hearing the click and whir of cameras and knowing that she would be seeing photographs of her angry face tomorrow, Catherine faced the reporter who had asked the question.

"Any suggestion that this administration would cynically manipulate the political process – and potentially put this country in danger – through such a stunt, is unworthy of a loyal American, and is the product of a paranoid and delusional mind."

Catherine turned on her heel and walked toward the waiting limousines.

She wondered whether she was going to regret that in the morning.

5

CATHERINE SAT ACROSS from Silverstein in the limo, with Zane at her side.

"So how is the President?" she asked, finally getting a private moment with his Chief of Staff.

Silverstein, a man with a heavy beard and little hair, ran his hands through what was left of it. "It's very serious, Madam Vice President" he said. "I'm sorry to say that it looks like they got it just in time. I hope he'll be all right."

"Oh my God," Catherine said. "I – what is the prognosis?"

"Apparently the President has been in pain for several days. He mentioned it to no one – not even the First Lady – but she saw him taking handfuls of Tums, and asked him what was going on. He didn't want to spend time being examined – you know how stubborn he can be."

Catherine nodded, smiling ruefully.

"When one of the kitchen staff mentioned to Mrs. Drummond that his midday meal was coming back barely touched, she insisted that he have the White House physician look at him. And by the time that happened, he could barely stand from the pain. So they took him by helicopter to the Naval Center, and got him on the table – as far as I understand, it had burst."

Catherine felt her throat tighten. "But he's not –"

"He's got the best doctors in the world for this," Silverstein said, lifting his hands from his knees as though to calm her. "They've assured us that he should be fine – but with a burst appendix, the recovery can be long and has to be very carefully monitored."

"So how long?" Zane asked. "Obviously the Vice President has a campaign that has to be run at the same time."

Catherine turned to him, knowing that her disapproval would sting, and not caring. It was rare for Zane to be so tin-eared. "Zane, I think we have more critical things to worry about at his point. My campaign can wait while the President needs me. Not to mention the country."

"Of course, Madam Vice President," Zane said, though he looked a bit peeved. "I completely agree that the country needs you. And that's why the campaign must go on."

She raised her eyebrows, then decided not to press the point until they were in private. Turning her attention to Silverstein, she asked, "So – can you tell me what's on the President's agenda that I'll need to cover? And how long do you think he'll be laid up... is there a prognosis for recovery?"

Silverstein nodded. "I think we're probably looking at two or three days at the least, before he's able to take back his duties."

He lifted the heavy leather briefcase on the limo floor and opened it. "First, I should give you a copy of this, which was faxed to the Speaker of the House and the president pro tempore of the Senate just an hour ago."

Silverstein handed Catherine a short letter signed with the President's typical scrawl. If he was in pain when he signed it, his signature didn't reveal any lack of will.

"This letter shall constitute my written declaration, according to the tenets of Section 3 of the 25th Amendment to the Constitution, that I am presently unable to discharge the Constitutional powers and duties of the office of the president of the United States, and I hereby appoint Vice President Catherine Maguire Young to execute said powers and duties until I am able to resume doing so."

§

Zane jerked to a stop at the corner of M Street and Wisconsin, fuming at the red light that delayed him from getting home – and getting to his stash of coke. He knew for sure now that he was getting in deep again. Just like the last time…was it already six years ago? Someone had tipped one of his colleagues off about his little addiction, and he'd been forced to go to the clinic and wean himself off.

Catherine knew all about it, of course. It had never been public knowledge on a large scale, but a lot of the folks Zane worked with now knew that he used to have a coke problem. Sometimes it seemed that it gave him a little frisson of danger – the druggy past proved he wasn't just a suit, but had a street life apart from that of most Capitol Hill power brokers. Which he did. He'd had a street life long before he acquired the pinstripes and the Harvard degree.

And Zane damn well knew it wasn't a good thing for him to be slipping back into bad habits.

To hell with it. With thoughts of Devon showing up around any corner – or in his backseat – Zane needed something to keep him going, and he'd worry about the consequences later.

His phone sounded, and he pulled it out of his pocket while revving the Porsche's motor. It was Maria.

"Zane," she said. "I need to see you."

"Now, baby? I've got some stuff to do at home…."

"I really…need you. You know?" Somehow she had turned her voice into that sexy purr he couldn't resist.

Well, damn. If a man couldn't come when a woman like Maria gave him a booty call, he wasn't much of a man.

"Gimme a half hour, and I'll be there, sugar."

"Thank you Zane. I'll leave the door unlocked. If you don't see me, look for me in the shower."

He gunned the motor and roared toward his house for what he knew was waiting there. Now he had two things to look forward to.

Tomorrow he would think about his big problem. Devon and the money. But for tonight, he would enjoy his blow, his girl, and the knowledge that his boss was – at least temporarily – President of the United States.

And somehow Zane was going to make that unexpected turn of events into the campaign opportunity that would put her candidacy over the top..

6

CATHERINE WALKED DOWN the hall in the West Wing of the White House, her assistant Lorraine trotting beside her in order to keep pace. There was a quiet formality, and a sense of history, in this hallway. Deep carpets, oil paintings, extravagant swoops and drapes around each window. The early morning sun slanted along the floor and gave the colors a special richness.

"So how are we doing this, Lorraine? What's on the schedule for today – now that I'm covering for the President?" Catherine nodded hello as they passed two Secret Service agents, wires snaking out of their collars, walking in the other direction.

"Well, Madam Vice President, one thing that's convenient, I suppose, is that you were supposed to be in California today, so you had nothing on your own agenda locally. Most of your new schedule will involve handling President Drummond's routine matters. In twenty minutes, you have a meeting with Mr. Leo and Mr. Jennings from the UAW, which was on the President's schedule, and then at 11:30 the limo will take you to a luncheon with the Washington chapter of the NAACP. Zane says you'll simply deliver one of the new campaign speeches you approved last week, with a customized finale Janet is typing up right now."

Lorraine was a short black woman with carefully coiffed hair wearing a navy blue suit. She looked down at a schedule grid on her iPad. "There's a meeting with Senator Jones at 2:00, in your office, and then you meet with a group about the education initiative that the President has been pushing..."

"But won't we put that off? Until he's well?"

"Um...Zane suggested that you go forward with that in the President's place. Big media coverage. Good exposure on kids and education."

"Fine." Catherine had reached her office. She turned to Lorraine. "And are the new campaign spots ready yet? I want to see them as soon as possible. Camilla and Zane will both need to be in on that."

Lorraine nodded. "Yes ma'am. I'm on top of it. I'll get a copy to you by lunchtime. It's supposed to be coming in from the agency in New York within a few hours."

"What is Camilla doing about the California campaign swing that should have been happening today?"

"She says she's going on the assumption that you might be able to travel again in about five days. I'm just getting the rescheduling details from her."

"Great. You're fabulous, Lorraine. Maybe you could be my Vice President." She grinned.

"Frankly, Madam Vice President, I'm not sure I want this job," Lorraine said, smiling. She handed Catherine a hard copy of the day's agenda and closed her tablet with a snap.

Catherine stepped into her office and sat down at the desk. Her briefing memo for the day lay in the middle of the blotter. The stack of routine correspondence was piled on the corner. Absently, she grabbed the first envelope and slit the top with a letter opener while skimming the memo.

Her hands automatically unfolded the sheet of paper inside, and it was only then that she looked down at the message.

I KNoW yOur SeCR*et*. YoU mUST PAY. $250 ThOUs*an*D iN unMarkEd b*i*LLs bY FRIDay. InsTRU*ct*IONS tO FOLLoW.

For a moment she stared down at the page. The letters were cut from some magazine and pasted unevenly across the paper.

"I know your secret." Catherine whispered, and gave an involuntary shudder.

Politicians got anonymous threatening letters all the time. And certainly, as the first woman to serve as Vice President, Catherine got a generous serving. But they didn't usually make it all the way to her desk.

How had this gotten here? Normally someone would have intercepted such a letter and given it directly to the Secret Service. Somehow this one had slipped through the cracks, maybe because of the unusual excitement of the last 24 hours and Catherine's surprising turn-around on the flight to California.

She looked down again at the letter. It was probably just some kook. There were no doubt hundreds of empty threats just like this in the "Crank File" her Secret Service guys kept. She should give the letter to them. Immediately.

She reached for the phone on her desk and then her hand paused. Not just yet. She didn't want to share this with anyone. She had to think.

Catherine folded the venomous letter and put it in her briefcase along with the envelope. She secured the lock and decided to hold onto it for just a little while longer.

All throughout the meeting with the UAW representatives, the predictable political lunch at the NAACP, and her own speech, Catherine was thinking of the letter in her briefcase.

Somewhere way in the back of her consciousness, there was a letting go. The message that she had always feared had finally come.

She knew what the letter meant. What else could it be? There was only one real secret. A secret which had cost her sleepless nights and sweat and guilt and prayer and struggle and fear...a million years ago when she was young. In a life so long in the past it almost seemed as though she must have imagined it. She could barely remember living it.

Sometimes in dreams now it came back to her, visions of that little dark-skinned girl she had named Elizabeth. Her first baby. A baby who must be grown now.

Catherine did the arithmetic, but she didn't really need to. She knew. Twenty-nine. Twenty-nine birthdays had gone by since her baby had been born and then sent off, with bittersweet tears and prayers that she have the best possible life, in the arms of a Catholic nun who promised she would find a good home.

That baby was a woman now. Older than Catherine had been then. Perhaps she had children of her own. For an instant, Catherine saw her imagined grandchildren...dark-skinned children, with smiles like...and then she cut the vision short.

No romanticizing. Catherine tried to be rational about the message. This note – this blackmail attempt – could have come from anyone. Even Elizabeth herself. From someone who had somehow found out. But who?

No one, not even her own family, had known Catherine was pregnant. She had gone to the most anonymous city she could think of – Paris – for the last five months, and had given birth in a Catholic charity hospital under another name. She had told Paul, years later, before she married him. But at the time...only one person had known...Nancy.

Nancy Eisen had been Catherine's closest friend since their days together at Mount Holyoke. When Catherine went to Ghana with the Peace Corps in 1980, Nancy got married. Their correspondence was a lifeline as each entered strange new territory. Nancy wrote of her struggles with married life, and then with her first baby, while Catherine's letters were filled with stories about digging wells and teaching adults to read. When Catherine fell in love with a fellow teacher at the school, she could confide in no one – fraternization with a married Ghanaian would mean swift dismissal – but she could write to Nancy about her feelings, and chronicle the powerful attraction that they resisted for three long years.

And Catherine told only Nancy when she and Chuka decided, knowing they'd never see each other again, to spend two stolen weeks together after her Peace Corps stint. They went to Geneva, to an international city full of diplomats where no one knew them. Catherine lost herself in the bliss of time alone with the man who was finally her lover, and after he left, she glowed with the memory of his adoration.

When the shock of pregnancy hit her, Catherine had sobbed out her pain and confusion to Nancy over a transoceanic line from Switzerland to Boston. The anguish of that phone call was etched in her mind.

"Nancy...I know it's late," Catherine had said, wedged into a phone booth at the Geneva post office. "Can you talk? What time is it there?"

"Catherine? Is that you?"

"Yes. Nance, did I wake you? I can call later."

"It's 3:00 a.m. here."

"Oh God. Go back to bed. I'm so sorry!"

"No, no, I'm up now. It's all right. Anyway, I have to feed the baby soon."

At the word baby, Catherine whimpered into the phone.

"You sound awful. Are you okay?" Nancy asked.

"I'm...okay. Nancy...God forgive me...I'm pregnant."

"Pregnant?" Nancy's voice was tentative. "Is it...?"

"Is it Chuka's? Yes, of course. There's no one else. He just left...a month ago...." Her words were lost in tears.

"Catherine, I'm so sorry. That is...should I be sorry? Are you sorry? Have you decided what to do?"

"What to do – what can I do? You mean not have the baby – an abortion? I couldn't. I'm Catholic. And it's Chuka's baby. I'm not... that's not...something I could do."

"Of course. So you...are you going to keep it?"

"God. Nancy. How can I?"

"I don't know. Do you want to?"

"I want to. Yes. I want to. I would cut off my right arm to keep this baby." Sobs broke from her mouth again. "He'll be a part of Chuka. He'll be wonderful."

"Or she," Nancy said.

"Or she. He or she – I would love to make a life for us together. I know we could manage. My parents would be disappointed – it would mean the end of my plan to start law school – and you know Dad always wanted me to follow him into politics." Catherine heard herself make a sound between sobbing and choking. "But I could give that up. And they aren't prejudiced...the color of the baby wouldn't matter to them. But Nancy...how about this baby... this child? He would have no father – I could never tell Chuka – "

"Why not?"

"Because he already has a family. A wife. A life of his own, in Ghana. I couldn't tear him away from that. And I couldn't ask him to somehow fit us in on the side." Catherine wiped tears from her face with the back of her hand. "No. I've already made my mind up about Chuka. He can never know this baby exists. The last thing I want to do is ruin his life."

"Catherine. Do you want the child to grow up without a father?"

"No. I don't. I want him to have a whole family."

"Is that what this is about?"

"Yes..." Catherine lowered her voice. "But, Nancy...if I'm honest...I also don't want him to grow up in a society where he'll suffer because the color of his skin is different than that of his mother's. I could love him. My family could love him. But what will that mean...when the world calls him names? And he doesn't fit in with anyone – no father in his life, and a white mother – when he doesn't know who he is?"

"You sound as though you've already made up your mind."

"I guess I have." Guttural sobs wracked her ribs. "What else can I do, Nancy?" It was almost a whisper. When she spoke again, her voice was clearer.

"It's Chuka's baby. A baby I'd love to raise, but I can't... I can't give him the life he deserves. I'm going to give him up for adoption...to a family where he can have both a mother and a father."

7

WHEN IT HAPPENS, if at all, the communion of body and soul comes but once in a lifetime. For Catherine, it took place in Geneva, in the spring, in her twenty-seventh year.

In the mornings he would make her a breakfast of pancakes or omelets, with the best of yesterday's market fruit on the side. They would sit down to strong coffee in their robes and look out over the spires of the old city. As she rose to rinse out the mugs, every brush past his body was a chance to touch. Her body became new to her, ripe and womanly. Her breasts brimmed like firm peaches blushing and smooth. Her taut waist begged for his reaching arms. Her hips grew full.

They saw the sights by day. They toured the gardens of Geneva and walked by her lake, watching flags from many nations ripple. They ran through the Chateau de Chillon giggling, ahead of the guide. They went to France for lunch and ate raclette – she fed him the sweet biting cheese. They drank white wine. He licked the last drop from her lower lip.

They climbed nearby mountains and looked across borders, being borderless countries themselves.

In the afternoon they went back to bed and rediscovered their flesh again. His touch on her warm smooth skin was a shimmer of electricity. She bathed in the glow of his desire, shining. Her shine made other men spiral in like moths to a flame and he would pull her with a strong arm tight to his side. She would look up at him and smile the smile of a well-desired woman.

At night, she would light dozens of thick white candles around their heavy wooden bed. He stroked each part of her back, all the way down her spine. Then he turned her over and worked his broad hands upward and every inch of skin, every hair follicle was singing. Her feet, her shins, her knees, her thighs, her hips, her belly, her waist, her breasts one at a time and kissing in between and nestling his head there while that maverick tongue slipped right and left and licked the tiny hairs around her nipples which were perfect and delightful after all. Then her neck, her face, his hands on the planes of her cheeks and soft like warm breath, each finger millimeters from skin and each tiny antenna hair at grateful attention.

He owned her mouth with kisses as many and surprising as the stars in the night. Each one different and hot, each one bright in its own spectrum, each one bringing his tongue and teeth right up into her wild spangled galaxy.

And then in the ripe achingness of the moment he would slide his body inside hers and zoom like a waterslide right up into her – splash.

The touch of his skin felt like black velvet and tasted like bee buzzing honey. Her throat sang a constant pulsing moan faintly astonishing to her ears.

Finally, the delicious exhaustion of lovers whose pleasure will not sustain them for a moment longer overtook them. He wrapped her up in his tall masted arms and shipped her to sleep.

Her lifetime in Geneva lasted only seventeen days but it was always the memory of love to Catherine.

8

CATHERINE SHOOK HERSELF out of the reverie the threatening letter had induced and found herself standing in middle of her office at the White House, with Lorraine gently knocking on the open door. She gathered herself for a moment before speaking.

"Lorraine, could you please get me Nancy on the phone – she should be in her law office – Kocot, Aronie at 1776 K Street? Interrupt her if you need to. Tell her secretary it's urgent."

"Of course," Lorraine answered, and disappeared from the door.

Catherine walked over to her desk. She was surprised to realize that her calves ached from clenching and unclenching her muscles. The phone rang and she reached for it.

"Catherine? It's Nancy."

"Nancy. Can you get here...now? I have to talk to you. In person. I wouldn't ask if it weren't – "

"If it's that important, I'll jog. I'll be there in 15 minutes."

"Thank you Nancy," Catherine said. Her voice was pinched. She ran her hands through her hair. She knew – she knew – Nancy could be trusted. But she had to ask.

She hung up the handset and buzzed Lorraine again. "Lorraine, will you call the Northwest Gate to let them know Nancy will be here in about 15 minutes? Tell them to escort her to my office." Catherine paused. "Oh, and Lorraine?"

"Yes, ma'am?"

"Do what you can to entertain Senator Jones. He'll have to be pushed back a few minutes – something important's come up."

"Will do."

Catherine released the intercom. She sat down and put her head in her hands.

Okay. Breathe in and out. Think logically.

What am I going to do?

She knew she needed someone to confide in – someone she could talk to and trust to keep the bombshell quiet. Nancy already knew about the baby. Nancy was brilliant. But she would be no help in talking through the political options. If it were a choice between World War III and Catherine, Nancy would save her friend and the world be damned. Which meant that she would never put the campaign ahead of her concern for Catherine's safety.

A few years ago, Catherine could have talked it over with her Dad, the man who had once been her biggest booster and wisest advisor. It was his background in local Democratic politics in Maryland that had helped propel her from the state legislature in Baltimore to Congress just as opportunities for women were opening up on the national level. But in the last two years, he had embarked on a swift and agonizing downhill slide into Alzheimer's. He wasn't really himself any more. No, she couldn't talk to her Dad.

If her beloved Paul had still been alive, she could have shared her dilemma with him. A strong man, he would have been able to look past his own feelings, and give her dispassionate counsel. Though he had been gone for nearly ten years now, Catherine often found herself thinking of Paul with bittersweet longing for the lost time together.

Of course she could tell Zane. He had been with her since he graduated from college – in fact, he had been a student intern during her first term as a Member of Congress. Only twenty when Catherine first met him, Zane had become a valuable member of the team early on. And though there had been some rocky times, especially when he'd battled, and conquered, a substance abuse problem, Catherine recognized in Zane the keenest political mind she had ever encountered – a natural instinct for reading the public, and the intelligence to craft a campaign which locked right in to the wishes of the voters.

At first, the brash and talented young Zane had been resented by Catherine's senior staff members. But he proved himself within the first three months, when his detailed analysis of her campaign polls revealed exactly how she could expand her constituency. She was strong with women, and strong with minorities. But many of the rank-and-file Democrats, including middle-income families where both parents worked, perceived her as a silver-spoon lawyer who had managed to slip into the typical political – WASP and male – ranks.

Zane had targeted new and old media outlets to address that perception and turned it upside down. He made it known that despite Catherine's status among the Ivy Leaguers and in the corridors of power, she had gotten there through hard work and thousands of hours of public service, starting in politics with the local school board ten years after she had put her law career on hold to be a soccer mom and raise her kids. His ad campaign was designed to show that she was just one of the folks.

Zane went back to Catherine's old neighborhood and got people on her street to talk about how she organized the block parties, led the Brownie troop, and baked the best chocolate chip cookies around. He found old photos of Catherine camping and swimming with her husband and kids, photos that held the golden shimmer of family summers past. He got her to pull out her wedding gown – she refused to model it – and he took a shot of it hanging in an artfully dusty attic beside a picture of her on her wedding day.

But the ad that everyone talked about was the one filmed in Ireland. Zane had hired someone to track down the Maguire family in County Cork, descendants of her paternal grandfather's siblings, and they turned out to be a photogenic lot who not only bore a striking resemblance to Catherine, but also enjoyed the gift of gab in full measure. The ad ended with the assembled Maguires standing in an Irish meadow in all their redheaded resplendence, wishing Catherine luck on her presidential campaign. The spot was designed to show that she had come from the same humble roots as millions of immigrant families of the last two generations – particularly the 40 percent of Americans who claimed some Irish blood – and it sure didn't hurt her appeal quotient on the Kennedy scale.

The poll numbers which resulted from the ad campaign brought such success that Zane was acknowledged as a key member of the team. He was now her trusted confidante and chief strategist as Catherine traveled what had been – until now – a fairly smooth path to the Democratic nomination and the final showdown for the presidency.

Should she confide in Zane about the "secret" referred to in the letter? She could count on his sharp instincts as to the reaction of the voters. She trusted him, but...this was so personal.

What would Zane think of her choice so long ago? He was particularly sensitive to racial discrimination, and with good reason. Observing his classic Italian good looks and ethnic last name, no one would suspect that Zane had grown up in an interracial family. As he had told Catherine one night years ago, his mother had gotten pregnant with Zane at 17, but Franco Zarillo abandoned the family within a few months of his son's birth. When she married three years later, it was to an African-American man whom Zane had described to Catherine as a devoted stepdad. Two other children followed for the family, his half-siblings Will and Jasmine.

Zane's connection to the black community had been a special asset to Catherine. From his days at Exeter through Harvard and his M.B.A., her campaign manager had moved comfortably amongst friends of all races, and seemed to be oblivious to color distinctions.

Zane, whose own mother had married a black man, might see Catherine's decision to give up her baby in a very different light. The young Catherine of three decades ago, concerned about raising a fatherless child, might just look like a liberal white woman – Peace Corps volunteer and all – who didn't want a dark-skinned baby that might interfere with her privileged life. But surely Zane knew her better than that.

No, she wouldn't share the truth with Zane. At least, not yet.

Catherine was standing by the window in her office, still reflecting on the threatening letter, when Nancy arrived.

"What's up?" Nancy asked. "I came as fast as I could."

"Close the door. Please."

"Sure." Nancy, a thin woman with tight black curls and quick movements, pulled the door closed behind her. "Catherine, what is it? Is everything okay?" She looked at her friend with concern.

"Oh God, Nancy." Catherine walked over to the sofa and sat down. She ran her hand over her forehead. "I have to ask you – did you ever tell anyone about my first pregnancy – about Elizabeth?"

Nancy looked blank. "Tell anyone? Who would I tell? Why?" Her brow tightened in dismay. "What do you think – that I'd sell your personal life to the National Enquirer?" She crossed her arms in front of her chest. "Your friendship is worth more to me than that."

Nancy backed up and looked Catherine directly in the eyes. "I would never betray you, Catherine, and I'm offended that you would think so. I told no one. Not even my husband. It wasn't my story to tell."

Catherine held up her hand. "You're right. I shouldn't have asked. Sorry." She bit her bottom lip, then took a deep breath. "I'm being blackmailed," Catherine said. "And I just had to make sure – "

"Oh no." Nancy's answer was a groan. She sat down beside Catherine.

"They're asking for money. Whoever it is wants a quarter of a million dollars. Hush money."

"But how did they find out?"

"I don't know. I never told anyone at the time – except you. Not even my parents. I told Paul, but it was years later."

"But then who could know?"

Catherine sat silent for a moment, her brow furrowed and her hands laced together. "I don't know. I can't imagine Paul would ever have told anyone, Nancy. He and I did once talk about the risk, when my political career was first starting. How damaging this information could be. But even then, it was so many years in the past, and the pregnancy... the fact that I had Elizabeth...seemed so well hidden. How could anyone have found out?"

"You're not going to pay it, of course," Nancy said. It wasn't a question.

"No. Not yet anyway.... I don't know."

"Catherine, you can't give in to this. Even if you paid, it wouldn't stop...they'd just ask for more the next time."

Catherine nodded her head slowly. "I know."

"Have you told anyone about the letter?" Nancy asked.

"Only you. I wanted to talk to someone I can trust. You're the only one I plan to tell, at this point."

"Catherine. You can't be serious. You have to tell the FBI." Nancy stood up. Her voice rose. "You have to! The FBI, or the Secret Service, or whoever handles these things. They're supposed to protect you! You have a presidential campaign to run. Not to mention doing whatever it is you're doing while President Drummond is in the hospital. And this guy – these guys – are criminals. They should be behind bars."

Catherine felt a quick flash of anger. "Nancy, I know that. I've been thinking of nothing else since I got the damn letter." Her voice became hard as steel. "If I tell the FBI, it will mean the end of my campaign. The minute word of this leaks – and it would, this is Washington – it would spread like a flashfire across the media until it hit the front page of the National Enquirer." She shook her head. "You can picture the headline: Secret Presidential Love Baby!"

Nancy nodded, looking at the same time pained and amused. "You're right. Of course."

Catherine let out an unhappy laugh. "They'd do one of those awful fake photos."

"The baby would have horns," Nancy said, smiling, but grimly.

"Two heads."

"And they'd claim the father was Elvis," Nancy said, laughing now.

"No. Better – Michael Jackson."

Catherine's laughter died. "Oh Jesus, Nancy, what am I going to do? If this gets out, my campaign is dead." She kneaded the tissue between her hands.

"I don't suppose you could just admit it? Bare your soul before the American public and take your chances?"

"I could, but my chances of election would be zero."

"Come on. If we made it through JFK and Clinton and...didn't Roosevelt have some secret hanky panky going on? Hmm...and Newt Gingrich and Rudy Giuliani and wait – I read that John McCain got engaged to wife No. 2 before he was divorced from wife No. 1...."

Catherine held up her hand. "Nancy. Can you honestly sit there and tell me that the American people would willingly elect me president if I admitted to an affair?"

"They've elected men who've had affairs!"

"Get serious, Nancy. The public allows men to have a sexual appetite. It's still shocking in a woman."

Nancy gave a grim smile. "Look...what did you do that was so awful? You had sex. Sex leads to babies."

"Right. So add up the people who wouldn't vote for me because I had sex before marriage, plus the people who wouldn't vote for me because I had sex with a married man, plus the people who wouldn't vote for me because I had sex with a black man – a foreigner! – and we haven't even started on the people who wouldn't vote for me because I gave the baby up."

"Maybe you could win the election with the 'no birth control' vote?" Nancy's voice attempted to be light.

Catherine put her hand on her forehead. "I did use birth control, Nancy. I'm not stupid. I got pregnant anyway."

"Oh." Nancy nodded, biting her lip. "Catherine, whoever wrote that letter could be dangerous. You have to go to the authorities."

"No."

"What, you're just going to sit here like a target and see what the blackmailer does next?"

"Of course not. You know me better than that." Catherine leaned forward. "I'm going to go after them."

"After them? How?"

Catherine stood and began pacing across the oriental rug.

"Nancy, there's nothing I've done in my life that I'm ashamed of. But there is nothing I've ever questioned more – worried about more – than the decision to give up Elizabeth. I would have given anything to know that everything had turned out all right. For years, I've resisted searching her out." Catherine twisted the Kleenex between her hands. "I could have tracked her down. Gotten peace of mind...with a couple of simple inquiries. But I let it be. I let it be because I thought – I hoped – that my daughter had found a new life somewhere, with a loving family, and she didn't deserve to get a phone call out of the blue saying I'm your mother, and I'm some white lady living in America. I stayed away out of love. And now this...."

"You know, Catherine, I never wanted to ask you about it..." Nancy's voice was low. "I never wanted to bring you pain. You must have wondered about her."

"My God, yes. I've done the best I could to shut off the worry...because it didn't do any good, and because I have a family of my own." Catherine's voice was ragged. "I have two other children. The hardest time in my life was after Lily and Mike were born. That was when I finally felt the pain of letting Elizabeth go...my first baby...the baby I would have loved so dearly."

Catherine turned to face Nancy.

"After I had the kids, I had second thoughts about giving her up. I struggled with the urge to find her. I thought of how I could fit her into my life. But it was too late! She was already seven years old by the time my youngest was born. It would have been crazy to pull her away from her adoptive family – even if I knew where she was! And once I had made my decision, I closed the door, emotionally. Or tried to. I gave her away with all the love in my heart, and sent her off to make a new life."

Nancy was quiet for moment. "But now...you're going to try to find her?"

"Nancy, this note could have come from Elizabeth, or one of her family. Maybe she just wants to meet me. Maybe she needs money. I would give her money. My God, I never wanted her to grow up in poverty! The nun I entrusted her to – she promised that she would find a good home for Elizabeth. I hope she's gotten an education, and...and grown up with a loving family, and...so many things I prayed that she would have." Catherine sat down suddenly, her shoulders shaking.

Nancy put an arm around Catherine.

"Catherine, I'm worried about you. I think it's dangerous to take these people – whoever they are – on. But you know I'll do anything to help you."

"Find me a private detective," Catherine said. Her voice grew stronger. "The best. The most discreet."

"What's that going to accomplish?"

"I'm going to follow the trail from the other end – from Paris, where it started. If I can find out what happened to Elizabeth, I can find out who knows she's my daughter. And maybe this detective will lead me right to..." Catherine's voice caught on the name, "Elizabeth."

Nancy sighed. "I don't like this, Catherine. I'm worried about your safety." She stood and walked away from the sofa. "But I'll make you a deal. I'll set up your detective – if you swear to me that you'll tell the FBI."

"I will. I promise I will. Just not yet. I want my guy to have a head start – maybe we can find her first, and head off any – any curiosity. The note gave me until Friday. That's five days."

"Five days is too long. Give him your head start – and then tell the FBI. For your own protection. You don't have to tell them about Elizabeth. Just tell them you're being blackmailed."

Catherine paused and then nodded her head. "It's a deal."

§

After the meeting with Senator Jones, Catherine was in her office on the phone when Zane stuck his head in her door. As part of the election staff, he was officially assigned to campaign headquarters, located in a building half a block down Pennsylvania Avenue. But he spent much of his time at the White House, and they had managed to find a small office down the hall that he "borrowed" regularly. She waved him in.

"I'll have to call you back," she said into the phone. As she placed it back in the cradle, she saw that Zane was holding an envelope. Her mind took a quick leap, and she knew what it had to be.

"I'm sorry to barge in like this, Madam Vice President," Zane said. "But there's something here you need to see." He handed her the envelope, and she saw the familiar cut-out letters forming his name on the front. She opened it.

I KNoW hEr SeCRet. Catherine mUST PAY. $250 ThOUsanD iN unmarked bills *bY FRIDay*. InsTRUctIONS tO FOLLoW.

Somehow the letter hit her harder the second time. She took a deep breath.

"I got one too." She punched in the combination for the electronic lock on her briefcase, and then pulled out the letter, taking it from the envelope and passing it to him.

Zane stood still in the center of the room, his eyes fixed on the message in his hands. "It's the same as the one I got." His brow wrinkled as he looked up at her, and there was something wary in his eyes. "Catherine. Is there…something I should know?"

Fighting furiously with the impulse to blush, Catherine straightened her back and attempted the ballet posture that had

been trained into her as a girl. She laughed, but it sounded
forced, at least to her ears.

"Zane, you know how these kooks are. Seeing conspiracies
everywhere. There's nothing that you need to worry about – no
secrets I'm ashamed of." Catherine turned quickly as she
realized that her left hand was trembling.

Snap out of it. No need to confess your past to Zane.
Probably whoever wrote this is talking about something
completely different. Or nothing at all.

Maybe.

Zane was looking at her closely when she turned back. His
mouth had something of a twist to it, an expression that she
couldn't interpret.

"You're going to show these to the FBI, of course. Right?"
Catherine faced him. "I will. Yes."

She tried to keep her expression neutral. She had the
ridiculous urge to cross her fingers behind her back. Yes, but
not just yet. Yes, but I won't tell them what I think the letters
are about. Yes, but I'm not telling you what I did all those years
ago, that I think someone has found out.

It felt almost like a child's game – keeping a secret from a
friend. But this game wasn't for children at all.

9

ZANE SWUNG WIDE around the corner in the underground parking garage, neatly missing a cement support. He pulled into a spot near the elevator that would take him to Maria's floor, and hit the brake. The Porsche bucked and stopped dead.

He pulled out the key and grabbed his jacket from the seat beside him in the same smooth motion. Pushing open the door and sliding past the side mirror, he caught a glimpse of someone behind him, closing fast.

A pivot, and an instinctive move to put the heavy car door between him and –

"Stop right there, Zane honey."

It was Devon. His blonded hair was full of product. His teeth were beautifully capped. He wore a navy sports jacket that bunched surprisingly at the biceps.

"Hey, Devon," Zane said. "Didn't expect to see you here. How's things?" Devon's cologne was nauseating.

"Oh Zane, you tease. You know I'm not visiting to chat with you. The boss sent me to get a progress report."

"A progress report?"

"Yes! About the money. You have until Saturday, remember? Not that it matters to me, of course, but that pretty face of yours – well, all I can say is that you really ought to be working on getting some cash."

"Right. I'm on it. I've got a plan. But you know, Devon, I was hoping we could maybe make another arrangement. Like more money if you give me a little more time. Double your investment, maybe." The car door was still open, and the security alarm yipped. Zane jumped.

Devon smiled.

"But we've already done that, Zane. Now it's pay up time. No extensions."

Zane didn't know what else to do but nod.

"Just so we're clear," Devon said, his manicured finger poking into Zane' chest, "I wouldn't mind taking you out, darling. You were always an arrogant son of a bitch." Devon pulled Zane toward him by the lapel. "I know you think you're pretty damn fancy with your White House job. They don't know the kind of a lowlife you really are – like I do. So when I come to see you on Saturday...if you haven't got the cash...it's going to be a pleasure." He bared his teeth in what must have been a smile, brushed Zane's chest as if to remove some lint, and turned to walk out of the garage.

Zane discovered that his hand was clutched tightly around the door. He slowly peeled his fingers away and massaged his fist.

§

Maria sat with Ester in Hotcakes, a small restaurant off Dupont Circle that had cheap but wonderful food. Between Ester's delicious curviness, coming in a short dark package, and Maria's long mocha beauty, the two women got a lot of stares. They were used to it, and swatted away the unwanted attention as one would a swarm of well-intentioned gnats.

Ester leaned across the table toward Maria, her generous bust making the move dangerously distracting for men nearby. She pushed away the plate which had recently held a succulent morsel of sea bass, and spoke in a low voice, in her native Brazilian Portugeuse. "So how are you enjoying being on your own… finally?"

"I love it. Now that I've got the apartment, I can come and go as I please," Maria said. She reached for her wine glass. "It was cheaper to live with my mom's cousin, but she was always reporting on me to the family back in Brazil. And feeding me too much. I was getting fat!" She laughed, and four men turned their heads.

"Now you can spend the night with Zane."

"Yes, but don't tell my mother," Maria said, smiling.

"Maria, you're twenty-nine years old! It's not a big deal."

"It is to my parents. They were very nervous about me going to America on my own. They're waiting for me to meet a nice Catholic man and bring him home to meet the family. And after we're engaged, maybe we can try kissing." She laughed.

"I know there's been lots more than kissing with your man Zane," Ester said. "Still yummy?"

"I see you looking at him, Ester. Are you trying to steal him away?"

"Maria! What kind of a friend do you think I am?" Not shocked at all, Ester practically purred.

"I know what kind of a friend you are – a hot Brazilian mama! And if you want him, just say so."

Ester raised her eyebrows. "Is that an offer? I thought you were in love with him."

"Maybe. Sometimes. I'm not sure."

"Wow. Just using him for stud service?" Ester's mouth became a smirk, and as she leaned back into her chair she once again attracted the attention of guys at several local tables. "You've come a long way, Maria! I thought you were the shy convent girl. I'm so proud."

Maria smiled and then brought her own voice low. "There's something weird going on, Ester. I think Zane has been snooping into my stuff. When I'm asleep, maybe. He's acting odd, too."

"Odd how?"

"Well, he's more attentive. Watching my every move."

"More attentive – isn't that good?"

"You'd think so. But he's normally pretty busy with the campaign. So I'm not sure what's going on."

"Are you going to cut him loose?"

"Oh, I don't know."

"And if you do, will he be everything I'm hoping for?"

"I guess you'd have to be the judge of that, Ester. You have way more experience in the stud department than I have." Maria laughed and signaled to the waiter, who was loitering nearby, apparently dazed by their gorgeousness.

"Can we have the check, please?" she asked him in English.

"Certainly," he said, springing to action and heading back to the kitchen.

Ester gave Maria a wicked smile. "You and I will have to compare notes about Zane," she said. "After you give me a chance to experience what he has to offer."

Maria rolled her eyes at her friend and shook her head. "I think America has corrupted you."

"America? It was Rio that corrupted me, honey. America is tame in comparison."

§

Catherine settled into her seat as the door of the Vice Presidential limousine was pushed shut from the outside. The second Secret Service agent took his position in the front seat. Zane sat beside her. They were headed for a fundraiser at the Washington Hilton.

"Lead car in place," the driver said quietly into the radio.

"Follow car in place," a voice responded.

"A follow car, Dan?" Catherine asked. "Is something going on?"

"Just a precaution, Madam Vice President," the Secret Service agent in the passenger seat answered. "There have been a few...threats. Probably just cranks. The usual. We simply don't want to take chances."

"What kind of threats?" Catherine adjusted her bearing, and her voice, to indicate her displeasure. "Why wasn't I told?"

"Well, we get phone and mail threats into the White House from time to time. We don't bother you and the President with every one." Catherine saw Dan give a small smile. "Besides, they're usually the same people we've heard from before. We keep a crank file on the regulars."

"If this is so common – to get threats – then why don't I always have a follow car?"

"The tempo picks up when election time comes around, and then there's...."

Catherine leaned forward. "If you don't give me a straight answer, I'm going to stop this motorcade right now, and report you to your boss for insubordination. I asked you – why do we have a follow car today, when I have never before seen one for a trip from 1600 Pennsylvania Avenue to the Washington Hilton?"

Dan wasn't smiling any more. "Of course, Madam Vice President. Since the Convention, death threat activity has doubled. And now of course you are the acting President, so you're more in the spotlight than ever. The Washington Hilton is a very public place. You'll recall that President Reagan was shot there."

Catherine sat back in her seat. "Thank you, Dan." As her annoyance wore off, she was sorry that she had been brusque. Dan Sweeney was one of her favorite agents. Putting her hand on the Secret Service man's shoulder, she was just about to say something apologetic when her cell trilled with Nancy's ring.

"Hi Nancy. What's up?" Catherine asked, turning herself slightly away from Zane.

"Hi there. I know you're on a tight schedule – I won't keep you a minute."

Catherine could hear the cautious tone in Nancy's voice. They were both aware of the risks of mobile communications.

"No problem."

"You know that package I sent to Paris? It went out yesterday."

"Good."

"But there's been a snag on the receiving end."

"Oh. And that would be because...?"

"The package is...in the dead letter office."

Catherine felt her throat tighten. Oh God. Elizabeth? Dead?

As if realizing the implications, Nancy quickly added, "The address I had was from several years ago. There's no longer anyone at that address."

Catherine realized Nancy must be talking about the nun who had promised to take Elizabeth to her convent.

"The addressee is probably deceased," Nancy said, "but I'm trying to see if anyone else there has the information necessary to send the package in the proper direction."

Of course. If that nun was dead, it would be difficult to track Elizabeth. Records of infants born 29 years ago in a Catholic charity hospital in Paris might not be perfectly maintained – especially since Catherine had done everything she could to disguise her identity. She had wanted to make sure no one could ever discover that she gave birth to her little girl.

"I hope it works out." Catherine's voice was perfectly controlled. "Let me know when you hear more."

"And Catherine," Nancy said, her voice growing more insistent. "Have you taken that step we talked about, in raising that matter with the appropriate people?"

Catherine sighed. "Not yet. But I will."

"When?"

"Nancy, only you could get away with talking to the Vice President of the United States like this...you and my kids." She laughed, and then noticed Zane regarding her quizzically. "Soon, okay? I promise."

"Okay. And if you don't, I'm going to talk to you this way again tomorrow."

"I'm sure you will." Catherine shook her head, still smiling. She said good-bye and clicked off.

10

"MOM, DON'T YOU like it? I went to Watergate Pastry to get that cake." Lily stuck her lower lip out in a mock pout.

Catherine sat across the kitchen table from her children and picked at the frosting on a piece of cake. The sturdy oak table was her own, brought from the home in which she and Paul had raised the kids, but much of the other furniture had come with – and would stay with – the house.

The Vice Presidential residence, located on the grounds of the Naval Observatory off Wisconsin Avenue, was acquired by Nelson Rockefeller when he served under President Ford. Rockefeller had donated the house to the government to be used by his successors in the office. Some twenty years later, when Catherine had moved in, the house had begged for a major rehaul. It had been gloriously – and rather formally – redone, courtesy of a historically precise and expensive decorator who had been thrilled with the generous budget Catherine provided. As a result, Catherine had felt as though she was living in a museum for much of the last four years. But the kitchen, with its skylights and tiled floor, Calphalon pots and old oak table, was home.

"I like the flavor," Lily said. "It's unusual. Almond, I think." She licked a dab of frosting from her deep green fingernail. A natural brunette, Lily's hair was bright red – this week. Her ivory skin and blue eyes made the choice of hair color startling. But she didn't particularly stand out among her generously pierced colleagues at the advertising firm where she had worked since graduating two years ago.

Catherine reached across the table and took her daughter's hand. "It's delicious, honey. I'm just not that hungry. They keep feeding me hors d'oeuvres at those fundraisers. If I have one more scallop wrapped in bacon, I'm going to bust out of my campaign suits."

"Mmm, scallops in bacon," Mike said. "I love those. Why don't you invite me to those fundraisers?" Mike sat in his chair backward, at 22 still a lanky man-boy. He tipped his head to the side in a gesture he had used since he was a toddler – one that looked slightly comical on a young man sporting the latest fad in facial hair.

"You know you're welcome to come, Mike. Any time. I just didn't think you'd be too interested. Of course when you show up there it brings out the paparazzi – who tend to follow you around once you get in the public eye. And I know you're busy studying."

"Mike? Studying?" Lily snorted and gave her not-so-little brother a chuck on the arm with her fist.

"Hey!" he said, nursing his bicep as though she had injured him, though his grin belied any soreness.

"I figured on putting you two on display more toward the end of the campaign," Catherine said, smiling at their act. "At a couple of rallies in the big cities – New York, Chicago – when we pull out all the stops and parade our good family values for all the world to see." Catherine laughed lightly and wondered if her voice gave away her fatigue.

Lily must have heard it, because she looked at her mother with concern. "Mom, are you getting enough rest? You look tired. It can't be easy running for office while you're also doing the work of the President." She reached out again and put her smooth hand on her mother's. "Which, by the way is very cool, Mom. Not that I doubt that you'll win – but you're already in the history books."

Mike nodded in agreement. "Yeah, in case I haven't mentioned – I think that's awesome. And let me tell you that the drinks were on the house from my buddies the day you got the word."

Catherine gave him a look. "Listen, I'm only in this position because President Drummond had a health scare. It's not something to celebrate."

"Yeah, we know," Mike said, slicing another generous piece of the cake. "But you didn't put him in the hospital. You're the hero – heroine – coming to the rescue of the country."

Lily stood up to get a napkin and hand it to her brother, who was eating the cake with his hands. "What's the latest on the President? Will he be back at work soon?"

"I hope so," Catherine said, and realized that it came out with an involuntary sigh.

"Mom – make sure you don't forget to take care of yourself." Now it was Mike's turn to look concerned.

"Oh, I'm okay. I'll manage. We're into the home stretch with the campaign – and hopefully with President Drummond's recuperation phase – and I've got to keep meeting and greeting."

"The polls have you way ahead, right?" Mike asked. "And all my friends are voting for you. I thought it was a sure thing. Especially with that airhead Jerusha and her Liberty Party friends as the opposition. You are going to win, aren't you, Mom?"

"Good question. I hope so."

"Of course she is!" Lily said. "She's going to win the presidency, and she's going to bring world peace to the entire planet." Lily smiled in a way that was gently maternal, and Catherine found herself touched by her children's belief in her. If they knew the whole truth.... She looked down at her plate. She fiddled with the almond cake for a moment, cutting a forkful and then putting it down.

"It was sweet of you to bring the cake, Lily." Once again she reached across the table to touch her daughter's arm.

Unbidden, she thought of Elizabeth. Her other daughter. Where was she tonight? Was she sitting across the table from her mother, the woman who had raised her? Was she warm and well fed? Was she happy?

Catherine shook her head and stood up from the table. Those kinds of questions had been banished to a locked room in her mind years ago. It was useless to ponder them now –

especially since the answers might finally be available to her very soon.

"I hope you kids will forgive me if I boot you out now. I've got a speech to go over for tomorrow." She began to cover the cake.

"Another speech?" Mike asked.

"And another and another and another. And you wonder why I'm tired?" Catherine gathered up the plates as Lily and Mike took the coffee mugs to the sink. When the table was clear, she walked with them to the front of the house. They opened the door and were hit in the face with the muggy Washington summer.

"Good night, Mom." Mike bobbed down to her level to kiss Catherine on the cheek.

"Take care of yourself, sweetheart. Is Lily going to drive you back to the dorm?"

"To the library. I have work to do."

Lily raised her eyebrows. "All right, brown nose. Isn't it enough that you're the smart one in the family? You have to show me up by taking summer classes? And then actually studying?"

"I have to take summer courses if I'm going to get this Masters in two years." Mike looked slightly insulted.

"I'm just teasing, you dweeb." Lily reached up and ruffled his hair. "I'm really proud of you."

"And I'm proud of you both," Catherine said. She hugged Lily and said good-bye. She stood in the doorway and watched as Lily's red BMW stopped at the gated entrance to the Observatory grounds. A pale hand waved out the window to the guard stationed in the booth, and the taillights disappeared from view.

Catherine closed and locked the front door, something she didn't always do. Between the Navy's security for the Observatory and her round-the-clock Secret Service protection, her house was one of the most secure in Washington. But she turned the bolt in the door, and then jumped when she heard her cell sound.

"Hello," she said.

"Hello, Madam Vice President. It's Zane. I hope I'm not calling too late."

Catherine looked at her watch. It was 9:00. "Not too late at all. But you startled me. I'm a little jumpy these days."

"I can believe that."

"What's up?"

"I'm still at the office, and if you needed me to stop by to tweak that speech – "

"For tomorrow? No, I think it's in pretty good shape, Zane. But I appreciate the offer."

"Good. Well...."

She waited for him to say good-bye, but he didn't.

"Zane." Catherine didn't bother to hide the weariness in her voice. "Do you have something on your mind? If you do, I wish you'd just come out and ask me."

Zane cleared his throat. "No. I just... I hope you're okay. You're got a lot on your plate right now, taking over the President's duties. I'm sure it's tough to handle that as well as the campaign."

Catherine felt the annoyance in her body before she heard it in her voice. "What do you suggest I do, Zane? Refuse to head the country while the President is lying in the hospital with stitches in his gut?"

"Of course not."

"It's my duty – and my honor – to stand in his place for as long as necessary."

"Yes. I know. I'm just hoping it won't be too much longer until you can dedicate all your energies toward campaigning. Jerusha Hutchins is all over the news all the time. While you're stuck in Washington."

"Stuck in Washington doing the President's bidding."

"Definitely. But even you can't do everything, Madam Vice President. I'm... well, I'm worried about you."

Catherine sighed. "Thanks for your concern, Zane." She tucked a strand of hair behind her ear. "Believe me, I am well aware that we need to get back to the campaign."

§

Catherine sat behind the desk in the West Wing office where she did most of her work. Like most recent Vice Presidents, she had been invited to make use of an office in the White House, and it was particularly convenient now that she was covering all of the duties the President couldn't attend to.

The fern-colored walls and elegant furnishings always made the office relaxing, even when there was a crisis – which was frequent. And Catherine loved being up close to the spare Asian paintings on loan from the Freer Gallery. This was art she could never own – but she could enjoy it while it hung on her walls.

Camilla knocked on the open door and held out a CD. "Are you ready for me, Madam Vice President? Zane should be with us any minute. He asked me to show you the final version of the ad that we plan to break out this weekend."

"Come on in," Catherine said, and moved her laptop over so that Camilla could get close to it.

Camilla pulled a chair beside Catherine and popped the CD in. The two of them watched as the ad began. The spot was called *Decades* and the first image was an old still photo of Jerusha Hutchins with a tiara on her head and wearing a frothy pink dress. Juxtaposed with that photo was one of Catherine in a college graduation gown with a mortarboard on her head. The day she graduated from Mount Holyoke.

A man's voice intoned, "It takes decades to be ready for a job as big as the presidency." At the bottom of the screen the number *1970's* floated.

Next was a shot of Jerusha as a stewardess, leaning over an airplane passenger and handing him a tray. Beside that was a photo of Catherine in Ghana, standing by a well she had helped dig, and surrounded by children from the village. Her heart lurched momentarily to see the scenery of Africa, which reminded her so much of her lost love.

The number *1980's* rolled across the two photos.

For the *90's* the shots were again in contrast. Jerusha was shown beside her husband Reverend Quigley Hutchins on their television show. She was holding a ukelele and had her mouth open. Catherine chuckled. Poor Jerusha wouldn't be pleased with that photo. She rarely took a bad one, but they had found it. Catherine's accompanying photo showed her standing in front of the Capitol building with the freshman congressional class her first year in national office.

Finally, in the *2000's,* the photo of Catherine showed her being sworn in as Vice President, her hand on a bible and President Drummond to her left. Jerusha's photo was taken at what appeared to be a country club. She was dressed in a long gown and had extra-large hair. She was dancing with someone other than Quigley, and she looked like she was having the time of her life.

The stirring tones of the man doing the voiceover began again.

"Dedication. Preparation. Experience. Who is ready to be your President?" the voice extolled.

Zane had walked in just as the ad was ending. He smiled at Catherine across the desk. "You like that?" he asked.

"Brilliant," Camilla said.

"Nicely done, Zane," Catherine said. "Just the right tone."

"We had to avoid anything that showed Jerusha with her kids – we didn't want to seem to be making light of her job as a mother. Or mocking her for having a lot of kids. And we also were careful not to use photos related to the ministry, so it didn't look like we were disparaging religion."

Catherine looked at Zane and smiled. "How do you always manage to hit that sweet spot with these ads?" She walked around the desk and shook his hand. "You've done it again, Zane. I bet this tested really well."

"Off the charts," said Camilla, "even with conservatives. They said it made them think about what each of the candidates had been doing with her time in the last 40 years…which is a long time."

"What I like is that it's not nasty. It's honest…and thought-provoking – though you did pick a pretty unflattering shot with that ukelele."

"Can you believe that?" Zane asked.

"Hilarious." Catherine gave Zane a slap on the back. "I'm so lucky you're on my team, Zane."

"It's my honor, Madam Vice President," he said, giving her a small bow.

"I'm off," Camilla said, leaving the two of them together and closing the door.

"Zane, how are our numbers looking?" Catherine asked.

"Pretty good, but still volatile," he said. "The more Jerusha Hutchins speaks, the better you look. I can't wait to get her into a debate situation."

"It's hard to understand what people see in her," Catherine said. "She doesn't seem serious, and she doesn't seem educated about the issues."

"That's what they like, I think," Zane said. "She's all spunk and instinct, with very little to back it up. But that appeals to a lot of folks who have stopped believing in government at all. The less experienced and 'tainted,' the more a candidate might represent something new. Something that could work differently than what they've seen before."

"So how do I persuade them, Zane? How do I get my years of working in the system to be an asset instead of a liability?"

Zane looked at her, his handsome brown eyes hard to read. "You just keep being the grown up. The woman who has worked her way up, paid her dues, and served at the right hand of the President – is serving, in fact, *as* the President – temporarily. Jerusha Hutchins may be blonde and perky, but she's not someone you'd turn to for leadership in a crisis."

Catherine leaned back in her office chair and swiveled toward the window, where she could see the a bit of greenery against the handsome edifices of Washington, D.C.

"I'm sure you're right, Zane. More voters want a leader than they want an entertainer."

Zane sat up. "You've just given me another idea for a campaign spot, Madam Vice President. We'll get some video of you speaking in Congress, appearing at the U.N., meeting with world leaders. And then we'll insert Jerusha, instead, and let the voters see what that would look like. Let them see and hear what kind of representative she would be."

Catherine nodded her head. "Good."

Zane continued thoughtfully. "What we always have to watch is the snark factor – it doesn't work if it looks like disdain, either for the fluffy bouffant hair or the Southern drawl – that just gets some people's backs up. We have to let the lack of coherence speak for itself. We've got to let Jerusha be Jerusha."

Catherine stood up. "I love that. Let Jerusha be Jerusha. Excellent, Zane." She walked him to the door. "I couldn't do it without you."

§

Catherine sat in her office on a sofa opposite Ralph Harwood, the head of the Secret Service. Harwood was an FBI man through and through. Though not tall, he had posture so ramrod straight he seemed to be always at attention. His intense blue eyes were focused on the blackmail letter, which had been placed into a plastic evidence bag. The letter to Zane, as well as the two envelopes, were in three more separate bags, sitting on the coffee table between them.

"Madam Vice President, I don't know why you didn't hand me these letters immediately. Speed is critical in matters like this."

"I'm sorry, Ralph. I know I should have brought this to your attention right away. I set up this meeting as soon as I had a spare minute – "

"When did you get these?" His tone was disapproving. "And exactly where?"

Catherine accepted the implied criticism, and decided further protest was pointless. "Two days ago. In the morning, as soon as I got in – around 8:30. And I found it right here.

Right on this corner of my desk...." She stood and walked to the desk, placing her hand on the spot where her personal correspondence was normally stacked.

"And who else has seen it?"

"Um...Zane has seen it."

"I should be more precise. Who else has touched it, as far as you're aware?"

"Ah...well, that would be Zane, again. Only Zane and me. I read the letter he received, and he read mine. I suppose you'll analyze the fingerprints?"

Harwood raised his brows. "We'll do more than that, Madam Vice President."

"Of course. I'm glad this is in your hands, and not mine. There's too much going on right now for me to try to play detective too." A little synapse fired in her brain, reminding her that she was doing exactly that, a continent away.

"Madam Vice President, I have to ask." Harwood's tone was cautious. "Can you say what 'secret' the extortionist might be referring to?"

Catherine had steeled herself for this question. She had thought of various responses, none of which she felt good about. She went with the one that felt more like a failure to tell the whole truth than a lie.

"Ralph, I've never done anything I would be ashamed for people to know." That much, at least, she could say honestly. She held his eyes.

Harwood actually blushed. "Madam Vice President, I sure didn't mean to imply...."

"Don't be silly, Ralph. You didn't imply anything." She almost chuckled. A straight arrow like Ralph probably got palpitations just imagining her doing something she would be ashamed of. "So why don't you take this matter into your capable hands, and see if you can get to the bottom of whatever – or whoever – this is. I'll cooperate with your agents in every way I can." Except by providing them with the truth, a little voice in her head nattered.

There was a quiet knock on the door, and Zane walked in.

"Lorraine said you wanted me to join you?" He looked over at Harwood and nodded.

"Yes, Zane. Thanks for coming. We're just about wrapped up here, though."

Zane took a chair at the side of the coffee table, and glanced down at the plastic bag in Harwood's hand.

"What?" Zane put his hands on the arms of the chair. He looked at Catherine, startled. "That's the – "

"The blackmail letter. Yes."

His tone became even. "I thought you decided – "

"Yes, as we agreed, I brought it to Ralph. He'll handle it from here. That way we don't have to worry about it any more. You and I have a campaign to run."

Catherine smiled and stood up. Both of the men hastened to stand. Harwood picked up the plastic bags. "I'll get these right over to the FBI for testing."

"Thank you, Ralph. Keep me informed."

"Of course."

Catherine reached out to shake his hand, and he transferred the bags to his left.

"I'll know you'll treat this with the utmost confidentiality," she said.

His hand seemed to turn chilly in hers, and he raised himself to his full 5'7" height. "Madam Vice President, the Secret Service is charged with protecting the lives of the Vice President and the President. You can rest assured that this matter will be handled on a need-to-know basis. There will be no leaks from our office."

"I appreciate hearing that, Ralph."

She ushered Harwood out the door and closed it, sensing that Zane was agitated.

"Yes?" she asked, turning back to him.

"So when did you decide to tell the FBI?" Zane asked.

"I had to tell them, Zane. It's too dangerous. Whoever this is – or they are – could be some sort of fanatic with an agenda – or a gun." She bit her lower lip. Catherine crossed the room, and spoke carefully, as though her hopes would come true if she said them out loud. "The FBI will find the blackmailers, or the Secret Service will protect me from them, and in the meantime, I can concentrate on running my campaign and doing my best to keep the Oval Office warm for the President." Catherine leaned against the back of the sofa and braced her arms stiffly.

"When is their deadline for the money?" Zane asked.

She looked up at him. "Two days from now," Catherine said. "Friday."

11

JERUSHA HUTCHINS STROLLED out onto the front porch of an antebellum mansion on the outskirts of Atlanta into the throng of well-wishers and reporters. Her hair was a high pouf of yellow-blonde and her peach-colored jacket was just shy of too tight. A black skirt and heels that showed off her still remarkable legs completed the look. Her face and her outfit would be all over the Internet and the MSM tomorrow, so she put on the beauty pageant smile honed to perfection in her teens.

She hadn't had this much fun since winning the race for Homecoming Queen at the University of Georgia.

No one was more astonished – and gratified – than she at the stunning success of her campaign for President. Even when Quigley had assured her that she was in a good position to win the GOP nomination, Jerusha had doubted that could be true. But Quigley was right. And as a Bible-following wife, she was continuously grateful at his leadership of the family and God's great blessing in providing her with such a wise mate.

Just last night she and her husband had knelt and prayed together, holding hands as they often did, asking for help and guidance in creating a campaign that would lead not simply to the presidency but to a better direction for the country and the world. Though Jerusha was humble enough to realize that her slim shoulders and modest intellect were unlikely qualifications for the role of leader of the free world, she had something that Ivy League graduates didn't – she had faith. With the help of the Lord, she would win. And if not, may His will be done.

All she had to do, as dear Quigley often reminded her, was be herself. "Just be Jerusha," he said, and they would love her. So she was Jerusha to the hilt, every time cameras were rolling. And gosh, but wasn't it a bushel of fun!

"Welcome folks! Isn't it a gorgeous day to be in Georgia?"

"Jerusha, do you have anything to say about the President's illness?" It was Billy Stranton, one of her favorite reporters from the local TV station. "What do you think of Vice President Young getting the opportunity to serve as acting President of the United States while she is campaigning as the Democratic nominee?"

Jerusha widened her smile. "Hey Billy! How are y'all today?" She gave a big wave, and then let the smile leave her face. "Well just like y'all and the whole country, I personally – along with Reverend Hutchins and the rest of our family – pray that our President get back to health as quickly as possible."

There were murmurs of assent from the crowd, and a loud "Amen" from the back.

"But what about Vice President Young?" Curly-haired Billy nodded and spoke up again. "Isn't she getting an unfair advantage...?"

"Oh, I'm not worried about that," Jerusha answered, raising her freshly arched eyebrows and shaking her head. "No matter what schemes they try – and they will try! – the Democrat party knows that the good folk of America want a change. So I am imminently confident that we are going to win! That we will be successful in taking back this country for the good of the people."

She turned and gave the signal to Annalee, God bless her, who opened the door and let the smallest five of the Hutchins children, all dressed in matching navy and white, come tumbling out to stand beside their mother. Jerusha knew a good photo op when she saw one, and this was it. She picked up little Ethan and gave him a kiss on top of his mess of blond curls, knowing that the cameras were rolling, catching her in a shaft of sunlight surrounded by beautiful, clean, and Christian children, all her fruit of her own womb.

"I do have to admit though, Billy, dontcha think? It's a mite bit of a coincidence that the President got laid up right about now." Jerusha puckered her brow in the cutest way she knew, and smiled into the camera.

There. That ought to give them something to chew on for the next 24 hours.

§

Catherine and Nancy sat in the small dining room across from the Vice President's office in the West Wing. It was done in dove gray and burgundy and the wall held a collection of pen and ink drawings of scenes on the C&O Canal. The table was a rich dark cherry.

They were eating a lunch of messy but delicious tacos Catherine wouldn't dare consume in public. She had a large cloth napkin tucked into her collar to protect the coral suit that had to take her through three more meetings and a speech to the Maryland chapter of the League of Women Voters.

"These tacos are delicious, Catherine. Who cooks this stuff?"

"The chef came with the President. He's from one of those L.A. restaurants. And I think he goes when Drummond goes — somewhere back in the rich hills of California." She put her hand to her mouth. "I can't believe I said that...when Drummond goes. I meant, when he leaves office. Not...you know."

"Don't worry." Nancy unbuttoned the top of her blouse. "See, no wires here. I'm not going to turn you in to the tabloids."

Catherine laughed. "I know."

"So how soon do they think he'll be out of the hospital?"

"Come on, don't you read the blogs? Or listen to Jerry Rash? The word is that the nefarious Democratic forces — including me — have got the President strapped down on a gurney screaming to get back to work — and this is all a big ploy to get me in power." Catherine nibbled another piece of taco and smiled ruefully.

"Wait. Wasn't that the plot of some movie a while ago? The real President is ill, and they pick a guy that looks just like him…"

"It does sound familiar."

"But seriously. How is he?"

"If all goes well, he'll be out by Friday."

"And then he'll come back to work?"

"On a limited schedule, they think," Catherine said. "So, what's up in France with the detective work? We have to talk quick. I've got another appointment in about 10 minutes. So much for leisurely executive lunches."

Nancy's voice became gentle. "The detective I hired – Stuart – went to that church in Paris near where you stayed. The nun you described turned out to be a Sister DelaCroix." She put her hand across the table and placed it on Catherine's arm. "They told him she died about four years ago. He made discreet inquiries about what might have happened to little orphans in the early 80's…but the answers were vague. No one knows who Elizabeth might have gone to. Right now he's going through hospital and court records for babies born on the right day. They have a formal way of recording these arrangements, of course, but it's not certain that every baby who got adopted would have gone through channels."

Catherine found that her appetite had gone. She put her fork down and lifted the napkin to her eyes, surprised at the sudden emotion. "Oh, Nance. I never imagined…I thought I had done the right thing. Giving Elizabeth a life with a real family." For a moment she saw the small but beautiful church where she had gone to pray every day while she was pregnant, asking God to help her know what was best for her child. She could see the light slanting through long stained glass windows, and hear the whispered French of the nuns as they walked quietly down the aisles. The smell of incense and the chill of stone all mixed together with the memory of awe and fear she felt during those six confusing months in Paris.

In the end, she had decided to trust in the charity of one of the nuns, a woman old enough to be Catherine's mother – a woman who looked at her with sympathetic eyes as she knelt and prayed and cried.

"I'm sorry, Catherine." Nancy's voice brought her back to the present, and she looked into the concerned eyes of her friend. "I wish I had more to tell you. He did say that with the exact birth date, he was hopeful that the trail could still be followed. They probably reissued the birth certificate in another name."

"We only have two days – before the payoff is due."

"Well…do you think these people really know? And your daughter is the secret they're talking about?"

Catherine put her head into her hands, and let herself sigh in a way that she could never do in public. "I don't know, Nancy. That's what's crazy. They may know nothing – they may know everything. But I… I just can't afford for this to get out. It's too much of a political bombshell." She untucked her napkin and stood up. "I need to find out where my daughter is so I can figure out what to do."

"I told the detective that time was critical. He's hired local people to comb the records."

"Okay. Thanks. Let me know if you hear anything else." Catherine dabbed at her mouth with the cloth napkin. She stood up. "I have to go over a briefing paper for my next meeting." She tried to keep the sadness out of her voice.

Nancy walked to the other side of the table and put her arms around the taller Catherine. "I know this must be painful," she said, her voice taut with compassion.

Catherine shook her head, holding back the tears that were always dangerously close to the surface these days. "It's just…that thinking about this has brought it all back. Pulled all those memories into my mind again. I thought I had wrapped them up and put them away for good." Catherine broke away from her friend, but gently. "Nancy, I don't have time to get emotional over this. If crying for Elizabeth would help her, or help me find her, I'd cry buckets. But it won't. And I've got an obligation to my constituents not to let this situation keep me from doing my job – and running for the next one." Catherine buttoned her jacket and squared her shoulders.

"Of course." Nancy put her hand on the door to the hallway. "You're very brave, you know. Carrying on, with this on your mind."

"Not brave, Nancy." Catherine said. She tried to smile, but her muscles trembled. "I'm like any mom, worried about my kids. It's just that I'm trying to run for president at the same time."

§

Zane stared at the ceiling, eyes open. The only thing that kept him awake in the daytime was coffee and blow. The only thing that put him to sleep at night was sex and liquor. And even that wasn't working anymore.

"Damn," he said, just under his breath, and punched the pillow. Maria stirred beside him. He checked the clock radio on the table. 4:17.

How the hell had he gotten himself into this box? And why?

He rolled off the side of the bed. He went into Maria's kitchen and grabbed what was left of a bag of chips from the cabinet, and the last bottle of beer from the fridge. He pried the cap open against the edge of the counter and sucked at the foamy top.

In the living room, he pushed the ON button and the TV glowed to life. CNN Headline News was reporting on negotiations between Israel and the Palestinians. The anchor had red hair and a lot of eye make-up. Behind her head, the icon changed to one that read "Election Update." Zane turned up the sound.

"A CNN poll shows that if the election were held today, 47% of registered voters would vote for Democratic Vice President Catherine Young in a race against GOP candidate

Governor Jerusha Hutchins. Hutchins would attract 36% of the vote, and other candidates combined for another 10%. The remaining 7% were undecided."

The screen showed a pie chart depicting the percentages in red, white and blue. Under the pie was a statement indicating that the poll had been taken by telephone from a random sample of the population and was accurate to within plus or minus four percentage points.

The scene changed to a rally for Governor Hutchins. Wearing her trademark red heels and bouffant hair, she was smiling at the crowd, looking like the Atlanta-born Georgia peach she was.

"How y'all doin'?" she yelled.

The crowd roared and the signs bobbed as a camera swung to cover the audience, most of them hoisting identical yellow diamonds with black letters that mimicked traffic signs – *LEFT LANE ENDS*. The flip side declared *Follow the Leader – Jerusha for President.*

As the camera continued to pan the enthusiastic faces of supporters, the CNN reporter continued, "These latest polls put Vice President and acting President Catherine Young, the Democratic nominee, eleven points ahead of GOP candidate Governor Jerusha Hutchins, despite the fervor of her Liberty Party supporters."

Zane felt an initial surge of excitement when he saw the numbers. A week ago the poll would have filled him with elation. Now it only made him wonder if he'd be there to savor the victory in November.

If he couldn't get some big cash soon, he would be…what? Floating at the bottom of the Potomac? He shuddered to think about it.

§

Catherine stepped into the room first as Zane held open the door. Six suited FBI and Secret Service agents stood as she entered.

"Good morning, Madam Vice President," they said, nearly as one.

"Sit down, ladies and gentleman," she said, waving her hands. "Let's get right to it. We're all busy."

The small conference room was not as ornate as some of the others in the White House. It held only a rectangular table, walnut chairs suitable for long meetings, and a sideboard on which muffins and Danish sat on a tray beside a coffee pot.

"So. What do you have for me?" she asked.

"Vice President Young, we've analyzed the paper, the glue, the pasted-on letters, and of course the fingerprints." Ralph Harwood passed a copy of a report across the table to her. "The paper on which the letters were written is standard computer paper – it's available at any Staples or office supply store. Comes in reams of 500 sheets. No detectable pressure markings on the paper itself which would give any clues."

"Pressure markings?" Catherine asked.

"Sometimes you can see indentations when something has been written by hand on a sheet above – but that didn't happen in this case."

"I see. Go on."

"The envelopes were a generic brand also sold by Staples. The glue used to affix the letters came from a glue stick produced by Dennison – available at office supply stores and many drug stores. The letters had no return addresses, only your name and Zane's name on the front in pasted letters. The letters in those names and the body of the letters came from this month's issue of Vogue, a fashion magazine."

"I'm familiar with Vogue," Catherine said. Her fingers drummed the table. "How did you figure it was Vogue?"

"We have analysts who compare the typeface to current periodicals. This was printed on glossy stock, and one of the strings of letters left a page number visible. We were able to trace that to the particular articles, both headline and body text, printed in the July Vogue."

"Good job."

"Which leads to the possibility that the blackmailer is a female."

Catherine arched one eyebrow. "There was always that possibility."

Harwood inclined his head. "Of course. But the likely profile for an individual who would make such threats is overwhelmingly male."

Zane scribbled something on his yellow pad. Catherine glanced over and saw the word Vogue followed by the female symbol.

"Anything else?" she asked.

"Unfortunately, the fingerprints which we could detect, as anticipated, consisted of only yours and Mr. Zarillo's. The perpetrator must have worn gloves."

Zane scrawled on his pad. No prints, it said. Gloves.

"The big question is how the two letters got on your desks," Harwood said.

"I assumed mine came in with the mail," Catherine said.

"It wasn't mailed. It only had your name on the front. No return address, no stamp of any kind."

Catherine nodded, feeling foolish that she hadn't noticed.

"It was placed there – though not necessarily by someone who was involved," Harwood said. "Your assistant left no prints on the envelope – and she doesn't recall seeing this letter. Which would surely stand out if she were paying attention."

"She always pays attention," Catherine said.

"Madam Vice President, I think you should consider the possibility that it's an insider."

"What?" Zane asked, then looked at Catherine.

"I find that hard to believe," she said.

"Nevertheless, there seems to be no other explanation for the letter simply appearing on your desk as it did. And the companion letter on Mr. Zarillo's desk."

Catherine shook her head. "No one on my staff would do this to me."

"Madam Vice President, I didn't mean to suggest that it was someone on your staff. Anyone with access to your office in the early morning hours could have done this. Cleaning or maintenance people, the clerical staff...any number of individuals. We're compiling data on everyone who was in here within 24 hours before the letter appeared."

Catherine pushed her chair back from the table. "Keep working on it. Let me know what you find out."

"Of course we haven't finished with the most critical part of the investigation – that will take a few days."

Catherine stood, and the whole table scrambled to stand with her. "And what is that, Ralph?" She moved toward the door and lifted a miniature bran muffin from the tray on the sideboard.

"The seal on the envelope. Someone licked the envelope to seal it closed."

"Ah. DNA. Of course," Catherine said, turning back to Harwood with interest.

Zane, right behind her, stumbled trying not to step on her foot.

Harwood smiled his approval. "Exactly, Madam Vice President. We're doing DNA testing on the saliva the perpetrator left on the seal. Then we'll take samples from everyone who was in the White House during the period in question."

"How long will it take?"

"With restriction fragment length polymorphisms, or RFLP – it used to take three to four weeks. But our lab is equipped to do PCR analysis, or polymerase chain reaction – "

"Spare me the jargon, Ralph. I appreciate that you all are the experts here. How long?"

"Three days, tops, Madam Vice President."

Catherine smiled. "Excellent job, ladies and gentlemen, Ralph." She put her hand on the doorknob. "I'll leave it in your capable hands."

"Yes ma'am."

"As far as I'm concerned, you can't find this bastard fast enough. Right Zane?"

Zane nodded. "Absolutely, Madam Vice President."

12

ZANE LOOKED OVER the FBI lab report on the blackmail note for the fifth time. His eyes were drawn to the last line on the second page.

Bodily Fluids: Saliva residue available in trace amounts mixed in with sealing glue on envelope flap. Sample forwarded to lab for analysis. Approximate time required for accurate test results: 2 - 3 days. PCR analysis of DNA may then be compared with cheek swab findings from potential suspects.

There was a quick double knock and the door to his office swung open. Zane sat up straight.

"Catherine." He pushed away from the desk. "I was just looking over the FBI report. It looks like only a matter of time before we find this guy – or guys. Whoever."

She nodded. "I hope so, Zane." She seemed distracted. "Do you think that the Hutchins-inspired idea that this whole Drummond in the hospital episode is a conspiracy will have any traction?"

"Well… with the crazies, maybe."

"But the crazies vote, don't they?"

Zane nodded. "More and more of them."

§

Maria stepped out of the shower and ran a towel over her moist skin. She walked through her tiny bathroom to her bureau and picked out a lacy bra and matching panties in turquoise. She'd be seeing Zane later.

He'd been completely stressed out recently, and wasn't all that pleasant to spend time with, but he was still important to her. She wanted to keep him satisfied.

After shimmying into the panties and hooking her bra, she flipped open her Mac and looked at the BuffBeast. A photo of the Vice President filled the front page, and Maria could feel her heart begin to beat faster.

As always, she examined the warm brown eyes and the fair, freckled skin, trying to see something in that face that would give her some answers. Shaking her head, Maria clicked the laptop shut and went over to her closet. But before she opened the door she turned around and went back to her bureau.

Rummaging in the back of her bottom drawer, she looked for the file she knew she'd find there. The one with information she had spent years collecting. For a moment she couldn't locate it. She started to toss clothes onto the floor, not caring about the mess in her rush to put her hands on the precious newspaper clippings and correspondence.

Ah. There!

Maria yanked the file out of the back of the drawer and opened it up.

It was empty.

§

"Nance, you want a drink? Wine?" Catherine stood in front of the open refrigerator in her kitchen and looked at the beverage possibilities. "Or I have Coke. Poland Springs?" She was wearing a thin white T-shirt over an old pair of jeans.

"Are you going to have wine? I will if you will," Nancy said. She sat on one of the old chairs around the oak table with one knee pulled against her chest. She looked like the yoga fan that she was.

"Not me. Sorry. I'll fall asleep if I have wine. And I've got more to do before I can turn in. Three more fundraising appearances tomorrow. It never ends." She filled a glass with spring water and another with wine. "But you go ahead." She handed the wine to Nancy.

"Catherine, you ought to make time for some relaxing. You know what you need?"

Catherine rolled her eyes as she sat down opposite her friend. "What – You're going to tell me I need a good lay?"

"Catherine!" Nancy pursed her lips and mimicked shock.

"What? I do need a good lay." Catherine laughed and put her elbows on the table to prop up her head. "I can't even remember how long it's been."

"I do."

"You do? Jeez, I'm in bad shape if you have better recall of my sex life than I do." She waited, and then reached across and slugged Nancy. "So are you going to tell me? Oh, now I remember. Greg Murphy – wow, that was six, seven years ago? Before I was elected Vice President."

"Wouldn't that make a great article for one of the confession magazines?" Nancy laughed as she held her hands up to frame the headline. "Starving For Sex Since I Joined The Drummond Administration."

"Well, how am I supposed to meet men in this job?"

"You're only surrounded by them every day."

Catherine gave her a withering look. "But they all report to me."

"So order them to be stand up guys. Tell them it's in the interests of national security. So you don't go bonkers from horniness and decide to blow up Kazakhstan." Nancy sipped her wine in one elegant hand while gesturing with the other. "You look great. Especially in that tight T-shirt. I'm sure no one would protest."

"Right." Catherine shook her head. "As if I don't have enough problems with what I already did. It would make good press for the Democratic party, don't you think? Perhaps an affair with a hot younger man."

Nancy groaned. "Maybe something involving a story about the Appalachian Trail? Or trolling around Craigslist for potential matches."

"Sure," Catherine said. "Though you have to admit that if it's an affair between people of the opposite sex it's considered tame these days." She picked up her water and took a drink. "Somehow I think my love life will have to wait until I get out of office. Which might be sooner than I thought it would be."

Nancy put her wine glass back on the table. Her face was serious. "So where are you on the blackmail scheme?"

"Nowhere. I'm prepared to come up with some money – if only to buy time. Though the FBI says that's just playing into their hands. But I haven't heard anything further – no instructions about where or when. I'm half afraid these guys will change their minds and just start giving out the information."

"Why the heck would they do that?"

"Nancy, I don't know why they'd do anything. I don't know what their motives are, or what they know...the whole thing could be a great big hoax. I spend hours lying in bed trying to puzzle this out. And I can't. The only thing I can do is keep on campaigning and react to their moves." Catherine got up from the table and moved to the sink to rinse out her glass. "I hate like hell to play their game, but I don't have any choice."

Catherine let out a pent-up breath and turned back to Nancy. "And what do you hear from our detective friend Stuart? Any progress on the Paris end?"

Nancy picked her glass up and brought it to the sink. "He called today. He has five people on it. There are a few leads. But lots and lots of birth certificates have to be checked out. After Elizabeth was adopted, he says, they would probably have reissued her birth certificate in her new name." Nancy put her hand on Catherine's arm. "Paris is a great big city. People come in and out from other parts of the world all the time."

"You're telling me that he may never find her."

Nancy nodded. "There's that possibility. At any rate, it looks like it will take a long time. Longer than you have."

"Nancy," Catherine said. Her throat suddenly tightened. "You don't think that anyone is hurting Elizabeth, do you? Because if I thought that she was in danger – "

"No, I don't. Catherine, you'll make yourself nuts if you keep thinking about that."

"You're right." Catherine walked over to Nancy and gave her a quick hug. "Now scoot, so I can look at two more speeches that I don't want to give and that nobody wants to hear. So this moderately horny, completely imperfect, nearly nutty woman can be elected president."

Nancy laughed. "And you think that's not an improvement over the men we've elected?"

§

Zane stood in Aisle 9 at People's Drug Store. He glanced toward the front. No one there.

Forget it, man. You're paranoid. No one here is looking at you.

Zane backed up slightly and looked toward the end of the aisle. There it was. The eyeball mirror, like Big Brother, catching the whole store in one round glance.

He paid and left the store, the glass door opening onto humid evening air. He walked across Pennsylvania Avenue amid the evening crush of traffic. One impatient Mercedes created a breeze beside him as it turned a corner seconds after he had cleared the lane.

Zane had reached the 1600 block, where cars were not allowed. He walked along the black wrought iron fence that surrounded the White House. During the day, there would be a long line of tourists waiting to see the East Wing. But tours were over for the day, and those that hurried along the broad sidewalk at this hour were mostly working people, hastening to the Metro station or to parking garages where cars were ready to take them home.

With one quick shudder, Zane became aware of someone walking behind him and to his left. Too close.

"Zane darling."

His heart lurched. Devon. The stink of his cologne was unmistakable.

"Devon." He kept walking. He didn't have the energy to pretend they were pals tonight.

"Have you found the money yet?"

"Working on it, Devon. I'll have it."

Devon gave a light chuckle. "But if you don't...." There was a bright flash in his right hand, held low and in front. Zane looked down. A blade.

His feet stopped, and his throat gave an involuntary swallow. Surely Devon wouldn't cut him, with White House security guards standing ten yards away. Zane glanced over at the guards. They were talking, leaning against the fence, arms crossed. It was too dark for them to see what was in Devon's hand, even if they had been looking.

When Zane looked back, the switchblade was gone. Devon brought his face close to Zane's. Cologne so thick it made him gag.

"It would be such a shame to have to cut your pretty face."

And then he turned and walked away, quickly disappearing into the dusky evening.

Zane found himself trembling. Jesus.

The adrenaline of relief coursed through his veins and turned to anger. Who did that asshole think he was? No prep school grad with a little blade was going to tell Zane what to do.

He's got more than a blade, though, doesn't he, Zane? Maybe you better get something to protect yourself. Because he sure as hell will be coming back.

Zane walked on toward the White House gate, waving to the guards as he passed them, and was allowed to walk onto the White House grounds without a search of his bag – they probably figured it was his dinner. He made his way through the wooden doors and up the stairs, nodding hello to the few staff members and Secret Service agents he passed.

He closed and locked his office door, emptying the contents of the bag onto his desk and pulling out an old Time Magazine from his drawer. He rustled around in his desk, hoping there might be an envelope in there. Nothing.

He left his office and made his way to the kitchen.

"Zane. Do you have a minute?" It was Ralph Harwood. For the second time tonight, Zane felt his heart leap with surprise.

"Sure. What can I do for you, Ralph?" He thought of hiding the sponge he was holding behind his back, but realized that would be suspicious. Instead he waved it in front of him. "Had a spill in my office." He gave a sheepish grin.

"Right. I've done that." Harwood was not interested in his sponge. His expression was serious. "We're coming up on the pay date for the blackmailer. I haven't been able to persuade the Vice President about the enormity of the mistake paying the blackmailer would be. Of course, I wouldn't presume to dictate – "

"Hey Ralph," Zane waved his free hand dismissively, "it's just you and me."

Harwood gave a perfunctory smile. He ran a hand over his head, as though smoothing down hair that was too short to require smoothing. "Of course. Anyway. I'm trying to make your boss understand that she can't pay these guys off. It sets a bad precedent, but more than that, it means they'll just keep coming back for more."

Zane nodded. "Makes sense to me."

"You can't reward criminals. You've got to punish them – give them an incentive to stop their misdeeds – not pay them for it."

Zane sensed in himself an urge to contradict this pompous windbag. But mouthing off now would be stupid.

"So you want me to talk to Catherine?" Zane asked.

"I'd appreciate it if you would." Harwood did look grateful. It was as though he found himself in a strange new world where women were in charge in unexpected areas, and he had not quite adjusted.

Zane relaxed. The guy was just trying to do his job. And keep Catherine out of trouble. He could understand that.

"Absolutely, Ralph. I'll talk to her." He switched the sponge to his left hand, and put the right one out to shake. Harwood grabbed it and gave him a hearty wringing.

"I know she listens to you," Harwood said.

"By the way, any leads yet?" Zane asked.

"We're counting on the DNA. Have you had a chance to give us a cheek swab?" Harwood seemed to realize the implication. "Just a formality, you understand. We have to do absolutely everybody. Me too, crazy as that sounds. So that we can assure the FBI nothing was overlooked."

Zane nodded. He wet his lips. "Haven't gotten a chance yet. You know how the campaign keeps me running."

"Just so we can put you in the 'clear' column." Harwood smiled with what was probably supposed to be humor.

Zane attempted a grin back. "Yup. Well, I'll do my best to get Catherine to understand your point."

"Appreciate it." Harwood gave a nod and walked down the hall.

13

CATHERINE GASPED AND let the letter fall onto her desk.

CoR*n*er of 7th and E, N.E. In a **duff***el* bag. $100k in
UNMarKed 100's. $100K in uNmark*ed* 50's. $50K in u*nm*ark**ed**
$20's. Fri*d*ay, lEAve it thERe at 1:00 p.m., tHen w*alk* awAy.
Not y**Ou** – some flUNky. No *Feds.*

Catherine buzzed Lorraine. "Get Ralph Harwood in here.
ASAP. And tell him to bring an evidence kit."

§

Harwood and three other agents stood over Catherine's
desk and watched as Harwood carefully lifted the letter with
tweezers, placing it into a polyurethane bag. He sealed the top
and carried it carefully by the edges over to a table near the wall.
The other agents were obviously eager to get a closer look, but
satisfied themselves by standing a polite distance away and
craning their necks to see. Harwood repeated the procedure
with the envelope.

"You just found this, Madam Vice President?" Harwood
asked.

Catherine ignored the possible barb. "I called you the
moment I saw it." She was standing in front of the two
documents, each in its own baggy. "Ralph, I don't think this
letter came in this envelope. The top had already been slit open
– which would be normal for correspondence that Lorraine

passed on to me for personal attention – but the first blackmail letter wasn't. It was still sealed. Plus, this one was addressed by hand, and the stamp was cancelled. I don't think our guy would risk that. At least not if he bothered to cut-and-paste the address on the outside of the first letter."

Harwood nodded, his face betraying the fact that he had come to the same conclusions. "We'll check this envelope flap for DNA too – and compare them."

"And if this is an envelope that was previously used, there could be a matching letter around here somewhere...." Catherine picked up the bag with the envelope.

Harwood quickly reached for the bag, and then stopped himself. "By the edges, please...Madam Vice President."

"Right. Sorry." Catherine moved her fingers to the edges of the bag and peered at the postmark. Oregon.

She walked the five steps to her desk and buzzed Lorraine. "Yes Ma'am?"

"Lorraine. Please check your correspondence logs and tell me what has come in in the last few days from Oregon."

"Right away," Lorraine said.

Catherine walked back to the table, where Harwood was again examining the letter. "I want to get these to the FBI lab immediately," he said. "We need to do a full analysis. The DNA testing on the first letter could be ready by as early as tomorrow."

"And tomorrow the money is due."

Harwood looked pained. "Madam Vice President, I think it would be a grave mistake to pay these guys off – "

"I know what you think, Ralph. I appreciate your input. But I've decided. I'm going to pay."

"Surely you don't intend to go down there yourself."

Catherine raised her eyebrows. "If you read the letter, you can see that I'm not invited. I tell you what – you can pick the guy who delivers the money. And you can put 20 agents in discreet spots within view of the corner. Any blackmailer with half a brain will anticipate that we'll do that, no matter what he wants."

"You're assuming this guy has half a brain."

Catherine didn't bother to respond.

Harwood gingerly picked up both baggies. "Please let me know if your secretary finds – "

He was interrupted by the buzz of the intercom. Catherine turned toward her desk with a smile. "That will be my amazing administrative assistant, Lorraine."

She punched the intercom button. "Find anything?"

"Yes ma'am. Four letters from Oregon that reached your office within the last week. All have been located, and I have them here for your review. Standard constituent letters. Unfortunately, we haven't been able to locate the envelope for one of them."

Catherine beamed. "Marvelous job, Lorraine. I'll need the one without the envelope. But don't touch it again. Just leave it wherever it is, and Agent Harwood will pick it up from you."

Harwood nodded, looking pleased, and moved toward the door with the two baggies. "Let's hope that the Oregon letter hasn't been through so many hands by now that we can't lift a few useful prints." He passed through a shaft of brilliant morning sun that was lighting up the swirling dust motes in the air.

"Wait." Catherine took two long steps and was by his side. She lifted the baggy containing the letter out of his hands, holding it by the edges. She turned it until the streak of sunlight was directly behind the letter. "There," she said, pointing to the bottom edge of the letter. "See it?"

"What?" Harwood moved close to her side, looking slightly self-conscious about standing right beside her. He let out a low whistle. "Will you look at that? The White House watermark. The paper came from this building."

Catherine turned to him, feeling a moment of triumph at having solved part of the riddle. But immediately her thrill turned to dread. This was not good news at all. This meant that someone close by – probably someone she trusted – was out to betray her.

§

Zane stabbed at the doorbell for the third time. His half-brother Will drove a UPS delivery truck, but he was sometimes home in the morning.

"Who is it?" asked a sleepy voice from behind small windowpanes.

"It's Zane. Open the door, Will."

The doorknob turned and Will stood there in his undershorts scratching his head. "Hey bro. You woke me up."

Zane pushed the door open farther and walked into the living room. The TV hummed with the sound from a music video channel and the plaid couch was littered with what looked like last night's pretzels. The trail of pretzels led to the end table where a couple of glasses and a Jack Daniels empty sat beside a white plastic bowl.

"You look like you could use a cup of coffee. Let me make some," Zane said, walking directly to the kitchen. "I need to talk to you."

"Thanks. I'm a little hung over. Had some friends over last night, after work." Will, chunky and medium-brown, one inch taller and four years younger than Zane, ran his hands across his eyes.

"No shit." Zane pulled a jar of instant coffee out of the cabinet and started water boiling.

"Come on," Will said. "Like you never had a drink yourself."

"But I know when to stop."

Will flopped into one of the two yellow plastic chairs beside his Formica table. He smiled. "Right. But don't tell me you ain't got your own jones. Just not booze." He yawned. "And how did I get lucky enough for a visit this early in the day? Your boss finally figure out what a bullshit artist you are? She kick you out?" He barked a laugh, then groaned and put his hands up to his head.

Zane gave an involuntary grimace. "No, I'm still employed, idiot." He looked hard at his kid brother, whom he hadn't seen in months. Will wasn't looking too good. Since getting involved in politics, Zane didn't come around for informal visits with his brother very often any more. Especially since his stint at the rehab center six years ago, and getting off the coke, Zane travelled in different circles than Will did.

But Will was the kind of guy who could help him with what he needed.

"Hey, bro – you're not boffin' her, are you?" Will asked, with a bleary grin. "I mean, she's single. And you're no slouch with the ladies."

"Shut up, man." The suggestion, which he had heard joked about before, suddenly made Zane very tired. He lifted the pot of boiling water from the stove.

"Ooh, looks like we hit a hot button. 'Sokay, Zane, your secret's safe with me."

"Drop it, Will. I'm not fucking her. No interest, either way." Zane poured water into a cracked mug. He put the coffee on the table and hunted for a spoon in what passed for the silverware drawer in Will's kitchen. He stirred the coffee and shoved it toward his brother. "Are you awake yet? I have something serious to discuss."

Will took the mug to his lips, and yelped when the hot liquid moved across his tongue. "You better keep that White House job. 'Cause you're sure as hell not ready for coffee making at 7-Eleven."

Zane turned one of the dinette chairs around and straddled it. "Can you get me a gun?"

Will put the mug down with a thump. "A gun? Are you in trouble?"

"Don't ask any questions. Just let me know. Can you get me a gun?"

"Hell, Zane, you can buy a gun yourself. They're legal. You got more money than I do. Fill out the papers – "

"I can't do it that way."

"You mean you want a street gun. No trail."

"That's right." Zane looked at his little brother. Was this something Will could do?

Will fingered the day-old growth on his chin. "Shit, man. What are you into? If you need a gun, that's serious."

Zane reached across the table and put his hand on Will's arm. "I need your help, Will. Can you do this for me?"

Will looked up. His eyes were slightly bloodshot. His face showed concern for his brother. Zane, the golden boy of the neighborhood. The street smart Italian kid from Jersey – the white guy with the black brothers – who made it all the way to Harvard Business School, and was now working in the White House. Zane knew Will was unhappy about his request, but he didn't know who else he could trust.

Will nodded, finally.

"I guess I could, Zane. But are you gonna tell me what's up?"

"I can't. Sorry. It's better you don't know."

Will looked at Zane for a slow moment, the conversation seeming to sober him as much as the coffee.

"If you need a gun, Zane, I'll get you a gun," he said.

"Thanks, Will," Zane said. He squeezed the arm he was still holding. "I knew I could count on you."

§

Catherine stood behind a wooden podium at the Mayflower Hotel, finishing her third speech of the day. As the applause washed over her, she soaked in the sensation of approval – and the opportunity to serve. Did it now feel especially sweet because her chance to stay in office seemed suddenly to be in jeopardy?

Catherine's rise through the ranks had been so all-consuming that she had rarely taken the time to stop and analyze her success. She simply put one foot in front of the other – and somehow what began as an interest in local politics had turned into a path to national office. A path that was just opening up to women as she ventured through each door along the way.

Catherine didn't see herself as a groundbreaker. She saw herself as the "good girl" her parents had always expected. She was born to educational privilege, and she had encountered little trouble in satisfying the requirements involved.

A well-respected women's college – Mount Holyoke. A stint in the Peace Corps following the ideals of her generation. Law School, for lack of any keener other clear ambition.

Her one rebellion – daring to love Chuka – had led to pain and heartache so unexpectedly sharp that it changed her forever. After she gave up her first child, nothing was the same. For a while, she simply went through the motions. She came home, traumatized and troubled by her pregnancy and her decision to let Elizabeth go. But she couldn't let it show. As far as her family knew, she had spent only a fun-filled extra six months living in Paris after her two years of service in Africa.

She started her first year of law school, and she hit the books hard. There was nothing else she wanted to do. She got such spectacular grades that she was first in her class. A summer job on Capitol Hill with one of her father's old school chums filled another few months. And then it was back to Georgetown in the fall, sleepwalking through Evidence and "Commie Trans" – Commercial Transactions – and spending hour upon hour in the library.

When she first met Paul, she recognized his interest in her. But Paul registered zero on her Geiger counter of desire. He was sweet, and quiet, and a bit on the geeky side. Without much encouragement, he made wooing Catherine a major subject in his second year of med school. And slowly he warmed the icy crust around her heart.

She finished Georgetown Law, and they married. She loved him, but in a tempered, placid way. He fit into the life she would create for herself – a life of safe, small steps. A life in which passion had little part.

Catherine started to practice law at a firm in suburban Maryland, and while Paul concentrated on his medical residency, she focused on her job. After Lily was born, Catherine kept working, but when Mike came along having two children suddenly made life tremendously complicated. Even though they had the money to hire a nanny, the children's life seemed to zip by so quickly that Catherine opted to leave the law firm and spend the rest of their preschool years at home. Her children suffused her life with more love than she had ever imagined. But mixed in with that joy was the bittersweet tug of wondering – always, and in secret – about her first baby.

Life went on, and the children grew. Her politics was part-time, first a term on the local School Board and then in the Maryland state legislature, as Catherine gradually gained in both political savvy and admirers. She was rather astonished at her election to Congress when the kids were 12 and 14 – and they were as proud as their Dad that Mom was going to Washington. Fortunately, the commute from Potomac to the Capitol was a convenient one. Catherine loved to gently nurture and then fight for bills as they made their torturous way from committee to the floor of Congress. She proved adept at patiently working the system by building coalitions. All of the struggling and often ugly infighting was worth it when something good was finally achieved.

Life was busy but happy during Catherine's fourth year in Congress when the stunning blow of Paul's heart attack tore her apart. Catherine had grown to love the gentle man completely, and to depend upon his steady hand in all things. When he died suddenly at the age of 47, she looked around and realized that he had been the foundation upon which her life was built. The kids were still teenagers, and Catherine turned to them for emotional support. Together, the family of three staggered through the next several years, leaning on each other. Catherine quenched her loneliness by working harder than ever.

Four years ago, when Tom Drummond had asked her to run as his Vice President, she had been amazed and humbled. She had never imagined holding such a position – but then again, girls born in 1955 grew up with visions of an apron-clad Donna Reed in front of a vacuum while Father Knows Best sat at the head of the table. Politics was for the guys.

Catherine had never had a model for a woman in the White House. So she became the model. A woman one part intelligence, one part warmth, and two parts ambition. The longer she was in politics, the more she realized that politicians were just people. And at this stage she knew that she was just as qualified to be president as anybody else — and a lot more qualified than some.

Today, as she looked out across the beaming faces of the audience at the Mayflower, she realized that these men and women saw in her proof that in America, anyone could grow up to be president. Except that it had never really been true for girls.

Until now.

Catherine nodded and smiled as she finished speaking and the applause swelled and died. She walked to her seat at the back of the stage, where Zane was applauding along with the other dignitaries.

"Did Harwood talk to you about the plan for tomorrow?" she whispered to him as the host stood at the podium wrapping up the event.

"Yes," Zane said. "He told me you were all set to bring the cash. But aren't you afraid that marked money will blow the deal?"

"No. It's marked with infrared ink. The FBI says it's undetectable." Catherine stood up, and Zane did too. "Besides, whoever it is won't get very far. The place is going to be crawling with agents. He couldn't possibly get away with that duffel bag."

The meeting was breaking up now, and the man who had just spoken was coming toward Catherine and Zane with a broad grin and an outstretched hand. Zane grabbed Catherine by the arm.

"Agents?" he asked. "But what about — "

"Ouch, Zane." Catherine pulled her arm out of his grip and frowned. The Secret Service agent standing in the wings with a wire snaking out of his collar began to move toward them.

"Sorry, Catherine. I didn't mean...."

Catherine stepped toward her smiling host and put out her hand to shake his. As she did, she whispered one more thing to Zane. "Tomorrow we're going to get that SOB."

14

ZANE WAS SWEATING.

He stood near the corner of M Street and Wisconsin in Georgetown and punched the numbers on the prepaid phone he had just bought with cash. Night music drifted through the summer air. People laughed as they passed him, groups of girls showing off their skimpy dresses and bare backs, couples linking arms and sliding hips together.

The sound of ringing came over the phone.

"Governor Hutchins for President. May I help you?"

"Uh, this is Zane Zarillo. I need to talk to Governor Hutchins's campaign manager."

"I'm sorry, Mr. Zarillo, but he's not here right now. May I take a message?"

"No. No." If he didn't act now, he would lose his nerve. He had to be sure that he would have cash by Saturday. Plan B had to be set in motion. "Uh...is there another number where I can reach him? It's very important. I've got to talk to him tonight."

"Just a moment, please."

There was a muffled sound as the phone was covered by a hand. Zane waited, his head down, turning into the shadows off one of the side streets.

"Mr. Zarillo?" It was a male voice, one with a hearty tone of false affection. "To what do we owe the honor?"

"Who is this?"

"I'm sorry. This is Chill Slavin. I'm Blair Faulkner's assistant." If this conversation had been held in person, Chill would have been pumping Zane's hand. "You were calling for Blair, weren't you? Carol said you asked for the Governor's campaign manager."

"Yes. I need to talk to him tonight – or to the Governor directly."

"Well, I'd sure like to help you out there, Zane. I always say, war goes easier when enemies cooperate." He let loose a booming laugh, and Zane had to pull the phone away from his ear.

"I have to talk to someone now."

"Can you give me a hint about what this is in reference to?"

"No. Sorry."

"Hmph. Well, then. Unfortunately, the Governor is out on the road giving a speech tonight. Another fundraiser – hell, you know the drill." More booming laughter.

"Is there a cell number? You must have some way to reach her."

"Well, sure I do, Zane. I just don't know why I should give it to you." Boom. The laugh.

"Chill...if you get me in touch with the Governor tonight, she'll be very grateful. I promise you."

"Really, Zane? Sounds intriguing. You guys sure do know how to sweet talk." Boom. A pause. "Let me see if I can get it from one of the ladies in charge of such things."

There was another moment of muffled discussion, and then Chill spoke again. "You can reach Blair in the limo. Just about now." Chill stopped and Zane could hear the rustle of a jacket sleeve being scrunched up to read a watch, "They should be between the rubber chicken at the Maryland CEO Club and the rubber chicken at Senator Dickson's Virginia estate. The number is 202-555-9306. Now don't make me sorry I did this."

"You won't be sorry," Zane said, and hung up quickly.

But I might be, he thought as he clicked off.

His fingers trembled as he held the cell in his left hand and looked down at the glowing buttons. He mumbled the number over and over. 555-9306. 555-9306. 555-9306.

Call. Do it now. Do it before you think about it too much.

He punched the numbers.

§

Catherine stepped into the dimly lit room and stood for a moment as her eyes adjusted. She cleared her throat quietly and saw the figure on the bed stir.

"Mr. President, sir? Is this a good time?" For a moment she felt awkward, wondering if she should have brought… what… flowers? That was silly. This was not a social call.

President Drummond sat up slowly, his hand reaching for the switch beside his bed. Both of them squinted as the harsh hospital light bloomed into whiteness.

"Catherine – yes, of course. I just dozed off… they told me you were coming. Please, take a seat."

She sat in one of the orange visitor chairs, noting that even though the President of the United States got a nice big private room, he didn't seem to get any better color scheme than the regular patients.

"How are you, Mr. President?"

"Doing better…coming along."

It was shocking to see him. His face was pinched and his body seemed wasted under the sheets. Tubes came out from the bedding, fluids moved up and down in the transparent plastic, and a bank of monitors beside his head registered his vital signs. For the first time, Catherine realized how close he must have come to death.

And how close she had come to suddenly taking his place permanently.

"So, how does it feel to be the most powerful leader of the free world?" Drummond managed a smile, and a tiny bit of the usual twinkle returned to his eyes.

"I…um…"

"Come on, Catherine, you can tell me the truth. It's pretty heady stuff, isn't it?"

She smiled. "Well, yes, it is. Also quite an awesome responsibility. I trust you'll be back soon to take over the reins."

As soon as she said it, she wished she could take it back. No reason to rush him. And she sure didn't want the poor man to feel guilty.

"Oh, have no fear, Catherine, I'll be back soon enough. They can't keep this old man down long." He turned a bit in his bed and grimaced at the effort. "I've convinced the docs that I can get out of here in a day or so – they have a full medical set-up at the White House anyway, and they keep me monitored every blessed minute – and then I can put in a few hours of work every day as I get my strength up."

"Sounds great," Catherine said, though she found it hard to believe that he would be ready to function that soon. She heard the door open and turned to see Jeffrey Silverstein entering with a bag from Cuisine Gourmet in his hand.

"Ah, my evening delivery has arrived," the President said, looking pleased. "Jeff has been kind enough to make sure that I don't have to subsist entirely on a hospital diet."

"Hello, Madam Vice President," Silverstein said, smiling as he took a small cardboard container out of the bag. "This will be our little secret, right?"

"Of course," she said. "So what is the secret executive meal? What's for dinner?"

"Not nearly as decadent as I might wish," Drummond said, carefully turning to open the container, "but at least it's not hospital cafeteria mush." He took out a small fruit tart and looked at it hungrily.

Catherine took that as her cue to stand up. "Well, I'll let you enjoy your dessert, and I look forward to hearing good reports about your progress. We'll keep the White House warm for you, Mr. President."

"Good night, my dear," he said, looking suddenly very tired. "Your country owes you a great debt. You're doing a wonderful job…and if all goes well, you'll soon have this job for real."

Catherine felt warm tears spring into her eyes, and found herself making a little bow as she left the room, her powers of speech having momentarily departed. Silverstein came out behind her, saying goodnight quietly, and closed the door behind him.

"So how is he doing?" Catherine asked when they had gotten a suitable distance from the room and from the several Secret Service agents who were stationed there.

"Despite how he looks, he's making excellent progress," Silverstein said. "He's a strong man." He put his hand on Catherine's arm. "And by the way? The special dessert – the doctors are all in on that. I wouldn't really put the safety of the country at risk to satisfy the President's sweet tooth."

Catherine smiled. "I'm glad to hear it." She hesitated, and then plunged in. "So when will he…"

"Take back the official reins of office? Pretty soon, I think. The day after tomorrow, probably. He's physically weak, but he's all there mentally. So we'll be getting a letter ready to formally hand back the power." He looked at Catherine and gave her a wry smile. "How has this been for you? Are you ready to go back to the minors?"

She nodded and smiled back at him. "It's not as though I have a say in the matter…but sure, I'm ready. It's been fun. A sort of dress rehearsal. And now I'll be happy – and Zane will definitely be happy – to be able to get back to my own campaign."

§

Zane rolled his car along the dirt driveway to where he could see a stone mansion aglow with lights. This must be the place. Cars were lined up in a grassy field on his right. He could see a half dozen chauffeurs in caps standing in front of the massive steps. One of them flicked his cigarette into a planter while another leaned against one of the sculpted lions guarding the entrance.

Zane felt a gut-deep urge to turn around. Twilight, a convergence of conservative politicians in a big house in Virginia. This was not a place where he wanted to be seen skulking in the dark. He turned the car carefully and drove back to the deserted dirt fork where Blair had told him to wait.

Fourteen minutes later a long black limousine pulled up beside him. The smoky rear window rolled down and he saw Blair Faulkner, the good ol' boy who worked for Hutchins, lean his fleshy face toward him.

"Zane. Now what in hell did you get me out of that fine party for?" Faulkner had the kind of reddened skin that made you wonder what he used for soap. His hair was the color of old wax, and lay pasted in a brilliantined mass across the dome of his head.

"I have some...information. For a price."

Faulkner grunted. "You're selling information."

"I said for a price. We have to talk payment first."

"Oh, sure. The Senator's good for it. But we need to know what it's worth before we'll talk payment."

Zane shook his head. "No negotiating. I want one hundred thousand dollars. By tomorrow. Then you get the information."

"You got to be shittin' me."

Zane felt his insides curl in anger. He said nothing.

"What the hell kind of information would be worth a hundred thousand bucks?" Faulkner slapped his thigh in amusement.

"It's...important information." Zane felt the sureness of his resolve slipping away. Why had he thought this would be easy? They had no reason to trust him. It made no sense that he would sell really damaging information on his own candidate. Unless he was the lowest kind of traitor.

The voices. Always there, a constant buzz, providing a background hum in his brain. Suddenly they saw their opening.

That's you, Zane. The lowest of the low. Scum. Fraud. Traitor.

He plowed ahead.

"Damaging information," he said.

"About who? The Governor?" Faulkner swung his head and looked toward someone in the dark recesses of the other side of the limo. For the first time Zane realized there could be other people listening.

Of course. They thought he was out to blackmail Hutchins. No doubt she had skeletons in her closet too...or more likely, her husband Quigley did. Zane would have laughed, but his stomach was clutching in spasms.

"No. About Catherine...about the Vice President."

There. That didn't feel so bad. Just the subject involved. He had to give them that.

"Catherine Young? Damaging information?" Faulkner slapped his thigh again. "So the perfect lady has some impurities in her heart." He gave a chuckle worthy of Goofy.

Zane saw smoke – and smelled it in the same instant. Pungent cigar smoke that drifted in the dark air behind Faulkner's porcine face.

"Right," Zane said. That was all he would give up. For now.

"Okay...what kind of information?" Faulkner asked. "No, don't tell me. She's a dyke!" Faulkner's chortling reached new heights.

"No." Zane didn't bother to remove the sneer from the word. "Look, don't try to guess. I'm not going to tell you. Pay me, and then we'll talk."

"Look son...." Faulkner might as well have had a piece of straw sticking out between his teeth, and if he realized it was patronizing to call Zane son, it didn't show. "I don't know how things work where you come from. But down in Georgia, we don't pay up until after we've seen the goods. And even then, we like to dicker some little while." More chortling.

"You'll have to take that risk. Believe me, this information is worth it."

"Forget it, Zarillo. I'm done encouraging your little fantasy." The window began to roll up.

"Stop!" Zane heard the panic in his voice. He knew they heard it too.

The window rolled down again.

"So?" Faulkner put his elbow on the windowsill and propped his face on his hand. "Tell me more. And maybe we'll talk money."

Inside his gut, Zane felt rage battling with fear. What could he do?

"This information...will knock Catherine out of contention." The voices in his head rose to a babble.

Faulkner raised his eyebrows and turned to the other side of the limo. When he turned back, he looked a bit less stupid and a bit more cunning.

"So why in Jesus' name are you tellin' us?"

Zane gritted his teeth. "I need money."

"You must need it bad." Faulkner whistled.

Zane didn't answer. He averted his eyes. For just an instant his mind drifted to the little bag of cocaine he still had in his pocket. Yes. Later. That would help.

There was a creak and then the sound of a car door slamming. Zane jumped. He looked over at the limo and saw Quigley Hutchins standing on the other side.

"Evening, Mr. Zarillo. I believe we've had the pleasure of meeting earlier – at the White House?" Hutchins took a last puff of his cigar and dropped it. He walked around the back of the limousine, toward Zane, slowly.

Reverend Quigley Hutchins was the quintessential Southern gentleman. Tall and spare with a full white mane and the kind of elegant dress that some men can manage without looking sissified. He wore a midnight blue vest under his suit and fondled the chain of a gold pocket watch.

After decades on the preaching circuit, each gesture was so smooth that he often appeared to be performing a well-rehearsed play. His civilized sheen was the antithesis of Faulkner's hoedown hick.

"Let's walk down the road a piece, shall we, Mr. Zarillo?"

Zane felt a deep recoiling in his stomach. He could nearly hear the hisssss of Hutchins' movement as he took a few steps across the grass into the darkness.

It wasn't too late to stop this, Zane realized, hesitating. He could just drive away. But he knew he wouldn't.

Zane opened his door and slid out.

"Cigar, son?" Hutchins asked. A chuckle.

"No. Thanks."

Zane was a tall man, but the Reverend Hutchins had an inch or two on him. They walked side by side, taking slow strides along the edge of the dirt road. Crickets sounded loudly in the field. The grass was dry and looked brown in spots, even in the near darkness. Fire flies blinked on and off in the random distance.

Hutchins said nothing.

"I expect you to pay me," Zane said.

Still Hutchins didn't reply.

Zane could feel the pulse in his neck throbbing. "This information," he continued, "it's devastating. I didn't want to...I would never sell Catherine out, you understand."

"Of course." Hutchins' voice was soothing. "Fine lady. Your candidate. You would never want to hurt Catherine."

"Right." Zane nodded his head, a thirsty man in the desert.

"I'm sure she knows that."

"Exactly. It's simply...well, when you hear what I found out, you'll see why I came to you. Why I have to tell...someone."

"I understand." Hutchins stopped in the dark and faced Zane. "This is something major."

"Yes."

"Something that troubles you."

"Exactly. I have to...."

"There are some truths, son, which are too much of a burden to carry alone." Hutchins let the sentence hang in the air for a moment. "Seems like you might be ready to put your burden down."

"Yes." Zane felt the sweet sensation of relief flood through him. Just let it go. Surrender. The voices were encouraging him now.

"And I'm here to listen. You can trust me to do the proper thing with this information. I'm guessing that it's something that the American people have a right to know."

A door opened in Zane's mind. Of course. Reverend Hutchins would make the decision about how best to handle this. It wouldn't be Zane's responsibility any more. He would pass on the facts and be out of the loop. It was simply a money transaction at this point.

After all, Zane hadn't gone looking for dirt on his candidate. Catherine's daughter had stumbled into his life, and it was only when Zane discovered that incredible file of newspaper clippings and correspondence that he had put the story together. Catherine had gotten pregnant by a black man from Africa. And Catherine – the woman he had so long admired – turned out to be a liar – and a racist. A woman who abandoned her own child to cover up her shame…and because of the color of that innocent baby's skin.

And now, through no fault of his own, Zane was stuck with this damaging information. Anybody else would have gone to the media instantly. And cleaned up.

Well, now it was time for Zane to get the payoff.

Hutchins must have made some sort of invisible signal, because suddenly Faulkner was behind them. Zane turned quickly in surprise. Faulkner said nothing, but in his hands was a thick manila envelope. It was unsealed, and out of the top showed a spread of 100 dollar bills.

Zane reached for it, and started to count. This couldn't be enough.

"Just a down payment, son," Hutchins said, waving his hand toward the envelope as though it were of no importance. He made a small gesture suggesting that the money disappear. Zane closed the clasp and slid it inside his waistband. Faulkner had gone so quietly it was as if he had never appeared.

"She had a child," Zane said. It felt good to say it. It felt good to stop holding in Catherine's dirty little secret.

"Yes?" Hutchins did not lose the smooth, easy delivery.

"Almost thirty years ago."

"Ah."

"A daughter."

"I see."

"The man was black."

Zane looked up at the minister. There was no acknowledgment of shock or even surprise.

Hutchins placed his hand on Zane's shoulder. His voice flowed like cool water over smooth stones. "Mr. Zarillo, you've done the right thing."

Zane nodded. He felt blood pumping through his body. He'd done it. "I need the money," he said. It was an apology.

Reverend Hutchins turned him gently by the arm and began walking him back toward the cars. "Don't you worry, son, you can rely on me. I take care of my friends. Money will not be a problem at all."

Zane could hardly hear him for all the voices clamoring loudly in his brain. Relief. Derision. Advice.

And now the information was out of his control.

Traitor! his head screamed.

15

THE MONEY WAS sitting there, at the corner of 7th and E Streets, Southeast. A nondescript intersection in a questionable part of town.

A duffel bag full of money. Two hundred fifty thousand dollars, practically in his grasp. Sure, it would be marked, with that infrared stuff, but that wouldn't stop Zane from giving it to Devon. His debt would be paid, and there would be no more threats. Let Devon have the dirty money. That suited Zane fine.

He couldn't stop to worry about Quigley Hutchins, and the troubling thing he'd set in motion last night. The money in the manila envelope had turned out to be only $10,000. That wouldn't touch his debt.

The voices kept directing him to go, do, run...keep acting until he was out of danger. Until he had the money. Doing something. Anything.

Right now Zane had to think about saving himself – anyway, how could he help Catherine keep her campaign going, stand in for the President – how could he squelch political rumors, if he were lying at the bottom of the Potomac? One thing at a time.

The cash would be surrounded by Feds. But he had to try anyway. It was so close he could taste it.

Zane sat in the Porsche, waiting for a red light to change at the intersection by the Capitol. He checked his watch. 12:47. If he didn't run into much traffic, he should be able to park and get to the corner by 1:00 without any problem.

It was a hot Friday in August, and the tourists straggling across Independence had that Washington droop – as though they were pushing their way through the wet blanket of humidity one step at a time. Zane had the air conditioning cranked up high and still he could feel sweat pooling under the arms of his Hugo Boss suit.

A couple of minutes later he was two blocks from the designated drop spot. The neighborhood was residential, but seedy. Zane worried about leaving the car on that street. Could he drive by and just pick up the duffel bag? Ridiculous. They would spot him and swoop down in an instant. How heavy was a bag with that much cash, anyway?

Zane pulled over to the side of the road just in time to see an unmarked sedan reach the intersection. A man he didn't recognize got out of the driver's door and walked back to the trunk. He lifted an army green duffel bag out of the car and tossed it onto the sidewalk in one fluid motion. He got back into the car and drove away.

Zane noticed another man walking rapidly down the sidewalk toward him. This man he did recognize. He was one of the Secret Service agents assigned to protect Catherine. He was wearing faded jeans and a T-shirt that said Howard University.

Shit. This guy knew him. He shouldn't have come. He'd been crazy to think he could grab the money with FBI all over the place. Crazy.

Before Zane could formulate a plan, the agent opened the passenger door to his Porsche and got in.

"What the fuck are you doing here?" the agent asked, his voice an angry accusation. "Did the Vice President send you?"

"Uh...well, she did ask me -- " Zane was running through the possibilities, but before he could pick one, the agent spoke again.

"Do you know you could have blown this whole operation? Jesus. What we don't need around here is amateurs." The man pointed ahead. "Drive. I want this car out of here, pronto." He reached into the neck of his T-shirt and placed a wire in his ear. After listening for a moment, he shook his head in disgust.

"Turn right here. Boss says I'm to escort you to the FBI stakeout headquarters. Seems you get a ringside seat." He pointed to a brick building halfway down the block. "Was up to me, I'd have you arrested."

Zane pulled into a parking lot behind the building and followed the agent inside. He walked down a hallway and into a room with a long metal table, several phones, and a large communications radio. Dust motes floated through the bright lines of sun that striped the otherwise darkened room. Facing the venetian blinds over the window were four men and two women, all in dark suits with bulges under their jackets. They turned as he entered.

"Zane." Ralph Harwood walked over to him and gave him a less than welcoming stare. "You could have asked if you wanted to be in on the stakeout."

"I'm sorry, Ralph. I sure didn't mean to jeopardize your operation."

The agent who had brought him in snorted.

"The Vice President didn't think we could handle this?" Harwood asked, turning back toward the window, where one of the slats was bent just enough to afford a view of the blindingly bright street. The duffel bag sat on the empty corner. A car passed as they watched.

Zane wondered how to answer. If he told them Catherine had sent him, Harwood would probably complain to her.

"I've got to admit, Ralph, it was my idea. Stupid, I know. Just looking out for the Vice President's interests. I should have known I'd be stepping into the middle of a delicate setup."

"No kidding." Harwood turned his attention to the street. Two young men were approaching the bag. One of them was smoking. He was black and square, and he walked with a calculated stroll. The other was white, with long dark hair gathered into a pony tail. He was pointing toward the duffel bag.

Somewhere there was a microphone, because as the men reached the corner, Zane heard distorted voices came out of a speaker on the table beside him.

"Look at that. I think this is our lucky day. Wanna guess what's inside?" the pointer asked.

"I don't know, man. Dead cats, maybe?" There was a cackle. The black man kicked the bag. "Well, it didn't blow up." He tried to lift the bag. "Shit man, it's heavy."

"You're just a wuss." The other man succeeded, with great effort, in lifting the bag onto his shoulder. "Help me. This thing's gonna knock me over."

His companion hefted the back of the bag with one arm. "Don't you want to look inside?"

"Hell no. Let's just get out of here. We can play show and tell later."

The two men started to walk down the street, struggling with their burden. Harwood picked up the radio speaker and pushed a button. "Okay, move in. Use caution. They may be armed."

As Zane watched, five men materialized from various points along the street. All five pointed guns at the young men, who dropped the bag and froze in palpable fear.

"Stop. FBI. You're under arrest."

§

Catherine pushed open the door to Ralph Harwood's office. It was perfectly arranged, right down to the black briefcase placed precisely in the center of his desk. A coffee mug sat on a coaster in the right corner, and photographs of aircraft carriers decorated the walls.

"Why wasn't I told that you have suspects in custody?" Catherine asked.

Harwood jumped up as soon as she entered. His face registered first surprise, then a brief flicker of annoyance. By the time she reached his desk in three quick strides, he had achieved the appropriate expression of respect.

"Madam Vice President. I was going to tell you – "

"But you didn't. Was there some reason why not?"

Harwood's voice took on an edge. "The truth is, we don't think they're the right guys. They're kids – teenagers. They show every sign of being completely in the dark."

"They picked up the bag, though, didn't they? They were at that corner at the right time. Was that just a coincidence?" Catherine crossed her arms.

Harwood sighed. "Yeah. We think so. It looks like these kids just stumbled onto the corner at an opportune moment and figured they'd lift the duffel bag."

Catherine put her hands on Harwood's desk and leaned toward him with her elbows locked.

"Where are these kids? I want to talk to them."

"You want to talk to them?" Harwood frowned.

"Yes. Immediately. Alone."

§

Zane sat in his office, dread pouring through his body, just as it had every day since Devon told him about the deadline. Now that deadline was tomorrow – Saturday. And he was no closer to getting a hundred thousand dollars than he had been a week ago.

The blackmail scheme had turned into a fiasco, and it was only a matter of time before the Secret Service insisted that Zane produce a DNA sample. Sooner or later they were going to figure out that he had licked the envelopes that held the blackmail letters.

Worse, he had played his trump card by spilling his collateral to Quigley Hutchins. With nothing but a few thousand bucks to show for it.

Zane pulled out the deep drawer at the bottom of his desk. He grabbed the bottle of cherry flavored Mylanta and screwed off the lid.

Stupid idiot! You can't go a day without fucking up.

Zane ran a hand across his forehead. How had he gotten to this point? When everyone thought he was so smart?

He wasn't smart. His only true gift was in reading people. He was just a little less dumb than the guys he grew up with in the old neighborhood, who were pretty dumb – or pretty uninterested in school. So when the folks from the private academy came looking for one of the "underprivileged" to sponsor, he charmed the socks off the interviewer lady. With his deep brown eyes and thick dark hair, Zane looked like a future movie star. Everyone wanted to help him.

So they helped him to Exeter and on to Harvard, one scholarship after another flowing to the needy kid from the bad neighborhood in Jersey. It was hard, but his mom and his stepdad were so proud of his success that he slogged on, squeaking through each semester with C's. Paying the occasional classmate to write a paper for him wasn't a problem – Zane ran the poker game at school, and always had cash. He had the cash for drugs and booze, too, and he was definitely up for a good time. Any disciplinary issues were decided in his favor after he showed his handsome, sincere face to those in a position to punish. It went especially well for Zane when there were women involved – he wasn't above bedding the random dowdy girl who supported him in his hour of need.

So where had all those street smarts gone? Gone with the stress and the coke and the panic that now filled his days. Something in Zane wanted to fail, and he was failing at one thing after another. He was definitely not good enough to be good, and he was bad at being bad.

As he tossed a mouthful of Mylanta down his throat, the phone rang.

"Zane Zarillo."

"Mr. Zarillo. This is Ellen Golding. I'm a producer for Fox News. We have information that indicates you may be available to give an exclusive interview regarding Vice President Catherine Young's candidacy."

"Of course. I'm available to talk about the Vice President any time."

"Yes. Well, I had in mind...something very particular. Fox is eager to talk to you on an exclusive basis. That is, we would be the first network to air the information – "

"What are you getting at?" The moment he asked the question, Zane understood. This was Hutchins' work. They expected him to leak the explosive news about Catherine's bastard daughter on live TV. And he hadn't even seen the rest of the money yet. "Did Quigley Hutchins tell you to call me?"

"Reverend Hutchins? No. And it wouldn't be appropriate for me to divulge my source."

Zane snorted. "So what is it you expect me to say?"

"Mr. Zarillo. I certainly don't know what you intend to say." The woman on the other end of the line suddenly changed her tone to a conspiratorial whisper. "But Fox is determined to be the first to air the interview which will – from what we've been told – destroy the Young candidacy."

Zane felt his throat give an involuntary swallow.

"How much?" he asked.

"How much what?"

"Money." What was she, an idiot? There was a pause.

"Mr. Zarillo, this news organization adheres to the highest journalistic standards. We cannot pay for interviews. Certainly we can cover your expenses – transportation to the studio, taxi cabs – "

"No money?" His breath came quickly.

"No reputable program will pay you. Surely you are aware of that. Although some of the so-called tabloid shows might pay."

He said nothing.

"Mr. Zarillo? Are you still there?"

"Yeah."

"Just remember that whenever you're ready to do that interview, we want you to call us first."

16

ZANE ROARED OUT of the parking garage across from the Old Executive Office Building and onto Pennsylvania Avenue. He knew he was going to see Hutchins, but beyond that he hadn't formulated a plan.

A dozen scenarios shimmered through his mind, one after another, as he drove. Hutchins laughing in his face. The FBI realizing that he was the extortionist, taking him out of the White House in handcuffs. Devon walking up to him, from behind, and putting a silent bullet into his brain. Devon grinning with his bright white teeth as Zane sank to the ground.

Zane reached instinctively for the semi-automatic handgun tucked under his bucket seat. Will had come through. At least he had that. There would be no instant, grinning death as long as Zane kept his wits about him when the day of judgment arrived.

Tomorrow. Jesus, could it really be tomorrow? But when? Was this a Cinderella thing – at the stroke of midnight he would be ripe for killing?

That seemed unnecessarily dramatic. Morning, afternoon, evening? Devon hadn't given him a precise time. How was Zane going to know when he'd be whacked? Not that it mattered.

A wild laugh escaped Zane as he swung the Porsche hard around the corner of Constitution Avenue and onto First Street. He had an appointment with destiny – but no one had told him the hour.

He pulled up to the curb in front of the Dirksen Office Building. It was past six, no cops would be around to ticket him. The absurdity of worrying about a parking ticket when he might be dead within hours didn't slow his steps as he jogged to the double doors and tried to pull one open. It was locked.

He pounded on the door. There was a light on at the end of the hall. He could see a security guard sitting by a table, a balding guy in a uniform. Slowly the man stood up and hefted his belt, adopting the deliberate gait of a man who would be there all night, no matter what happened.

Zane pounded again, knowing that it wouldn't speed up the guard. Somehow the pain in his knuckles was a small counterweight for the pain in his head.

The man took out his keys and opened the door.

"Closed," he said.

"I know you're closed. I have to get in. To see Reverend Hutchins."

An elaborate shrug.

"I can't let you in unless someone from his office comes down here."

"Well, call them then."

"Call who?"

Zane felt the fever of anger well up and it was good. "Hutchins. Call Hutchins!"

The man seemed to consider this. "They expecting you?"

"Yes," he lied.

"What's your name?"

"Zane Zarillo. I work for the Vice President. Tell them I'm here to see Faulkner and Hutchins."

"Hang on." The man closed and locked the door and made his bearish way back to the table, where a telephone sat. He turned his back to make the call, as though Zane could somehow gain advantage from watching his face.

Two minutes later, he returned.

"They're coming," he said, opening the door and allowing Zane into the building. "You can wait here," he indicated a chair by the table, and walked ahead down the hallway.

After five minutes the elevator lit up, and Blair Faulkner emerged.

"Zane. Good to see you." He held out a red hand and gave a smile that must have been meant as welcoming.

Zane didn't return the smile or the handshake. "Where's Hutchins?"

Faulkner gave a glance at the guard and nodded his head toward the elevator. "Why don't you come up to my office, and we can talk?"

Zane followed him and waited until the elevator doors closed with a metal whoosh. "Who the fuck called Fox News?"

"What?"

"You heard me."

"I don't know anything about that."

"Like hell you don't." Zane bunched his fists and saw the flabby Faulkner look down at them and then back away slightly toward the other side of the tight space.

"I swear to you, Zane. Reverend Hutchins didn't even tell me what your information was – whatever you told him, he kept it to himself."

"Then why am I getting phone calls about it?"

Faulkner was now standing in the opposite corner of the elevator. "I don't know. I don't know anything about it."

Zane took two steps toward Faulkner. "And where's the rest of my money." It was not a question but a threat.

Faulkner held up his hands in front of his chest. "I didn't get any instructions – "

Zane boxed a quick right to his temple, lightly, just to get his attention.

"Listen, you asshole. I want the money. Now."

Faulkner was quivering. "I'd be happy to give you the money. But I don't – "

A left jab to his other side.

"Where's Hutchins?"

A small trickle of blood came from Faulkner's ear. "Not here. He's not here." His hands were scared rabbits, trying to cover up his ears and his face at the same time. He was almost to the floor, sinking down in terror.

The elevator dinged and the doors slid open. Zane wanted to kick Faulkner as he cowered in the corner, but didn't. Instead, he walked out of the elevator and jogged to the end of the hall, pulling the door open to the stairs. No point in beating up Faulkner any more. He sure didn't have that much cash on him.

Zane knew his behavior was out of the range of what was acceptable, even during an election year. But what were they going to do? Call the Feds to report that he was threatening them for the rest of his bribe money? No more than Zane would go to the police because the Reverend Hutchins had reneged on a deal to pay for dirt on Catherine.

He was fucked. He had to get that money. Or tomorrow he'd be dead.

§

Catherine looked at the two young men in the holding cell. One was black and solid, while the other was lean and tall and pasty white. Both of them looked miserable.

"We picked these guys up at the corner, just after they attempted to grab the bag. But as I told you – "

"Enough, Ralph." Catherine held up her hand to stop him. "I'll take it from here." She nodded to the detective who had brought them back to the cell, and he opened the door. "Leave me, please." She stepped into the barred room.

"Are you sure – " Harwood began.

"Yes. Now go." She turned her back on Harwood and the detective and focused on the men. One looked surly and the other frightened. She checked her watch. 9:13. They'd been in custody for about eight hours.

The cell had nothing but an open toilet and a bench along the side. She crossed her arms and leaned against the bars.

"Are they treating you okay?"

The taller man gave a sort of snort. "What – you the lawyer we been asking for?"

Catherine smiled. "I'm a lawyer, but I'm not representing you. I didn't realize you had asked for counsel. I'll make sure you get it."

The black man had been staring. "You're the Vice President."

"No shit, man," his companion said. "I knew that."

"Yes," Catherine said. "I'd like to ask you some questions."

"I ain't answering no more questions until I get me a lawyer. Shorty and I, we been answering questions all day, and we still sitting in here." The tall man kicked a corner of the bench. "What the fuck this all about anyway?"

"Hey, Darryl! She's the Vice President," Shorty said. "Don't be dissin' her."

"Whole damn FBI been dissin' me," Darryl said. He seemed more annoyed than angry.

"Yeah, but she can get us out. She's on top of the FBI."

This seemed to be a new notion to Darryl. He looked up at Catherine with some interest.

Catherine relaxed her posture and uncrossed her arms. "Did you write me a letter?"

The scowl came back to Darryl's face. "Shit no. We don't know nothing about no damn letter. They been asking us about that all day."

"Honest, um, Mrs. Vice President, we don't even know why we're in here. Just found a bag – figured we'd drag it home and check it out." Shorty shook his head. "Last time I touch some stranger's shit," he said with a mumble.

"So the letter...about my daughter...." Catherine let her voice trail off.

"Don't even know your daughter," Darryl said. "Seen her picture once, in the paper. In one of those flat top hats – graduating from college, I guess. Kind of a babe."

"Shut up, man! That's her daughter."

"Why were you on that corner?" Catherine asked.

"We was going over to Shorty's house to get something to eat. Wasn't nothin' to eat at my house."

"Why would you bother to steal some duffel bag sitting on the street?"

Shorty looked at Darryl. "His idea," he said.

"My idea? You was the one pointed at it."

"You didn't know what was in it?"

"Naw. Just...just figured some jerk left his shit – sorry, stuff – hangin' out on the street. He deserved to lose it," Shorty said.

"So you took it. For no particular reason."

Shorty looked like his Mom had shamed him. "That's about it, ma'am."

Catherine held up her hands. "Okay. I'm done with the questions. I don't think you guys will be here much longer."

She pushed a button on the security beeper she had been given, and Harwood came quickly through the heavy door into the hall.

"You okay?" He gestured for the detective following him to open the locked cell door.

"Of course. I'm finished here."

She stepped out of the cell and walked toward the door leading to the front of the station.

"Nice meeting you, Mrs. Vice President," called Shorty from the cell.

Catherine turned and waved. "Nice meeting you, Shorty."

Harwood opened the door and she walked through. When it closed with a thud after them, she looked at him. "Those kids said they wanted a lawyer, and weren't given one."

Harwood exchanged glances with the detective. "Well, they aren't under arrest. And they weren't explicit about asking for counsel."

"They were pretty explicit with me."

"Did you learn anything?"

Catherine shrugged her shoulders. "Only that they don't know what the heck is going on. I think you're right. These aren't the guys. You ought to let them go home."

The detective cleared his throat. "Uh...we thought, ma'am, that we would hold them overnight, just to give them a chance to sleep on their story."

Catherine raised her eyebrows. "Then get them a lawyer, or let them out. Tonight."

Harwood gave her a worried look and moved slightly away from the detective. He lowered his voice to a stage whisper. "If a lawyer gets wind of this whole thing, we'll have a sticky time explaining why six FBI agents were staked out at a quiet corner in the middle of a Friday afternoon."

Catherine turned toward him, her voice tightly controlled. "Yeah, I'm aware of that Ralph. And I'm not looking forward to word of this getting out. But we can't trample on the constitutional rights of those two poor guys, just to keep my name out of the papers. That's been tried before, but it's not something we do in this administration."

Harwood motioned to the detective, who had suddenly discovered a stack of files that needed examining. "Let them out," Harwood said, resigned. "Tonight."

Catherine walked out beside Harwood. "Since these don't seem to be the guys, I guess the blackmailer is still out there," she said. "So what do we do now? Wait to hear from him again?"

"We keep doing what we're doing to identify the extortionist. And yes, in the meantime, we wait."

Catherine turned to Harwood. "I don't like to be in a passive position, just waiting."

"Agreed, Madam Vice President. But I don't see any other options."

"I hate like hell letting him call the shots," she said, feeling her hands curl into fists.

§

Catherine sat at her desk, her head pounding with exhaustion. It was 11:30, and she had been examining the FBI reports on the blackmail letters for half an hour and they still hadn't yielded any answers. There must be a clue. Somewhere. She took off her reading glasses and rubbed her eyes.

The corner of the second page swam before her, somewhat blurred. It was the same phrase she'd read six times.

First communication -
Fingerprints: Vice President Catherine Young and
Campaign Chairman Zane Zarillo. Letter and envelope.

There was something wrong. She read it again.
Fingerprints... letter and envelope.

Wait.

This was the report on the first letter, the one addressed to
her. She had slit open the envelope without looking at the
pasted-on address, then read the letter. When Zane had come in,
she had handed him the letter only...right? The envelope was
locked in her briefcase the whole time. He never touched that.

He must have, or the report wouldn't say that his prints
were found there. Maybe she was remembering it wrong. It had
been five days, after all. And a lot of things had happened. Or
maybe the report was wrong?

But she remembered locking the envelope and letter in her
briefcase, and then taking out only the blackmail letter to show
to Zane...was that how it happened? She needed to talk to
Harwood.

She buzzed her intercom. No answer. Lorraine had gone
home.

Of course. She had told her to go home, at around 10:00
p.m., after Lorraine had ordered Catherine a sandwich from the
White House kitchen. The sandwich was still sitting there, half
eaten, on the side of her desk.

Catherine put her other glasses on and stood up, feeling the
stiffness in her legs. She crossed the carpeted office in stocking
feet, and then padded down the hallway to the office where she
knew at least three Secret Service agents would be waiting to
accompany her home. As she approached the door, she heard
restrained laughter coming from the agents' "limbo room."
When they were in there, they usually played cards and did paper
work to pass the time.

The four agents gave a collective start and rose when she
entered the doorway to the limbo room.

"Madam Vice President. Uh...are you ready to go home? You didn't have to come down here. We would have come to your office." Dan Sweeney was one of her favorites, and he looked a little embarrassed that she had caught them by surprise. They were in their shirtsleeves, their guns strapped into shoulder holsters hanging on the chairs behind them, sitting around a table with cards and bills in the middle. Two men and two women, all in navy blue or gray.

"No, I'm not ready to go yet. Sorry." She grinned. "I'm just looking for Ralph's home number. Do you have it?"

"Sure." Dan went over to a desk in the corner of the room and unlocked a drawer. He took out a list. "Here it is. He's in Alexandria. 703-555-3185. Do you want me to write it down?"

Catherine grabbed a scrap of paper from the pad they were using to keep score. She scribbled the number.

"No. Thanks. Got it," she said. "I should be leaving in about fifteen minutes, so get ready to pack up." She headed toward the hallway, then turned back. "By the way, how come there are four of you here tonight?"

"I'm just leaving," said Dan. "My shift was over a while ago. Just cleaning up some work."

"Just cleaning up, you mean?" She grinned. "You look like you're winning tonight." She turned as they laughed, and walked back to her office, punching Harwood's number into her phone as she walked. She reached her desk just as he picked up.

"Ralph? It's Catherine. I apologize for calling so late. Hope I didn't wake you."

"No problem, Madam Vice President. I was just watching TV. What can I do for you?"

"Ralph, this FBI report – concerning the first letter to me. It says they found Zane's fingerprints on the envelope. Do you think the FBI lab could have made a mistake?"

There was a pause. "I doubt it. Why? Are you saying you never saw Zane handle the envelope?"

"Well...I'm not sure."

"Catherine – "

"Look, don't worry about it. I don't for a minute suspect Zane of blackmailing me."

"We can't take anything for granted."

"And I don't. Let me straighten this out myself."

"We should question Zane."

"If it comes to that, you can. But let me talk to him first. Tomorrow, as soon as he gets in in the morning. Then he's all yours. I just want to make sure my memory is correct – that there's not some simple explanation."

The voice on the other end of the phone was reluctant. "All right. I'll wait until you speak to him."

"Yes. Tomorrow."

17

ZANE DROVE THROUGH Georgetown. The sidewalks were
packed with pedestrians on a hot Friday night. He watched the
slow crawl of people along M Street from one bar to another and
wished that he could just jump in – step into a bar, have a drink
or three, and wash his troubles away. But he couldn't do that.
Because trouble was on his doorstep, and tomorrow it would
ring the bell.

What the fuck am I going to do?

Tomorrow Devon was coming. Zane checked his watch.
Jesus. It was almost midnight. What if Devon showed up right
on the stroke of twelve? But the Cinderella theory was
ridiculous. No way he would come in the middle of the night.
Or would he? To catch Zane by surprise?

He wants the money, you idiot. He'd rather have the
money than kill you before you can give it to him. Of course,
you don't have the money.

Zane patted the handgun under his seat. At least he had
protection.

He made a sudden change of plans, and swung a wide U-
turn in front of Mr. H's Bar. Honks and shouts greeted his
maneuver, but didn't slow him down. He had to avoid his place
tonight. Just to be safe, he'd head for Maria's and spend the
night there. She'd be pissed when he woke her up – but it was
for a good cause.

Of course, Maria was totally unaware of his money troubles,
along with the letters to Catherine, so he couldn't tell her he was
in danger. He had intended to explain his brilliant plan, and how

it was the perfect way for Catherine to pay for the heartless abandonment of her mixed-race daughter, but the right moment had never seemed to materialize. And at this point, it didn't feel so brilliant any more.

Just let him get to her apartment building – get one good night's sleep – and then he'd figure out something...in the morning. Too many things on his mind. Devon, the FBI, Catherine, Hutchins.... Too much pressure.

Zane reached over to the glove compartment and took out the new baggy full of coke. At least he had the cash to buy coke again. But the $10,000 – well, less than that now – wasn't going to impress Devon and company.

He'd park in Maria's garage and do a line or two before going up. His spirits rose as he contemplated the heavenly white powder. Zane pushed the Porsche a little faster as he headed toward Connecticut Avenue.

§

Dan Sweeney felt more than a little uneasy as he realized how many cardinal rules he was breaking tonight. Eavesdropping on the Vice President's phone call to his boss – though he hadn't really meant to. Going to question a suspect alone, something a Secret Service agent was not supposed to do. And countermanding the explicit request of the Vice President that she be allowed to talk to the suspect first.

But he was going anyway. There was nothing worse for an ongoing investigation than to have the perp anticipating your moves. And if Catherine tipped Zane off about their suspicions, he would have a smooth explanation all worked out by the time Harwood and the FBI could get to him.

Dan had heard only Catherine's end of the conversation, but that alone was enough to make it clear that the lab had found Zane's prints on the blackmailer's envelope when there should not have been prints. Would a campaign strategist extort money from his own candidate? Hard to believe, but stranger things had happened in politics. And while Zane was generally thought of as a good guy, he was known to have had drug troubles in the past – and who knew how deep his loyalties were rooted? The right amount of money could tempt almost anyone.

Dan would simply drop in unexpectedly and test the waters. Get a read on Zane's initial reaction to the question of how those fingerprints got to be on the envelope. He wouldn't press. This way Zane would be caught unprepared.

Dan had no trouble locating Zane's Georgetown row house. He pulled up to the 33rd Street curb and looked for lights. Nothing. He checked the clock on the dash. 11:47. Maybe Zane was asleep, maybe out. Dan got out of the car and rang the bell. No answer. Another two rings. Nothing.

Damn. It was important to get to him tonight. Catherine, not normally a sentimental person, was a true believer when it came to Zane. He had kept her campaign alive – or so she believed. She would bend over backward to give him the benefit of the doubt. Dan needed to talk to him before she gave away the tactical advantage of surprise.

Ah. The girlfriend. Now what was her name? Maria. Something. Something hyphenated? He grabbed his briefcase from the passenger's seat and opened the lock. Yes! One of the events he had covered was the Vice President's acceptance speech at the Convention. Every guest at the private reception had been identified by name, address, and social security number. He had turned in the report, but his rough notes should be here somewhere.... He riffled through scraps of paper and torn-off legal sheets until he came to the right one.

There it was, scribbled below Zane's name:

Maria Flores-Jenkins. 4800 Connecticut Avenue. Apartment 17-L.

He put the car into drive and pulled away from the curb. Zane was going to get a surprise visit tonight.

§

Zane sat behind the steering wheel in the dimly lit underground garage. It was so late now that it didn't matter when he got upstairs – Maria would already be asleep. He steadied the mirror on the storage compartment between the plush leather seats of the Porsche and sucked up another line through a rolled-up bill.

Man-o-man. So sweet.

It went right up to his temples and then blissed out the top of his head. Nothing like a little cocaine when you needed a lift. He licked his right pinkie finger and picked up the faint powdery residue left on the mirror, applying it directly to his nostril. His heart was pounding and his blood was singing. Sleep held no appeal at all. But the thought of Maria coming to the door in that half-awake state where dreams were still clinging – and in nothing but some filmy nightie – was enough to get him moving.

He put away the mirror and the baggy, and pulled the Glock out from under the seat. His movements were jerky. He glanced at the clock. 12:42. Past the witching hour. Today was the day when Devon would come.

Footsteps sounded from somewhere behind the car.

Jesus! He was here. Now!

Zane grabbed the gun and undid the safety. He opened the car door as quietly as he was able, though his muscles felt spastic. He looked down the line of cars at the approaching figure. In the shadowy light he could only see a shape. Broad shoulders. An arrogant step.

Yes! It was Devon. With his senses on high alert, Zane caught a whiff of the sickening cologne Devon wore. A wave of hate swept over him.

The bastard was not going to get him. Not tonight, not any night.

Zane squeezed the trigger and the astonishing noise of a semiautomatic exploded off the concrete ceilings and walls of the garage. As the fire raked Devon, Zane could see the path of bullets sweep across his chest. There was no blood, in front. But there was a terrible groan and a nearly instantaneous series of physical responses to each shot as the body was pummeled from left to right. Then he collapsed backward onto the concrete, and it was over.

Jesus, Zane. What have you done now?

Zane remembered to breathe. His arm shook so hard it hit the car door.

With a start he remembered the security cameras at the entrance to the garage. They'd have his car and his license plate on videotape. They'd identify Zane, and it wouldn't look like self-defense to anybody else. It would look like murder.

I've got to get out of here.

He latched the safety on the gun and tossed it under the seat, slammed the car door and backed out of his spot. He screeched down the ramp and up to the body and as he came even with it he jerked to a stop. Something was wrong.

He opened the door and looked at the dead man on the concrete.

It wasn't Devon..

18

CATHERINE HIT THE button on the answering machine as she kicked off her pumps. Three messages. She peeled off her jacket and flopped onto the bed. Home at last.

She carefully rolled her pantyhose down each leg and then crushed them into a ball in order to improve their trajectory as they sailed toward the laundry basket. It didn't help.

Forget it. She'd pick them up in the morning. She was not leaving this bed.

"Hi Mom!" It was Lily's voice on the machine. "Just wanted to let you know that I'm available for the rally next week, if you need me. Let me know when. If you're going to have me on stage, I'll skip the nose ring. But I can't take the one out of my tongue, or the hole will close up." Catherine cringed. Yuck. Had she really done that? Stuck metal through her tongue?

Then Lily let out a whoop of laughter as the tape kept rolling. "Just kidding! Scared you, didn't I? By the way – Mom? If you want Mike to be there, you better remind him to buy some new pants. All he has are jeans and ratty T-shirts, and those pants I bought him for his last birthday look too short. He either shrunk them or he's still growing. Is that possible, at 22? You know, it's not fair. I'm the one who needs a couple more inches, and he's past six feet. Why couldn't you have passed on the tall genes to me? Gotta go, Mom. Call me. Love you." The machine beeped to indicate the end of the message.

Catherine smiled as she listened to the voice. Lily had always been a bundle of energy. Now that it was channeled in a positive direction, she was having a ball learning the advertising business.

The second message was from Nancy. "Hey, are you out making another speech? I don't know how you keep going, day after day. Anyway, I wanted to let you know that Stuart is on the job, and thinks he's made progress. I'll relay the details when he reports further." Beep.

"Catherine?"

She was startled to hear the voice of President Drummond on her answering machine. He sounded stronger, but certainly not the vigorous man she knew him to be. "Sorry to leave this on your machine – I tried your other phone. Didn't want to do this through official channels…it's just between us. I need to talk to you in the morning."

The voice paused, and Catherine heard him take a heavy breath. "I got a peculiar call from Reverend Quigley Hutchins today. He was implying something, but I'm damned if I could figure it out. See me in the morning – I'll be coming into the office for a few hours just to get my feet wet – and maybe you can shed some light on what he had in mind. Good night."

Catherine, now fully undressed, pulled the covers over her head and firmly resolved to think about that one tomorrow. She punched the remote beside her bed and found a news channel.

Jerusha and her large blonde hair appeared on the screen wearing a big smile and perfect eye makeup, despite apparently standing in the heat of the Washington sun. She had taken a tour of D.C. earlier in the day, explaining to the press contingent that had followed her through the streets of Georgetown and around the monuments that she was just checking out her new neighborhood.

"Well, y'all know I don't need to look at open houses… I've got myself a nice big white one all picked out. Sixteen hundred Pennsylvania Avenue is available, right?" The supporters in the crowd cheered, and the reporters leaned in with more shouted questions.

"Governor, what did you think of the Washington Monument?"

"That's my favorite spot. Love the majestic height of it –
shows our strength. And Washington is my favorite president!
The way he fought for the freedom of the American. Against
the British. Standing up for the right to bear arms, and not buy
their English tea. Because they charged too much for the
colonists. Remember that tea party in Boston – they threw the
tea right into the river!"

At least one reporter was grinning as the microphones were
tilted in the Governor's direction. Jerusha glowed with
conviction and patriotic fervor. "General Washington rowing
across the water – y'all remember the famous painting – to get
through the long winter and fight for our freedom against
tyranny. And that's what we have today! Financial tyranny –
under the Democrat party. Taxes! Which is what I intend to
stage a revolution about. I think it's time we were revolting.
America, are you with me?"

Huge waves of applause and cheers rang up from the crowd
that had formed around her on Independence Avenue.
Catherine pushed the button on the remote and turned the TV
to black. She finally dropped off into fitful dreams featuring
President Washington pouring his tea into the Delaware River,
pierced tongues, and Parisian nurseries full of little babies, crying.

§

Zane kept one hand on the wheel as the other raked
through his hair. He didn't know where he was going, but he
was driving there fast.

He realized with a spasm of fear that he was heading toward
his house. No. Not there. They would be sure to look for him
there, as soon as they figured out who had shot that man. That
man – Dan Sweeney, Secret Service agent – would be missed,
certainly by morning. And it wouldn't be too long before his
dead body, lying in the parking garage under the apartment
building where Zane's girlfriend lived, was connected to Zane.

And then there was Devon – still out there, still looking for
his money. Expecting to be paid sometime today.

Zane couldn't go home.

Will. He would go to Will's house. His little brother would let him in.

Zane swung the car around, grateful that at 1:14 in the morning the traffic was sparse. He went as fast as he could, screeching to a halt in front of those traffic lights which weren't blinking yellow by this time of night. When he got to Will's neighborhood, he pulled onto the dark street and parked the car behind his brother's dented LeMans. He didn't like to park here, but worrying about his precious leased car was a luxury he could no longer afford.

He rang the doorbell and then knocked loudly. There were no lights and no sounds from inside. He knocked again. A third time, and finally he saw movement. Will opened the door and stood there in his shorts, blinking at the street light outside.

"Zane? Hey man, I was asleep."

"I'm sorry, Will. It's an emergency."

Will backed away from the door to let him in. Zane closed and locked it behind him.

"Can you put me up for the night?" Zane asked.

"Here? I got the sofa." He gestured to the bumpy plaid couch beside them. "But why? Something going on at your place?"

Zane shook his head. "Don't ask any questions, Will. Believe me, you don't want to know."

Will led the way into the kitchen. He pulled out a half-empty bottle of Jack Daniels and set it on the Formica table. "I'm worried about you, Zane." He pulled a couple of glasses from a cabinet and sat backwards on a chair, then splashed liquor into both glasses.

Zane sat down and lifted one of them to his lips. The whiskey burned as it slid down his throat. Will took a long drink and drained his glass. As he filled it again, he looked up at his brother.

"I'm guessing this is about that gun – and whatever trouble you're in," Will said.

"I'm serious about not asking, Will," Zane said, downing the rest of his drink. He shook his head and moved his left hand as if to push the facts away.

Will looked offended. "If you're in trouble, Zane, I want to help. You know you're not going to get much help from those fancy friends of yours. I've been thinking you'd be grateful for having a brother one of these days."

Zane sighed. "I am grateful, Will. I'm trying to protect you, don't you understand?"

"I understand – I do! I know better than you do – with your grand education and your impressive title – that you're the same slick Zane Zarillo you always were – just that now you're got up in nice suits." Will's voice sounded more sad than triumphant. "Strung out on coke – I see it! You may fool the folks at the White House, but you can't fool me. You've been heading for a fall all these years. And who but your family to catch you when you do?"

Zane put his head in his hands. "Do you really want to know?"

"Spill it."

So Zane went through the long story of how he had gotten to this point, telling it in a way that made it clear he was just the unfortunate victim of a series of well-meant miscalculations. Will raised his eyebrows in astonishment when Zane told him that Maria was the Vice President's daughter, and how he had discovered their relationship the night of Catherine's convention speech when he looked at the file that Maria kept in her bureau. A file full of notes and research into the woman who turned out to be her mother.

But when Zane got to the part about sending the blackmail letter, Will was out of his chair. "Are you shitting me, Zane? What the hell were you thinking, trying to pull something like that against the Vice President of the United States? You must have been crazy."

Zane tightened his mouth. "I don't know what was so crazy about it. You said yourself you thought she should be called on this – disowning that precious baby – not wanting to bring Maria home to her white family because her daddy was an African. And I had these money guys threatening to kill me if I didn't come up with the cash."

Will sat back down, still shaking his head. "No wonder you're in trouble. I'd hide out too."

"But tonight..." Zane didn't look directly at Will. "I had to use your gun – shot an agent. Thought he was Devon, looking for the dough."

"What?" Will's eyes were open wide.

"You heard me. That's why I'm here."

"A Federal agent? Damn. Is he dead? What are you going to do?"

"Yeah, he's dead." Zane let out a groan. "And I don't know what I'm going to do. I didn't mean to kill him – but that's not going to help much. I need a place to hide out for a while. I need some leverage."

"Where did you shoot him?"

"In Maria's garage. There were security cameras at the entrance. They'll pin it on me pretty quick. I'll have to ditch the Porsche."

"Yeah, and then they'll check out your brother Will's place, to see if you're sleeping on the couch." Will gave a glance toward the door.

Zane looked at his watch. It was after 3:00. "They must have found the body by now. I don't know if people heard the shots or not – it was a couple floors below ground – but it sure sounded like it would wake the whole building."

"We got to find somewhere to put you. Let me think."

"I'm starving. Do you have anything to eat?"

"I got – frozen pizza. You want that?"

"Yeah." Zane bit the knuckle of his left hand as he thought about his next move. Will opened the freezer for the pizza and slid it into the oven. He sat back down.

"The girl – how much does she know about this?" Will asked.

"Maria? Nothing."

"She wasn't in on the money thing? The letter?"

"No. She wouldn't do anything like that. Nice girl. Never wanted to hurt Catherine. She just wanted to meet her. Came all the way from Brazil, managed to get a job at the embassy. All to meet her real mother. But when she finally got a chance to see Catherine, it just hurt worse."

"So you mean she's completely out of this? No clue?"

"Yeah. I didn't want her messed up in any of this. She's kind of innocent, to tell the truth. Raised pretty religious. Keeps asking me if I'm serious about her. I think she expects to marry me one of these days."

"Hell, you're great marriage material, Zane. Running from the law." Will smiled, but it was a sad smile. "And you sure as hell can't stay here. I know you're my brother, but I can't afford to get messed up in your shit."

"You must have a friend, right? Someone with a floor I can crash on?"

Will nodded his head. "Hunh. Well, maybe…"

"Think. I gotta go somewhere."

"Okay. There's this church – the Glory Baptist Church on 15th Street. They let me sleep there once, when I couldn't make rent."

"How's that gonna help me?" Zane looked at his brother.

"They'll give you – what is it they call it when you need protection? Asylum. It's a church, right? Nobody can bust in there. Until we can figure this thing out. Buy you some time to get a lawyer and make a plan."

"Asylum?" Zane paused. "That's an idea. Show there's a political threat against me…"

"Hell, they're going to threaten you. Soon as they find out you killed a Fed."

Zane nodded slowly. "Exactly. But the good folks at the church won't know that." He stood up and slapped Will on the back. "Give me some of that pizza, bro, and then you're going to take me to the Glory Baptist Church."

19

CATHERINE WALKED PAST Lorraine's desk at an energetic clip. There were quite a few people in, despite the fact that it was a Saturday, and only 8:00 in the morning. Then she remembered that the President was making an appearance in his office this morning. And that he wanted to see her.

"Is Zane in?" she asked Lorraine.

"No, he's not, ma'am. Would you like me to call him?"

"No, I'm sure he's on his way. He usually beats me here. I don't know when the man sleeps. Make sure he talks to me as soon as he comes in – or as soon as I get back from seeing the President, which is where I'm going right now. Did I remember to put lipstick on?" Catherine stopped her forward motion long enough to turn and face Lorraine.

"Yes."

"Thanks." She smiled as she turned and headed toward the Oval Office.

Catherine passed a group of Secret Service agents standing outside of the limbo room. They were deep in conversation, and only two of them even acknowledged her with a "Good morning, Madam Vice President."

She walked briskly down the hall past the portraits of presidents and other statesmen, turning into the outer rooms of the President's suite of offices.

Mrs. Greenfield, President Drummond's personal assistant, saw her as she entered. "Madam Vice President. Good morning. Shall I tell the President that you're here?" She was a perfectly coifed, thin-lipped woman who had the largest collection of pearl necklaces Catherine had ever seen. Today she wore a double strand over a navy jacket.

"Please, Mrs. Greenfield. I hope I didn't keep him waiting."

"Oh no. The President just came downstairs from the residence. He's expecting you." She opened the door to the Oval Office and stepped back for Catherine to proceed.

"Good morning, Mr. President," Catherine said, entering the famous room. She had been here a hundred times by now, but it always gave her a little thrill each time she walked in. And it was especially wonderful to see President Drummond back in his rightful place.

"Ah, good morning, Catherine. Please, come in and sit down. I hope you'll forgive me for not standing." Tom Drummond was taller than Catherine, but he seemed smaller now, pale and depleted in spite of his broad shoulders. His still-dark hair was rumored to be his own. He had a bent, aquiline nose that gave him the appearance of a bird, but somehow it enhanced his powerful expression. It was easy to believe the official bio that listed him as being one quarter Cherokee.

"Thank you, Mr. President." She took her seat on one of two sofas facing each other in the center of the large room. He sat across from her, with a steaming mug on the table in front of him.

"Coffee for you?" he asked. "I'm just having mine."

"No thank you, sir. I'm sufficiently coffeed this morning."

He laughed. "All right, then."

"May I ask, Mr. President, how you're feeling?"

"Better. Much better now. Not one hundred percent, but on the mend. I know I gave everybody a scare. Damn foolish of me not to have the doc look at me sooner. As my lovely wife Brenda keeps reminding me."

Catherine wasn't sure what to say to that, so she just smiled.

"You've done a great job, though," Drummond said, wincing a bit as he leaned over to pick up his mug. "I'm grateful that you were here to step in."

"Mr. President, it was my honor to—"

"No, you don't have to give me the official line, Catherine. I know it was inconvenient for you, in the middle of your own campaign, to have to hold down the fort here in Washington."

"I—" Catherine started, but the President held up his hand.

"Look, you got all the dull parts and none of the power – playing President for a week means a lot of speechifying and boring meetings. It doesn't add up to much in terms of a chance to make policy and change the path of the United States government."

Drummond paused and smiled, raising his coffee mug toward Catherine.

"But I feel confident that you'll get your own chance – soon – to do all that." His eyes smiled at her over the top of his steaming coffee. "That will be a historic day, when the first woman is sworn in as the President of the United States. This country is obviously ready to see that. And I know I'm ready."

He grinned, and when he did he looked almost like the relaxed man Catherine had worked with at the Capitol a decade ago. "A few more months of the excitement and headaches of the presidency, and by next January I'll be sunning myself on my little boat. I keep a place on Santa Catalina Island. Do you know it?"

"No, I can't say that I've ever been there. I've heard the old song, though."

"Beautiful place. Little jewel of an island, right off the California coast." He began singing quietly. "Twenty-six miles across the sea, Santa Catalina is waiting for me, Santa Catalina, the island of romance, romance, romance, romance." He stopped and blinked, looking sheepish. "You'll think I'm ready for retirement, after that."

Catherine laughed. "I thought it was charming, Mr. President. I haven't had a man sing to me in years."

His expression changed to one of concern. "Right. That brings me to the reason I wanted to speak to you. Quigley Hutchins, who is not a man whose personal opinions normally concern me, has indicated that he has some doubts about your fitness for office."

Catherine felt anger rise. "In what way?"

"Well, he seemed to be saying something...and I can't imagine what he had in mind...about your 'womanly virtue.'"

"My womanly virtue?" Catherine was aware of the blood rushing to her face.

"I thought perhaps it had something to do with this blackmail letter – unfortunate thing, but the FBI tell me they have it under control – which of course I've been kept apprised of. Though I don't expect he's gotten wind of that. Hope not anyway."

"Mr. President, I assure you – "

"No need, Catherine, no need. It's none of my business – or Hutchins', for that matter – what your romantic life is like. I know you're a single woman...."

Catherine resisted the urge to jump up from the couch. "There is nothing...nothing in my behavior, since I've been a public figure...which would cause you or the party any embarrassment, Mr. President." She kept her voice carefully modulated, despite her anger. That statement wasn't a lie, after all. But she didn't feel good saying it.

Drummond looked sheepish. "I don't for a minute think that there is any cause for – embarrassment, Catherine. I simply wanted you to be aware of Hutchins' latest tactic. You know the political climate – there's a blogger on every corner waiting to spread rumors. Even the most blameless in public office have to be very careful." He took a swallow of coffee. "I'm sure this came from some rumor with no basis in fact, which Hutchins is floating to see how many political points it gets for him and Jerusha Hutchins and their ticket."

Drummond looked down at his mug and seemed to be speaking to himself. "Never understood how that man could have been a minister. Much too slick for my taste. Anyway, I'm not worried about it, and I don't think you should be."

He started to stand up and Catherine quickly put up her hands. "Please, Mr. President. You don't need –"

With a clear effort, Drummond raised himself, took her by the arm and walked her toward the door.

"I'm truly sorry, Catherine, if I've upset you. Perhaps I should have dealt with someone else. I called Zane Zarillo first, yesterday, actually. Didn't get a call back, and I wanted to give you a heads up about this as soon as I got an inkling. With the political pundits on TV on the weekends, you never know what the Hutchins campaign might come out with."

Catherine had regained her composure. "I appreciate your telling me, Mr. President. It's always an advantage to be prepared. Thank you."

As they reached the door, she turned to him and gently put her hand on his arm. "I hope I'm not stepping out of line if I ask you to go easy on yourself, sir."

Drummond waved her concerns away. "Be prepared." He repeated, smiling. "A good motto – for the Boy Scouts and for future presidents," he said, and opened the door for her to leave.

§

"Maria? It's me, Zane. Sorry to wake you up." He was calling from Will's kitchen, leaning against the doorjamb with his foot up on one of the ratty chairs.

"Zane?" Her voice was groggy. "It's Saturday."

"Sorry, baby. It's important. I need you to meet me somewhere. An emergency."

"Meet you." She spoke slowly. "When?"

"Start getting ready. In fact, bring some clothes, just a couple days' worth. Actually, make sure you have a nice dress or something – something you wouldn't mind being seen in."

"Clothes? Where are we going?" Her voice was turning from sleepy to annoyed. "I am supposed to see a friend. Why did you not tell me if you were planning a trip?"

"It's not exactly a trip. I'll explain it when you get there."

"Where is 'there'?"

"It's a church. On 15th Street. The Glory Baptist Church. Just come in...the minister will be there. Reverend Ezekia Abraham. She's expecting us."

"A church? A minister?" Maria's voice sounded more awake. Her questions took on a coy edge. "Zane – are you planning a surprise?" She started to laugh. "Because if you are thinking of a romantic ceremony, it is very sweet – but you know I must be married by a Catholic priest. And my parents! They should be here. They would be heartbroken if I – "

"Maria! Look, this has nothing to do with a wedding. I'm sorry if you thought…"

"Oh." There was an embarrassed pause.

"Maria, you know how much I love you. This is really important. It involves – well, it involves you, and your safety."

"What do you mean, my safety?"

"Listen, I can't talk about it now. Just do as I say, okay? I promise that I'll explain it when I can. I'll be at the church by 8:30. Get there as soon as you can."

"All right, Zane." Her voice was dubious.

"I'm only trying to protect you. You have to trust me on this."

§

Catherine was back in her office after talking to the President. She sensed a somber tone amongst the staff, and she was about to get up and ask Lorraine what was going on when Ralph Harwood appeared in her doorway. He wore an expression that made his usually stiff face look even more so.

"Madam Vice President. May I come in?"

"Of course, Ralph. Is something wrong?" Catherine stood up and came around her desk. She leaned backward against it, making the difference in their heights disappear.

"I'm afraid so. We lost one of our agents last night – Dan Sweeney. He was shot and killed."

Catherine gasped. "Dan. Oh my God. Where? Why? What was he doing?"

"That's what we can't figure out. As far as we know, he was here late last night, after his shift finished, working on some reports that were due...." Catherine watched while the stoic Harwood sought to keep his composure.

"Yes. I saw him! He was in the limbo room, playing cards, and then he said he was going home. It was...maybe 11:30? Pretty late." Catherine shook her head. "Ralph, I'm so sorry to hear it. Dan was a great guy. How horrible." She crossed her arms. "So...how did it happen?"

"He was found this morning in a garage – under an apartment building on Connecticut Avenue. We don't know why he was there. He was a single guy, and there are lots of people in that building – he could have been going to see a new girlfriend, whatever. But his buddies don't know of anyone he was dating. For all we know, it was some random thing." Harwood sighed, and suddenly looked older. Catherine was struck by the understanding that the agents were like his family, since he had none of his own.

"No signs of a robbery," Harwood said. "And the shooter was not right on top of him. He took quite a few hits." A heavy sigh slipped out of the side of his mouth, and Catherine took a step toward him and put her arms around him. The action seemed to embarrass him, but instead of pulling away he became stiff. He kept his arms rigidly at his side. After a moment, Catherine let go.

"You saw the body?" she asked, looking into his eyes.

"Yes." Now his voice was gruff.

"Ralph, this is just...I am so terribly sorry. I'd like to call the family – his parents would be the next-of-kin?"

"Yes." Harwood's face softened with appreciation.

"And please let me know about the arrangements for the funeral. I'll do my very best to be there."

"Thank you, Madam Vice President. I know he would have been honored."

"It's the least I can do. He did a lot for me." Catherine walked toward her door with Harwood. "Do you have any leads?"

He shook his head. "There was a security camera at the entrance to the garage, but the damn thing wasn't maintained –

which happens a lot. The mechanism that was supposed to keep the tape looping through didn't work. So basically, we have nothing to go on except the usual forensics."

Catherine put her hand on his arm. "Ralph, please let me know what happens. I want to make sure we find the creep who killed him."

"Yes indeed, ma'am. You can be certain we'll find him."

20

THE GLORY BAPTIST Church sat on the corner of Fifteenth Street beside a store with bars across the entrance called "The Wild Shoe." The church was an elegant brick building with an arched entrance way. Its name was spelled out in large white letters, overlaid with gilt.

Zane had insisted that Will take his own car, though that meant leaving the precious Porsche unattended. Paranoid as he was, Zane was going to swap vehicles with Will, and take over the dented LeMans, until he realized that the Porsche would be sought after – with no consideration as to which brother was behind the wheel – by every law enforcement officer within 100 miles of the crime, as soon as they saw the videotape from the garage. So he settled for instructing Will to stash the Porsche in a secure garage, and hoped that by the time this whole mess was unsnarled, he would be flush enough to get it out of hock.

Will dropped him off at the back door of the church, then left to attend to the ditching of the sports car. Zane mounted the small steps leading to the church office, and rang the bell. The day was bright but not yet hot, and when the minister opened the door, it was impossible to see inside.

"Mr. Zarillo?" asked Reverend Abraham, waving him in. "Your brother William – he is your brother?" She looked at Zane's face and seemed to be trying to reconcile it with that of Will's.

"Yes, indeed, Reverend. And Will has told me wonderful things about you."

The Reverend raised her eyebrows before leading him down the hallway. "Pardon our humble quarters. We don't have a fancy place here. That's always the way, when you're doing the Lord's work with the people." She looked nevertheless very proud of her humble quarters, which included a beautifully grained wood desk and a sitting area consisting of a sofa, loveseat, and matching stuffed chair in a gray and purple floral pattern. The walls were adorned with photographs of the Reverend with political and religious notables, as well as various proclamations attesting to her good works.

"Please sit down. I understand you are looking for assistance from this institution." The Reverend sat her ample bulk down on the chair, folding her arms in prayerful repose on her likewise ample lap. Her round face displayed childlike, almost beatific features, set off by golden spectacles that complimented the gold of a pin at her throat. She wore a ruffled white blouse and a dark blue suit. Her hair was carefully coifed and showed not a touch of gray.

Zane leaned forward. "Reverend, I do appreciate your seeing me this morning...."

The Reverend nodded. "William has said something about... he tells me you are seeking some sort of asylum?"

"Yes. My girlfriend and I – Maria...she should be arriving soon – are seeking the assistance of you and your church for a few days." Zane hesitated, trying to gauge her reaction. "It's really Maria who is in jeopardy here. She has a lot to be afraid of."

Reverend Abraham nodded. "Go on."

"Reverend, this may be difficult to believe...I didn't believe it myself, at first...but," Zane looked down, then continued, "Maria is the illegitimate daughter of Vice President Young."

The reverend sat up higher. "The Vice President?"

"Yes."

"This is an extraordinary claim."

"I recognize that, Reverend Abraham."

The Reverend looked hard at him. "What is the likelihood of such a secret child? Do you have any proof of this alleged relationship?"

Zane took Maria's manila envelope out of the case he had kept under the front seat of his car since the night of Catherine's acceptance speech. He handed the Reverend a French document.

"What is this? This is… in French?"

"See – here is her birth date, the 8th of May, 1983. She was born in Paris. After Catherine Young served two years in the Peace Corps, in Ghana. Her name is listed as Elizabeth Anne Webster."

"So what does that prove?"

"The false name that the Vice President used was Webster."

"And?" Reverend Abraham's dark eyes looked up at Zane's.

Zane pulled out a clipping. "This is from a French newspaper. Maria got this from the nun who took care of her as an infant – the nun who gave her as a baby to her Brazilian mother." He stood up to lean over the Reverend's shoulder. "See that word she wrote above the photo? 'Mere'? French for mother. The nun recognized Catherine – who was then a Member of Congress – from a trip she took to France in 1997."

"So you feel this claim has a basis in reality."

"I do. All the dates match. And Maria looks like Catherine – if you factor in a much darker father."

"An African, you say?"

"That's my assumption, because of the Peace Corps years in Ghana. But who knows." Zane sat down. He could feel the Reverend beginning to believe.

Reverend Abraham looked at him in silence for a moment, and then shook her head sadly. "So if this is true, Mr. Zarillo – and I am not at all sure that it is – why does this concern us?"

"Because they're trying to kill her."

"Indeed?" The Reverend raised her dark eyebrows, and it wasn't clear if she was stunned at his making such a claim, or stunned that such a thing could be true.

"A man came… to her apartment. He was from the government, and he was armed."

Reverend Abraham shook her head. "A lot of men in the government are armed, and that doesn't mean they come ready to kill innocents."

"But this one tried to kill her. I was there. He would have succeeded if she had been alone. And there are more of them out there on the hunt."

Zane could see the wheels turning. He waited. He watched the Reverends chest rise and fall under her tailored suit. He saw her breathing become more rapid. She was turning.

Yes.

"And so she is a threat to the Vice President – the Democratic nominee for president. And those in power seek to silence her." Reverend Abraham was nodding now, and her voice was taking on the deep timbre of an orator. She nodded. "Your brother William had explained to me that your companion was a black woman, who somehow needed our protection. And now I understand."

The Reverend raised both of her hands to her broad face. "So your girlfriend – Maria – herself embodies the physical evidence of an interracial relationship."

Zane realized that he need say nothing more. He nodded, and he could see the chain of reactions in the Reverend's face. Her shoulders lifted, and her jaw set.

"I never thought I'd see the day that here, in these United States of America, in the birthplace of liberty and democracy, an official of this government would try to hunt down an innocent girl-child because she is the black daughter of one who covets political office." She shook her head and held her hands up in consternation. "Her own mother."

Zane nodded. "It is difficult to believe." He looked over at the Reverend. "And so I am hoping that you will consider taking us under the protection of your church. I have to warn you, though, that Maria knows nothing about the danger she's in. I've done my best to shield her from the frightening truth." Zane found the words tripping across his tongue, each sentence rolling out like a discovered jewel. It felt just like in second grade, when he told the other kids that his real Daddy – who hadn't been seen since Zane's birth – was rich and owned the biggest store in town, and they could all go down and pick out any toy they wanted. He was good at stories.

Zane's voice took on the burnished tones of a true believer. "It was lucky that Maria met me, a man who had access to the government's plans because of my position. If we hadn't crossed paths, she would already have been snatched off the street by the Federal goons – or worse."

After a pause appropriate to the gravity of the statement, the Reverend gave a quiet smile. "Son, that was not luck. That was the Lord's hand here on earth, making things happen according to divine plan. And it is divine plan that has brought you here to our church today. I think it is appropriate now that we bow our heads and thank the good Lord for his providence."

The Reverend folded her hands and began intoning. "Lord Jesus, we thank you for bringing this young man to us, a man who is in need of the protection your house of worship can convey. And we vow, with all our hearts and all our strength, to keep these children out of harm's way for as long as they are in danger from the political forces which have power in the secular world. Amen."

"Amen," Zane said.

§

"Lorraine, have you seen Zane yet?" Catherine looked at her watch as she walked out of her office. "It's almost 9:00. He must be in by now."

Lorraine stopped typing and looked up from her computer screen. "He hasn't come into the White House yet, ma'am. I taped a note to his desk here, and I've called his personal phone three times. Would you like me to try him at home?"

"Yes. Please do that. Thanks." Catherine started to step into her office, and then turned back. "Lorraine, if you don't find him at home, try his girlfriend's place – Maria, I think? I'm sure you've met her – the gorgeous Brazilian one. I think Zane spends a lot of time with her these days." Catherine frowned. "And when you find him, tell him to get his butt in here pronto."

§

Zane and Will sat on a narrow bed covered in an aqua chenille spread in the room down the hall from the Reverend's office. The small space had yellow walls and a portrait of Jesus looking heavenward. Beside the bed sat a card table and a folding chair. A small television was on the table.

The morning news was just starting, and the face of Kelton Burl, a local anchor, filled the screen.

"The Treasury Department reports that Secret Service Agent Daniel Sweeney was shot and killed sometime around midnight last night. He was found dead in the parking garage under a large apartment building at 4800 Connecticut Avenue. No suspect has yet been identified, and the FBI is asking that any individual who has information about the shooting contact the Bureau at the number you see on your screen."

Zane watched as the man's face was replaced by a star-shaped badge graphic, and underneath, the words FBI Special Investigations Unit, followed by the number 800-FBI-INFO.

"For once I got a lucky break," Zane said. "Something must have gone wrong with the video camera at the entrance. Because they sure don't seem to know it was me. Unless...do you think this is a trap or something? They actually have my license plate number, and they're trying to fool me into thinking I'm in the clear?"

"Hell if I know, Zane. What I do know is that you're in deep this time," Will said, his voice low.

Zane stood up and walked to the door of the small room. He made a sort of snort, and punched a tight fist against the wall. It hurt like hell, but he wasn't going to show that to Will. "Where'd you put my coke?" he asked.

"Just where you told me. I stuck it in the trunk under the tire-changing stuff."

"Well, go out there and get it."

"You want me to bring cocaine into a church?"

Zane looked at Will with scorn. "Like you never had a drink before church."

"Not the same thing. You know I put my neck on the line for you here. Reverend Abraham trusted me that you were legit."

Zane shook his head and gave a short laugh. "Legit or not, she smells an opportunity. This is politics, bro. I'm here because your Reverend Abraham wants to stir up the waters with my story. She took the bait and ran with it...I didn't even have to tell her that story."

"Well, you can't blame her for figuring it's logical the Vice President would want Maria out of the way." Will was scowling.

"I don't blame her. I just recognize her. She's one of us, Will. A politician." Zane put a hand on his brother's shoulder. "Now go get me that coke. I want to have it on me. I'll make sure your Reverend never gets a whiff."

"I'm not your flunky, you know," Will said, turning to go.

"I know that. You're my brother, Will, and you've been great. You've always taken care of me." He slapped Will on the back as he walked through the doorway. "And Will – now that the stores are open, can you see if you can get me some clothes? These look slept in, and I'm going to be here for a while. Obviously, I can't go back to my house to pack a suitcase."

At this, Will stopped and looked at his Zane. "You want me to buy you some clothes?" His expression was sour. "And with what damn money am I supposed to buy you clothes?"

"Oh, I got money." Zane reached into the chest pocket of his suit and pulled out his wallet. "Here's my ATM card. Get me some shirts, pants, socks, the whole bit. May as well clean out the bank. Pretty soon, they'll be watching my account. There's about...a thousand in there. I think."

"You sure you can trust me with this, Zane?" Will grinned.

"Will, I already trusted you with my life. And you came through. If not for you, I might be dead already."

"That's a little dramatic, don't you think? The FBI wasn't going to shoot you down in cold blood today."

Zane looked at him. "I wasn't talking about the FBI – I'm talking about the other guy."

21

CATHERINE LOOKED UP to find Ralph Harwood standing in the doorway to her office. He looked unsure about whether or not to come in.

"Madam Vice President?" he asked.

"Yes, Ralph? Come in. Are there any developments on Dan Sweeney?" She stood up.

"Nothing significant yet. We're canvassing the area. We've asked the media to publicize the location, to see if we might get a witness that way." He looked drained.

"Do you want to sit down?" Catherine gestured toward her sofa.

"Yes. Thank you." He sat down with an uncharacteristic slump, not waiting for Catherine to sit first. "Could we close the door?"

"Of course." Catherine shut the door and sat opposite him. "I spoke to Dan's parents. Very nice people. Such a shame."

Harwood nodded his head, looking down. "Right. A tragedy. He was only 29."

"Was he? So young."

Harwood sighed. "I need to talk to you about Zane."

Catherine was hit with a dull pain in her chest. It was time to admit that there was something terribly wrong. Thinking about what Harwood was going to say next actually hurt.

He looked up at her as if he knew how reluctant she was. "It's time for us to consider Zane as a suspect." Almost gently, Harwood began ticking points off on his fingers. "He has access to your office 24 hours a day. He was here during the period in which the letter was placed on your desk. His fingerprints were on the envelope, which you yourself could not explain – "

"But – "

"Please let me finish." He waved his hand as if to apologize for taking control of the conversation. "And I have to add that Zane hasn't provided a saliva sample so that we can check his DNA against that found on the envelope flap. The lab tells me that the test results will be ready later today. And if the DNA shows that Zane could be a member of the population identified...."

Catherine put her hands to her cheeks. "Oh no."

"I'm afraid we need to bring him in now."

§

"Zane?" The voice came from the sanctuary of the church, and it sounded tentative.

Maria. Finally.

Zane flipped off the television and swung open the door to leave the cramped quarters that would be his – and Maria's – while they were under the protection of the church. He called out to her. "Maria? I'm back here."

"Where?"

He opened the side door that led to the sanctuary, and saw Maria standing in the center of the high-ceilinged church with a small suitcase. She was stunning in her vulnerable beauty.

For just a moment, Zane believed the whole story he had concocted. Here was Maria, the brown-skinned innocent whose mere existence could shake up the government of the privileged... the government of the United States of America. Through no fault of her own, she had been born to a woman who chose to disown her, and now that she had come seeking a child's birthright – to know her mother – she had become a threat to the power structure. It was only a matter of time before the gods of politics would swoop in to sacrifice this blameless lamb on the altar of propriety. Only Zane could save her, and turn her certain death into redemption and truth revealed. And if it cost America a Democratic president, then so be it.

"Zane!" She saw him, then, in the doorway. The spell was broken. It was just Maria, standing in a church. "Something awful has happened." She dropped her bag and rushed up the aisle to reach his arms. But before she did so, she genuflected quickly before the altar and made the sign of the cross. "It was frightening."

"What? What happened?" Zane's protective instincts were on high alert, and he was ready to do battle with whoever had threatened her.

"They found a body – a dead body. In the garage under my building. It happened last night...someone said it was a policeman."

"Did you talk to anybody?" His hands went around her wrists of their own accord.

"No – what do you mean? Talk to anybody? Ay – you are hurting me!" She pulled her hands away, looking at him. "I did not – I spoke to the neighbors only. Everyone was in the hallway early this morning. We were afraid. A murder!"

"Do they have any idea who did it?" Now his voice was carefully calm.

"No, I...I do not know. I did not hear anything from the police. The tenants were talking about it. And then I saw it on the news. Awful."

Zane saw that she was trembling, and he felt bad. He took her into his arms and then walked back with her to retrieve the bag.

"There were police all over the lobby, and the garage. They had people taking pictures – I saw the blood." Her eyes were glistening, those fabulous golden eyes. Eyes that she inherited from Catherine, Zane remembered.

"Come with me," he said, and put his arm around her waist. He held the bag in his other hand, and walked with her through the doorway that led to the Reverend's office and the back hallway. Now was the moment when Zane had to decide exactly what to tell her. He had thought about it all morning. He brought her to the little bedroom, and closed the door.

Maria looked around, puzzlement clear in her face.

"Sit down," he said. "Please."

She sat beside him on the chenille bedspread. "Zane, what is this about?"

He put his hand on her arm. "You trust me, Maria, don't you?"

"Of course I do. You know I love you."

"Well, then you'll believe me when I tell you that everything I am doing is for you. I can't tell you the whole story now – I don't want you to be frightened – and I'm trying to protect you, in case I'm caught – "

"Caught?" She clutched his arm. Her eyes clouded. "Zane, what do you mean, caught? Is someone chasing you?"

"Maria, don't...don't ask questions. There's no one chasing me – yet. And you don't have to worry about that. Let me do the worrying."

"Are you in trouble? Is it the drugs?" Her eyes were loving, but the question made him suddenly angry.

"No, there's no drug problem. I've told you – that's not a big deal to me. Forget about drugs." He softened his tone. "All you need to know is that you need to stay here – with me – for a few days. Until everything is cleared up. I know it's difficult to leave everything in the hands of someone else, but believe me, it's for your own good."

She straightened up and looked at him seriously. "Zane. Is this about what I told you – about Catherine Young being my birth mother?"

Zane made a quick decision. He nodded slightly. "It's best that we don't discuss it. But you should know this – you are a threat to the people in power."

Her eyes widened and her nostrils flared. "A threat? I am a threat...to whom? To her? To Catherine? All I wanted to do was to meet her... to have her know me, and to get to know her...." She stood up, and paced as far as was possible in the tiny space allowed by the room. Her fists were clenched into tight balls.

"This is monstrous! Meu Deus! My own mother – the one who abandoned me. And now she is alarmed that I have the...the...strength of will to seek her out...." Her fierceness dissolved into a flood of tears. The shimmering eyes filled and as the wetness slipped down her face, she looked at Zane. There was stark fear.

"Zane. What are you saying? Are they trying to kill me?"

§

Catherine sat in the family room with her hands cradling her head. She was in a long sleep shirt, and her feet were tucked underneath her on the old velour sofa. A cup of untouched coffee was left to make a ring on the scuffed end table. She had called Nancy to come over and talk about what to do next. Nancy, who was the only person who seemed to be a true friend these days, sat on a lumpy chair across from her.

"Oh God, Nance. What a mess I've made of this. What an utter mess." When she raised her head from her hands, tears wet her cheeks, leaving mascara trails. She wiped the back of a hand across her nose and sniffed.

"Why do you say that, Catherine? You haven't done anything wrong. I don't know where you think you've made the mess. What choices did you have? Did you ask to be blackmailed?" Nancy shook her head and her dark curls flew. "You're the victim here. Though nobody likes to use that word any more. And I know it's not a role you like to play."

Catherine didn't hear everything she said. She was working it out in her mind, looking through a long tunnel backwards to the day she had met Chuka in Ghana. Chechuka, his whole name, meant "God is everywhere," he had told her. And he had worked steadily alongside her for the next three years, while their friendship grew into a forbidden love.

When they decided to act on their love – a move that had seemed completely natural and spiritually honest, back when she was young and naïve – Catherine had never imagined that the diaphragm she dutifully inserted might let her down.

And here she was, 30 years later, dealing with the consequences of what seemed a lifetime ago. She noticed that Nancy was staring at her.

"Catherine? Are you listening to me? Or should I just wait until you beam back?" Nancy wasn't smiling – she looked concerned.

Catherine stood, unfolding her long legs. "I have to tell them," she said.

"Tell who? Tell what?"

"Tell the truth. First to my children. Then to the FBI."

"Catherine...wait. Are you sure you want to do this? You were the one that said it would leak the minute you told the authorities."

Catherine walked across the room and looked out at the dark night. She turned back to her friend. "Nancy, I'm not worried about leaks any more. It will get out. It's just a matter of when, now." She crossed her arms. "And if it was Zane who set this in motion...."

Catherine could feel another tear balanced on the edge of her lower lid. She bit her lip. "I – I just don't get that. Zane. I can't understand how he could do this to me. I thought we were...friends. I trusted him."

"I know you did."

"Nancy, he was like family. You remember...of course you remember...when Lily was in high school and got involved with cocaine. I was up nights...pacing the floor, afraid that one of those dawns would bring a phone call that my sweet girl had been in an accident – or worse...."

Nancy put her hand on Catherine's arm. "Yes. And Zane – "

"Zane went downtown to wherever she was. He never told me, you know? Wherever she was, in some sketchy neighborhood where kids from the suburbs went to score drugs, and he found her and hauled her back home. And he somehow got through to her – when I couldn't. I mean, she didn't have a father, and she wouldn't listen to me. Stupid mother, that's what she thought then, old and out of touch, stuffy, didn't know what fun was – "

Catherine knew that tears were falling down her cheeks, and she was laughing and sobbing at the same time.

Nancy wrapped her arms around her. "Yeah, I've had teenagers too. I know all about that stage."

Catherine pulled away, sniffling, and grabbed for a Kleenex on the table beside her.

"Nancy, I've always figured Zane saved her life. I mean, if he hadn't pulled her back to reality – "

"Right."

"And, the part I never told you…Lily had a crush on Zane after that. I could see it. She was throwing herself at him, despite – or maybe because of – the difference in ages. I mean, she was…what? Seventeen then? And he was about 25, 26. She was shameless."

"Really? No, that I didn't know."

"And Zane was a perfect gentleman. Acted like an older brother, just letting all her flirting roll off and not embarrassing her a bit. Despite the slutty outfits, etc. Oh, she was out of control! I was embarrassed. But Zane was just cool. Never took advantage. Never blinked. And then it was over, just like that. And she grew up and found a boyfriend who was closer to her own age."

"Good for him."

"So you see why I think of Zane as family. Or…I did."

"Catherine, you don't know for sure that it's him."

"Nancy, all the evidence points to him. And he's disappeared. Harwood was trying to spare me by not raising Zane as a suspect until it became so glaring…." She trailed off.

Nancy took a deep breath. "But Catherine…if you tell…do you think the public will…accept it? Forgive you for having this child? Not that there's anything to forgive."

Catherine sighed. She put a hand to her forehead and pushed her hair away. "It's crazy to think so. No. I don't. I think when it gets out – and it will – it will mean the end of my chances at the presidency."

"Then how can you tell them about the baby?"

Catherine smiled the tiniest bit. Her eyes were hooded. "Nancy, how can I not?"

22

CATHERINE PLUCKED OUT the raspberries from her bowl of All-Bran as she waited for the kids to arrive. She picked up the remote and turned on the television in the family room. The season for political commentary was in full swing, and the guests on The McCallister Clan were just warming up to their Sunday talk.

"Word on the street is that there's a political bombshell soon to be dropped concerning Vice President Young." White-haired, patrician Roddy McCallister looked at the panel members sitting in a horseshoe around him. They each nodded. "So you've all heard this? What do we think it could be? Predictions?"

E.J. Molly leaned forward, pushing her glasses up farther onto her long nose. "I've heard about this so-called bombshell. Something having to do with Catherine Young's 'female virtue,' whatever that might mean. But I don't expect anything to derail this White House-bound train. Let the right wingers try to smear her – there couldn't possibly be anything truly scandalous, because we would have heard about it by now." She threw up her hands in mock exasperation. "My Lord, the woman's been in the national spotlight for more than a decade. She made it through her Congressional years and most of her Vice Presidency without anybody uncovering any dirt. Do you think we'll suddenly discover that she's got a thing for wearing leather and whips? And who would care if we did?"

"What say you all?" McCallister asked. "Is this but a partisan balloon being floated to see if it bursts in the Vice President's face?"

Mary St. Claire, former staffer for the recent GOP administration, spoke up. "Don't be too quick to dismiss this, John. I've heard on good authority that this is major news. Something that will absolutely blow Catherine Young out of the race."

"That's ridiculous." James Deauville, the liberal half of the well-known political couple, turned to his wife in mock annoyance. "First of all, you can't blow a candidate out of the race who's already got the nomination of the Democratic Party." His eyebrows tilted up as far as they could go. "And secondly, I know what this supposedly shocking secret is going to be. It's the only thing it could be. These boys can't stand to be beaten by a girl. So what would the Republicans say about a single woman who's threatening to embarrass their candidate with a landslide win?" He gave an exaggerated shrug. "They're going to claim she's not a 'real woman.'" He wiggled his fingers to make quote marks in the air.

Annie Horseman crossed her long legs and added her throaty voice to the discussion. "What about Jerusha Hutchins? She's a woman! Why aren't they afraid of her?"

Deauville leapt in, voices rising and overlapping now. "Gov'nah Hutchins has eight children, last I counted. She's paid her dues, so to speak, as a woman – "

"So what about Young's children – " St. Claire interjected.

"What, you mean if the Vice President isn't the mother of a whole litter of kids, she's not woman enough?" E.J. Molly asked.

"Maybe Catherine Young is a transsexual," Horseman said, her voice mocking. "Now that would be news, right?"

The other members of the panel laughed but kept speaking over each other.

"Maybe James is talking about steroids," McCallister said. "Vice President Young is taking steroids to be up for the heretofore manly task of the presidency?" He let loose with a chortle at full volume.

"Naw. You're not getting it." Deauville held up one hand. "They are going to say – I kid you not! – that Catherine Young is a lesbian. What else could it be?"

"And what if she were…I ask you, panel, would that be a dealbreaker?" McCallister looked at the pundits sitting around him.

"Listen, if the Catherine Young flamed out of this race because of some heretofore unknown characteristic that made her unelectable, there would be a third party candidate in there as fast as you can say President Jerusha Hutchins!" Deauville was almost apoplectic now. "The majority of the people in this country will not vote for a woman, no matter how cute and blonde she might be, who is as ill-informed as she is…so God help us if the Vice President turns out to be a lesbian."

"But imagine the catfight!" Horseman chimed in, grinning wickedly. "Don't all men fantasize about girl-on-girl action?"

Catherine watched the glib commentators double up with laughter. It was fascinating and grotesque to watch them discuss her as though she were some toy to be fought over and then discarded. She listened to the gruesome ribaldry as one would watch the aftermath of a car accident, knowing that it was a twisted impulse, but compelled to stay and see exactly how bad the damage was.

The doorbell rang, and she punched the "off" button on the remote. Enough of that.

"Hi Mom," Lily said, as she hugged Catherine tightly and walked into the foyer. "You said it was urgent, so I just came in my home duds."

Her "home duds" were men's plaid shorts that were at least two sizes too big, held up by suspenders over a lime green midriff tee. Today, her hair was blond.

"Come on in, Lily. Let's sit in the family room." She was heading toward the back of the house when the doorbell rang again.

"Mom, can I just get myself something to eat? I'm starved. You always have real food."

Catherine smiled. "I can tell you where to buy some, honey. You can have real food in your refrigerator too." She opened the door and saw, not Mike as she expected, but Ralph Harwood. "Ralph." She realized that she didn't really want to see him. Something in the depth of her stomach was afraid of what he might say.

Harwood held his hands in front of his groin in the official government pose. He was wearing a dark blue suit. "Madam Vice President, I certainly apologize for surprising you this way. I know that it's a Sunday, and – "

"It's no problem, Ralph." Catherine pushed aside the urge to tell him to go away. "Please, come in." She calculated that the kids would give her a good opportunity to make his visit short. "I thought you'd be Mike. Lily is here, and we were going to have breakfast...."

Harwood began to back up instead of entering the house. He put his hands in front of him. "Your family is here. I apologize. This can wait."

"No, don't be silly." Suddenly Catherine felt sorry for the poor man. "Why don't you come in and we'll sit down until Mike gets here."

"If you're sure." He looked at her as though he really did need to talk now. He walked a few steps into the foyer.

"Yes – come on in. Let me tell Lily I'll be a minute."

"No need, Mom." Lily was behind her in the hallway. "I heard. I'll just hang out in the family room. I'm sure if it's official business you'd kick me out anyway. Hi, Mr. Harwood." She waved as she turned toward the back of the house, balancing a bagel and a knife covered in cream cheese in one hand, while the other carried a bottle of Poland Springs. Catherine resisted the urge to remind her not to get cheese on the furniture. Lily was 24, after all. But she ought to know about the use of plates by now.

"Hi, Miss Young," Harwood called to the retreating figure. He was clearly reining in the eyebrows which tempted to rise in response to her peculiar outfit.

"You should have brought the cone of silence!" Lily yelled from the hallway before she closed the door to the family room with a thud.

Catherine smiled as she got the reference. "The cone of silence. Remember Maxwell Smart?"

"One of my favorite shows." Harwood grinned, and Catherine realized that he was really a nice guy most of the time. He simply had a difficult job, and she was the boss lady. He probably had some strong feelings about her, too.

"Coffee, Ralph?"

"Uh, no thank you, ma'am. I don't need but a moment of your time. I could have telephoned...." He looked down at his polished black shoes. "But I thought I should tell you in person."

Catherine knew it was bad. Suddenly she was afraid. Could Zane be dead? Like Dan Sweeney? Was that the news he came to deliver in person?

"It's Zane," he said.

A pain like a knife hit her. In an instant, all was forgiven – the horrible thing he had done was forgotten. Zane, her friend, her trusted confidante, was dead.

"He's dead?" She could not breathe.

"No, no, he's not dead." Harwood looked oddly annoyed. "No. We don't know where he is, but there's no reason to think he's dead. What I came to tell you is that he's the one. He's the blackmailer."

Catherine found herself reeling, and had to put a hand on the wall.

"Are you all right, Madam Vice President?" He made a move to touch her, then stopped. "Should I call somebody?"

She waved him away, angry at herself. "I'm fine. Sorry. Stupid of me. I'm not even surprised. I just...never mind. Got the wrong impression." She pushed her hair behind one ear. How stupid to have let him see her sentimentality about Zane. "So. It's Zane. How did you find out?"

"The DNA results came in late last night. Of course, Zane had never given a saliva sample, and that had made me suspicious – since nearly everybody was prompt. Every single person, right down to the vacuum brigade. Zane didn't come in, and when I finally mentioned it to him, he said he'd been too busy...and would come to the office the next day. It was hard to see why he would be too busy for a 30-second cheek swab."

Catherine nodded. "So you don't have a sample."

"But then we realized that we did. Most people would need to give us saliva. But not Zane."

Catherine was getting impatient. "Why not?"

"Do you remember when we put those medical emergency plans in place for key people on your team? We always did this for the President, the Vice President, and a few Cabinet Officers – those who would be in succession for the presidency if there were some kind of catastrophe."

"Yes?"

"And this year we did it for some of the top staff too."

Catherine made a rolling motion with her hand. Get to the point.

"We have Zane's blood," Harwood said. "In a medical storage facility. In case he was in some kind of accident. We had some of the top staffers for you and the President store blood to have on hand for self-transfusions."

Catherine nodded. "So you compared the DNA with that from his blood." Her head was pounding. It seemed there was no doubt. All of the bewilderment and anger of her earlier feelings about Zane were tangled up with the sorrow and pity that came rushing in. "And how did it compare?"

"An exact match!" Harwood sounded about as excited as he ever got. His eyes were shining. Then he seemed to realize how inappropriate that was. "I'm sorry, ma'am. I know this can't be happy news for you. I really was anticipating...well, I had a head start. The DNA revealed that we were definitely looking for a male who was probably of Mediterranean background, and that put Zane in the target group."

Catherine put on her best professional voice. "Thank you for telling me in person, Ralph. That was considerate of you."

"Yes." He looked uncertain about what to do now.

She gently moved him backward toward the door. It was easy, because he was so wary of inadvertently touching her. "So...Mike should be here any minute. Thanks, again, for coming by with this." She opened the door and saw that Mike was parking his car. "There he is." She gave her best June Cleaver wave to her son. She willed the tears to stay back. Harwood should not see her cry.

She would have made it, but Harwood reached out and grabbed the hand that fluttered down from the phony wave in both of his. "I am so sorry. I am really sorry. I know he was your friend." Harwood released her hand immediately and practically stumbled down the steps. He muttered something to Mike and got into his government-issue car.

Catherine was sobbing by the time Mike got to the door. "Mom, what's wrong. Are you okay? Is something...did he say something to you?" Mike seemed about to run after Harwood's departing car.

"No, no." She managed to say, hugging him and wiping the tears away. "It's not him. Come in. I have to tell you...I have to tell you and Lily something."

Mike walked in and closed the door behind them.

"Are you sure you're okay?"

"Yes. No. Get your sister. She's in – no. I'll come there. The family room." Catherine grabbed a box of tissues as she walked by the table in the foyer. "Do you want something?" She waved vaguely toward the kitchen.

"No. I'm okay." Mike followed her down the hall to Lily. When they opened the door, they found Lily picking up the bagel, which had landed cream cheese-side down on the carpet.

"Sorry Mom." She grimaced. "Hi Mike." She looked at Catherine. "Hey, why are you crying?" She put the fuzzy bagel on the end table and walked over to her mother. "What did you do to her, Mike?"

Mike looked insulted. "Don't look at me, I didn't do anything. She was crying when I got here."

Catherine sniffled through her Kleenex and shook her head. "Sit down, both of you. Nobody did this to me. I did this." She wiped her eyes, and then her nose. "It's a long story, and it's one I probably should have told you years ago."

Catherine began the story in Ghana, and ended up in Paris after she gave birth to Elizabeth. When she was finished, both of her children were looking at her as though she were someone they had never met.

"So...we have a sister?" Lily asked. Her voice was angry.

"Yes. A half-sister."

"Where is she?" Mike asked. He looked troubled.

"I don't know. That's what I'm trying to find out now. I have a detective in Paris...trying to find the trail."

"We have a sister?" Lily seemed to be unsure of what to say, which was a rare circumstance for her. "Why now, Mom? Why the hell tell us now, after keeping this a secret for so many years?"

Catherine sighed. She didn't know what she had expected, when she decided to tell them. But it wasn't this eerie feeling of having them think she was a stranger. "It wasn't my idea to tell now, honey. I...I don't know if it was a good decision to keep it from you all these years – "

"But Dad knew," Mike said. "Right?" His eyes beseeched her, and Catherine realized with a start how much of a betrayal he thought this was.

"Yes, Mike. Your Dad knew. He knew – and he accepted it as a part of my life that happened long before I ever met and fell in love with him."

"So. Why are you telling us now?" Lily had her arms across her chest, and her tone was cold.

Catherine wanted to cry in hurt and frustration. Why did this have to be so hard? Why was something she decided with the very best of intentions hurting people she loved three decades later?

"I'm telling you now...because I've been blackmailed. Someone found out about this child – Elizabeth." Catherine saw another layer of shock register on Lily's face at the fact that this new mystery sister had a name. "And that person, who found out that I had an illegitimate child 29 years ago, decided it would be worth money to me to keep it quiet. He figured it wouldn't play well with the public if the first woman president had a past."

Lily stood up. A parade of emotions seemed to sweep across her face. "Who would do such a thing?"

Catherine bit her lip. "Who?" She struggled with a groan that was threatening to burst out.

"Oh, honey. I'm so sorry to tell you, but it looks as though it was Zane."

23

ZANE SAT IN Reverend Abraham's office with Maria at his side. It was 10:15, and they could hear the commotion of people arriving for services through the door to the sanctuary, which was just behind the Reverend.

"Today we will ask the congregation for their support." Ezekia Abraham, resplendent in her pastoral robes, was firmly in charge. "You can be certain that the brothers and sisters of Glory Baptist will come to your aid. I will ask Mrs. Brown to organize the ladies to do some cooking, so you will have proper meals. I will have a couple of the young men set up a small podium – yes, right out front on the church steps, our lovely church will be the backdrop – aren't we lucky it's summertime? Perfect for outdoor press conferences. And I'll need to have someone handle the media." She looked at Zane. "Of course you're the expert here, Mr. Zarillo. Perhaps you can give us the names of some contacts – "

"The media? But we...but what do you intend to say?" Maria had been becoming increasingly agitated, and finally she interrupted.

The Reverend gave Zane a significant look. She reached across the space between her chair and the couch occupied by Zane and Maria. She put her hand on Maria's arm. "My dear, don't be concerned. This is only for your own protection."

"Maria, maybe it's best if I talk to the Reverend privately for a few minutes. Can you go into the church and see if Will is here? I sent him off yesterday to get me some clothes – and I haven't seen him since."

"But Zane," Maria whispered into his ear as he walked her toward the hallway, "Even if she does not welcome me, I do not seek to make trouble for my mother – for Catherine. I never wanted that."

"Honey, this is really something you should let me handle. I'm the one who knows how politics works, right? Don't worry about Catherine. The party has been putting pressure on her to project a certain image – that's probably the reason she hasn't tried to find you before this. They wouldn't let her. It's the guys behind the scenes that are in control. By making this public, we take away their power. And then you'll be safe."

Maria nodded, looking only partially convinced, and Zane marveled once again at his natural gift for putting just the right spin on things. A kind of brilliance, really. He gave her a brief kiss and she went into the hallway to find the side door to the sanctuary. Zane closed the office door behind her, and sat down on the couch across from the Reverend, who had picked up a pad of paper and a pen.

"All right, Mr. Zarillo. I intend to have everything in place for a press conference tomorrow at, say, 10:00 a.m. Who do we call to get the proper attention for this matter?"

§

Catherine opened the door to Harwood's office in the Secret Service command center just under the Oval Office. He rose quickly to greet her. "Madam Vice President?" His surprise was tinged with a slight annoyance. No doubt he was busy, Catherine realized, and knew that her unexpected visit would throw off his tight schedule.

"Ralph – I apologize for barging in. I know you've got things to do. But this couldn't wait." She realized that she was rubbing her hands together nervously. She stopped. "May I sit down?" She didn't wait for his permission, but sat in one of the hard chairs in front of his desk.

"Of course." He sat down himself, looking at her quizzically.

Catherine glanced at her lap and then up again. There was nothing to do except jump in. "I have something to tell you. I should have told you a long time ago. You're going to want to shoot me – "

"Madam Vice President, I would never – "

"Shut up, Ralph, until you hear what I have to say." She smiled grimly and shook her head. "That 'secret' that the blackmail letter – which we now know came from Zane – talked about? The secret, which I kept for 30 years, is that I had a baby out of wedlock. A daughter, whom I gave up for adoption."

Ralph Harwood's mouth was open.

"The father of the baby was a married man, a Ghanaian – a black man – whom I met when I served in the Peace Corps. We fell in love. He never knew I was pregnant, or had a baby. I was...with the father...in Switzerland. And then I went to Paris to have the baby."

Harwood had recovered enough to close his mouth. "And what did you do with her?"

Catherine let out a breath. "I had my baby under an assumed name, in a Catholic charity hospital in the poorest section of Paris. There were a lot of people there from different backgrounds. Algerians, Moroccans, people from many continents. A lot of different skin colors. That's why I chose Paris. I thought my child would be less...memorable...if I had it there."

Catherine looked up, and saw in Harwood's eyes an expression she couldn't read. Was it disgust? Was it pity? She didn't like seeing it.

She rushed to finish. There was something crowding her throat and making it hard to breathe. It made her angry. Her voice came out in staccato bursts. "So I handed my baby – Elizabeth – over to one of the nuns there. I asked her to find a loving home for my daughter."

Damn it, she was not going to cry. She marshaled her pain into anger instead of hurt.

"And so you... shared this information with Zane," Harwood said, nodding.

"What?" Catherine was caught by surprise. "Zane? No, I never told him. I never told anybody – not my parents, not even the father. The only people who knew about the pregnancy were my friend Nancy from college and the nun in Paris. Oh, and before I got married – several years later – I told the whole story to my husband Paul."

"So how did Zane find out?" Harwood was like a hound on a trail now. "Do you trust this friend Nancy? Could she be the one?"

Catherine raised her hands in protest. "Not Nancy. She would never betray me." She let her hands drop. "And of course I asked her, even though I was sure, as soon as I got the first letter."

Catherine looked at Ralph. "I don't know how Zane found out. I didn't even imagine, until the last couple of days, that it could be him. I...I still find that difficult to believe."

Catherine put her hand up to her head. "Oh my God. Oh God! Ralph, do you think Zane knows her?" A piece of the puzzle had just come together. "I don't know why it never occurred to me – so many different things have happened. I never considered...."

Harwood's brow was furrowed. He ignored her question. "So where did she go? Who raised her – who raised this Elizabeth?"

"I don't know. I don't know." Catherine felt a small tear fall down her face. She didn't make any noise, but she trembled.

Harwood looked at her in alarm. "I'm so sorry, Catherine – Madam Vice President. I'm so sorry! Can I get you a tissue?" He opened one drawer after another until he found some, pulled out three, then walked around the desk to hand her the whole box.

Catherine took one and blotted her eyes, then grabbed another and blew her nose loudly. She tried to keep her voice level. "Oh, Ralph, I'm so embarrassed. Please don't share this with anyone." She looked up at him, knowing that her mascara must be all over her face, and her nose would be a rosy red. "The newspapers would have a field day."

"Of course not," he said, patting her shoulder awkwardly. "You know I wouldn't do that."

She reached up to hold the hand on her shoulder. "You're right. I know you wouldn't do that. You're a good guy, Ralph. You've done a lot for me." She sniffled and wiped her eyes with the Kleenex.

For a moment, they stayed like that. A tiny flicker of amusement came to life in Catherine's mind as she realized something – Ralph Harwood had a crush on her.

She released his hand and he returned to his desk, looking oddly goofy and a little sheepish.

"So how did Zane get this information? Do you think he knows the girl? Or just learned that she existed?"

Catherine's head hurt from all the hypotheticals. "Since I don't know where she went, who raised her, or even what her name is, I can't even guess as to the answers to those questions. I know he never heard anything about it from me – until after the first letter was received."

"And then you told him?"

"No. I never told him." Catherine put her head in her hands. "But once I got the letter – his letter – I broadcast my every move to him. I was so stupid.... I trusted him."

"Catherine. He was your campaign manager. Of course you trusted him."

"He was my friend. Or so I thought."

Harwood nodded. "Well, this makes things a lot clearer, anyway. About the whole blackmail scenario." He put his hands together in a steeple under his chin. "Of course, you haven't heard from Zane."

"Nothing. Since yesterday. You've been looking for him, I assume?"

"All day. No sign of him. We've had an A.P.B. out since we verified that the DNA matched his. We've checked his house – no car, but no sign of a planned departure, either – and of course he hasn't been near the White House. We're in the process of following up on other leads – family, friends."

Catherine nodded. "Zane is probably not the only one who knows by now. There have been hints from the media. This whole thing is going to blow soon. I told my kids this morning. I didn't want them to hear it on TV first. Told them about the baby, and about Zane writing the blackmail letter."

"How did they take it?"

Catherine spread her hands. "I think they were in shock. By the time they heard about Zane, it didn't really register." She looked across the desk at Harwood. "I have to apologize, Ralph, for not coming clean from the beginning. It was stupid of me to try to hide this from you and the FBI. Somehow I thought I could contain it. I thought of it as something...personal. And now," she gave an irritated shrug of her shoulders, "there are rumors floating around about my 'virtue.' That's got to be code for a woman sleeping around before marriage – even if it is ancient history."

Harwood looked embarrassed, but said nothing. There was a knock on the door, and Catherine turned around when it was pushed in. Ben Rickerby strode in rapidly, holding a document in his hand. When he saw her he stopped.

"Please excuse me, Madam Vice President. I didn't know you were – "

"What is it, Ben?" Harwood asked.

"Kelleher and I were going over some records, sir, to locate Zarillo's relatives and acquaintances. And we realized that his current girlfriend lived at 4800 Connecticut Avenue – the same apartment building where Sweeney was murdered." He gestured with the paper in his hand, to indicate where the information came from. "We figured that Dan probably made the same deduction, and might have been heading out there to question Zarillo."

"So you think Zane was the shooter," Harwood said. It was not a question.

"It would fit," Rickerby said. "The murder happened Friday night, probably around midnight. And when did Zane disappear?"

"We haven't seen him since Friday." Catherine said. Her mouth was moving slowly, it seemed. Her tongue was thick. "He was supposed to come in Saturday morning, and he never did."

Harwood stood up and moved toward the door. "He might be out of the country by now. Maybe we can still pick up the girlfriend – Maria."

"Right," Rickerby said. "We thought of that. Turns out, though, she's a Brazilian citizen. Works for the embassy. She might have been able to get him documents in another name."

Another agent, Donna Kelleher, showed up in the doorway beside Rickerby. "Afternoon, Madam Vice President," she said quickly. "I called and had Boyle and Cooke stop by the Connecticut Avenue building. There's no sign of the girlfriend. They got someone to let them in her place, and it looks as though she left in a hurry – but with a suitcase. There were signs of packing."

Catherine stood slowly and put a hand on the back of the chair to steady herself. She felt as though she were in a bright spotlight. Everyone was staring. Or did it just seem that way?

"Does that piece of paper include her date of birth?" She articulated carefully, as though the question were a difficult one that took special effort to enunciate.

Rickerby looked at the sheet in his hand. "Yes, ma'am. Her birthdate is...May 8, 1983."

"Thank you," Catherine said, and sat back down. It was then that the face came back to her – Zane's girlfriend – the Brazilian girl with the stunning golden eyes. The girl whose eyes had glistened with tears when she shook Catherine's hand.

"It is an honor to meet you," she had said.

If only she had known. Her daughter – that beautiful stranger. And Zane – a killer? A cold finger of fear touched Catherine's heart. She gripped the arms of the chair while all around her swirled the language of murder and apprehension. Her heart beat strange patterns in her chest.

The earth shifted on its axis, and she realized that her future was teetering out of balance.

24

Ezekia Abraham wore her black robe, a heavy gold medallion, and a purple lipstick called Kissable Plum. She stood in the brilliant morning sunshine on 15th Street in front of the Glory Baptist Church, and she was indeed in her glory. It was an otherwise uneventful Monday morning during the dog days of summer, and today her alleged campaign bombshell was the hottest news going.

The Washington Post was there. Politico, BuffBeast, and The Drudge Report were there. The New York Times was there. ABC, CBS, NBC and Fox were there. CNN was most definitely there.

The press had been primed by the rumors floating around in the last two days that the Young candidacy was about to run aground. And Ezekia had promised that a visit to her humble church would guarantee them all the answers they had been looking for.

Behind her, arranged on folding chairs, were twelve respected members of her congregation. There were two doctors, a lawyer, a pharmacist, a nurse, a school principal, three merchants, two teachers, and a lady who had given birth to two sets of twins. Without fertility drugs.

When the appointed hour of ten o'clock arrived, Ezekia unfolded her prepared text. She didn't read it, however. Like any good orator, she merely used it as a basis for the points she wished to cover. In fact, she and her quickly assembled "Emergency People's Committee" had prepared the paper to be used as a formal press release. But they had decided not to pass it out until after the Reverend had spoken. It would not do to distract the listeners with reading material.

Reverend Abraham raised herself to her full height, which was considerable. She gathered her breath in one mighty heave. "Brothers and sisters of America. I have come before you today to focus your attention on a grave injustice. A grave injustice." She looked out over the collection of reporters and cameras, and thought about how good it was that they were here. Good for her – and good for them. They were about to learn something.

She continued, relishing her rolling tones as they swept out over the assembled parishioners, who were outnumbered five to one by media. "There is something going on in this country, right this very minute, which is antithetical to the cornerstones of life, liberty, and the pursuit of happiness on which this nation was formed. Though you are unaware of it, the government of the United States of America has been engaged in a frightening conspiracy – a conspiracy! – to hunt down, and bring to ground, an innocent child who is guilty of nothing but the sin of being born. This church, the Glory Baptist Church, and I, its pastor, Ezekia Abraham, along with the twelve apostles you see behind me today – fine citizens of this city and this nation, who have pledged to lend their strength and support to this brave child – are sworn to grant asylum, to protect and defend this sweet girl against the evil powers of governmental racism and the Federal manhunt which has been organized to erase and destroy and expunge her until she shall cease to exist and shall perish from the Lord's green earth!"

Reverend Abraham was at full bore, but she sensed an impatience in the crowd. They were not used to her brand of rhetoric, and they were not yet with her. This was a crowd for hard evidence, rather than flashy words. So be it.

She flung her hand back toward the doorway to the church. "Ladies and gentlemen, I give you the disowned – the downtrodden – the cast out and denied child, who has been rejected by her own blood because of the color of her skin – the denied, disavowed, disclaimed and unacknowledged – the innocent victim of murderous black-booted government thugs! –

the so-called bastard daughter of the leading candidate for
President of the United States, Vice President Catherine Maguire
Young." There was a frantic scramble by the still and video
camera operators to get a good angle. They hadn't been ready
for action so quickly.

The twelve apostles, now standing, parted to let Maria and
Zane through to the front of the steps. Zane had his arm around
Maria's shoulders, and was urging her forward. For a moment
she stood there, the combination of her summer dress and the
bright sunlight revealing her body's silhouette. The noise of
camera shutters sounding one after another was all that was
heard. Then Maria turned, her face an unreadable mask, and
pushed her way back into the front door of the church.

"What's her name?" someone shouted.

"Wasn't that Zane Zarillo? Why is he here? Did he bring
her to you... why would he do this to his own candidate?" said
the next person, in quick succession.

"Can you prove she's Catherine Young's daughter?"

Ezekia Abraham raised her hands, and the babbling ceased.
This was the way she liked it. Right in the center, and in control.
She smiled, a smile of serenity and infinite patience. "Lucas, will
you hand out those press releases, please? Ladies and gentlemen,
this document will answer many of your factual questions."

"Why can't we talk to the girl – the daughter – herself?"
someone called out. "What's the matter with her?"

Reverend Abraham gave him a stern look. "There's
nothing the matter with her. She is a very intelligent, perfectly
wonderful young lady. A girl any woman would be proud to
claim as a daughter. But she has recently been through a very
traumatic ordeal. She has been the subject of a manhunt! It is
Mr. Zarillo who has been protecting her. He's the hero who
shepherded her to this sanctuary – and that's why I want her safe
inside my church. You can never be certain where government
sharpshooters might be lurking." She looked accusingly into the
crowd, now swelled by the addition of a significant number of
passersby. Most of them responded by looking around keenly at

each other. "Ms. Flores-Jenkins has asked me to handle press inquiries at this juncture."

The babble of questions began again. Still and video cameras were jockeying for position. Half the reporters were quickly skimming the press release, while the other half decided to shout questions. A few heads were bent over as the hot news flashed out to the Twitter world in staccato bursts of 140 characters.

"Has the Vice President admitted she's the mother?"

"What's her racial make-up? Who's the father? How old is she?"

"Has she been tested to see if...wait, is there a maternity test?"

The Reverend looked modestly down at the podium. "I am not prepared to answer individual questions beyond the information provided in our press release, at this time. I am, however, making myself available for media appearances, should it be necessary. I have told Maria that she may consider me and this institution at her disposal for the remainder of this crisis." She raised her head and let the fire come into her voice. The apostles stationed behind her were joined by 20 choir members in black and purple robes.

The Reverend looked over the crowd. "We of the Glory Baptist Church intend to ensure — with our very bodies, if necessary — that no harm is done to this precious child of God. Let the government dare to take us on! Let them come with their soldiers and their guns and their weapons of destruction. We welcome the opportunity to fight back — to fight for truth and justice — as the righteous have always fought in His name."

"Amen!" someone from the crowd shouted.

"Amen!" the voices in the choir began. And all of 15th Street, along with the cameras from ABC, CBS, NBC, Fox and CNN, was treated to clapping and rocking and singing; to the joyously united voices of the Glory Baptist Church's Celestial Choir, all ready, willing, and deliriously able to protect an innocent child in three-part harmony.

§

Inside the church, Maria ran up the aisle and through the door into the back hallway. The sanctuary was empty. Zane followed her, calling her name. He heard a door slam.

When he caught up she had locked the door to their little bedroom. Sobs came from behind it.

"Maria? Let me in, honey."

There was only the sound of crying.

"Please let me in, Maria. I'm sorry you're so upset. I didn't know it was going to be like that – I told Reverend Abraham that you shouldn't be paraded around. I didn't know that she was going to display you that way."

"Go away!"

Zane jiggled the doorknob and pleaded again. "Can I come in? Please?"

"You have brought shame to me, and to my family. How could you do this to me?"

"Maria, darling. Please. I didn't know. I'm sorry – look, I'm down on my knees out here." He knelt on the hard floor. He hoped she'd open the damn door soon.

The sniffles continued but the sound was coming closer to him. He heard the lock being released, and then the door opened. Maria looked down at him with nothing but disdain.

"Why did you do this to me? You told Catherine about me – I do not even know what you told her – without my permission. You claim that I am in danger, and you must protect me. And now you bring the television cameras and the newspapers here – to this church, so that they can point and stare at the poor Brazilian girl." Her arms were crossed tightly in front of her chest. "You asked me to bring something nice to wear – to display me to the world like a side show whore – the girl who is the Vice President's bastard!"

Zane got up from the floor and put his hands on her bare shoulders over the narrow straps of her dress. "Maria, I know that's how it looks. But believe me, that's not what I intended."

He thought quickly now. How best to explain? "When I first told Catherine...I know I should have asked you first, but I wanted – I wanted to set it all up for you. I – I was going to give you both this incredible gift, and bring you together myself. In my mind, Catherine would have been thrilled to meet you – to know you – it was supposed to be the kind of reunion you had always imagined. Because I know how hurt you were when she didn't recognize you that first time. So I wanted to pave the way. For you, baby." He dropped his hands to his side. "Only it didn't work that way." He stepped into the bedroom, closing and locking the door. He gently guided Maria toward the bed.

He sat down beside her and looked into her gorgeous, angry eyes. "What I wanted – what I hoped – was that Catherine would be thrilled to meet her daughter. Even though there would be some complications, I thought she was the kind of person who would embrace you...bring you into her life, and make you a part of her family. You are family, after all." Now he was getting somewhere. The glint of tears in Maria's eyes looked more tender than mad. "But – and this shocked me – she started talking about how she couldn't let this get out. Not with the election coming up in less than four months." He felt what could have been tears start to form in his eyes. "It was then that I knew I'd made a mistake. My attempt to reunite you was what put you in danger. I'm so sorry, Maria. What I didn't know – what I couldn't imagine..." he reached for her arm, "is that Catherine wants to be President more than she wants you."

Maria turned away, and there was a small sound like a gulp before she turned back. The moisture trembled on the edge of her eyelids, but her voice sounded as angry as it did hurt.

"So – she would rather be President." Zane saw her swallow to keep her tears in check. "Why could I not go home then? If she did not want me, you could have simply told me...and I could forget that I ever tried to meet her."

Zane shook his head, taking one of her soft hands in his. "Maria, it's not that easy. Once her people knew that you existed – and that you knew she was your mother – they had to eliminate you. And that's why we're here." It all fit so smoothly together, like the pieces of a fine jigsaw puzzle. Zane could picture the scene in which he had told Catherine, pleading with her to have some motherly instincts toward Maria. It unrolled before him like a movie he had seen somewhere in his dreams. And in that movie, Catherine was absolutely firm in her resolve that the "Maria problem" could never be allowed to be made public. The imagined conversation was so convincing that he almost believed it had happened.

"What, she ordered me killed?" Maria's voice was accompanied by a ragged laugh.

"Of course not. Catherine isn't heartless. She just said she could never acknowledge you – that it was more critical to the country that she be elected president." Zane saw the pain in Maria's eyes. He found it gave him a strange surge of excitement. "It was Harwood – the head of Secret Service. He's the one that was making threatening noises. And I knew I had to get you out of danger – quickly." He arranged his face into its most sincere. "Maria, the truth is that even if you went back to Brazil, you could be tracked. The CIA is everywhere."

Maria's face registered fear and confusion.

"By taking this public – even though I knew it would be painful for you..." Zane put a warm hand on her cheek, still wet with tears, "we were making sure the world would be on your side. Now everyone knows. Catherine can't pretend she doesn't know-

and they can't hurt you any more."

"Zane – "

"Sshhh," he said, bringing the hand on her check over so that one finger gently closed her lips. "Catherine may not want you – but I do. You can be my baby now. Zane will take care of you."

His mouth moved onto hers and he tasted the salty tang of her moist swollen lips. With a little cry, Maria wrapped her arms around him. He slipped one hand down to her shoulder and pushed the strap off. He reached under the filmy fabric and cupped her breast. She let him pull the dress up over her head and begin caressing her gorgeous tawny skin.

He pressed her against the narrow bed and ran his tongue down her chin and neck until it hit the spongy hardness of her right nipple. His hands were busy unfastening his belt and fumbling with his button. He felt the delicious throb of hardness against his pants. A quick unzip and it was released.

"Baby, don't cry. I'll take care of everything."

25

QUIGLEY HUTCHINS WAS having a very good Monday. Every time he turned on the news it seemed to get better. He had now seen the clip of Reverend Abraham introducing Maria Flores-Jenkins at least three times, at the top of every hour and half-hour as it played on all the news channels, and it made him happier every time he saw it. Dozens of television reporters were busy explaining who the lovely mystery woman was. Stations all over the country were showing the footage. It was gaining hits on YouTube by the minute, and talk radio hosts were foaming at the mouth to give their reactions.

Intrepid reporters were seeking out Catherine Young's Peace Corps colleagues in an attempt to find out who the baby daddy could have been. He was African, of course. Was he married? Was he... Muslim? The possibilities were numerous and wonderful. The blogs were going wild.

The Vice President's candidacy was dead, he was sure of it. And that meant that Jerusha's candidacy – which for all intents and purposes was his – was bound to be successful. She was all but elected already.

Here in Texas the local noontime anchors were having a thrillingly difficult time threading through the morass of politically correct language required to describe Maria, and the fact that she was illegitimate and interracial. Mostly they simply let Reverend Abraham's words tell the story as they rolled the clip again and again: " – the innocent victim of murderous black-booted government thugs! – the so-called bastard daughter of the leading candidate for President of the United States, Vice

President Catherine Maguire Young." It made his heart sing. He couldn't wait for the next set of presidential polls to come out. He and his wife Jerusha would wipe that bitch Catherine Young off the scoreboard.

"Reverend Hutchins? Ready for the speech?" Blair Faulkner's pink face glowed with happiness. It was a good day for him, too.

"I couldn't be readier."

"Then let's get on with it, Senator." Blair led the way down the hallway to the back of the Houston Marriott stage where the crowd was sitting fat and happy after a luncheon of well-marbled beef. When Hutchins heard the last line of the introduction, "Ladies and gentlemen, I give you Reverend Quigley Hutchins, the husband and most fervent supporter of Republican nominee, Liberty Party champion, Governor of the great State of Georgia and the next President of the United States, Jerusha Hutchins," he stepped out from the wings and the crowd got to its feet, whooping and hollering.

Hutchins strode to the spot behind the podium, and felt the powerful lights on his face. He noted with pleasure the television cameras pointed his way. They were looking for the sound bite from the opposing candidate to complement the bastard daughter story.

He waved his hands for quiet. "Now that's what I call a Texas-size welcome!" More whooping and cheers. "I am so pleased to be here today, in your fair state, in the lovely city of Houston, where my many dear friends and supporters have encouraged my wife's candidacy from the get-go." Hutchins launched into his regular speech, savoring the fact that the audience was chomping at the bit to introduce the topic of the day as soon as he opened the floor to questions. When he closed his prepared remarks with a resounding flourish, and asked for questions, the volley came quickly.

"Reverend Hutchins, what do you think of the revelations about Vice President Young?"

"Do you think a woman with sexual misconduct in her past should run for national office?"

"Are you going to call on the President to ask Catherine Young to step down?"

Hutchins carefully mastered the smile that threatened to appear on his face. It would not do to gloat. A well-worn principle of political strategy was to let your opponent bury him- or in this case her- self. He waved his hands for silence, shaking his head and looking sober. He projected cautiousness and respect.

"First of all, ladies and gentlemen, I cannot pretend ignorance as to what you all refer to. I, too, have seen the news, and I must confess that I have felt surprise and some discomfort regarding the allegations which have been brought in connection with Vice President Young's past conduct." There was another hubbub while people tried to shout more questions. Hutchins put his hands in the air to silence them.

"Let me say this at the outset. I would never criticize a lady on her personal moral behavior, no matter how shocking or abased it might be. And this would be my policy even if we knew that the statements being made were true, which is not the case, as yet. This entire story may well be fabricated."

Hutchins drew his white brows together in serious thought. "What I will say is that it is an outrage if the current Democrat administration – and the Democrat nominee for the next presidential election – are involved in an immoral and unethical personal witch hunt, against an innocent child of God, because of her mixed-race heritage. If this is true, it is to be condemned in the strongest terms. I will not tolerate such an abuse of power! Whether or not Vice President Young was involved in a scandalous sexual liaison with a married man, an African – and possibly a Muslim, as some have suggested – and let me remind you good people that we have as yet no basis on which to judge the truth of these allegations! – I am prepared to stand up in the halls of Congress and protest the use of government resources to hunt down and destroy the guiltless spawn of such a hypothetical illicit union."

"Reverend Hutchins, some people are suggesting that the girl undergo testing to see if she is really the daughter of the Vice President. Do you support this?"

"What does Jerusha think? Have you spoken to her about this?"

"What is your position on mothers giving away their children?"

"Do you personally find miscegenation objectionable on moral or religious grounds?"

Hutchins knew that this was the moment. Wrap up the discussion while the reporters were still salivating for more. He clasped his hands in front of his chest and looked down as if in prayer. He spoke quietly. "Ladies and gentlemen, I think it would be inappropriate for me to comment further at this point. But I do think that this is an occasion when we all might look into our own hearts, and into the deepest, darkest corners of our soul, and reflect on our own imperfections. Because God is willing to forgive the most base and sinful among us. And I want you to know that, as is natural between married men and women, Governor Hutchins and I have spoken about this latest — this rather stunning accusation."

Now the room got quiet, as the word from Jerusha was about to be handed down. Cameras focused, and pens hovered above notebooks. What would Jerusha say?

"As you all certainly recognize, Governor Hutchins is a God-fearing woman, and as she leads the Republican Party into office in November, we will have the Lord with us as our staff and our shield. So despite the putative sins of Catherine Young, Jerusha and I both recognize that she is not irredeemable. No man — and no woman — is irredeemable!"

Hutchins stood at the podium, his arms raised and his eyes beseeching God, and slowly made his voice quiet. "Ladies, and gentlemen, no matter what abominations we have committed, we are all welcome back into the loving arms of the Lord. The only thing necessary to achieve His forgiveness is that we repent and resolve to sin no more."

§

The radio was tuned to a talk station.

"Unbelievable, folks. Simply unbelievable. The virgin princess of the Left, Catherine Young, caught with her pants down. Or should I say her skirt up?" The chortles which accompanied Jerry Rash's voice assailed Zane as he walked into Reverend Abraham's office. Along with the sounds came the scents – cigarettes and booze. Will was slouched in the Reverend's chair with a glass in his hand and a butt in his mouth. A pack of Camels and a bottle of Jack Daniels sat on the table.

"Where the hell have you been?" Zane asked his brother, pulling him up by the lapels of a suit that looked better than anything he'd ever seen on him.

"Hey, Zane. Watch it! This is new, man." Will looked with dismay at the splashed whiskey that had missed his creased pants by inches and landed on the carpet.

"Yeah, I can see that," Zane said. "Is that what you spent my money on? I've been looking for you since Saturday. You were supposed to buy me some clothes."

"I did buy you clothes. I just bought myself some too." Will sat back down and poured himself another glass from the nearly empty bottle. "Yep, I got you some nice threads – nicer than mine, even."

Zane sat down across from him and glared. "You better not have spent all my money on clothes and booze. I'm going to need that cash. If you fucked up – "

Will sat up. "Who's a fuck up, brother? Who killed the cop?"

Zane stood. "I don't need this shit, Will."

"Come on, Zane. We need to hang together, man." Will took a long drag on his cigarette. "I did just what you said. Got your cash, got you clothes, and got you something else might cheer you up." He smiled and reached into the inside pocket of his jacket. "Just took me some time to get back in – it's crazy outside. All those vans with little satellites on the roof. 'Bout 12

reporters wanted to talk to me." He pulled out a plasticine bag
filled with white powder.

Zane felt his pulse spring to life when he saw the coke. He
had finished the stash from the car, and since the church was
under siege by the media, he hadn't figured on getting more any
time soon.

Suddenly he felt very warm toward Will. He had been too
harsh on his little brother. "Will, man, you came through." He
held his hand up for a high five, and sat back down, taking the
bag and setting up a few lines on the back of a Bible pulled from
the Reverend's shelf. He figured he was safe from discovery for
the moment. Maria was sleeping in their tiny quarters, and
Reverend Abraham was downstairs with her media committee
discussing which of many interview offers to accept.

As the first cool-hot explosion reached his cortex, Zane
relaxed. It had been a rough day. He'd had all he could handle
in keeping Maria from falling apart. The coke hit the spot.

"Listen, man," Will said. He was pointing at the radio, still
tuned to Rash.

"Why are you listening to this guy? I didn't think you knew
who he was."

"Sure I do. Jerry Rash. Somebody outside – a TV guy –
was asking me what I thought of what Rash says about this.
That if Maria's really her daughter, Vice President Young should
pull out of the race."

The voice on the radio was different now. It was a caller, a
man, practically foaming in anger. "I'm a Republican, but I was
ready to vote for Catherine Young in November. I thought she
was a darn sight sharper than Governor Hutchins, for sure. But
after this...why, I'd sooner have a five dollar...ahem...prostitute
in the White House."

"Now hold on a moment, just hold on," Rash's voice broke
in, relishing the caller's ire. "Whatever you do, don't say I called
her a slut!" His booming laugh sounded. "Really now... what
horrible thing has she done? Come on, people. She had a little
fling... before she was married, according to the alleged birth date
of this so-called daughter. O' course, he might have been

married, as some have suggested, which is purportedly the reason that she gave the babe up for adoption. But, for all we know, this is a simple case of sex out of wedlock. That's not a crime. Well, actually it is in some states. However, I doubt that it's a crime in Africa – or wherever she was when she did the dirty deed." He stopped to laugh. "Of course, if she was in South Africa at the time, it might have been a capital offense, since we can imply from the skin tone of the young lady claiming to be her progeny that Virgin Princess Young must have been consorting with a fellow of a somewhat darker hue."

Rash's trademark sound of rustling paper came over the airwaves.

"Let's hear from someone else. Here's Linda from Los Angeles, the City of the Angels."

"Mega-claps, Jerry. I'm a big fan."

"Thank you, Linda."

"I am just so glad that you are bringing the news to us in a fair and unbiased way. The lamestream liberal media is already busy saying that this is perfectly all right, and it's the Vice President's business. That what kind of morals she has is totally unrelated to her fitness to be president. Well, we've heard that before! That's the usual Democrat line. I wouldn't vote for a woman – or a man, either – to be dogcatcher, if I thought she had gone and made a baby with some married guy before she got into politics. Not to mention the race thing at all. I'm not prejudiced, but I mean, what if we found out that one of our children's teachers had a secret black Muslim baby? A bastard – whoops! I'm sorry. Can you say that on the radio?"

"That's all right, Linda, if the FCC threatens our license here on the Rash Network, I'll just get me one of those First Amendment lawyers who's always defending the liberals' right to spread pornography. You have a right to your opinions, and I'll defend to the death your right to express them here on my show."

Rash paused and the sound of papers shuffling came over the radio again. "Folks, I'll tell you frankly, that I've heard a lot of pretty peculiar takes on this already from the liberal press.

Yes, ladies and gentlemen, there are some in the left-leaning media who are saying that the fallen Virgin, Vice President Young, should be congratulated on her humanitarian decision of lo these many years ago not to abort the young lady who has just been introduced to the American public. I ask you, what is this country coming to when a mother is congratulated for not destroying her own flesh and blood? Even though the lovely hyphenated Maria Flores-Jenkins" – Rash trilled the 'r' extravagantly – "was in fact banished to a dark continent of the Third World where she was raised far from her natural mother.

"It reminds one of the fairytale, which one is it, Mr. Wombley? The one where the beautiful young girl is sent away to be killed by the woodcutter? Snow White, that's it! Except in this case, the Wicked Queen is actually the snow white one, and the beautiful daughter is of a noticeably darker shade!" Rash laughed.

"No, ladies and gentlemen, what's shocking to me, and to all of you out there listening, I'm certain, is the fact that the current liberal Democrat administration – a bastion of tolerance and racial understanding, as they are always reminding us – is going after this lovely young lady because she is an embarrassment to Vice President Young! I mean, can you believe it? All these years of lecturing others on how they should be more understanding... these bleeding heart liberals who think that all traditional social norms should be tossed aside, and as soon as one of their own steps out of line they do everything they can to eradicate the evidence! So when Catherine Young is exposed as having birthed an illegitimate child, she sends government thugs out to erase her own spawn! To murder the poor girl! With my tax dollars and yours!"

Zane finally walked over to the radio and punched the power button off. His stomach was burning with a deep shame for Catherine. And Maria. To be trotted out for ridicule by a clown like this was unbearable.

He bent over to snort some more forgetfulness into his nostrils.

26

THE DOORBELL RANG and Catherine stood up to open it. She
had just dumped most of her uneaten Lean Cuisine dinner into
the garbage compactor after hearing from the security people at
the gate that Nancy had come by. She padded to the front door
in bare feet and the long T-shirt she wore on hot nights. The
words across the front read, "A woman's place is in the House,
and in the Senate...." Scrawled across the bottom in cursive was
the addendum, "and in the White House!"

Catherine reached the front door and peered through the
security peephole. When she saw that it was Nancy, she swung
open the door.

"Nancy, what are you doing here at this hour?" Catherine
asked, her hands on her hips.

"Well, that's a nice welcome," Nancy said, holding up a
bottle of Glenfiddich 12 Year Old Reserve. When Catherine
made no move to step aside, she pushed past her. "So, are you
going to invite me in, or do you enjoy giving the Secret Service
guys out there an eyeful of presidential thigh through their night
vision goggles?"

Catherine backed away and closed the door. "That's vice
presidential leg – and at the rate I'm going, it may not be that for
very long. Frankly, flashing my thighs to the Secret Service is
one of the tamer things I have to worry about these days."

Nancy put the bottle down on a table in the hallway and
wrapped her arms around her old friend. "Catherine. I'm so
sorry. So sorry about how all this turned out. I saw that awful
press conference – at least the part they showed on the 6:00

news. I couldn't believe my eyes when Zane brought her out. You don't deserve this."

Catherine let her head rest above Nancy's curly one for just a moment. She pulled away, trying to blink back her tears. "Nancy, don't get me blubbering. I've been one step short of falling apart all day. I'm either distraught or livid about Zane. Or both, depending on the time of day. And then, finally seeing Elizabeth...Maria? My daughter." Tears crossed over into laughter that became a rasping sob. She walked rapidly over to the hall table and pulled a Kleenex to her eyes. "But I can't afford to look all puffy and red tomorrow – God knows I'm going to have to come up with some kind of public response to this. The press is smelling blood, and they're looking for the President's next move."

"What do you mean? What move?"

Catherine walked toward the kitchen with Nancy following. She shook her head. "You mean that you haven't heard? Word is that I should pull out of the race for President, to save the party the embarrassment of having to boot me out. People are calling for my immediate resignation from the vice presidency. And on the Hill, they're talking impeachment."

"Catherine, you know that's ridiculous. People say all sorts of things when they think they'll get a few minutes on the news. Nobody's serious about that."

Catherine took two glasses out of the cabinet. She raised her eyebrows as she looked at Nancy. "Ha." It was supposed to be an arch laugh, but it came out as a broken sort of moan. "Don't underestimate the power of a political juggernaut, Nancy. This is the most fun people inside the Beltway have had since the Bill Clinton era. Sex and politics – an irresistible cocktail." She leaned her elbows on the counter and dropped her head onto her hands. "And this is even more juicy than talking about the typical male politician's sexual peccadilloes... a woman with a sexual secret in her past – a scarlet woman! In fact, I think the GOP is going to introduce a bill forcing me to wear an 'A' on my chest after they cast me out of Washington."

Nancy took the glasses and filled them generously. She handed one to Catherine. "Here. Drink this. I wish I had some Valium – or maybe Prozac? But this will have to do."

Catherine took the drink and swallowed a hard gulp. It burned as it made its way down her throat. "So how did you get past the guards? I told them no visitors tonight."

"Oh, I said you just meant media. That you and I were going to get seriously drunk and talk about your sex life."

Catherine put her glass down. "My God. You didn't, did you?"

"Of course not, silly." Nancy looked at her directly. "But Catherine, don't make the mistake of underestimating the people. There's a lot of sympathy for you out there – and not just from women. You're getting stoned – " she stopped and giggled slightly, "in the biblical sense, I mean – when there are a lot of people throwing from glass houses who have no right to talk."

"Nancy, that is a dangerously bad metaphor."

"Yeah, yeah, you know what I mean. And Catherine – I think you may be overlooking an important piece of the puzzle here."

"What would that be? I can't imagine I haven't thought of every horrible possibility."

"Who says this Maria is your daughter? As far as I've seen, she hasn't provided any proof."

Catherine shook her head. "Nancy, that's wishful thinking. If she isn't my daughter, how did Zane find out that I had a daughter at all? She has the right birth date – that can't be coincidence. And why would she want to go through this charade if she didn't have a real claim?"

"Who knows what their motivation is, Catherine? Or how Zane heard about your past? He could have hired someone to pose as your long-lost daughter – did you ever think of that?"

Catherine crossed her arms. "Zane go looking for dirt on me? And then hiring some stranger to play a role? To screw me and ruin my chances of being elected? " She pushed her hair back from her face. "All that does is destroy his career too. It strikes me as nuts. And I don't think he's that."

"You don't think he's nuts? I do. But I'm just reminding you not to make assumptions. Stuart is still digging away in Paris, and he's going to find out exactly what happened to Elizabeth."

Catherine sighed. "Nancy, I'm sure I've found my daughter. But for the sake of thoroughness, let him keep searching. So at least we'll have proof."

"Right. Now let's go watch the show." Nancy took her drink and the bottle and started to head toward the den at the back of the house.

"What show? What are you talking about?"

"You know perfectly well what I'm talking about. Bernie Schwartz is going to interview the indomitable Reverend Abraham. And you're dying to watch it." Nancy swung through the door into the den, put down the whiskey and picked up the remote. She pushed on the power.

Catherine sat down on the old couch and gave in. "You're right. I was going to watch it and pretend that I hadn't. So I could say that I couldn't respond to whatever she says."

"Great. You can still say that. I won't rat on you." Nancy sat down beside Catherine and tucked her feet beside her on the couch. "But this way you'll know what happened."

Bernie Schwartz's face, sporting his trademark glasses, appeared on the screen. "...And tonight, ladies and gentlemen, we will be speaking to the Reverend Ezekia Abraham, spokeswoman for Maria Flores-Jenkins, who claims to be the biological daughter of Vice President Catherine Young. Up until now, Vice President Young, who is the Democratic nominee, has been the front-runner in the race for the presidency. Please join us for what we hope will be an informative discussion about today's allegations. Allegations that include a claim that the administration has been trying to suppress knowledge of the existence of Ms. Flores-Jenkin's relationship to the Vice President, up to and including threats of physical violence. We'll be back." Schwartz's finger pointed toward the camera, the theme music came up, and the screen showed a black Mercedes cornering on a wet road.

Catherine held out her hand for the bottle. "I think I need another drink."

Nancy passed her the whiskey. "It's nuts to think that your election would be derailed by something like this – something perfectly legal, and absolutely personal – that happened thirty years ago."

Catherine shook her head. "Nance, I always knew that if this came out, it would be the end of the line for me. People can't handle women being sexual. At least women politicians. If the women in entertainment are seen as the whores, who do you think has to play the madonnas?" Catherine pushed a strand of hair behind her ear. "Once Paul died I was obliged to be the sober widow – I know you always told me to lighten up, but it's nearly impossible for a woman in Washington to pull that off without tongues wagging."

Catherine turned back to the television as the music for Bernie Schwartz came up. Schwartz was sitting across a desk from Reverend Abraham, who was dressed in a black suit with yellow piping.

"Reverend Abraham, you claim that Maria Flores-Jenkins has brought this matter to the attention of the American people not because she wanted to be acknowledged as the daughter of the Vice President, but because her life was in danger – and that if she had not done so, she might have been kidnapped or even killed by agents for the Federal government. Do you have any proof for this astonishing accusation?"

Reverend Abraham smiled. She had a wide smile, and it shone forth as though she were conferring a blessing on Bernie Schwartz.

"Mr. Schwartz, Ms. Flores-Jenkins has nothing to gain here." Reverend Abraham sat with her hands clasped on the desk in front of her chest. "She is not looking for money, as some in the media have maintained. She is not looking for prestige, or fame. In fact, until she discovered that her very existence was a threat to the political power structure, she was quite content to let her status as the unacknowledged daughter of Vice President Young remain a confidential matter between herself and her mother. She had – and has – no desire to embarrass or expose her mother. Ms. Flores-Jenkins wanted merely to be treated with a little dignity." Reverend Abraham's voice was getting louder. "She wanted her mother to grant her a modicum of respect – a nod, a shake of the hand, a private conversation. Surely she is entitled to this."

Her voice began to swell with righteousness. "This is an outrage. What we have here is a motherless child – a child cast out by her white mother because of the shame of her dark skin. And we have a presidential administration willing to support this astonishing bigotry. What is particularly shocking – unbelievably so! – is that her mother is the very same woman who has called upon, and received, the support of my people throughout her entire political career."

Schwartz nodded. "It is shocking, if you accept the premise that Ms. Flores-Jenkins is in fact the Vice President's daughter."

At this, the Reverend bristled. "Maria is willing and eager to submit whatever evidence is deemed necessary in order to prove parentage. In fact, we plan to ask the Vice President to supply tissue samples so that a DNA comparison can be made as soon as possible."

"So Ms. Flores-Jenkins is not demanding money, or other compensation?"

"Nothing. The sole reason that this matter has been brought to the attention of the people is that Maria's life was in danger. This was the only way to keep her safe."

"And how, exactly, was her life endangered?"

"I am not at liberty to discuss the details of the actions taken by the government against Ms. Flores-Jenkins, since they may become the subject of a civil suit. I can say that various surveillance activities were undertaken, including an illegal investigation into her background by the Secret Service agents protecting the Vice President. This was only one incident in the pattern of harassment dictated by the government's attempts to silence her."

"You say they investigated her?" Schwartz leaned forward.

"Yes indeed. They went to her neighbors and asked questions about her character."

Catherine found that her mouth was open. "Unbelievable," she said to Nancy, shaking her head. "That would have happened as a routine...when Zane listed her as his guest for the reception after the Convention."

On the screen, Schwartz frowned for a moment, and then nodded his head. "Reverend Abraham, we have a call from the Reverend Walter Freeman. Reverend Freeman, you're on the air."

"Bernie, Reverend Abraham." It was the carefully enunciated tones of Walter Freeman. "I have been discussing the treatment of this young lady – Ms. Flores-Jenkins – with black leaders throughout the country today. In fact, I will be holding a press conference alongside the President of the NAACP tomorrow. However, I must tell you that I am personally disappointed to learn that Vice President Young, whom I had considered a true friend to our people and our community, has rejected her own flesh and blood, this child of God, Ms. Flores-Jenkins."

Reverend Abraham smiled. "Amen," she said.

Bernie Schwartz put his finger against his earpiece. "Reverend Abraham, I'm being told that a Secret Service agent was found murdered early Saturday morning in the Connecticut Avenue apartment building where Ms. Flores-Jenkins lives. To your knowledge, is this death connected to her dispute with the government?"

The camera was directly on the Reverend's face. Her expression was momentarily startled and then settled into a cautious resolve.

"This is news to me, Mr. Schwartz. I have no knowledge as to whether this alleged murder is connected to Mr. Zarillo or Ms. Flores-Jenkins. I can say that if government thugs were sent to hunt Maria down, bloodshed could well have been the inevitable result."

Schwartz's brow came together in consternation. "Are you saying that Mr. Zarillo might have killed a Federal agent?"

"I am saying nothing of the kind. What I am telling you is that Federal agents were attempting to kidnap or murder Ms. Flores-Jenkins, a Brazilian national, for the sole purpose of silencing her and sparing the powerful Washington political machine the embarrassment of acknowledging the inconvenient black daughter of the Vice President of the United States!" Reverend Abraham was no longer smiling. Her nostrils flared and her shoulders heaved.

Catherine turned to Nancy. "I think I'm going to be sick."

Nancy took her hand. "Maybe the whiskey wasn't such a great idea. You want me to make some coffee?"

Before Catherine could answer, the phone rang. It was her private line. She picked it up. "Hello?"

President Drummond's voice came over the phone. "Catherine. Are you watching Bernie Schwartz?"

She gulped, and hesitated. No point in lying. "Yes sir."

"We have to contain this thing, and quickly. Before it gets to be even more of a circus than it is. Zane is going to be arrested – tomorrow. I've got the Attorney General here, and the head of the FBI. I need you at the White House."

"I'll be right there."

Catherine put down the phone.

"Was that who I think it was?" Nancy asked.

"Yep. The President. Wants me at the White House. Now." She looked down at her T-shirt. "Probably in something more than this. And only after liberal doses of mouthwash and mascara." She ran both hands down her cheeks. "Nancy, can I take you up on that offer of coffee – strong? This is going to be one hell of a night."

27

ZANE AND MARIA headed downstairs with Will to the church basement, where the Reverend had stationed a large-screen TV that had been donated by a 14th Street store. The basement was only a big concrete room with small windows, but good smells emanated from the kitchen on one side. Long Formica tables with folding chairs around them were still set up from the last church supper, and a dozen or so people sat by them. On the tables were fliers in fluorescent orange, green and pink. A large yellow poster had been started, with the words, "Save Maria and Zane! Support the Glory Baptist Church and their political asilem," but the teenage writer apparently suspected a mistake, because the last word was smudged in an attempt to change a letter.

As Zane and Maria entered the room, several of the people gathered around the tables applauded. Zane smiled while Will gave a mock bow and started clapping in his brother's direction. Maria gave a stiff smile and averted her eyes. Zane led her up to the first row of chairs, where they sat in front of the television.

The screen showed the White House pressroom, and the rows of reporters were just sitting down as President Drummond reached the podium. It was clear to all watching that the President's recent illness had taken a toll on his usual vigor.

"Ladies and gentlemen, I'm sure you know why I've decided to talk to you this morning. Some shocking and troublesome claims about a member of this administration have been made in the last 24 hours, and I cannot let them go unchallenged. Particularly when they are so completely and virulently false."

He paused, and then looked to the left side of the room, and the camera panned over to where Catherine was standing. Zane was startled to see the grim lines beside her mouth and the paleness of her skin. They should get some better make-up on her, he thought reflexively, and then realized how absurd it was for him to worry about her television image. The camera swung back to the President.

"First of all, I want to state here and now that I support Vice President Young and her continued candidacy for this office." Drummond's voice took on an edge. "The Vice President has done nothing to shake my faith in her competence and her fitness to serve as president." Once again, the camera swung wide to take in Catherine's face. This time, she nodded slightly, and the paleness in her face was replaced by a light shade of pink. The sudden recognition of her pain hit Zane suddenly in the stomach.

Drummond was once more in the center of the screen. "Since this matter is primarily one of law enforcement, I'm turning the podium over to the Attorney General." There was a quick babble of questions, but the President waved them off and stepped aside for Harold Leighton, a medium-sized black man with the rolling gait of a former police officer accustomed to packing a heavy belt.

"Ladies and gentlemen. We have issued a warrant for the arrest of Zane Zarillo. The charges include extortion, conspiracy, and felony-murder in connection with the death of a Federal agent." Zane felt his throat close up. He sensed Maria turning to look at him.

Leighton held up his hand for quiet as the reporters reacted noisily. "The version of this story you have heard up to the present time has been completely fabricated. The truth includes attempted blackmail of the Vice President by a member of her own campaign staff. For this we have indisputable proof, in the form of a letter demanding 250 thousand dollars to keep this alleged relationship secret. The saliva on the envelope containing that letter has been shown via DNA testing, to a 99.3% certainty, to be that of Mr. Zarillo. Further, the true story includes the cold-blooded and premeditated murder of a 29-year-old Secret Service agent who was doing nothing more sinister than attempting to ask Mr. Zarillo some questions concerning the above extortion attempt. And since Mr. Zarillo was privy to all of the government's strategy in seeking to apprehend the blackmailer, he decided to lie in wait for this agent, and kill him before the man even suspected that he was in danger. The agent's gun was still holstered when his body was found riddled with bullets the next morning."

"That's a lie! That man is lyin'!" A young man sitting behind Zane stood and pointed his finger at the television screen.

"Amen, brother." A thin woman in a polka dot dress was standing in the kitchen door drying off a pot. "Ain't it a crime when the government starts lying to protect its own."

The small crowd in the basement was getting vocal. "Can you imagine?" a man with a deep voice boomed out. "The police put that gun back in his holster, so the Feds look completely innocent. I tell you, it's O.J. all over again."

"And blackmail. What's that about?" asked a teenage girl wearing cut-offs and a form-fitting top. "Like Zane needs any money." And she shot him such a look of desire that Zane felt the heat across the room.

"Shut up, shut up. I wanna hear what's going on," said another man, pointing at the TV.

Leighton was answering questions now. "What about the statements made earlier this morning by the NAACP and Reverend Freeman claiming that the shooting was likely to be justified on the grounds of self-defense – that Mr. Zarillo believed the government was trying to kill this woman because she claims to be the Vice President's daughter?" asked a reporter in the front row.

"That is utter nonsense. The evidence will show that Agent Dan Sweeney was caught completely by surprise – with his weapon in his holster, with the safety on. Unfortunately, he's no longer around to testify – but we can demonstrate through ballistics precisely what his position was when he was gunned down."

"How are you going to arrest Zarillo? He's holed up in a church, isn't he?"

The people in the basement suddenly stilled. This they wanted to hear.

Leighton nodded. "We are aware of the fact that Mr. Zarillo has claimed some sort of protection – asylum, he calls it – from prosecution while he is at this church. And we certainly respect the good intentions of those who were unwittingly hoodwinked into believing his false and frightening claims. We are confident, however, that with the truth now apparent, we can obtain Mr. Zarillo's cooperation – and that of the church which has lent him the cloak of legitimacy – in bringing this matter to a close without any possibility of harm to innocent bystanders."

"What about that, Zane? You ain't just gonna lay down and give in to this B.S., are you?" It was the young man who had first talked back to the TV.

The anxious faces all turned toward Zane. The deep-voiced man and the polka-dot woman, the angry young one and the seductive teenage girl awaited his answer. Reverend Abraham, who had come down the stairs and stood in the back, looked at him closely. Will shrugged his shoulders, as if to say he was on his own. Maria regarded him with a gaze part suspicion and part expectation.

"No I'm not," Zane heard himself say. A murmur of approval rumbled through the basement.

Read their faces. What do they want?

"No!" His voice was louder now. "I'm not going to crawl back on my hands and knees and beg the man for justice. Let them come get me!" He punched his fist hard and high, and the people roared their support.

§

Zane sat in the Reverend's office while she stood and paced the length of the room.

"Mr. Zarillo, you came to me and represented yourself as an honest man wronged. I put myself, my reputation, and my parishioners behind you...gave you legitimacy, and a forum...and the protection of the Glory Baptist Church! And now I find that you have held back half the story." She turned and placed her considerable bulk directly in front of him. Her finger pointed like the wrath of God.

Zane put on his best smile. He turned up the wattage in his eyes to maximum charm. He could get past this woman.

"Reverend Abraham, I can imagine how you must feel. I can only offer my sincere apologies that I didn't fill you in...didn't know you well enough...to tell you that part of the story." He put his hands in his lap. "Yes, I did shoot that agent. But it was self-defense. I did it to protect Maria. And I was afraid to explain that part...think of what you would have said. Would you have taken me in if I had told you I'd shot a Secret Service agent?"

Her face was granite. "Mr. Zarillo, we'll never know what I might have said. But the time for honesty was then. You asked me to put my church, and my congregation, on the line for you. And you didn't mention killing a man?" Her purple mouth made a thin line. "I am not willing to give you another chance to deceive me. This is now a matter for the courts to decide." She put her hands on her waist. "It is time to move on, Mr. Zarillo."

Zane looked at her in amazement. She didn't believe him.

"But Maria...she needs protection – "

"Nonsense!" The Reverend released her powerful voice. There was no doubt that the sound was making its way down the hall and into the church sanctuary. "I know a con artist when I see one, Mr. Zarillo. I don't know if your little lady is in on this or not...but you are not dealing with a fool. I will not have you using me or my pulpit any longer."

"Maria is the Vice President's daughter!"

"She may well be. So you've gotten your press conference, and your media spotlight. Do with that what you can. No one is going to kidnap or kill her now." The Reverend sat down and put her hand on his knee. Her tone was kinder. "It's time to turn yourself in, son, and deal with the truth, whatever it may be, about the extortion letter and the death of that Federal agent. The FBI will be arriving in…" she looked at her watch, "one half hour. I expect you to be ready to go when they come to collect you…and go peacefully, so that no one in my church community is put in a position of having to choose between you and complying with the law. Because that is not what we are about."

She nodded and looked him directly in the eye.

"And I'm afraid, Mr. Zarillo, that the FBI is going to take you out of the Glory Baptist Church in handcuffs."

§

Catherine clutched a coffee cup bearing the presidential seal. Her stomach was bitterly empty, but she found no urge to eat the generous sandwich sitting before her. President Drummond was pacing behind the sofa opposite hers in the Oval Office. She wished to hell he would sit down.

"Catherine, I never thought of you as a quitter." He stopped and leaned over the back of the sofa, his arms braced against the carved wooden frame. His brows were drawn together over the hawk-like nose, and he looked as much like a member of the Cherokee nation as she had ever seen him.

"I'm not a quitter, Mr. President." She did her level best to keep the rancor out of her voice. She didn't look at him. "But I'm not an idiot, either. And there is no reason to punish you, or the party, or anyone else, because of my behavior. Why would I want to take the Democrats down with me?"

"Catherine." He moved slowly around the sofa and sat down. His arms spread in the air. "You're giving up too soon. This thing is a long way from over. The public hasn't even had time to digest our first volley — all they were getting was Zane's side, until just now. Now they'll have the truth to chew on. Blackmail. Murder. Why should they support this guy — or his girlfriend? Why should they believe him?"

Catherine leaned forward, her throat clenched. What she meant to be a shout came out as a raw whisper. "Because it's true."

"Yes. So you told me. It's true." Drummond pushed on his lanky knees and stood. He walked again, ticking off the points on his hand. "You had an affair, you had a daughter, you gave her up for adoption. It's true. So what?" He turned quickly and glared at her. "Who gives a fuck?"

Catherine moved backward as if hit.

"Catherine – this is the big leagues. I know you know that – only maybe you didn't realize it until right now. People have immense stakes in who's president, and that includes your candidacy. They bribe, steal, lie, cheat, murder...and that's only in this country. Do you think Richard Nixon would have let a little thing like this get in his way?"

"I hardly think of him as my role model." Catherine didn't bother to cover her distaste.

"And that's my point. You're too prissy. Too much of a lady. This is a damn big job, and somehow I'm not sure any more that you have the cojones to do it."

Catherine felt her temper rising. Prissy! After all the years that she had put in getting to this point, to have the President tell her that she wasn't strong enough was enraging.

She stood up, knowing that he would hear the anger in her voice, but not caring. "Mr. President, you weren't worried about my competence for the last four years. Not when you depended upon my counsel during the terrorism crisis, and not when you relied on me and my constituents to pull out the voters and help you get elected. In fact, you just told a roomful of reporters that you still supported me." Catherine was pissed now. She walked toward Drummond and let the adrenalin surge through her body. She was a tall woman, and she moved right up to his face.

"So what the hell does my sex life of 30 years ago have to do with my fitness to serve as President?"

Drummond backed up, and put his hands up in mock fear. "My point exactly, Catherine. You're right. You're competent –

you're more than competent. You're smart, you're hard-working, you're the perfect woman for the job."

Drummond was smiling now. "Don't you see? Don't let them take this incredible chance away! Fight! Don't run away with your tail between your legs.

"Catherine, people in this town don't care what you've done, as much as they care about how you react. From Clarence Thomas to Bill Clinton to – who was the senator caught playing footsie in the bathroom stall? – if you're going to survive, you've got to stand your ground and take the punches."

Catherine looked Drummond in the eye. "I refuse to lie. The presidency isn't worth my integrity."

He walked across to her and took her hand in his. His hands were big, and gnarled. Strong.

"I'm not asking you to. I don't want you to lie. That's your strength here... you haven't lied, protesting your innocence. You never denied it. And because of that... you may survive. I'm asking you to wait – give it a little time to percolate. Don't throw yourself down in abject penitence and let the people stomp all over you. At least not until you have to."

Catherine gave a weak grin. "No mea culpa? It must be the Catholic in me, dying to confess after all these years."

He nodded. "That's the trouble. You're embarrassed by this. You feel shamed. You don't like people knowing your private business – and I don't blame you – so now you want to pick up your ball and go home. But this is too important.

"It's too late in the game for us to get another – a better – candidate. We'll be irretrievably damaged if you quit now." Drummond's voice turned gentler. "And you'd be surprised how many folks will rally to your side if you fight against this."

"So what should I do? Ignore the press, the blogs, the tabloids, the folks standing on street corners chatting about whether Maria is my daughter?"

"Right. Hold your head up high, keep campaigning, and don't answer the question. There's plenty of time for DNA tests and family reconciliations later. We've managed to shift the focus to Zane, and exactly what he did to get himself into this predicament." Drummond finally let her hand go. "Catherine, if you can make it through the heat generated for the next few weeks, you'll have earned a place in the kitchen." He smiled.

Catherine gave a bark that might have been a laugh. "As long as they don't want me there barefoot and pregnant."

Drummond put his hands in his pockets, and looked for a moment like the country boy he was. "You know you wouldn't be the first president of the United States who had an illegitimate child out there somewhere. Though you would be the first woman." He smiled.

"President of the United States," Catherine said, wondering at the feel of those words in her mouth. Words that had never tasted quite so delicious, and yet so impossibly remote.

Drummond crossed his arms. "Catherine, I believe you can ride this through. If you don't – if you quit now, and let your party take this one on the chin, we will not have a liberal female candidate for another decade. Maybe another generation. Only super-conservative women like Jerusha Hutchins will be considered squeaky clean enough to apply.

"Because you're the first from our party, you will be remembered. And the next time the Democrats consider a woman for the top spot, they'll shake their heads and say, 'Don't forget what happened with Catherine Young. Let's not make that mistake again.'" Drummond pointed his finger at her. "You don't deserve this burden, Catherine. To be the standard bearer for your gender. But that's the way it worked out. If you walk away from this – admitting that what you did was so wrong that you don't deserve to be president, the next female candidate will have to be a nun. I mean, where does it stop? Everyone is entitled to a life, a history...a youth. What was your mistake? That you had sex before marriage? Yes. You and nearly everybody. And most of them don't think it's such a terrible thing."

"I thought you called me in here to gently suggest that I drop out of the race – and maybe resign," Catherine said.

"Forget it. I'm not losing you as my Vice President, and I don't think you should leave the presidential race. We're a long way from that. Ride the wave a little bit, Catherine. Take the shots. It hurts, but it won't kill you. And I think you'll be the better for it. A little sex scandal is nothing compared to sending soldiers to die."

Catherine looked at Drummond's dark eyes. "When you put it that way, it does sound pretty small."

"It is small." He put his hand on her shoulder. "So will you stay in the running?"

"Okay," she said. "I'll stay in." She put out her hand. "Thank you, Mr. President."

28

"MARIA, IT'S TIME to get out of here." Zane was standing beside the bed, dressed, with an athletic bag in his hand. There were no sounds from the church hallway outside.

"What?" Maria rolled over, shading her eyes as he turned on the lamp by the bed. "Zane. What time is it?"

"We have to go."

"Go where? What are you talking about?" She sat up, and her sleepiness was slowly replaced by a look of annoyance. "I am not going anywhere."

"Yes you are. We both are. Look, Reverend Abraham told me it's time for us to turn ourselves in. The big players – the NAACP, and Reverend Freeman – don't want this to blow up. There are kids dying to fight for us, but the Glory Baptist Church can't stand up to the whole United States government, and it's going to get ugly. So they made a deal."

"A deal?"

"Right. We're supposed to go peacefully – the Feds are expecting us to turn ourselves over to the authorities."

"What do you mean us?"

"Maria – you must understand that they're going to implicate you in this."

"You mean – the blackmail? The murder? But it is not true." She frowned. "You told me they made all that up. To frame you."

"Exactly. It was a setup. They put the gun back in the holster. Repositioned the body. The kind of stuff the police always do to protect their own."

"What about the DNA?" Maria's glorious hair fell
backward as she shook it out of her face. The golden eyes were
wide awake now. She sat on her haunches on the edge of the
bed, perfectly manicured nails spread like talons on each side of
her black nightie. She looked like some primitive goddess about
to pounce.

For a moment Zane was taken aback. He had already been
over all this, and thought she was satisfied with his explanation.

"Like I told you, they faked it. I don't know how, but they
did."

She crossed her arms, making her breasts come together in
a honey-colored crevice. "Faked it."

Zane found himself aroused. This was a lioness to tame.
He sat down beside her. "Baby. I can't leave you here. They'd
just haul you into jail."

"What do you mean? They cannot put me in jail. I am not
even an American citizen. Plus, I'm the Vice President's
daughter. She would not let them do that."

Another emotion stirred in his breast. The desire to protect
her. From more pain.

"Maria, the truth is that Catherine may never admit that
you're her daughter. I hate to say it this harshly, but she might
be the happiest mother in America if you were convicted of
conspiracy to commit murder. And the penalty for killing a
Federal agent? Death."

Maria gasped. "No. It is not possible. I did not even know
you had a gun."

Zane sighed. "We know that, but they might be able to
persuade a jury otherwise. And juries can be bought. You have
to remember that you're dealing with the most powerful
organization in the world – the United States government."

Once again she seemed to rouse herself from fear and fight
back. "Zane, the Attorney General, he talked about a warrant
for you. Not for me. No one said my name in connection with
these crimes."

Zane put his arm around her. "It's only a matter of time,
Maria. They kept it light because they were still negotiating with

the people who believe I'm innocent. But once they get you incarcerated, no one will be able to protect you from the system." He turned her shoulders toward him and looked in her tiger eyes. "Maria, do you have a lawyer? Do you know any American lawyers? Do you have the money to hire one?"

Her head nodded slowly. "I know the Brazilian Ambassador. He would help me. And my parents have money. I am sure – "

"Maria, wake up! If this were a matter of a traffic accident, your foreign immunity and your charm would get you off. But we're talking murder here! These people are very angry. And they are ruthless." He found himself enjoying this. It was like telling a ghost story to a roomful of kids. "Once you're in their custody, Maria, do you think your Ambassador will be able to protect you? From the guards? From the other prisoners? What if they found you with a rope around your neck one morning, before you were due in court to get bailed out? What if they claimed it was a suicide? Who could prove otherwise? These people can do anything they want."

Her eyes widened and she looked less and less sure. "That is not possible!"

"It is. I'm so sorry," he said.

Finally she crumbled. She collapsed into his waiting arms and sobbed. "I am afraid, Zane."

"Sshhh. Baby, don't cry. I've got it all worked out. Will is waiting for us. He's going to get someone to create a diversion in front of the church, while you and I get out the back."

"Where will we go?"

"He's taking care of everything. Just follow me into the back of the van. We have a whole lot of friends out there." He pulled her up off the bed. He looked at the black nightie, and wished there were time...but there wasn't. "Now get dressed, in something comfortable. Pants. Dark ones, if you've got any."

In a moment she was in jeans and a black T-shirt. She had pulled her hair back into a ponytail. They stepped quietly into the hall and then walked to the door of the sanctuary. Will was sitting in the front pew.

"Where you been, man? I been waiting." Will stood up and wavered a little. As Zane approached him, he got a strong whiff of liquor.

"Sorry." Zane motioned toward the rear parking lot. "You ready to go?"

"Don't say thanks or nothing, Zane," Will said. "Man, all the favors I called in for you? Arranging this whole thing to get you out of here – my ass on the line, again. And you not playing straight with these people."

Zane glanced over at Maria, and gave his brother a look that he hoped would make him shut up. "Will, you know how grateful I am for your help. Maria and I would be in rough shape without everything you've done for us. And you know I'd do the same for you."

Will nodded, looking somewhat mollified. "Okay – so you want me to go out front first and make a lot of noise, roust up all those sleepy reporters camped outside, so they come around to the front doors of the church?"

"Exactly," Zane said. "You go out, then give us two minutes. We'll wait till we hear the rear contingent move off before we leave the church."

Will walked toward the front doors of the church. Zane and Maria went toward the back, and into the dark hallway. For a minute nothing happened, and then they could hear shouts and the noise of people rushing to get around to the front of the building. Zane cracked the door open. The small back parking lot was full of cars, but they were empty. Sharp shadows were cast across the edges of the lot by bright lights set up in front. A police cruiser slowly headed by on a street behind them.

"Come on," he whispered, and took Maria by the hand. He headed straight for a purple customized van with the motor running. He walked purposefully but didn't run. As he approached the doors, they swung open.

"Come on in, Brother Zane and Sister Maria. We got a spot just right for you." Holding open the door was a 60-something black man in a three-piece suit and a striped tie with a diamond tie tack. His fussy dress was in sharp contrast to the thick carpeting and colorful decor of the van's interior. He waved them in, and Zane helped Maria step up.

Inside, they sat down on an orange beanbag chair large enough for two. The man shook each of their hands in turn. "So proud to meet you both. I'm Brother Jules Hopkins. But most folks call me Gem." As he spoke, the van lurched to the left, and began moving. "That's my wife, Josephine, up front driving. She's better on the clutch than I am. I would have introduced you, but I knew that we needed to make a quick getaway." At that he smiled, and was silent.

"We really appreciate your help here, Mr. Hopkins. Everyone in the church has been very generous."

Hopkins, sitting cross-legged on the floor beside the beanbag, reached up and patted Zane on the knee. "I haven't done much, young man. My part in this is very small. But even the smallest efforts can come together to make a mighty movement."

Zane elbowed Maria gently. It was time for her to show some gratitude.

"Mr. Hopkins," she said, "I also thank you."

"No need, Sister Maria. It's not every day that I have the honor of riding with the daughter of the Vice President of the U.S." He smiled at her. "And I see the resemblance." He made that observation quietly, as if to himself.

The van proceeded with some rather uncomfortable bumps until it came to a sudden stop. Zane and Maria slid forward off the beanbag and onto the carpet.

Hopkins laughed as he crawled to the back doors. "That chair could use some seatbelts, right? This isn't really my van. Borrowed it for the occasion." He pulled open one of the doors and peered out. "We seem to have a welcoming committee."

When Hopkins stepped out, Zane looked through the open door and was amazed. There were at least 30 people of all ages standing on the lawn behind the van. They were dressed, mostly, in sleepwear, their faces, both pale and dark, looking up at him with an expression mixing awe and curiosity. Behind the crowd was a row of neat houses, each with a small porch in front.

"Who are these people?" Zane asked their host as he got out and gave a hand to Maria. "I thought this operation was going to be confidential."

Hopkins nodded. He walked over to one of the younger men. "Reginald? What all are these folks doing here? I told you that this was a secret."

"Heck, I didn't tell nobody, grandpa." Reginald walked back to the front of the van, where the door was opening on the driver's side.

"Well, somebody must have," Hopkins said. He walked up to the driver's door. "Josephine?" His tone was annoyed but tolerant. "Did you blab about this to everybody on the block?"

Josephine, a plump woman with gray hair and lace-up shoes, stepped heavily down from the van with the help of her husband. She looked around at the crowd, and her eyebrows rose. "I told Shantel. She's the only one I told. I didn't know she was going to tell half the neighborhood." She walked over to a woman on the edge of the crowd. "Shantel! What did you do, girl? I told you this was supposed to be a secret."

Zane stood beside the van with his arm around Maria. A lean black man in his thirties approached him and reached out his hand. "Good luck, brother. We're with you. You need to know that a lot of black folks believe in you."

After the first contact, the whole crowd surged forward. "God bless you, my dear," said an older woman with a Spanish accent, addressing Maria. "I know the Lord is watching over you."

"I think you're very brave for doing what you did," a blonde teenager said to Zane. She had piercings in her eyebrows and gauges in her ears. "Standing up to the government."

They reached out, one after another, to shake hands or merely to touch the couple. For a moment, Zane fought the urge to back away. He didn't know these people or why they wanted to touch him. And then it washed over him like warm rain. He was a hero. He was a celebrity. He, Zane, was finally in the spotlight, instead of in the reflected glow of Catherine.

And then the voices started up again.

Yeah, right. You a hero. What bullshit. You're nothing. You're worse than nothing — you're a fraud. Taking these good people for a ride to protect your sorry ass. But someday they're gonna find out. And you're gonna fall so far....

He started talking to drown out the voices. "Thank you, sir," he said to a tall man with dreadlocks. He reached out and clutched hands as they came his way. He smiled at a bashful 5-year-old boy, and hugged his mother. "I appreciate your support." As he spoke to the people, the crowd seemed to swell. Lights went on in the houses all the way down the street. Someone put on music, and turned it up loud. It was a warm night in between hot days, and the feel of summer was still in the pavement. Zane found himself sweating. He shook another hand. "Yes, thanks. It was tough, but I'm glad I did it. You got to stand up to the man sometimes." Maria seemed nonplussed as the people came up to shake their hands and give them fist bumps or hugs. She said little, but nodded her head and mumbled thanks from time to time.

Soon he and Maria were walking down a gauntlet of congratulations, as Hopkins led them along a walkway to his house. On the covered porch, Zane turned and looked back at the crowd, now numbering more than 50. He raised his hands for silence. "I am overwhelmed by your kindness. I didn't do this to be a hero."

"But you are, brother," came a shout from the crowd.

Zane shook his head. "No, I'm just a regular guy. But it's good to know that there are folks like you out there willing to stand up for what is right. Even if that means taking on the President of the United States."

"Amen," shouted a woman in the back.

Hopkins stepped up beside Zane and motioned for silence. "I think that we should all thank the good Lord for keeping Brother Zane and Sister Maria out of harm's way, and say a prayer that He continues to keep them in His good graces. Now let's go get some sleep."

He turned and led Zane and Maria into the house. Once inside, Josephine bustled by them and into the dining room.

"We thought you might be hungry," she said, proudly displaying a table laden with enough food for dozens of people. There were macaroni casseroles and buttered vegetables, chicken and ham and roast beef, corn on the cob and biscuits, and at least five pies.

Maria looked at Zane. "You are so kind," she said. "But we — "

"Mrs. Hopkins, this is such a feast," Zane said. "We couldn't possibly do justice to all this...."

Zane realized his error when he heard Mrs. Hopkins laugh and noticed that a good portion of the crowd had followed them into the house. As the people swirled into the small dining room and took plates, he located Gem Hopkins near the pies.

"Mr. Hopkins, you know that Maria and I are very thankful for your help." Hopkins nodded, his mouth working efficiently on a piece of strawberry rhubarb. "But I'm a little concerned about all the folks who know exactly where we are." Zane reached out to touch the older man's arm. "Please don't misunderstand me. I trust your neighbors — it's just that it's so easy for a careless word to spread the information — "

Hopkins held up his hand. "Don't you worry, Brother Zane. You won't be here long. This is just your first stop. We got it all worked out." He laughed and wiped a little strawberry from the side of his mouth. "I don't think even the President of the United States will be able to find you once we get the word out that you need help."

29

"MADAM VICE PRESIDENT?" It was Harwood's voice, coming over the speakerphone. Catherine grabbed the handset and stood beside her desk. Her jacket was draped over the back of her chair, ready to be pulled on as soon as the President agreed that she should talk to the press.

As far as Catherine was concerned, it couldn't come too soon. She was dying to talk. It was excruciating to see the screaming headlines online and to hear the babble of TV criticism without being able to say a word in her defense. But that might finally be over. Harwood's call should mean that Zane and Maria had turned themselves in, as agreed.

"Yes, Ralph. Are they in custody?" She realized that she was clutching the phone so tightly that her hand hurt.

"Sorry, ma'am. I don't have good news. They've left the church." Harwood's voice was strained.

"What?" An icy hand gripped her middle. "But didn't we have assurances that they would come in? The FBI wanted to storm the place right away, but we were promised – "

"I know. I know." Harwood sounded less angry than tired. "And believe me, the people who vouched for Zane and Maria – the Reverend Abraham, Walter Freeman and the people from the NAACP – are just as ticked off as we are. They realize how guilty this makes Zane look."

Catherine didn't say anything for a minute. "So where are they?" she asked finally. "Have we got any idea?"

"We think we know where they were last night. Apparently they crossed over into Maryland. There was some kind of excitement early in the a.m. in a normally quiet neighborhood. It looks as though the church people might have smuggled them out."

Catherine sat down. She started to chew on a nail, and when she realized what she was doing to her manicure, she decided she didn't care. "So how do we find them?"

"Well, there's an APB out now. Since their faces have been in the news for the last two days, anyone who goes online or watches TV would spot them in a minute. We're setting up a hotline, and we're going to offer a reward. That should flush them out pretty soon."

"But how do we know they're still in the country?"

"They're just too recognizable. The warrant for Zane was issued yesterday around 11:00 in the morning. We would have heard if they tried to board a plane, or even a train. What's more likely is that they're driving."

Catherine finished one nail and started on the next. "Right." Her shoulders slumped. "Well, keep me informed."

"Madam Vice President?" Harwood's voice sounded tentative.

"Yes Ralph?"

"I hope you're not being too hard on yourself over this. You know, you have a lot of supporters."

Catherine kicked her pumps off and gave a small snort that was not quite a laugh. "Thanks, Ralph. I appreciate that."

§

Maria and Zane sat in a cool basement under someone's house. There were about 15 people gathered around a television set, sitting on the blue flowered couch or on the floor. The noontime news was about to start.

It was the third place they had landed since the escape from the Glory Baptist Church late last night. Zane wasn't even sure which state they were in at this point. But he sure liked the treatment he was getting.

Underground hero. He had gotten more back slaps and admiring hugs in the last 12 hours than he had gotten in his entire life. And it felt good.

At each stop, the folks had turned out to welcome them with speeches and hallelujahs and enough food to feed a small nation. It was becoming clear to Zane that he had created a movement. A grassroots movement in which the people were being empowered to fight back against prejudice. And if it meant that he was going to have to remain a fugitive for a little longer, then so be it. Life on the lam wasn't so bad.

Then the voices started.

A movement? You're fulla shit, Zane. This is all about you getting out of a loan you couldn't pay off. You don't believe that story you're telling about how poor little Maria was gonna be killed by government thugs, do you? If you are starting to believe your own BS, you have finally gone certifiably crazy.

He excused himself from the small group sitting in front of the TV to go to the bathroom. Once there, he locked the door and knelt on the pink shag rug in front of the toilet lid. With the top closed, it made a slick porcelain table for his snow. He set up five quick lines and snorted them with a tightly rolled bill. He felt the bitter drip down the back of his throat and leaned against the wall for the last exquisite lift.

He checked his stash. Plenty left. For now. It was good to have along, because he wasn't getting much sleep, and he needed to have his wits about him while he chatted with people at every stop.

He stood up and looked at himself in the mirror. A little drawn around the eyes. At least he'd managed to shave this morning. And he'd have to see about getting some clothes. He'd been in the same shirt for more than a day now.

Zane smiled at himself. The cocaine made the voices in his head dim into a mellow background buzz. They couldn't torment him now. He smoothed his hair and unlocked the bathroom door. When he came back in the room, all eyes were on the TV. Longtime anchorman John Cadwallader's face appeared on the screen, backed by a photo of Zane and Maria.

Zane recognized the tie – it was the Hermes silk he had worn the night Maria first met Catherine. The night he learned that Devon wanted the money immediately. And the night he wrote the blackmail note.

It seemed a very long time ago.

A poll had been taken by the network, dated last night. As Zane watched, the screen was filled with a table showing the results. Cadwallader's voice read each percentage aloud.

"According to our research, 32% of those polled believe that Vice President Young should resign from office and leave the race for President, while 49% find her fit to continue in office. Another 19% are undecided or need more information."

The screen changed and showed another poll.

"In other results, 29% believe Ms. Flores-Jenkins' claim to a relationship with the Vice President, while 17% do not. Another 54% of those polled are undecided or need more information." Cadwallader paused while the chart on the screen dissolved and different percentages appeared.

"Further results show that 32% feel that the fugitive couple has been the victim of government oppression, as compared to 35% who believe that the government did nothing improper," Cadwallader's smooth voice intoned. "Another 33% responded that they are undecided or need more information."

Just above the newscaster's head appeared a new graphic.

"However, when this last poll is broken down by race, pollsters report a wide discrepancy between the views held by white and black Americans," Cadwallader said. Now the numbers were split into two columns.

"When asked whether these individuals were victims of a government set-up, those identifying themselves as white said yes only 9% of the time, while African-Americans answered in the affirmative 73% of the time. When the individuals polled were asked whether they agreed with the statement that the government had done nothing improper, whites answered in the affirmative 57% of the time, while those identifying themselves as African-American agreed only 12% of the time." Cadwallader looked gravely into the camera. "Those who declared themselves undecided or in need of more information came to 34% of whites and 15% of the African-Americans polled."

John Cadwallader's face was replaced by a scene in which a man was standing behind a bank of microphones. Zane tried to remember who it was. He had met him somewhere. The man was tall and thickly built, with tanned skin and black hair.

"The Ambassador!" Maria said, sounding as though she had been floating in the sea, and a lifeline had just been tossed.

Someone turned up the sound.

"The President of Brazil has asked me to convey to the American people our deep concern with the events of the past two days, and to assure the United States government that we intend to make certain that Senhorina Flores-Jenkins is held accountable for any misdeeds." Maria sat suddenly upright. Her eyes were wide.

"However, we also remain adamant that she be afforded the opportunity to explain her actions with the full protection of her own government. We urge anyone who has had contact with her to please assist us in locating her." The Ambassador looked into the camera directly. "Maria, if you are out there, there is no need to run in fear. This situation can and will be resolved in a just and civilized manner. Maria, tudo vai ficar bem!"

"What did he say?" Zane asked, turning to Maria.

"He said...it will be all right. It will turn out okay." She did not look reassured.

Cadwallader's face came back on the screen, and behind him now was a graphic to accompany the unfolding news story. It showed a picture of the White House covered by the words "Blackmail in the Inner Circle."

"The Attorney General is asking for cooperation from the public in locating Mr. Zarillo and Ms. Flores-Jenkins," Cadwallader said. "There are warrants out for both the Vice President's staff member and the young lady, a Brazilian national, who claims to be the Vice President Young's biological daughter. Both are wanted in connection with an extortion attempt and the murder of a Federal agent. A fifty thousand dollar reward is being offered for information leading to the arrest of either of these individuals. The FBI has set up a hotline to handle calls concerning their whereabouts. The public is asked to report sightings as soon as possible." An 800 number appeared on the screen along with the words "Fugitive Sighting Hotline."

There was a sudden electricity in the room. As Zane looked around at the people sitting in the basement, he saw the rush of small movements. Heads turning to catch a friend's eye. Raised eyebrows. And people looking at him with new intensity.

Some of the teens had phones in their hands, and their texting stopped while an idea took root.

"Shew," one woman said. "Fifty thousand dollars? I know folks'd turn in their mother for that kind of money." A general nodding of heads and mutters of agreement followed. "But don't you worry, honey, we're gonna stand by you."

A few people seemed seized by the urge to get coffee upstairs in the kitchen or go home and check on the children. As a half dozen of those assembled made an awkward beeline for the stairs, Zane saw that their eyes were averted.

They were going to turn him in. And each of them wanted to be the first to do it.

He looked at Maria, and she knew the same thing. She stood up and came over to him.

"Just stay with me. Real cool," he said quietly. The time to move was now.

Zane did a quick mental inventory. He had cash. He had the cocaine. There was no point in trying to get to his gym bag upstairs for clean underwear. Hats would be useful, though. Especially to hide Maria's long hair.

What he needed was a car. But first, a way out.

He grasped Maria's hand as he walked toward the back of the house. There was another door from the basement level, he was sure of it. No one would stop them – the people who had seen the reward offer were too busy examining their loyalties. They quickly made their way to the rear door. It was open, with only the screen door in place.

Outside on the scruffy lawn were about five kids and a dog. They were in bathing suits, running through a hose held by one of the kids. Zane walked up to a boy about eight years old. He was skinny, and he had a scab on his right knee.

"Hey there. What's your name?"

"Ezra." The boy knew who Zane was, and was smiling up at him.

"Ezra, do you know where I can find a couple of hats?"

Ezra stared at him. "What kinda hats?"

"Any kind. This is like a scavenger hunt. We need some hats – two hats. Do you think you can get some? I'll pay you – five bucks."

Ezra smiled again. "You don't need to pay me, Mr. Zane. I know where some hats are." Then his smile faded. "But I can't reach 'em."

"Where are they? Like in a closet or something?"

"Yeah. In my brother's closet, at home."

"Is home far?"

"Naw. Next block."

"Great. I'll come with you, and get the hats down. Thanks a lot, man."

"Sure." Ezra looked proud. He took off at a run through the backyard of the house behind them, and Zane and Maria followed, looking as casual as possible. It was a weekday, and there weren't many people around. When they reached the sidewalk, they saw Ezra go into a house.

The door was open when they got there, only the screen keeping the flies out. It was dark inside, compared to the high hot sun on the street. Zane looked into the hallway before he entered.

"Ezra?"

"Come on in. I'm up here." The voice came from another level.

"Your Mom home? Or your Dad?" Zane hesitated at the doorway.

"Dad don't live here. Mom's at the store. Aunt Ruby's watchin' me and my sister."

"Where's Aunt Ruby?" Zane opened the screen door and walked into the hall. "Is she here?"

"She's talking to her friend. Down the street. I'm allowed to come home by myself. To change." Ezra appeared at the top of the stairs. "Come on up. The hats are up here. I can see them, but I can't reach 'em."

Zane motioned for Maria to stay by the door. He walked up the stairs and into the room Ezra entered. It was neat, with lace curtains on the window and a flowered bedspread carefully smoothed. He made his way over to the closet.

"See? Right there."

Ezra pointed to a baseball cap with the letter "X" on the front. Beside it was a cowboy hat. Zane pulled them both down. They would have to do. He gave a quick scan of the contents of the closet and pulled out a dark sweatshirt and a navy jacket.

"Hey. You didn't say nothin' about takin' clothes too. Those are my brothers!"

Zane reached into his pocket and found some bills. He took a twenty and showed it to Ezra. "Twenty dollars. That's for you. It's a lot of money – you can share it with your brother to pay him back for the clothes. Tell him I really appreciate it."

Ezra grinned. "Thanks. I never had twenty dollars for myself."

Zane gave the little boy's head a rub and then took the stairs two at a time. He looked past Maria, standing by the front door, and saw a beat-up gray Honda pull up right next to the house.

"Shit," he said. He grabbed her and backed into the living room, outside of the view from the front hallway.

Ezra saw his reaction. "Those ain't cops or nothing. That's my brother." When Zane didn't move, he added, "He won't mind about the stuff. I'll tell him who you are."

Zane was about to tell Ezra not to say anything, when the brother and two friends burst through the door. "Damn it's hot," one of them said.

"We got some beer," the brother answered.

"Hey Kevin," Ezra said. His voice was bursting with pride. "Guess who's here." He pointed to Zane and Maria, standing just inside the doorframe of the living room.

Kevin and his friends stopped and looked at them. After a quick moment of recognition, Kevin immediately stuck out his hand. "Zane Zarillo? Pleased to meet you. You're a hero, man."

Zane took his hand and smiled. "Thanks. But I'm just a guy who had to stand up when the government came after Maria here."

The other young men shook his hand, mumbled politely to Maria, beautiful as ever despite a day on the run, and then stood awkwardly regarding them.

"So. Can I offer you a beer or something?" Kevin pointed toward the kitchen.

"No, thanks, Kevin. The truth is, we're on the move. Gotta find a new hiding place. The police, you know."

"Right, sure. Yeah. Anything I can do?"

"As a matter of fact, your brother Ezra here was helping us with some threads. A couple of hats, a sweatshirt. Hope you don't mind. I gave him some cash." Zane lifted the hats, which had been sitting on a chair beside him.

"No problem, man. I can spare a couple hats. For a good cause." Kevin smiled, and raised his fist in a quick salute.

Zane saw an opportunity. "You know what I really need, Kevin? Transportation. Would you be willing to sell me that car? I wouldn't ask, but it's an emergency."

Kevin leaned his angular body against the door frame. "How much?"

"All I can spare is a few hundred bucks."

Kevin's expression showed disappointment. "Listen man, I'm sorry. You know I want to help you-all out – "

"A thousand? Cash?" Zane reached into his pocket and pulled out a wad of bills. He started counting.

Kevin looked at his friends. "Now that you put it that way...." He smiled. "You got yourself a car, man."

30

MARIA STARED AT Zane as he turned onto a street filled with boarded-up houses. The car was stifling, even with the windows open. Trickles of sweat had long since pooled stickily on her back, making sucking noises whenever she moved against the vinyl seat.

"Where are we going?" she asked.

"I know what I'm doing," Zane said. His voice was not tired, like hers. It was full of excitement.

There was no mystery about where that energy came from. An hour ago, when Zane had finally pulled up beside a gas station and let her go to the bathroom — after she had pleaded for 20 minutes — Maria had come back to find him shoving a bag of white powder into his pocket. He had used the chance to snort some cocaine.

Now she recognized the trademark sniffle and the constant nose rubbing. There it was again. Maria shook her head.

"You may know what you are doing, but I do not," Maria said. "Why are we here?"

He turned to look at her.

"I'm looking for the right spot for us to hide out."

"Hide out?" For once, she didn't bother to cover the disdain in her voice. "From the FBI? From the police? From all of the people who want a fifty thousand dollars? Zane — you are crazy to believe that we can—"

"Don't call me crazy!" He braked the car to a sudden stop. A car behind them honked, then drove around, shouting obscenities. Zane didn't even look. He was staring at her. The venom in his eyes took her by surprise.

"Okay," she said.

"Don't ever say that to me again." He still stared. "I am not crazy!"

The fear and despair started deep inside her, and crept slowly through each of her organs. And as the feeling spread, she realized that she had known it all along.

She had been a fool.

This was a man she had lulled herself into relying upon, letting the aphrodisiac of political power and romantic fantasies about a new life in America – maybe as the daughter of the President! – put her into some long hypnotic sleep. It had been so easy to go along with the parties, the glamorous social life, the sex appeal of being on the arm of a man as attractive as Zane.

After she had discovered the identity of her mother – it seemed like so long ago, now – on that fateful trip to Paris with her family, Maria had turned to the Internet. Patient research had yielded a detailed biography of Catherine's life, including a precious newspaper photo of her mother as a young girl standing beside her father in the Maryland of the 1960's.

Maria had tracked Catherine's life from childhood through college, law school, marriage and motherhood, and then into Congress and the White House. And when she felt she had uncovered all she could about this woman who had given birth to her and then given her away to be raised by others, she decided it was time to look her in the face. To stand in front of Catherine Maguire Young, her mother.

At that point, Maria's plan took on a new urgency. Obtaining a job at the Brazilian embassy in Washington took a year and a lot of patience. Once in D.C., she was hit with the reality that meeting with Catherine in person would not be easy. It was only after she showed up at the Vice President's office in the Executive Office Building that she encountered a stroke of luck – she met Zane. As she waited in the hallway to speak to one of the aides who would probably have sent her packing, Zane spotted her and apparently decided to talk to her himself.

A lucky break. Of course, Maria couldn't tell him at that point what her real agenda was.

It was natural to fall into a dating relationship with Zane. She knew that he was far more sophisticated than she, and she was alarmed at his drug use. But as a girl raised in a quiet, protective environment, Maria figured she had a lot to learn about the way things worked in America. Expensive clothes and fancy restaurants, fast cars and cocaine. Wasn't this what young powerful men did here?

And so Maria had fallen into a stupor, spending time with her first real boyfriend and enjoying the D.C. social whirl. At 29, she was finally living her own life, far from the family who had raised her. And dreaming that as soon as her real mother – Catherine – saw her face, the Vice President would wrap her arms around her long-lost daughter, and they would become one big, happy family.

But she was awake now.

She fought the urge to jump out of the car and run away from Zane. But she couldn't escape this crazy man, who thought that they could somehow face down the United States government with their little band of supporters – most of which were ready to turn them in when the offer of money came along.

Waves of recrimination hit Maria with a physical thud. She had a moment of nausea. How had she let herself be so blind? Following Zane like a meek puppy, letting him make the decisions after she realized that he had discovered – stolen – the file that told the truth about her mother. Letting him take her urge to make a personal connection with the Vice President and turn it into an international scandal.

The life Maria had lived for the last few months had been an exotic journey beyond anything she had ever imagined. Educated at a convent school in the mountains, she had been shielded by a strong religious upbringing and her insular adoptive family from the attentions of strangers. But Zane Zarillo had looked like the grand prize – a Prince Charming who would also lead her back to her true mother. And Maria had somehow become Sleeping Beauty, ignoring troubles as long as she could dream of the sound of church bells and a happily ever future with Zane.

She wanted to cry. It was all so painfully stupid now.

Maria's fists tightened into balls, but she didn't feel the fingernails digging. The heat in the car made her dizzy. Zane kept going around the same blighted blocks, over and over. Looking for the refuge his fevered brain imagined.

She needed to plan. To take some time to think through her options, and then make a careful break from Zane. She was in a bad position, but she was not without resources. The Ambassador had asked her to come in, and she trusted him.

"I got it," he said suddenly, and looked over to her with eyes that she didn't recognize. For the first time, she allowed herself to see the real Zane. A liar. A coke addict. A murderer.

"I'm brilliant!" he said, making a wide U-turn and narrowly missing a junked car on the side of the road. "Hang on. We're going for a ride, Maria."

She clutched the door handle as the car picked up speed and rounded a curve on two wheels. There was no getting out yet.

§

Catherine stood beside the President in the residential quarters of the White House. She had the eerie feeling that she was watching a movie of her life – and not a good one. On the television in front of them was the face of Don Samuelson, who was standing on the White House lawn in the lengthening shadows of early evening.

"In less than 20 minutes, the Vice President will be coming out to speak to reporters concerning the charges and counter-charges surrounding Zane Zarillo, who served until recently as a member of her campaign organization. The hunt for Mr. Zarillo and Ms. Flores-Jenkins, who claims to be the biological daughter of Vice President Young, has been riveting the country since yesterday morning, when it was learned that the couple had left the Glory Baptist Church on 15th Street in the District, where they had earlier sought political asylum, rather than turning themselves in to authorities as negotiated by their representatives." Samuelson brought his considerable eyebrows together and peered into the camera. "Throughout the day, reports have surfaced regarding the couple's whereabouts, and the FBI – along with the media – have been playing a cat-and-mouse game with the fugitives, keeping residents of Maryland, Virginia and the District of Columbia on high alert. Maureen Graves has more on the chase which has mesmerized the public since early yesterday."

"Thanks, Don," the reporter said. She was standing with a microphone in her hand in front of a small house in a suburban neighborhood. Behind her was a crowd of onlookers. "Just behind me, you can see the house where Mr. Zarillo and Ms. Flores-Jenkins were last sighted. People in this quiet Granville, Maryland neighborhood have reported that the couple spent at least part of the early morning hours here, and then disappeared suddenly around noontime. Police were alerted to Zarillo and Flores-Jenkins' whereabouts when several residents called the FBI hotline claiming the fifty thousand dollar reward which is being offered for information leading to their arrest."

The scene changed to the same reporter talking to a resident of the neighborhood. The brightness of the sun indicated that it was the middle of the day. On the bottom of the screen were the words "Taped Earlier Today."

"They were here. I saw them." The speaker was a young black man wearing an oversize T-shirt and low-hanging jeans. Behind him a dozen people stood listening, some of the kids mugging for the camera. "Go Zane!" shouted one of them.

The reporter gestured to someone outside of camera range and a boy of about eight came up to the microphone, looking shy. "Ezra Greene," said the line at the bottom of the screen.

"I gave him a hat," the boy said, his new and uneven front teeth exposed as he burst into a grin. "I helped him."

The reporter came back onto the screen. "After the couple left this neighborhood, they were spotted at a Seven-11 in Alexandria, Virginia. Justin Brentwood has that report."

"Thank you, Maureen. As you can see, I'm standing in front of a Seven-11 at Bailey's Crossroad's in Virginia. I'm joined by Herman Lang, an assistant manager here, who reports that Mr. Zarillo and Ms. Flores-Jenkins visited the store at approximately 3:30 this afternoon. Could you tell us what happened?" He nodded to Lang, a heavy bearded man in his twenties wearing a button-down shirt and perspiring noticeably.

"Only the man came in," Lang said. He held onto a hat and twisted it as he spoke. "I didn't recognize him at first. He asked me for two Cokes – jumbo size. He bought some sandwiches, and he kept looking around, like he was in trouble." Lang nodded his head rapidly. "He left real fast, and then I saw the lady in the car, and I grabbed one of the newspapers off the rack – it was them. I called the police. They haven't told me yet if I get the reward money."

"Thank you, Mr. Lang. Back to you, Don."

Samuelson was holding his earpiece when he came back on the screen. "I'm being told that we may have a live sighting of the vehicle in which Mr. Zarillo and his companion were traveling. If you'll bear with us just a minute, we'll try to get you that picture."

Catherine had barely moved during the last few minutes, feeling so much like a bug under a microscope that it seemed futile to do anything other than watch numbly as her life unraveled. But she was startled out of her trance when Drummond spoke.

"The media is eating this up. It's on every channel." As if to prove himself correct, Drummond grabbed the remote from the table beside them and flipped through ABC, NBC, CBS, Fox, and CNN. Every single network had a reporter talking about the hunt for Zane Zarillo. On CNN, the voice of Serge Rothman could be heard over the rotors of a helicopter. The screen showed a small gray car hurtling along a tree-lined highway. The C&O Canal could be seen alongside.

"I'm being told that this is the vehicle in which Mr. Zarillo and Ms. Flores-Jenkins were last seen," Rothman said. "If this is indeed their car, they are heading at a rapid pace back into the

District of Columbia. They are at present on Canal Road, which is on the Maryland side of the Potomac River, and are approaching the District line." His voice was difficult to hear over the noise of the helicopter, but suddenly that noise was gone, as the studio cut out the audio feed but left the picture.

"I think you can hear me better now? Yes. The vehicle has just now passed into Washington, and is right at the edge of the section of the District known as Georgetown. However, instead of taking the Whitehurst Freeway into downtown Washington, the car has made a sudden lane change and gone straight, along M Street."

There was a moment of static, and then Rothman's voice resumed. "We are being informed, in no uncertain terms, that our helicopter, as well as those of other news organizations, is making it dangerous for the FBI to follow the vehicle in its own helicopters. In fact, you can see two large green government helicopters to the left of your screen, which are continuing to pursue the car. CNN is being told to back off a considerable distance, on pain of criminal charges." The gray car receded into the distance as the helicopter camera moved away.

"I do see, however, that the car has turned right down Wisconsin Avenue, and it seems a reasonable assumption that it will follow O Street as it runs under the Whitehurst Freeway, thus making it impossible for the helicopters to track it. I am also being told that a number of police and FBI vehicles have caught up with the car, and the authorities are optimistic that they will soon have Mr. Zarillo and Ms. Flores-Jenkins in custody."

Serge Rothman's face reappeared on the screen. "We are expecting the White House to make a statement very shortly. The Vice President scheduled a press conference for 5:30 this afternoon, and Candy Mabry is standing by waiting for that to begin. Candy?"

The face of Candy Mabry filled the television. "Serge, there seems to be some confusion here as to whether this appearance by the Vice President will take place as scheduled, or whether there will be some delay. A spokeswoman for the administration gave an indication a couple of minutes ago that the White House might postpone it, since the capture of Mr. Zarillo and Ms. Flores-Jenkins appears imminent."

Catherine heard herself groan. "Whose idea was that? What – are we going to sit here waiting until they get him in handcuffs?"

President Drummond shook his head in frustration. He turned to an aide. "Jimmy, find out what the hell is going on with this thing, and whose bright idea it was to hold it up?"

Jimmy pulled a phone from his pocket. He punched in some numbers, and then spoke rapidly. "What's going on? The President wants to know." He nodded, then turned to Drummond, looking sheepish. "It was Silverstein, Mr. President. He was afraid we'd be upstaged. He didn't want the networks missing the press conference because they were hot to show Zarillo getting grabbed."

"Jesus!" Drummond said, his head bobbing rapidly. "Who's running this country? The government, or the networks?" When no one replied, he spoke reluctantly. "Tell Silverstein to find out what's going on with the arrest. If they think it'll be quick, we'll wait."

Jimmy mumbled some quick directions into the phone. A phone on the President's desk rang, and a woman picked it up. Her shoulders jerked in response to the message. She turned to Drummond.

"Mr. President? I'm afraid that they weren't in the car."

On the television, Serge Rothman said nearly the same thing a fraction of a second later. "Ladies and gentlemen, we have just been informed that the driver of the vehicle we were following earlier with our helicopter was not in fact Mr. Zarillo, or Ms. Flores-Jenkins. It seems that there was a decoy."

The scene changed to a deeply shadowed shot of a car surrounded by police and FBI vehicles. At the center of a chaotic push for camera space was a woman in a pink tank top and cut-off jeans, her dirty blonde hair spilling over her shoulders. She was being handcuffed by police, who were propelling her none too gently toward a patrol car. Reporters were shouting out questions on the chance that someone would answer.

"Did you get the car from Zane?"

"Why did you want to help them?"

"Her name. What's her name? Is she under arrest?" This last was yelled out to the FBI agents who were doing their best to block the view of the young woman as she was folded into the back seat.

"No comment. We have no comment at this time," answered the frustrated voice of one of the agents.

"Ouch!" was heard over the din, and then in a loud female voice, "Freedom for Maria and Zane!"

The door closed with a decisive thud, and the car carrying the blonde squealed off with an escort of six flashing police vehicles.

Rothman's face reappeared on the screen. "Well, it seems that the FBI was fooled into following this young woman, as were most of the reporters on the trail. We'll bring you details of her identity and how she fits into the story as soon as we are able. In the meantime, I suspect that the Vice President's press conference will be starting shortly."

Drummond turned to Catherine, his expression a mixture of frustration and amused resignation. "Well, Catherine? If Serge says we should start, I think we should start. May I escort you to the toughest 20 minutes of scrutiny I hope you'll ever have to endure?" He offered his arm, and Catherine placed hers carefully on top.

She didn't feel afraid. She felt hardly anything at all.

31

As ZANE ZIGGED and zagged the car through the streets of Washington, Maria kept her head averted from passersby who might recognize her face from the news. She hoped that the cowboy hat she had tucked her hair into would help

She and Zane were in a different vehicle now – an old Corolla they had traded another $1000 and Kevin's gray Honda for. That money, plus some coke and a little quick talking on Zane's part, had persuaded the young blonde woman who was in the seedy section of Southeast looking for a drug connection to give them her keys and take the Honda for a joyride – in a very visible way.

"Okay," Zane said. "We should be all right for a while now. Here's the spot." He pulled the car over to the side of the road beside an industrial building with boarded-over windows, and then jumped the curb, driving onto the dirt. He maneuvered until they were behind a car that had been thoroughly stripped. Wiping his brow, he opened the door and pulled the keys from the ignition. "I figure she'll give us up right away – and they may have her in custody already. But the police will be looking anywhere except the District."

"Zane." Now was the time to make him understand. Maria opened her door and walked around to the driver's side, where Zane had gotten out of the car. "I do not want to run any more."

"What?" He looked at her. She tried to read his face.

"I will call the Ambassador. Turn myself in. Whatever they might think, I have done nothing wrong. And when I tell them that – "

"Maria." His face took on the patient look of a parent explaining something to a child. "We talked about this. They won't believe you. You're involved in something bigger than you understand – "

She reached her hand out for the keys. "No. I am a foreign national. They would not dare to throw me in jail. I will get a good lawyer. My parents – they have connections. It was my father's cousin who got me the position with the Embassy – "

Zane backed away, the keys still in his hand. He laughed. "Maria. Your connections...they can't help you. Don't you think I have connections?"

"But I did not kill anyone." Her eyes stayed on his, looking for danger.

What those eyes did surprised her. They didn't turn hot and angry. They turned cold. "That's what you say," he said.

She nearly gasped when it hit her. No one knew who had been in the garage – the garage under her apartment. No one could say who had pulled the trigger. Maria struggled for breath in the hot, fetid air. For a moment, she was drowning. He was pulling her down with him.

"No!" Her voice echoed on the brick building beside them. "I will tell them the truth. I killed no one." Now she moved closer. "I would rather take my chances with your American justice system, than try to hide out from the law. The sooner I turn myself in the better it will go for me."

Her hand reached toward the keys again. She would be firm. He had never hurt her. He might not agree – but he would let her choose. "Give me the car. I will do no more running."

Zane wound his arm up and lofted the keys as far as he could. Somewhere in the scrubby bushes behind the building, there sounded a whoosh and a clink.

"No keys," he said. There was no pretense of friendliness.

Maria turned her back and started to walk down the street. No one else was in sight in this blighted corner of D.C. She took a bare arm and wiped it across her forehead.

Stay calm. Something will appear. A car. A friendly stranger. She was not prepared when she heard his voice again.

"Stop right there. You're not leaving."

Maria turned, and saw the gun.

"Zane?" Her mind was in free fall, part disbelieving, part having known it would come to this all along. Of course. It was predictable. If she had not been busy thinking about her own wishes – getting close to the Vice President – she would have seen it. Zane was a cruel, arrogant, selfish man. He had always been so. He cared nothing about her. How could she have been so foolish as to believe she could walk away?

Maria didn't move a muscle. "What will you do? Kill me too?" Her voice was level but her knees were trembling. The gun was pointed at her chest. He had killed before.

"I don't want to kill you Maria, don't be ridiculous. You know I love you, baby," he said.

She wanted to vomit.

"Why do you need me, Zane? Why can I not...simply turn myself in? I promise I will not tell them where you are." As she said this, she realized how pathetic it sounded. Of course she would tell them. And he knew it. She looked at him for a moment, hoping her eyes had not betrayed her thoughts.

"Right. You won't want to, I know. But you'll tell them. They are very good at getting information out of people. Especially kind, trusting people like you, Maria."

She said nothing. There was nothing to say.

"Maria, I can't let you go, sweetheart. Even if I believed that you could keep a secret – which I don't," he laughed, "don't you realize that you're my ace in the hole?"

She stared at him. Understanding hit her full force. Her need to stay close to Zane – and thus to her mother – had blinded her to the obvious.

"Don't you get it, Maria? They'll negotiate with me if I have you – remember, Brazilian citizen, innocent pawn...daughter of the Vice President?" His attempt at a smile made her skin crawl. How many different stories did he have? His mind was an ever-changing kaleidoscope of versions of the truth. But which one did he believe? One, none, all?

"What do you want me to do, Zane?" The gun was still pointed at her chest. Do what the man says. Whatever it takes to survive.

"Come back here. Help me take the license plates off." He motioned with the gun toward the back of the car.

Maria felt her body respond. Walk ten steps to the car. Bend over. Look at the license plate. Screws. They're held on by screws. Try to turn them with your fingers.

She couldn't.

She looked back at Zane, trying not to see the gun. "I cannot get it off. You must help me."

He laughed again, that boyish laugh. "And then what? You run off while I'm busy unscrewing the plates?"

"No. I promise."

"You promise." His voice was mocking. "Forget taking them off. If somebody in this neighborhood sees them, they'll just lift them for another car anyway. Go get some branches – and that old rag. Cover them up." She looked to where he pointed with the gun. There was a piece of white cloth – maybe an old T-shirt. She walked over and picked it up. Each step was a journey as she wondered...would the gun go off now, and make her body explode with pain? But he only watched, while she draped the rag over the rear plate.

She got leaves from the dead-looking bushes behind the building, and did her best to cover the front plate. Her hands trembled. Her mouth was a desert.

What time was it? When would this be over? Would it ever end, or would these sensations of fear, heat and paralysis continue forever, a hell on earth she had never imagined?

Zane seemed satisfied with her efforts, because he grunted in approval. "Okay. Let's go." She tried to make her posture look willing. If he would tell her where to go, she would move. "Wait a minute." He looked at the car. "We should check the trunk. Maybe there's...some food. Something." He reached in his pockets and felt for the keys. "Shit," he said, remembering they were in the bushes. "There must be another way to open it. Try the glove compartment."

She moved to the other side of the car and opened the door. The glove compartment was sticky. When it finally opened, she saw no way to open the trunk.

"I do not see anything," she said. Her head was down as she responded to Zane and avoided looking into his eyes.

"What, are you stupid or something? Look again." His use of the word stupid meant nothing to her. But she had become a creature living by careful observation, watching for nuances of behavior that might signal a sudden change in his intentions. A split second could be the difference between survival and death.

She looked in the glove compartment again. "There is nothing. I am sorry."

He gave a disgusted sound and opened the driver's door. There must have been a button, because the trunk clicked and bounced upward. He walked back and peered in. "Books," he said, throwing one aside. "A blanket. Well, we might use that. Beer. Hey...a phone!" His voice took on that tone that she knew meant he was pleased with himself. "Good thing I thought to look in here. Power ran out in mine. Hmm. A druggie like her... must use it to make deals. That'll come in handy. You take the blanket." He tucked the phone into his pocket.

Maria took the blanket and folded it over her arm. It was the scratchy brown of army surplus, and her arm immediately began to sweat underneath it.

Zane grabbed the three cans of beer left of a sixpack and closed the trunk with his elbow. He still held the gun in his right hand. He pointed it at Maria. "Walk," he said.

She headed up the littered walkway to the front of the brick building. It was three stories. The rusting metal door was swirled top to bottom with graffiti, and slightly ajar. Every window on the bottom floor was covered with boards. When she reached the door, she pushed it with the blanketed arm. A smell assailed her, and she shrank back from the fetid stench of urine.

"Go in!" Zane shouted, and Maria forced herself to move forward into the dark hallway. Some animal scurried off at the approach of her feet. She looked back at Zane, silhouetted for a moment against the brilliant sun outside.

"Where do you want me to go?" she asked. Ahead was only fear.

Behind Zane she saw a little girl on a bicycle, looking back over her shoulder at the man with the gun, and peddling as fast as her legs would carry her.

32

CATHERINE STOOD BEFORE the bank of microphones, wondering at the reasoning behind having this press conference outside. Perhaps someone thought that the American public would go easier on her if she explained herself while standing in the Rose Garden. It seemed a hopeless effort.

The President, standing beside her, squeezed her elbow. Yes. Of course. Time to begin.

She had, naturally, prepared her remarks. She had discussed the matter with pollsters, lawyers, aides and advisors. She had sought the President's opinion as well as those of her children and Nancy. They'd all had different advice, but each and every one of them was adamant that it was premature to address the allegations of Maria's birth. Wait till Zane is in custody, leave it up to the lawyers and the DNA tests – stall the inevitable as long as possible. Keep the emphasis on Zane. Express sympathy for the young woman who seemed to be caught in the middle of his delusional scheme, and assure the public that she – and the administration – felt absolutely no ill will toward her and had no reason to think she was guilty of any wrongdoing.

And it was good advice. She fully intended to say everything but what people wanted to hear. She would tell them about Zane, whom she had considered family. The shock of the blackmail letters, the betrayal, and the killing of poor Dan Sweeney. She would tell them that she was still eager and willing to serve. She would talk about rumor-mongering and being in the public eye, and the way the media scrutinized every little thing until no one in political life could come out looking clean....

And then she began to speak.

"Ladies and gentlemen." She licked her lips. "A very long time ago, I was young."

Startled laughter ran through the crowd. Catherine was surprised to realize that her statement was funny.

"A very long time ago, I was a college graduate with high ideals and a lifetime in front of me. I joined the Peace Corps, which seemed a wonderful way to give back something to the world – a world which had given so much to me, a woman growing up with enough money, and family support, to get a good education. I believed in the dreams of racial equality and a class-free society. I still do." Catherine looked around, but she didn't really see the faces in front of her. What she saw was her first love, Chuka, her mind turning back three decades to the memory of his face. She let the words fall out of her lips as they would.

"I worked in Africa – in Ghana. I grew to admire the hard-working people there. I made many friends during my two years of service. But there was one man who was more than a friend. He was...." Here she looked down. She wasn't telling it right. How could she make them understand?

Her knees began to buckle, and she clutched the podium to keep from falling. She noticed her white knuckles, tight from squeezing. She looked at all the faces staring back at her. Staring, staring. In the back of the crowd, standing beside a video camera, was a black man with sweat on his brow. He nodded, and suddenly there was one person who believed.

It was enough.

"I fell in love." Now the words tumbled out, a torrent which had been dammed for too long. Catherine felt wetness and didn't know if it was tears or sweat. It didn't matter. "I fell in love, with a wonderful, caring, wise man. He was Ghanaian. I loved him. He was easy to love." The man in the audience smiled. "And he loved me." Catherine smiled.

"As strong as this love was, we knew it was going to be over when I left Africa. He was married to another woman – and he had children. I was going back to America. We...we accepted the fact that we had separate paths in life." Catherine couldn't tell if the faces were with her or not. "In the Peace Corps, it was forbidden to become romantically involved with the local people. We worked side by side for two years, building a school, teaching children, praying for the strength to avoid giving in to our physical desire. And we didn't. It was torture." She stopped for a moment as a wave of memory hit her – the smell of his skin, the touch of his lips on her cheek. When had desire been so strong? So long, long ago.

"I was very young," she said, for no particular reason. In remembering, the fire of sexual heat seemed unbelievably powerful. A brute force. And the need to resist seemed some ancient taboo, written on brittle parchment. Why had they fought it so?

"In 1981, I was 26. I was the only virgin there." The laughter spilled over her from the crowd and she noted it without understanding why it happened.

"When my time in the Peace Corps was over, we took a trip – to Geneva, in Switzerland. It was beautiful. We made love. Finally." She was caught for a stunned moment by what she had just said. In a press conference being covered by media from all over the world. The crimson blush of shame crept up her face. She looked in panic at the faces. But now a few of them were coming into focus. Her man with the video camera was nodding, but so were others. A woman wearing red. A young white man with a shy grin. Yes. There were some people who knew, who remembered. When it was beautiful. Irresistible.

"It only lasted...17 days. And then he was gone. Back to Ghana, and his life. And I, planning to go back to the United States and to law school, learned something astonishing – I was carrying his baby." Catherine felt the urge to explain. "I had used birth control," she said, and then stopped. That was silly. They didn't care. No excuses. She held her head up. "I loved him." Her hand ran over her upper lip. She tasted the salt on her fingers.

"I did not want to end the pregnancy. I could not. For me. And because the baby would be his. I prayed that God would take the pregnancy away. It didn't happen." She had a momentary thought – I should talk about supporting reproductive choice. But this was not the time. "I didn't believe I could raise it – her – as a child who would never know her father – a mixed-race baby in a country going through its own painful racial divide. So...I gave her up."

An astonishing pain gripped Catherine in the middle of her gut. She bent over, turning away from the microphones. She grabbed at her stomach, knowing that it was over. The speech. The campaign. The dream of leading the country.

Wrenching herself upward with a force of will she didn't know she had, Catherine leaned into the microphones, whispering. "I gave her up. May God forgive me, I gave her up."

And then she felt the President's arm around her as she looked one final time at the faces. Wide-eyed, shaking their heads, a few crying.

She left the podium, supported by President Drummond and Ralph Harwood, wondering exactly when the future had flown away.

§

Zane had set them up on the third floor of the building. It was hot, but it had the advantage of a view. He was sure as hell not going to be taken by surprise. There was nothing in the room at all, so the blanket would be a seat and a bed. He settled down at the end of the room opposite the window.

On the way up the stairs, they had seen trash piled in corners, but the smell of urine abated after the entranceway. They had passed a bathroom, and Zane had waited while Maria used it. No water in the bathroom – just cracked mirrors, empty porcelain, and dusty, dry sinks. He flipped switches on the walls as they passed, but got no response.

"Want a beer?" he asked, from his post against the wall.

Maria shook her head.

"You understand, Maria, that I feel really bad about this. I didn't intend for you to be a prisoner."

There was no response.

"Maria, you've got to understand. This whole thing – I don't know how it got out of control. But don't you worry. You stick with Zane..." he laughed. "You'll see, I'll get us out of this. I'm figuring Catherine won't be getting elected President in this lifetime, which kind of blows my shot at an important post there – not to mention that she might not be my biggest fan anymore." He didn't really want to think about that too long. "But you and me, we got a story to tell. Books, movies, talk shows. After this is all over, and folks understand exactly what happened, we'll be heroes."

She wasn't answering, and it was getting annoying. He looked down at the little collection of items on the blanket beside him. "I'm going to put the gun down, so I can have a beer. But don't try running, because it's right here."

Maria nodded.

"Hey, we got this phone." He picked it up and punched on the power button. "It has power. Want to order a pizza?" He laughed. Maria looked away. She wasn't much damn company.

"Actually, we're going to need some food pretty soon." He regarded the numbers on the phone. "Maybe Will is home."

Zane pushed the numbers for Will's phone. He held the phone to his ear. It gave a series of beeps, but didn't connect. Shit.

"Maria." She looked up. Damn, she still looked sexy to him, hot and sweaty and prisoner that she was – she turned him on. Well, why couldn't he order her to service him? But the idea lost its appeal when he looked at the hate in her eyes. Bitch would probably run out the door just after he came, when the muscles had stopped twitching and pheromones made him sleepy as a cat.

"Do you know anyone you could trust to bring us supplies? We're going to need some food, some water."

Maria just stared at him again. He couldn't trust her to call anyone anyway – she'd just give up their location. Happily, she didn't really know where they were. But she might call the police. He tucked the phone into his pocket.

He was hungry. They hadn't eaten since leaving the basement this morning after the reward was announced. There was a handy antidote to hunger, though. He pulled out his baggy, now half full, and was overcome with a feeling of gratitude for the powdery white substance inside. This, he could count on. Coke never let him down.

He picked up a piece of cardboard from a pile of trash in the corner, and brought it over to the blanket. He used it to set out some short lines. He looked over at Maria.

Nothing to do but wait now. He felt a momentary panic as the babble of voices rose in his head.

Right. You da man now, Zane. Cokehead, extortionist, murderer. Getting it over on your girlfriend with a gun. Fucked up your life for good now. Nowhere to go from here.

Zane snorted up the lines, one by one, desperate to drown out the voices. He ignored Maria's eyes on him. He knew what she thought.

The hit was just reaching his head in a satisfying rush of snow when he heard the sirens coming.

33

CATHERINE WAS IN the President's private quarters, on the third floor. She was sitting on a sofa with a pitcher of water at her side. Several worried people stood around her. President Drummond, his wife Brenda, the President's personal physician, and Nancy, whom she had asked for when she got back into the White House from the Rose Garden.

After Catherine had left the microphones, she held onto the President's arm as he helped her get back into the building. Secret Service men several deep were walking within three feet on all sides. Everything seemed close and hot. Her lungs struggled to pull oxygen out of the solid air around her as she concentrated on staying upright.

But the coolness of the White House hit her like a startling dose of reality. Immediately it struck her as ridiculously Victorian for a woman to swoon from describing a doomed love affair that had taken place three decades ago. So she asked for a glass of water and had been protesting that she was fine ever since.

The people standing around her now weren't buying it, however. They kept taking her pulse and asking her if she wanted to lie down. Finally, she got mad.

She stood up. "No, I don't want to lie down, and if one more person asks me to, I'm going to hit him. I'm fine. A little embarrassed, for damn sure, but fine. I certainly am not suffering from anything physical – anything that medicine can fix. Now if you have something to revive a presidential campaign, I just might be interested. Otherwise, I would kindly request that you all get the hell out of here and let me recuperate from what I just inflicted on the American public all by myself." By the time she finished, her hands were on her hips.

Nancy started clapping slowly, and the others laughed.

"Yup. You're fine, all right." Drummond shook his head. "Though I sure thought you'd gone off the deep end when you started that speech outside."

Catherine put both hands to her face. "Don't remind me. I barely know what I said. But whatever it was, I'm sure I'll never live it down. Do you think I can plead temporary insanity?"

Nancy came over and touched her arm. "Catherine, I saw it on CNN. You have nothing to be ashamed of. It was true, and it was real, and I was...so proud of you." There were tears in her eyes.

Catherine hugged her friend close. "Ah, Nance, it was stupid. It was probably the stupidest thing I've done in my life. I don't know why I did it – maybe I really was crazy for a minute."

She pulled away from Nancy's curly head and looked at her dark loving eyes. "At the time, it seemed to make sense. I guess it was the confession I've been dying to make for 30 years. I should have picked a priest instead of an international audience and a press conference in the Rose Garden."

Catherine looked around at the kind people gathered in the room. "Anyway, it was a hell of a way to leave the campaign, eh? Out with a bang." She laughed. "So to speak."

"Why are you talking as though it's over?" Drummond asked. "You didn't quit. You told the truth." His voice was both wry and sympathetic. "More politicians should try that."

Catherine was about to respond when the phone rang on the table to the right of Drummond. He picked it up.

"Yes?" he said.

His eyebrows shot up. He looked over at Catherine. "They've found them. Zane and the girl. Right here in D.C."

Catherine felt frightening and contradictory reactions fight for space in her throat. "So – are they taking them into custody?"

Drummond signaled for quiet. His face registered concern at whatever he was hearing, and then he replaced the phone in its cradle.

He turned and looked at Catherine. "Zane is holding the girl – your daughter – hostage. He's got a gun."

§

First the police cars had come. The sirens, the twirling lights. Flashing red in the twilight of a hot D.C. night. The "whoop, whooop, whooooop" of a cruiser's mating call. A bullhorn.

"It's the FBI! We know you're in there, Mr. Zarillo. We have you surrounded! Come out with your hands up!"

Maria had cowered against the wall then, her eyes a terrified gold, like some kind of exotic tiger trapped in a cage. She said nothing. She hadn't spoken to him in a long time now. It was hard to remember just a few hours ago, when she had been his lover, his girl, his partner and confidante.

Now she was his prisoner.

"No!" He shouted out the window to the Feds below. "We're not coming out. And if you come in, I'll shoot her!" He pulled Maria to the window by her long curly hair, and made her lean out so they could see. Her face was twisted with fear. That beautiful face, which had once looked on him with such adoration. She knew he was just doing this because he had to! Why did she have to look that way?

He wanted to punish her for changing her face.

She hates you. Why shouldn't she?

He yanked Maria's hair tightly against the side of the window so he could shove the gun up to her head. "See? I've got a gun. Back off! Or I'll blow her away."

A small part of his brain sat back and observed. This was like a play, or a movie. He was trying out for the role of the bad guy. He was the villain of the piece, but it was just acting. This wasn't the real Zane. Everyone who knew him would recognize that.

For just a moment he thought about Devon – Devon the flunky for the big loan shark, who had managed to turn Zane into a trembling boy – a boy who barfed on the side of the road at the thought of violence. Had that conversation happened only...ten days ago? Devon would be proud of him. Not a wuss at all, now. Zane twisted his fist in the delicious black hair. Show that motherfucker it's dangerous to mess with Zane Zarillo.

Already, a crowd of people had gathered, kids on foot from the streets nearby and people in cars who were attracted by the noise and lights. It was a big event. Something to do on a Wednesday night. Better than TV, even. Real life. With guns, and police, and a beautiful girl in jeopardy. They paid big bucks for scripts like this.

A mobile camera van screamed around the corner, narrowly missing one of the police cars. Now it really would be on TV. The sound of a helicopter approached. He was the big news. Zane Zarillo, on every channel, news at 6. He could see the glow of dozens of cell phones, capturing video footage that would go right up on YouTube.

With a nauseating jerk, another realization hit Zane. His mom would see this, his stepdad, all his friends. Will, Catherine, everybody who ever had an opinion about him, good or bad, would be watching Zane Zarillo on CNN.

Anger blazed within him at the unfairness of it all. They would make him out to be crazy. They would portray him as the hotblooded Italian guy, undoubtedly mob-connected, murderous and unstable. Never worthy of the high-level campaign position he held. The betrayer of a fine lady like Catherine Young.

"Get back," he screamed out. "Back off, or I'll shoot her."

The FBI pulled back rapidly. The initial flurry of motion had waned. This was a hostage situation, their stance seemed to say. We're in for the long haul. He could see the experienced hands organizing things. Setting up yellow police tape to keep the crowd contained. Staking out a good vantage point for the top brass to set up a communications table. Corralling the media into a roped-off press area.

As he watched, another camera crew hustled up to the front. More people were arriving. He realized that he was still holding Maria by the hair. The gun was by her skull. She hadn't moved.

He relaxed his grip. "Come over here, sweetheart" he said, gesturing for her to follow him across the room, onto the blanket, where they were out of range of the rifles the FBI were no doubt positioning right now. "You know I won't hurt you, Maria. This is just for their benefit. Sorry about the gun." He gave her his best charming smile. "You know I love you, baby."

Her face told him she didn't believe him any more. How could he convince the world he was innocent if he couldn't convince her? They weren't hearing his side of the story. Suddenly he realized he had to tell the story himself.

Of course. P.R. was always his forte. Spin the story; interpret the visuals. Give them your point of view. He needed some allies. Some folks who would see his perspective a little bit better than cop with the bullhorn and the dozens of telescopic rifles. And he just might be able to get them.

He remembered the cell in his pocket. He pulled it out and dialed Will's number again. The voice that answered was like a long-lost dream.

"Will, my man." Zane was smiling big. "Brother, am I glad to hear your voice. I need you to rally the true believers."

34

CATHERINE SAT IN the President's quarters with Drummond and Nancy. They were getting telephone updates from FBI agents at the scene, but nothing matched the instant reporting available on live TV. She watched in amazement as a circus unfolded before the cameras.

Though it was after sundown, the hot white lights of the police and the media had created a glow that was as bright as high noon on the street corner. A reporter, a black woman with almond eyes, was standing with her back to the chaotic scene and trying to keep from being jostled by the crowd behind her.

"As you can see, the police and FBI have laid siege to the building over my shoulder, an abandoned commercial building here in Northeast Washington. We've been told that Zane Zarillo and Maria Flores-Jenkins, both fugitives from justice since the issuance of warrants for their arrest, are holed up inside. However, it appears that Ms. Flores-Jenkins is no longer a willing accomplice, but is being held hostage. While the FBI has made no official pronouncements about her status, we have an eye witness report regarding the situation."

She turned and the camera panned backward to reveal the eyewitness. "Beside me is Keisha Morgan, a resident of a nearby neighborhood, who has been at the scene for some time. Can you tell us what you saw earlier, Ms. Morgan?"

Keisha Morgan was a skinny woman in her twenties. She looked at the camera seriously, and then back at the reporter.

"We come down when we first heard the sirens. Wasn't hardly nobody here at first. Police, that's all. And then that man

– Zane – he stuck his head on out the window and told the police to stand back, else he's gonna blow her away." Keisha pointed back toward the top floor window. "I seen the gun – pointed right at her head."

"Thank you," the reporter said, and nodded her head to indicate that the girl should step out of camera range, which Keisha obediently did. Immediately behind the reporter were a number of kids, ranging from ten to 18, who were mugging for the camera and making hand gestures. They looked like they were celebrating after a big win.

Just as the reporter began to open her mouth to speak again, the crowd surged toward her, perhaps in response to a police directive, and she was forced toward the camera. It was a surreal moment as she gripped her mic and silently attempted to maintain decorum. As she got closer, her face was out of focus, and she began to scream into the mic, "Watch out! Hey! The camera – "

And then her distorted face disappeared to the left and down as she fell, clutching at the camera for balance. Immediately the camera made a crazy arc through the sky, flashing past brutal white lights that threatened to blind the lens, and a momentary view of the cameraman's surprised face. Then the screen went dark.

The gray-white of static filled the television screen. Catherine gave a start when the President grabbed the remote to change channels. Now it was a local affiliate of ABC. Another reporter was standing in front of the same scene, with almost the same vantage point. His florid face showed the near-panic of someone whose senses are on high alert.

"...Camera didn't catch it, but just outside of range, a reporter from another network came dangerously close to being trampled by the unruly crowd which has gathered here as news of this stand-off has spread. I see an ambulance making its way through the crowd – " the camera swung to show the vehicle cautiously approaching a small cluster of people looking toward the ground, " – and we certainly hope that it won't turn out to be anything serious. In the meantime – "

President Drummond pushed a button on the remote and that reporter disappeared. "Where the hell is Serge? Which channel is he on?"

Catherine would have found it funny if she hadn't been in so much emotional pain watching the scene. "Serge Rothman, Mr. President? CNN is on channel 40."

He punched the numbers and absent-mindedly thumped Catherine on the knee in thanks as she sat beside him on the sofa. The screen showed Darwin Andrews, far enough away from the building that he was in no danger from the crowd, holding a microphone in front of a well-dressed black man in his forties. The corner of the screen said "CNN Live." It took Catherine a moment to register the fact that the man smiling into the camera was Will Jones.

"That's Zane's brother," she said to no one in particular.

"...Mr. Jones, you are saying that the charges against your brother are completely false?" the reporter asked.

"Absolutely." Will looked both nervous and eager to be on camera. "Zane didn't blackmail anyone. He was framed, by people in the administration who wanted Maria to disappear."

Andrews looked puzzled. "I'm not following you, I'm afraid, Mr. Jones. Are you saying that Mr. Zarillo did not kill the Secret Service agent?"

Will suddenly changed from enjoying the airtime to acting annoyed at being put on the spot. "I ain't saying he did or he didn't. I'm just saying that if he did, it was 'cause he had to."

"We've heard reports that Ms. Flores-Jenkins is now being held against her will. That your brother – Mr. Zarillo – held a gun to her head and ordered the police back, threatening to shoot her if they did not respond. What do you make of this?"

Will shrugged. "Man, if his life is in danger, I wouldn't blame him for doing anything. The FBI would shoot him in a minute."

The reporter nodded in polite dismissal, and was about to say something into the microphone when Will grabbed it and pulled it back to his own mouth.

"I'm asking the people out there to come join us here in Northeast tonight." Will was shouting, and Darwin Andrews seemed to be trying to decide if he should wrestle the mic away from him – or if he could. "Zane needs you!" Will yelled into the microphone. He thrust his closed fist into the air, then turned and started chanting "Free Zane! Free Zane! Free Zane," until the chant was taken up by the crowd which had gathered behind them to watch the reporter.

Andrews took the mike as Will shoved it back in his direction. The reporter pushed his finger against the tiny transmitter in his ear. "This is Darwin Andrews, reporting from the scene. Back to you, Serge."

Serge Rothman's face appeared on the screen. "Thank you, Darwin. It's evident that the crowd at the hostage site is getting increasingly more volatile. I think we have a helicopter shot." He hesitated for a moment, apparently listening to the voice coming from his own earpiece. "Yes...here's the way the scene looks from the air."

Immediately the sound of helicopter rotors joined a static-covered voice that played over an aerial scene. A new voice spoke. "This is Vic Leslie in the CNN helicopter. We are looking down on the crowd now, which has grown to several hundred already. To the right is the FBI command post. Onlookers are being held back by the D.C. police, but it is clear that the force is being stretched thin. No one anticipated the kind of crowd which would show up on the corner of Downey Street, here in Northeast D.C., to watch what initially might have been a simple arrest."

The helicopter changed its position, and angled down so that its camera was level with the windows on the third story of the brick building. "This is where the couple are believed to be hiding. They have not been seen for some time, since Zane Zarillo's initial threats to kill Ms. Flores-Jenkins if the police tried to storm the building."

Once again the helicopter moved, rising rapidly into the air so that the streets were visible for many blocks around. There was a line of lights moving slowly along a parallel main street, heading toward the hostage scene. "It is evident that people are still coming. It's eight o'clock in the evening in the District, and there appear to be many dozens of vehicles heading this way. In addition, local residents are arriving on foot in large numbers. We will continue to report new developments as they occur. Serge?"

Rothman appeared once again on the screen. "Thank you, Vic. Now we take our viewers to Pamela Kane, who is positioned on a roof two buildings down from the one where this hostage drama is unfolding. Pamela, can you hear me?"

A short redheaded woman was standing on the roof in what sounded and looked like gale force winds. She too held her finger in her ear. "Serge, I can barely hear you. This wind we're experiencing is from the numerous helicopters at the scene. The FBI is now telling the private helicopters from the television networks that they will have to leave the vicinity, to allow maneuverability for the government 'copters which have recently arrived." As she spoke, a man in a dark suit and tie hurried over to her and began to gesture with his finger. "Serge, I think we're going to have to leave. The FBI is telling us they need this roof. Back to you in the studio, Serge."

Catherine, sitting on the sofa beside the President, was swept away by the prickly unreality of what she was watching. It was difficult – impossible – to comprehend that her actions were central to the dangerous drama being played out on TV tonight. She found herself buffeted by an emotional hurricane, at the center of which was Elizabeth – Maria – her daughter. Whatever role Maria had played up to this point, whether willing accomplice or foolish pawn in plans masterminded by Zane, right now she was in danger.

Catherine discovered that her long-dormant feelings of maternal concern were alive and well. And fully ready to forgive any understandable anger that might have fueled Maria's actions. After all, this was her child. A child who had grown up without knowing how much Catherine had always cared. Always wondered. Always wished.

She reached mechanically for one of the sandwiches sitting on the low table in front of her. She wasn't hungry, but she knew she should be.

A phone sounded and an aide, standing in the open door beside the President's living room, strode in.

"Mr. President?" she asked.

"Yes?" he said, turning.

"The Brazilian Ambassador is in the White House. He requests an immediate audience in order to convey a diplomatic message on behalf of the President of Brazil."

"Aw, hell," Drummond said. He sighed. "I don't mind seeing him – I have to see him, if I want to avoid a political crisis with Brazil. But can you ask him if he's willing to dispense with the diplomatic formalities and just come up to my private quarters? Be a lot faster than if I have to put on a jacket and meet him in the Oval Office over tea."

"Absolutely, sir. I'll convey that." She disappeared back into the hallway.

§

Maria sat against the wall, numb with fear and hunger, but pleased to have a moment of relative peace. Zane was lying back on the blanket. His gun was on his chest, pointed toward her, and his finger was on the trigger.

Unbidden, her thoughts went back to her parents – the parents who had raised her. They had been loving but strict, and always grateful. Grateful for the beautiful daughter they said that God had brought to them. In Paris, as Maria had always known.

Her father's cousin had spent a year there, and that's where the "miracle" happened, as her mother always called it. The miracle of finding Maria.

Her parents were visiting the cousin in Paris, their only trip away from their mountain home in Brazil since they had been married seven years before. Despite her mother's prayers, there had been no children yet. Three pregnancies, but no baby. Maria's father had taken his wife to France to cheer her up.

When the cousin came home one day to tell them about a newborn baby girl that was available for adoption, Maria's mother rushed to the Parisian convent to talk to the nun who was taking care of the baby. She knew no French, and could only repeat, "Bébé, bébé!" The French nun, though perplexed, had placed the infant Maria in her mother's arms. When her French-speaking cousin arrived to explain, the mother was weeping tears of joy and Maria was sleeping peacefully in her lap. She didn't put her down again until she had completed a rosary on her knees in front of a statue of the Virgin. There Maria was dedicated to Mary and acknowledged to be a gift from God.

"My miracle baby," as her mother called her.

Her parents had taken Maria to that same church in Paris just two years ago and introduced her to the old nun. One evening, while her mother and father were having dinner, Maria went to the convent on her own and begged the nun, Sister DelaCroix, to tell her what she knew about the woman who had given birth to her.

At first the sister refused, but when Maria came back again, first praying by the same statue of Mary that her mother had knelt before so many years ago, the nun relented. She handed to Maria, who had only rudimentary French, a newspaper clipping from years before. It showed a delegation of American politicians who had visited the city, and one of the faces was circled. That face was Catherine's, and beneath it was her real name.

Pointing to it, the old nun said, "Ta mere, ma petite. Voila, c'est ta mere."

And that information had led her to her biological mother, to Zane, and finally to this point. Depleted and sure that her life would soon be over, Maria sat in the rubbish on the floor of an abandoned building, praying to God, to Jesus, to the Virgin, for intercession. For a miracle.

Why had she needed to meet Catherine? Why hadn't her beautiful, devoted Brazilian family been enough? They had been enough… until she learned that her mother was a powerful politician in America. And she wanted to be part of that. It was because of Maria's pride – her desire to be someone important, someone who left her little mountain town and made something of herself in the world, that she was here.

In the control of a madman with a gun, who was deranged from drugs and paranoia… and who could kill her at any moment.

She looked over at Zane and he opened his eyes. His fingers tightened on the trigger and he smiled.

"Maria," he said. "Come here."

§

Catherine, sitting beside the President, leaned forward toward the television. Rothman was on the screen again, and he hesitated a moment, apparently listening to information being fed into his ear. "Ladies and gentlemen, we have just learned that the government is bringing in riot police. There is concern that there are so many people now converging on this area, with so many different agendas, that they are becoming unruly. In addition, the FBI is setting up sharpshooters on the roof where Pamela Kane was just reporting."

His brow furrowed as he listened again. "One of the people who may be able to shed light on this situation is Reverend Ezekia Abraham, the pastor of Glory Baptist Church, where Mr. Zarillo and Ms. Flores-Jenkins initially sought asylum. George Dubay is there now."

"Thank you, Serge." The man speaking into the camera was a handsome man in his thirties. He stood beside the Reverend in the basement of her church. A number of well-dressed people sat on chairs in the background.

Ezekia Abraham was magnificent and powerful in a turquoise jacket and a scarf that provided a swirl of color beneath her face. "Reverend Abraham, what do you make of the standoff we are currently witnessing?"

The Reverend looked not at the reporter but straight into the camera. "I stand before you tonight, along with the apostles of the Glory Baptist Church, to urge calmness and restraint on the part of the law enforcement officials as well as the residents of the District of Columbia. It is clear that this is a volatile situation, and at least one life has already been lost. Let us contain our emotions – let us proceed cautiously – so that we have no further violence."

"As you have seen, Reverend Abraham, Mr. Zarillo is now threatening Ms. Flores-Jenkins, the very woman he claimed to be defending. Do you still maintain his innocence when he is holding a gun to her head?"

Reverend Abraham drew herself up to her full height and looked at the reporter. "I stand for peace, Mr. Dubay. Though I certainly condemn the use of a hostage in this situation, I am not making any accusations of guilt until I know the entire story. Desperate men do desperate things."

"So do you contend that this crisis is the result of actions that were racially motivated?"

"Let us speak realistically. We both recognize that, had Ms. Flores-Jenkins not been born of a black father, there may well have been no story – her white mother might have brought her home to America instead of giving her up to be raised by strangers."

"Reverend Abraham, are you saying that Vice President Young bears responsibility for the dangerous hostage situation unfolding before us tonight?"

The Reverend's voice rang with conviction. "We all bear responsibility, sir. The American people, you and I, the Vice President, Mr. Zarillo – and our ancestors." She looked directly at the camera. "This racial crisis is the legacy of slavery, an institution which holds sway over our nation to this very day."

Dubay turned to the camera and said, "We return now to the scene of the hostage standoff in Northeast D.C."

Darwin Andrews appeared on the screen, gesturing toward the ever-increasing crowds around the building. "Serge, as you can see, this incident has attracted hundreds to the corner of Downey Street this evening. A minute ago we began to see riot troops arriving, wearing helmets and carrying the familiar Plexiglas shields. The FBI is reporting that the crowd may be as large as a thousand, and they are doing their best to control the area. Privately, a law enforcement official has told CNN that the number of people outside the building has become as serious a threat as the man inside. Normally, they would have blocked this hostage scene off for several street blocks around, if only to stop onlookers from complicating their ability to negotiate safely. But because so many people streamed in so quickly, they are now attempting to play catch-up, and move the crowd back."

As he spoke, a voice through a bullhorn could be heard faintly: "Ladies and gentlemen, we will have to ask you to clear this area. Move back. That's it. Folks behind, please allow these people to move back."

Rothman's face once again appeared. "We have a reaction now from the Reverend Quigley Hutchins."

The familiar visage of Quigley Hutchins appeared. He wore a pale gray suit, and perfectly-coiffed white hair framed his smiling face.

A voice off-camera asked Hutchins for his views on the hostage crisis.

"While I don't for a moment believe that President Drummond's administration was terrorizing this girl, I have to admit that Vice President Young's actions were the impetus for a violent standoff which is sure to inflame race relations in this country. And what the American people have to ask themselves now, is whether this woman is fit to continue to serve – "

"Who decided to put this ass on TV?" Drummond blasted from the sofa beside Catherine, jolting her back to the reality of the president's private quarters. She turned in her seat as someone knocked. The door was in fact open, but the aide who had spoken to the President earlier was waiting to be acknowledged.

"Mr. President," the aide said, looking slightly pink of face with the formality, "His Excellency, Mr. Edson Pereira, Ambassador, Republic of Brazil." She stepped aside, and, with a flourish, ushered the Ambassador in.

Drummond hastened to stand, and seemed to reach for the buttons on a jacket he wasn't wearing. He might not have realized that he was also shoeless. He walked over to the Ambassador.

"Ambassador Pereira, welcome. I hope you can forgive the extreme informality of this meeting."

Pereira, nearly as tall as the President, nodded stiffly as he took the extended handshake. "I understand, Mr. President. I too, have been watching the events unfold on television." He looked toward the set, which was showing footage taken a few minutes earlier from the air. "It makes one wonder what we did before we had 24-hour news."

Drummond smiled, and then introduced Catherine and Nancy. "Madame Vice President, Attorney Eisen, would you excuse us for a moment? The Ambassador would no doubt prefer to convey the message in a confidential manner."

"I do appreciate – " the Ambassador seemed about to agree when all conversation stopped. A scream came from the television. A loud, female scream.

On the screen, telephoto lenses captured close up a scene that made Catherine's stomach leap into her throat. Zane's face was visible in the corner of the third-floor window, his right hand clutching a gun, his left crossing over Maria's pelvis as he held her there. Her torso was upside down, and her ocean of black hair spilled against the ruddy brick of the outside wall. With her body balanced over the fulcrum of the windowsill, only his arm kept her from plunging to the ground.

35

ZANE WAS HUNGRY. But there was no food. He'd had the last
of the beers hours ago, just after all the noise started outside. He
thought for a minute, about ways to get food. Probably he
should send Maria out there. Yeah, they wouldn't shoot her.
She could go get something...or maybe they would shoot her.
He didn't care. She had changed. Bitch. Didn't talk to him
anymore. Looked at him like he was some kind of crazy man.
Pissed him off.

He looked across the room at Maria. She no longer shared
this side of the room with him – the side with the blanket, the
empty beer bottles, and the phone. His little collection of stuff.

She sat directly under the window, where she had fallen
down, trembling, when he pulled her back in. He wasn't exactly
sure why he had pulled her to the window and dangled her
upside down. But he had needed to look out – see what was
going on. And he couldn't do it without Maria to cover him.
Just for fun, he had shouted "Back off!" one more time, and then
disappeared from the window, before they could pick him off.
There were guys with rifles everywhere. Roofs, windows,
probably in the helicopters circling above. He knew how this
worked. He'd been around.

After he pulled away from the window, he heard a roar.
Lots of people out there. That was Will's doing. Will had said
he'd get some folks out for Zane. Good old Will. Who could
you count on but your brother?

Once in a while he heard chanting. "Free Zane! Free
Zane!" That was nice. Free Zane.

Or the police would try to bait him. "Zane, it's the FBI. We'd like to talk to you. Please come to the window. We'd like to find out what you want."

Did they think he was stupid? Come to the window alone, and he'd be a dead man within 30 seconds. They'd pick him off clean if he gave them an instant's opportunity. He was going to take his time, wait until he'd worn them down a bit. Wait until they were anxious. And then he would talk. He didn't know yet exactly what he would say.

Zane looked across the room, in the shadows under the window. Maria was lying down, her left arm tucked under her head. Beautiful girl. He'd done all this for her, and she didn't even appreciate it. Defended her – protected her honor. Even shot a man for her. If not for Zane, Maria would be some orphan in Brazil.

Perhaps that wasn't quite right. But it didn't matter anymore. He couldn't get all the things that had gone on exactly straight, but it would be okay. He had Maria – she would buy his freedom.

Zane reached into his jacket and started to pull out his best pal – his only pal. His little baggy. As he unzipped the top, he realized that the stash was almost gone. Couldn't worry about that. Good Lord would provide. That's what his grandmother used to say. He needed some now.

Him and coke. Coke and him. Best buds.

He poured some out onto the cardboard. He lined it up and sniffed it in. Head clouds. Jesus. Mmmm.

For a moment he leaned against the wall, loving the shoots of delight that zipped through his body. And then a funny thought caught him. Devon. Scary old Devon. Maybe he was outside talking to the Feds about Zane. Sitting down with the head of the FBI to say, "Hey, this guy Zane owes me some bread. I want a piece of him!"

Zane laughed out loud, and Maria stirred. Sweet little thing. He'd protect her. So cute when she slept. Catherine's grown-up girl.

He picked up the cardboard and licked it. That was the end. No more. He tossed it across the room.

Maria jumped at the noise, in such fear that she was on her feet instantly, a wild woman with hair tumbling across her face. The noise outside picked up, "There she is!" someone screamed. She dropped to the floor immediately.

The cell phone rang.

What the hell? Zane picked it up and pushed the talk button. "Yeah?"

"Zane Zarillo?"

"Yeah. Who is this?"

"This is Ray. I'm with the FBI. We'd like to talk to you."

Zane gave a snort. "FBI? How'd you get this number?"

The voice on the other end didn't answer for a moment. "Zane, I want you to be honest with me, so I'll be honest with you. There's no reason I can't tell you the answer to that question. Someone heard your call to Will. Someone with a scanner."

Zane didn't say anything.

"So, Zane. Let's talk. We're anxious to resolve this thing without anybody getting hurt."

"Right." He'd play it cagey. Don't give them anything.

"Why don't you let the girl go? Then we can work it out."

"Forget it."

"Zane, listen. I'm here to help you. You're not a bad guy, right?"

Zane didn't answer.

"I know you went to bat for this girl. You were doing your best to take care of Maria in a dangerous situation. Everybody understands that. Let her go...and you come out, and we'll talk about your options."

Zane laughed. "What options, Ray?" Use his name. Make him feel like he was buddy-buddy.

"Zane. Listen to me. You were – you are – a respected public servant. With your clout in this administration – and with the Vice President on your side, which I know she is – you're going to get heard. Your side of the story will come out. I promise you."

"You're full of shit. They think I killed an agent in cold blood. They're gonna shoot me as soon as they can see me."

"No, Zane. The Bureau doesn't work that way."

Zane laughed.

"I admit, there are more than a few guys who are steamed, who'd like to get away with that," the man said. "No judge, no jury, just a rifle shot or two. But this is the United States. We don't do that anymore."

"Yeah? Tell that to all the kids who get shot in the back by police."

The man seemed to take that to heart. Or maybe he was just conferring with his pals.

"Zane? I have someone here who'd like to talk to you."

The phone made clicking noises, and then Zane heard a female voice.

"Hello? Zane?" The voice sounded frightened. It sounded like his mother.

"Mom? Have they got you? Jesus...." For a moment his mind raced with possibilities. They had her. In some dark room with only a chair. Maybe she was blindfolded, chained –

"Zane, honey, what do you mean 'got me?' I'm standing with the FBI, outside of the building where you are. Son, won't you please come out? We love you, and we don't want you hurt." Now a sob pushed through her brave words.

"Don't you worry, Mom. I'll be okay."

"But what are you doing? That beautiful girl – Maria. They told me you threatened her. I thought you loved her."

He couldn't bear to hear the anguish in his mother's voice.

"I do, Mom. It's all for her." Jesus. Didn't anybody understand?

"How could it be for her, Zane honey? You held a gun to her head. She must be terrified."

"No, she's not terrified. She's fine. She's asleep. I explained it to her – that it was just for show." He waved his arm across at Maria, as if they could see. She wasn't asleep, though, she was staring at him as though he ought to be in a cage. He hated that face.

"I can't talk any more. Gotta go." He hung up the phone, and dropped it on to the blanket.

It rang again, and he picked it up. "I told you I can't talk any more." His head felt as though it might explode. He stalked along the one dark wall.

"Zane?" It was the man's voice again. "It's Ray."

"What do you want?"

"Zane, that's what we want to know. What do you want? Tell me what it would take to get you and Maria out of there safely. Whatever it is, as long as it's within reason, I'll do my level best to get it for you."

"What, you mean like money?" For a moment, Zane had the dizzying thought that his troubles were over. Ask for the money he needed to pay Devon, and he would be out of danger. And then the smothering weight of where he was crushed that instant of hope.

"Money, or – a plea bargain. Your side of the story told. Whatever would help you walk out now."

Somehow the earnest tones of this guy and all his government friends, sitting outside trying to outsmart him, infuriated Zane. He pulled the phone away from his ear and punched the power button off. He looked at Maria, who was careful to avert her eyes.

"They got my mother out there, can you believe it?"

Maria didn't respond.

"Say something."

Her eyes moved around the room, as though she wanted to, but she'd forgotten how to speak.

He lifted the gun and pointed it. "Say something!"

"Of course. Yes. I will say whatever you want. What do you want me to say?" Maria was plastered against the opposite wall, her arms up, looking as though she would will her body through solid brick and out into the open air. "Let us talk, Zane. Yes, we should talk."

Zane smiled. He liked this kind of responsiveness. It was only what he deserved.

"What do you want to talk about?" He was flirting now, and he could tell she liked it. His baby was still hot for him, even with police surrounding the building. He remembered the warmth of her hot salty lips on his.

"Whatever you want, Zane. You tell me. We can talk about whatever you want."

"Come over here." Something in her reluctant moves told him she knew what he wanted. It turned him on. This time, she'd do it for him.

He waved the gun lazily in the air, then looked at her as she crouched low and made her way across the floor, avoiding the stripes of brightness that came in from flood lights hooked up by the government. He pulled the blanket into the corner, where no lights could find them. An idea hit him. A delicious, wicked idea.

"Stand in the light."

"What?" she asked. She looked out at the floodlights mounted across the street. "But they'll see me."

"So?"

"They will...they will shoot."

"Shoot you? No baby. You're the angel in this show. Don't you know? You're the innocent – my lamb. You've done nothing to be ashamed of." His voice was caressing her now, a lullaby.

"But you said...." She was puzzled, angry. Spent.

"I said a lot of things, baby. You ought to know by now not to listen to everything Zane tells you." He smiled. He loved her so. And she was so beautiful.

Beautiful, innocent Maria. Catherine's daughter. Her family, her blood. At his command. "Take off your clothes."

"What?" A note of fear in her voice.

You're sick, man. What do you think? You're getting it over on Catherine by humiliating her daughter? They're calling you crazy out there. They're right.

He lifted the gun, still lying heavy and throbbing in his hand, and pointed it at her chest. "Take them off."

She stood and began to lift the T-shirt over her head.

"No," he said. "In the light."

Her eyes didn't leave him as she moved into the light. It was so bright he could see her shape through the T-shirt. Her back was to the window.

"Wait. Face that way."

She knew what he meant. She turned, and pulled the T-shirt over her head. Her movements were neither sultry nor fearful. She just did it. Jeans. Bra, quickly unhooked. Panties, sliding down to the dirty floor. When she was finished, she stood in the flood lights, waiting for his direction.

"Come over here, baby." He was on the blanket, in the shadows. Everything was out of control. Except Maria. She was his.

She walked across the room to him and lay down. Her eyes were dead.

He held the gun in his right hand. A smile lit his face as he reminded himself not to shoot.

36

CATHERINE HAD LEFT the White House around midnight after watching for several horrifying moments as Maria dangled upside down from the window. When Zane finally pulled her back to safety, Catherine knew she was going to burst into tears or start screaming, and neither seemed appropriate in front of the President and the Brazilian Ambassador. She excused herself, and she and Nancy were driven home by a couple of very discreet Secret Service agents who pretended to ignore the mumbles, wails and curses she finally let loose in the back seat of the limo.

Now home, she was sitting with Nancy in the comfortable back den. She was still wearing the pink summer suit and white silk blouse she had worn for the press conference. She hadn't had the energy to change, but she peeled away the jacket and kicked off her shoes as soon as she hit the couch.

At 3:30 a.m. Nancy made them strong coffee with shots of something even stronger. It didn't help, much. They had been up all night, talking, commiserating, watching the events unfold. Nancy had tried to persuade her to turn off the TV, but Catherine had refused. She wanted to know what was happening – no matter how horrible – as it happened. As if by watching, she could keep the worst from coming to pass.

Neither Zane nor Maria had been seen since his threat to propel her out of the window and down into the scraggly dirt yard below. But there had been a moment when Serge Rothman had listened to his earpiece and started to report something. "Ladies and gentlemen, we are unable to see Mr. Zarillo or Ms.

Flores-Jenkins from where our cameras are situated, but our sources have learned that the FBI has seen movement inside the room on the third floor where they are holed up. It seems that Ms. Flores-Jenkins is visible in the window right now, and she appears to be...."

Rothman stopped speaking, his brow knit, and then understanding passed across his face. "Right. The report is that she was simply visible for a moment. Unfortunately, we couldn't get anything on camera."

Pain was coming over Catherine in waves as she watched the talking faces, the aerial shots, the taped footage of Zane dangling Maria from the window. This was the daughter, the little baby girl she had never known. The child she had cried over in her dreams and in her secret memories for nearly 30 years. And now it might be too late to ever know her.

Catherine had wanted to rush to Downey Street the moment she had seen what was happening. But Drummond and Nancy had persuaded her that it would be better for Maria if she didn't show up. Her presence might get Zane spinning out of control, and his threats to kill might turn from braggadocio into metal bullets singing through the air. No matter how untrue, they argued, he believed that Catherine had betrayed him by giving up her daughter, and fanning those flames would be the wrong thing to do. Let the FBI work it out, Drummond kept repeating.

But it was getting harder to bear every minute.

The doorbell rang, and Nancy jumped up to get it. It was almost 6:00 a.m. "Expecting someone?" she asked, a puzzled look on her face.

Catherine shook her head.

In a moment, Nancy came back down the hallway, trailed by Lily and Mike. Lily ran into her mother's arms. "Oh, Mom. I feel so rotten." She hugged Catherine tightly. "I'm sorry I didn't come sooner. I know I've been missing in action. It's just...it took a while for me to adjust to the idea of this...sister." Now she looked up, tears glowing in her eyes. "But I saw your speech today – great speech by the way – " she laughed but it came out as a hiccup, "and then I saw...um...Maria...in the window with Zane and the gun...." Her voice petered out.

Catherine felt great sobs building up in her chest, and wondered for a moment why she always fought them so. In her own damn house, in the middle of a night when her newly-found daughter was being held hostage, she could cry. And so she did, with one arm around Lily and the other around Mike, who looked slightly alarmed to see his mother in tears. For several minutes they stayed that way, Lily and Catherine both sobbing together, and Mike an uncomfortable silent third.

Finally Catherine turned to him alone. "Mike. Thanks for coming over." She pulled him to her again, though he was nearly a head taller.

"Sure, Mom," he said. "Is there anything...anything we can do?"

"No." She patted him on the cheek. "Just being here is good. This way I know the two of you are safe." She pulled both of them down on the old sofa, and just for a moment saw them as children again, jumping over the back of this same couch.

Lily, at seven, her hair in a pixie cut, taunting her brother. She was the quick one, with a height advantage at that stage and two years seniority. But Mike made up for lack of speed by fearlessness. Tears sprung to Catherine's eyes as she pictured them playing together, all those years ago. How would their lives have been different if there had been a big sister, a child from another relationship, who was not their father's baby? Could her husband have accepted Maria? Paul was a wonderful man, but.... Swiftly, Catherine banished the vision. There was no point now in imagining what might have been. She grabbed a tissue and mopped her eyes for the fiftieth time.

Nancy was asking the children if they wanted something to eat, which Catherine recognized as an attempt to let the family talk alone, when the phone rang. Catherine picked it up.

"Catherine Young," she said automatically, her eyes still on the television.

"Catherine?" She did not know the voice, she could not place the voice. But it was a voice that had never left the memories in her heart. And when she heard it, a part of her came back to life.

"Catherine? Is it you? It is – "

"Chuka," she said, barely breathing.

"Yes." He did not continue. And it was enough. It was enough, after 30 years, to know that his mouth was next to the phone somewhere, someplace far away, listening to her breathe.

Catherine noticed, as if from a distance, that Nancy and the kids were looking at her. Whether Nancy had heard the name or not, she sensed that this was important. "Come on in to the kitchen," she said, herding Lily and Mike along. "Are you guys old enough to drink yet?" They left sharing a slightly forced laugh, and Nancy pulled the door shut behind them.

Catherine sat down, her legs twisted tightly around each other, her hand gripping the phone. He was here, on the other end of a satellite connection, and she was not going to let go. It had been at least a thousand years, and it might well be a thousand more, before she got this close again.

"How are you?" he said.

"I'm..." she considered all the levels of politeness, and then abandoned them. "I'm in pain. You've seen...the news."

"Yes. I was in South Africa, on government business."

She was ashamed of the joy that bloomed in her heart when he spoke. It was like rain in the desert. She had not known she was so parched.

"Catherine… we have a daughter! Catherine." His voice was an extraordinarily kind rebuke. "How is it that you did not tell me?"

There were no words to answer that question. Only days and nights of longing and excruciating wonder. Yes. Exactly so. How is it that I did not tell him?

Had it all been a mistake? These years, this life, her American lawyer mother Vice President life? When all along she might have been in Ghana, with Chuka and Elizabeth – Maria – at her side, living another reality.

For a moment, Catherine felt the room swing around her. Everything was tilted crazy. She reached for the arm of the sofa. She reached out, and as she felt the old, softened fabric, she heard the shouts of Lily and Mike tumbling over its back. Laughing. Her other children. Children who would have been erased from the picture if she had stayed in Ghana with Chuka. And they made her choice worthy. Much, much more than worthy.

"Catherine?" His voice was worried now. She had been silent a long time.

"Yes. Chuka. It's so good of you to call."

He laughed as though it were a funny statement. "You bore my child, Catherine. And that child is in mortal danger. I got on the first plane, as soon as I heard – before she left the church, and went with that bastard who has her now."

"Plane?" Catherine recognized that the question sounded absurd. "Where are you?"

"I'm at your front gate. They would not let me in, of course. You are the Vice President of the United States – even with my diplomatic credentials, they do not admit old suitors without a lady's permission." There was pride in his voice, almost awe. For the first time, Catherine realized that the static she had assumed came from an international connection was only that of a cell phone.

"You're here."

"Yes. Right outside."

"Then come. I'll call the gate. Immediately."

She pushed the button to end the call and then gasped as though an artery had been severed. His voice was gone. What if he wasn't really here? What if he couldn't get in? If something happened between the time she hung up, and...?

She shook her head at her own foolishness and tried to swallow a dose of reality. An old friend...a love affair from three decades ago. He was married, she was widowed. They were both much older. They had been through a lifetime apart. Nothing there but fond memories.

How absurd that her heart beat quickly and her hands trembled. He was coming. She punched in the number for the front gate, and told them to let him in. And then it hit her – the children were in the kitchen. What could she say?

The truth, of course. Catherine swung the door of the den open and headed for the front of the house. As she passed a mirror, she turned to look at herself. It was a habit she had cultivated for many years – a politician never knew when she might meet a constituent. A woman like Catherine had better keep her hair neat, her mouth lipsticked, and her pantyhose run-free. She never passed a mirror without checking. But she had not passed a mirror – in thirty years – knowing that Chuka would be looking at her any minute.

She gazed at the copper brown eyes, surrounded by crow's feet. It was so hard to remember what she had looked like. Long hair, red-brown, and braided, in the hot African sun. A hat, or bandanna, always. Bare freckled arms. So very very young.

She was startled to hear Nancy's voice a few steps away.

"Anything important?" Nancy asked. She stopped when she saw Catherine's expression. "Are you all right? You look like you've just seen...."

Catherine saw Lily and Mike right behind Nancy, carrying tall glasses with ice. Mike had a bag of pretzels in one hand. They were looking at her, waiting for a response. Nancy had her head tipped, as though waiting for a signal to take action, to know whether to hustle the kids out of there or not.

Just tell them. Catherine opened her mouth to say it, and found that she had been holding her breath.

"It's Maria's father. From Ghana. Chuka."

The doorbell rang, and she went to the door before she could register their responses. She swung it open, and right behind the door was a miracle.

He looked just the same, just the same and much older, like his own father. He had the old glorious smile and eyes that were deeper than the center of the ocean. She reached out with one hand and found that hand gathered into his.

And then she was in his arms again. The arms of a life passed by..

37

ZANE PULLED OUT his baggie. There was the smallest dusting of white powder at the bottom. The thought of no more coke made him want it bad. He poured out what there was, nudging it into a narrow row on his left hand, and snorted it. He waited for the rush, but got only a tingle. He turned the baggie inside out and licked it to get the last hint of powder.

His body ached from sitting on the wooden floor all night long. He hadn't wanted to sleep. Had to keep alert.

He looked at his watch. 6:17. Dawn was turning the walls of the room red. The crowd outside, nearly half a block away, was held back by cops in riot gear and regular bullhorn warnings to stay back. The street, which had been largely silent since about midnight, when a choir ran through a solid hour of gospel music, was waking up. Occasionally a police siren sounded a short whoop, or the heavy rotors of a helicopter came nearer overhead.

They were waiting for him. Waiting him out.

Zane hadn't thought about the waiting. Hadn't thought about a lot of things. Like water. Food he could do without, as long as he had coke. But since the beer was gone, there was nothing to drink. No water in the bathrooms – though they used them anyway. He had walked Maria to the bathroom more than once, bringing the gun along in case she tried to bolt, and now the stench was beginning to drift down the hall. It was humid already, and the day would be hot.

Zane looked over to Maria, sleeping on the dirty floor. After her little strip show last night, he'd slumped on top of her, satisfied, and she had shrugged him off and crawled to where her clothes were. Pulling her T-shirt back on, she tightened into a ball and closed her eyes.

As he watched, she opened them. There was nothing there but fear and reproach. It pissed him off.

He shuffled to his feet and grabbed the gun. It seemed heavier. For a moment he found his balance off, and put a hand on the wall to steady himself. He shook his head.

"Get up," he said.

She scrambled up, and still in her wild disarray looked like a tousled goddess, dirty, tired, T-shirted and barefoot. He still wanted her, and this made him madder yet. His mind was buffeted by gusts of fear, confusion, desire, and the need to prove something. He no longer knew what.

One memory rose from his center and pierced his gut with pain. He remembered the night – only just over a week ago? Was it possible? – when he rifled through her underwear drawer while she was sleeping and discovered the astonishing truth about Maria. And all that it had meant to him rushed back in.

This is Catherine's daughter.

Catherine must acknowledge her.

"Come with me," he said, and this time there was a hint of tenderness in his voice. He moved toward the window, the gun in his right hand. Maria followed, her eyes wide, alert. He took her by the left upper arm, and put her body in front of his. She was tall enough to protect his chest and neck, while he looked over her right shoulder and kept the gun at her head. Zane could feel the rigid fear in her back. She trembled.

Jesus! He'd told her this was just a charade. He would never hurt Maria. The woman didn't appreciate what he was doing? He was standing up for her. Putting his own ass on the line so she would no longer be a little black bastard disowned by her family.

He knew all about families where some were dark and some were light. He knew about it from both sides. Back in Jersey, growing up, people couldn't believe Will was his brother. Especially the teachers. Zane went through school slick and handsome and Italian-looking, courtesy of the father he never knew, and Will went into first grade as a little black kid that didn't get the same kind of welcome.

Sweet. He was so sweet, Will. His big brother Zane had looked out for him as a kid, knocking out any kid who dissed Will. And now Will was looking out for Zane. By getting folks to rally to his cause. He could hear them down below. They were with him, right?

Or were they just here for the show?

For a moment Zane felt the agony of where he was, and wondered how he had gotten here. Last week he worked in the White House for the Vice President, and now he was a fugitive running from a murder charge.

You always knew you'd end up in trouble. Or dead. You always knew you were faking it. A bullshit artist. A con.

His brain bubbled over with rage. He had to do something, anything, to stop the voices, which were almost constant now. Zane pushed Maria with his body toward the window. He could hear the noise change, below.

"Look. There they are!" bellowed a voice from the street. Scraping and stamping noises followed as hundreds of people stood and pointed upward. They all wanted to see him. Babies were crying, and the shouts of police could be heard, trying to contain the crowd.

"Stand back. Ladies and gentlemen, please stand back," someone with a bullhorn was droning repeatedly. The helicopter noises got louder, as they pulled closer to the building. Zane clutched Maria to his chest.

He looked down. For an instant, it felt as though the building were moving, and he steadied himself against the edge of the window with his shoulder.

There were people...everywhere. People of all ages and all shades of skin, looking as though they'd spent a night waiting for tickets to a rock concert. Some had chairs and blankets. Some had coolers. There was music, blasting out of boom boxes, thumping in the pale morning air. The police had kept them back behind a yellow tape, but they were surging inward now, their numbers so large that the simple movement of standing and stretching created a bulge which might push the crowd through the tape.

"Back!" shouted the cop with the bullhorn. As Zane watched, police on horseback came around the corner. They had riot helmets and sunglasses on, and they made sure to clatter right up to the folks at the front of the police line. It had the desired effect – the front row shrunk back, afraid, and the crowd behind them felt the push.

"Hey! Watch it!" There were screams from the crowd as some people fell and others were stepped on. "Juanita! Where are you, Juanita?" a mother yelled, panicked. "Where's my baby?"

On the right the FBI had cordoned off an area with a table and telephones in the center. On the left was the media contingent. Reporters and cameramen with equipment on their shoulders, microphone stands and light stands, and slightly down the street, dozens of logo'd cars, along with vans sprouting satellites.

"We're with you, Brother Zane," a young white man in the middle of the crowd yelled.

"Amen to that. Don't give up!" shouted a golden-skinned woman.

"Free Zane. Free Zane!" The chant began again, and it gave Zane a warm feeling in his empty belly. He might be thirsty, and he might be tired, but he wasn't ready to crawl. The warmth turned into a fire, and the fire a blaze.

"Listen, Maria," he said and smiled. "They believe in us. They believe in you. Your momma's gonna love you yet."

He leaned into her curly black hair and kissed it. "See what I did for you baby? It's gonna be all right. Zane is gonna fix up this whole mess. You'll see."

Placing the gun directly against her temple, he leaned forward, pressing his body against Maria's, and shouted to the crowd. "You know I wouldn't hurt this precious sister, right?"

Faces looked up directly into his, pressing at the tape holding them back, as though surprised that he was talking to them. "Right!" yelled the crowd on cue.

"Amen, brother," someone shouted. "We're behind you!"

"You believe this is Catherine Young's daughter, right?" His heart pounded.

"Right." They had their arms raised toward him. He was the preacher.

"She gave away her own baby girl! Her flesh and blood! She wouldn't have her in the house, 'cause her Daddy was a black man!"

The crowd roared and surged. The cops on horseback held up their batons. The helicopters buzzed overhead, moving in.

Zane leaned out further, swaying a bit, squeezing Maria's belly against the window. He smiled.

"You tell Catherine Young I want to see her face down here. If her child dies, the blood is on Catherine's hands."

§

Catherine stood riveted in the doorway of the den, watching Zane and Maria act out the horrifying dance on TV. She tasted bile as she tried to choke back the fear and anger rising in her throat. After the blessed moment at the door in Chuka's arms, all of the pain had crowded back in. And now she slumped toward him as they stared together at the television.

Their daughter, Maria, with a gun to her head.

Catherine heard the words before she knew she'd spoken. "I'm going down there," she said.

"Catherine, you can't. It's not safe," Nancy said, grabbing her arm. "Don't try to play hero here. This isn't a game."

Catherine shrugged her arm out of Nancy's grip. "I know." She felt a cleansing flush of anger. "This is my daughter. Why would I think it's a game?" She didn't let Nancy's reaction register. It was time to take action.

"Mom?" Lily ran over and gave her a hug. "Oh my God. Do you have to?"

Catherine hugged her and then Mike. She looked closely into her daughter's eyes. "You understand, don't you Lily? Mike?" She bit her lip. "It's not that I put her first – I hardly know her. But Maria...never had any of me...." She wanted to explain it better, but she didn't have the words.

"Go, Mom," Mike said. He nodded slowly.

"I'm coming with you," Chuka said. Catherine walked swiftly ahead of him down the hallway and to the front of the house. She called to one of the Secret Service agents by the door, and soon they were in the backseat of a limousine, making their way through the morning rush hour along Massachusetts Avenue.

Catherine's emotions were now under tight rein. She needed to call on every reserve, and tears would not help any more than screaming would. She found herself twisting a Kleenex in her hand as the embassy buildings passed by the window. They were heading toward the hub of D.C. – the Capitol building. From there they would cross into the Northeast section of the District, where Downey Street lay in a struggling section of boarded-up buildings and trashed lots.

And when she got there, what would she say? What would she say to Zane – a man she thought she knew – but perhaps never had. In his angry statement from the window, she had seen the rage that burned because of her actions. A part of her could understand that rage – if not the things he had done. To Zane, it must have looked like a betrayal of everything she claimed to stand for. A betrayal of him, and his family, and certainly Elizabeth – Maria.

Catherine was startled to feel a movement beside her, and to realize that Chuka was touching her arm. She smiled at him, but it was an automatic, polite smile.

"This is not what I would have planned for our first meeting in thirty years," he said, his dark eyes warm but sorrowful.

"Right." Catherine felt the tiniest flicker of annoyance. Surely he wasn't going to expect attention, at a time like this. There was so much going on. Zane, and Maria...and the hopeless campaign. Her political future was going down the drain as she watched the child she had never known – a child she might finally have welcomed into her life – in mortal danger.

Catherine felt powerless. It was a sensation unfamiliar to her. And it made her want to fight back.

"Catherine." Chuka's broad face was tight with misery. "I am as afraid for our daughter as you are. This is a terrible day for us – nevertheless, I feel joy in my heart, merely because I sit beside you now."

Catherine felt something move in her heart. A tiny fissure opened in a thick wall.

"Chuka – "

"Say nothing today," he said, holding up his hand. "You are in the center of a storm. Someday – there will be time."

"Your wife?" she asked, angry at herself the moment she said it. How could she even be entertaining romantic memories, when their daughter was suffering through such horrendous fear?

"I am a widower," Chuka said. "Kalla gave me 25 wonderful years, and when she died, I thanked God for our life together. But I never stopped thinking about my Catherine in America." He brought his hand toward her cheek but didn't touch it. "I never planned to come – with your political prominence and your family, you did not need a visit from an ancient lover – perhaps especially one from Africa. But now that I am here, my soul could not be silenced."

Catherine knew that she should discourage him immediately. Yet somehow the words didn't come. She looked into his face, a face she had known intimately so long ago. Could he really still care for her? And did she want to rekindle that flame in her own heart? They had been children – now they were strangers.

With a start she realized that her automatic reason for rebuffing him – the presidential campaign – might soon be a thing of the past. And then she asked herself if Chuka's race had to do with her instinctive belief that a renewed relationship was

impossible. Could Zane be right? Had she never taken Chuka
seriously as a potential life partner?

The phone rang beside her and she picked it up.

"Catherine?" It was the President.

"Yes, Mr. President."

"Surely you realize how dangerous it is to go down there."

"Yes sir."

"I don't suppose I can talk you out of it?"

"No sir."

"Harwood wants me to order you to turn the limo around.
For that matter, so does the Attorney General."

"I'll understand if you feel that you have to do that, Mr.
President. And I hope you'll understand if I tell you that I would
then have to resign, effective immediately, as Vice President."
Catherine paused. She sighed. "I owe this to my daughter. I'm
going to her. And nothing will stop me."

38

THE LIMO MOVED slowly down the street, pausing to wait as the crowd was parted by the police cruiser in front. The siren gave two quick blats every few yards. Catherine watched the faces stare in, most curious, some hostile.

They pulled up to the corner where the FBI had set up. She opened the door, and was immediately assaulted by the hot excitement of the mob. There was something dangerous in the air.

FBI agents surrounded her and walked her over to the man in charge. He was a tall man with a bald dome and intense blue eyes. He held out his hand.

"Rick Forrest, Madam Vice President. FBI." Forrest was looking at Chuka with an air of expectation.

"This is Chuka Obi, Maria's father." Catherine did not bother to process the reactions of those around her.

Forrest nodded at another agent who was sitting at the table with a headset and a phone bank. "We've been trying to reach them on a cell phone they've got inside, ma'am. Mr. Zarillo turned it off last night – but we figure he might turn it on again when he feels like talking."

"Has he spoken to anyone?"

"When we first reached him, he talked briefly to one of our negotiators and to his mother. He wasn't ready to deal."

Catherine looked around at the throbbing crowd, held back by the yellow police tape. It was hemmed in by dozens of police on horseback and on foot, each of whom had the edgy movements of someone on high alert. The FBI stakeout table was an oasis of men in dark suits, surrounded by police cars and government vehicles. She felt more than saw the firepower under their jackets and in the cruisers. Above her head were SWAT Team shooters, visible only because of the long-range rifle bores jutting out of windows and from rooftops. And in the air, Army helicopters hovered, their rotors chopping like memories of Vietnam.

Catherine saw Forrest turn as the man in the headphones signaled. "It's ringing," Forrest said. "He must have turned on the power. Do you want to talk to him?"

Catherine nodded. Forrest passed her a phone, and she heard the click as it was picked up.

"Yeah?" It was Zane. He sounded different.

"Zane. It's Catherine. I'm here – outside."

"About time." His voice was ragged.

"Zane, I...I wish you had come to me. This whole thing...it didn't have to happen." He said nothing. Catherine, afraid he would hang up, continued. "I know you must think – I'm a hypocrite, or worse. I'd like a chance to explain."

There was no answer.

"Zane?" She waited, and then spoke again. "Please... Maria is an innocent. Could you let her go?"

"Let her go?" He gave a harsh laugh. "Forget it."

"Zane...this is between you and me. Not Maria. I want you to let her leave the building...so she's safe. Let her go, and I'll come in – in her place."

Catherine felt a still coldness in her center when she said those words. She had known, deep in her being, that it would come to this. But she had not allowed to herself to think about it. And now it was obvious.

She must ransom herself for her daughter. It felt terrible and inevitable.

"You?" Zane gave another rasping laugh.

"Yes. I'm a more valuable hostage – the Vice President of the United States. Swap her for me."

Catherine could see the shocked look on Forrest's face. She didn't look at Chuka. Zane didn't answer for a minute.

"Okay," he said. "You come in. But no guns. And nobody else. If the FBI tries anything, I'll have to kill her."

There was a deadly sound to his voice that Catherine didn't recognize. She felt the pressure of time. He was on the edge, if not over it.

"I'm coming in now," she said. She handed the phone back to Forrest.

"You can't go in there, Madam Vice President!" Forrest looked at her as though she were the crazy one.

"He'll let Maria out if I go."

"But you can't...it would be impossible to protect you." His keen blue eyes looked at her with a measurement that was amazement tinged with disapproval.

"I can and I will. This is my decision."

"It's crazy...ma'am. You'll be shot. Let us send a man with you."

"No."

"Somebody could go in the back, while you're going in the front. We've checked the perimeter, there's a back door."

"No."

"Um...I'm sorry to sound disrespectful, Madam Vice President, but I think I'll have to check with the President on this — "

"Agent Forrest! Is that your name?" Catherine grabbed him by one lapel, and didn't care if he was losing face with his subordinates. She pulled him close to her face. "Are you aware that I am the Vice President of the United States?"

"Yes, ma'am." He swallowed, and she felt his Adam's apple bob. "We could physically restrain you, um...ma'am."

Catherine's voice held a sneer. "You want that on camera? You and your men tussling with the Vice President while I claw my way out of your grasp to go in and save her? This is my child. I'm not some crazy mother running into a burning building...I'm an adult in full control of my emotions, and I want to go in there and trade myself for her. I'm a more valuable hostage than Maria is — and Zane knows it. He won't kill me. He'll use me to get away.

"I do not need to get permission from anyone, including the President. He is not my husband, and he is not my father. And neither are you. I am going into that building now to save my daughter's life, and I don't give a fuck if you approve or not. The only way you keep me from walking through that door is by shooting me in the back. Are we clear on this?"

When she released him, he pulled his jacket down. "Absolutely," he said. There was high color in his cheeks.

Forrest turned to an agent at his side. "Get the Vice President a bulletproof vest."

Catherine became aware of Chuka standing quietly beside her. She turned to him. A shiver of grief hit her spine when she looked into his eyes. Was this a brave act, or a foolhardy move that would rob her of the joy of knowing him again?

He didn't touch her, but he looked as though he wanted to. "You know that I would do this for you. And for our daughter. If you would let me."

"No. No." Catherine shook her head quickly before she let the rush of relief flow into her brain. Don't think about the fear. Just act.

She took off her pink jacket and shrugged the vest Forrest had brought onto her shoulders. She secured it, and put her jacket back on. It was heavy, and already hot on her torso. For a moment she thought about removing the jacket. But she didn't want to look like any more of a Rambo than she had to. And wasn't that the idea of a bulletproof vest? That they shot you where they thought it would kill you, and it didn't.

Catherine repressed a shudder at the notion of bullets being stopped millimeters short of her chest. It was time to walk.

The FBI escorted her through the police line to the walkway in front of the building, and she began the trek to the stairs. It seemed a long journey. She had the absurd thought of Dorothy on the yellow brick road, walking in a spiral as the munchkins cheered her on.

"Hey. Look! It's the Vice President!"

"About time you owned up to that baby."

"Good for you. You go in there and get her."

A ripple of applause met her ears as she reached the front step. She opened the heavy door to the building. She stepped into the dark and left the sunlight behind.

39

CATHERINE WALKED SLOWLY down the hallway, willing her eyes to adjust to the darkness. The place smelled. Her shoes made crunching noises, and she wondered what she might be stepping on. There was a sudden skittering of tiny claws. She didn't jump – there were far deadlier threats than mice ahead.

She had her hand on the railing beside the stairs when she first heard him.

"Hey, Catherine!" There was a pounding noise reverberating down the stairwell. Like someone banging on the wall.

"Yes. Zane?" What did he want her to do?

"I'm up here."

Catherine walked up to the landing on the second floor. There he was, with Maria in front of him, her arm twisted behind her where Zane held it. She was barefoot, wearing a T-shirt and jeans. Her eyes met Catherine's and there was a slight quickening in their golden depths.

Catherine's heart dropped one beat. This is my child.

She looked at Maria's face, searching for signs of a resemblance. How beautiful she was. How mysterious, this adult woman who had grown to maturity as a stranger to her.

And how she longed to know that stranger.

Catherine waited for Zane to instruct her. There would not be a chance to correct any mistakes.

"Hold up your hands," he said. She did so. "Take off your jacket." She did. "A bulletproof vest? What, did they think I was going to kill you?"

Catherine had not looked at Zane closely. She had been half afraid to, fearing it might be seen as a challenge. So she had fixed her attention on Maria. Finally, she brought her eyes to his.

They were bloodshot, and his chin was covered with black stubble. He had an odd smile, and he waved the heavy gun in the air near Maria's head while he held her tightly by the arm. He was laughing.

"They thought I was just gonna go crazy and kill my boss, is that it?"

Catherine didn't know what to say. Her first priority was to get Maria out. She tried to think of what he wanted to hear.

"No – " she began, but he interrupted her.

"Take it off. Take the vest off!"

She took it off, and dropped it carefully to the floor. The stickiness of her silk blouse became cooler as the air hit it. She would rather have been hot. The security of the vest now felt like a blissful memory.

Don't be ridiculous. He's not going to shoot you in cold blood. She looked at him again, this Zane she had never met.

Is he?

"Do you have a gun?" he asked, his voice just barely slurred.

"No." She raised her arms high, and turned slowly 360 degrees. He seemed satisfied.

She pointed toward Maria. "Can she go now?"

Zane used the request to twist Maria's arm a little more tightly. She made a noise of surprised pain, and then quickly closed her mouth.

"You come over here," Zane said. He pointed his chin toward Maria's spot, and waited for Catherine to approach. As she did, he let Maria go and grabbed Catherine by the arm. It hurt. He twisted her arm just enough to apply pressure, and pulled her back against his body. The gun was six inches from her head.

Catherine could not breathe. This was too real. This was not some romantic gesture she owed her motherless infant of 30 years ago. This was Zane, a madman, sweaty and unpredictable, gleefully bruising her arm and holding a gun to her brain. This was death.

She was wrong to have come in. She didn't feel brave. She felt sick. Her gut was roiling with fear. What would it feel like to have a bullet slam into your skull?

Maria's wide eyes, relieved but concerned, held Catherine's as she backed away.

"I am so sorry," Maria said. Her voice was a parched croak. "I never wanted...." She shook her head.

A moment of serenity hit Catherine. A mother is meant to die before her child. It was better this way.

Horrible. But better.

"Go," she said.

Maria looked at Catherine for one moment longer. "I thank you," she said.

There were tears in Maria's eyes when she turned and ran down the stairs.

40

ZANE TIGHTENED HIS grip on Catherine's arm, pushing her ahead of him up the stairs to the third floor.

It felt strange to him to be so close to her. There had been times over the years when she had hugged him, in victory, or during a personal moment. But it had always been at her initiative. You didn't grab the Vice President and give her a squeeze, especially when you worked for her.

And now she was completely under his control. It felt good. A wicked notion crept into Zane's mind...nah. Bitch didn't turn him on that way.

It was awkward getting up the stairs with her in front of him. They made their way up, slowly, like some trundling beast whose center of gravity had been misplaced. He pushed her along the hallway until they got to the same third-floor room where he had sat with Maria. The scratchy blanket was still on the floor, and the empty beer bottles lay on their sides near the cell phone.

The crowd sounds came through the window loudly. They were reacting to Maria's release. Shouts and cheers rose up. Zane pushed Catherine with him toward the sounds. He made sure her body was protecting his as they stood in front of the window.

She was nearly the same height as Maria, but not as slim. And the feel of her body against his was not that of a trembling victim. It was calm. This made him angry. He tightened the twist on her arm until she panted. Still, she did not cry out.

He put the gun right against her temple. She rewarded him
with a quick shiver. He smiled.

Sick bastard. You're crazy now for sure, brother!

On the street below, Maria had reached the FBI agents.
They surrounded her in a quick swarm suggesting both
protection and imprisonment. Zane knew they would get her
story, and she would blame it all on him.

He watched as a well-dressed black man – African black –
approached Maria. He didn't have the look of an agent. Of
course. Maria's father.

"This is the guy you fucked?" He gave a vicious pull on
Catherine's arm, and she gasped.

"That's Maria's father, yes." He heard the pain in her voice,
and he liked it.

"So you finally admit it? That she's your daughter? Little
black baby you abandoned so you wouldn't spoil your lily-white
life?"

Catherine's labored breathing might have come from
physical pain, or from her emotions. He didn't care.

"Zane, I admitted it – yesterday. I held a press conference.
At the White House. I told everyone...that I fell in love with
Chuka in Ghana, and I got pregnant. That Maria is my
daughter." She stopped, and he felt the throbbing of her pulse in
the wrist he was pressing against her back. He could smell the
expensive perfume she wore. White Shoulders, she had told him
once. Of course.

"I admitted everything, Zane. The whole world knows
she's my daughter."

A howl of fury raged through his brain. She admitted it.
She did it.

She fucked that man. She let him put his hot hands on her.
She let him inside her. Suddenly Zane wanted to be inside her
too.

He pulled her back from the window and threw her to the
floor so hard that she slid into the wall. Her head hit and her
body slumped into unconsciousness. There was a trickle of
blood on her face and her white blouse was gray where the sweat

had picked up the dirt from the floor. He put his hand in front of her mouth and felt breath.

The voices in his head started up instantly.

You're lucky she's alive, motherfucker! What kind of plan do you have now, Zane? It was only a matter of time before you screwed up totally, and flushed your large life down the toilet.

The phone rang, and he crossed the floor in two strides to pick it up.

"Yeah?"

"Zane, it's Ray. Everything all right up there?"

"Sure."

"Can I speak to the Vice President?"

"No. You can't." His head was filled with darkness, and he couldn't see very well. He sat down on the blanket and shook his head to clear it. The man was talking, but none of it made sense.

You're gonna die, bro.

This was the endgame now. Maria was gone. He had Catherine. He looked over at the limp body against the wall. Right. Catherine. He had to keep them straight. She was out, but she wasn't dead. Not a good move to kill her.

Have to think, now. Nobody understands – nobody is ever gonna understand how he had to do this for Maria. Even she didn't get it.

It was always Zane, on his own, doing what was necessary. Fighting to get Maria recognized. He would never give up. But wait...hadn't Catherine said that she admitted...? Couldn't remember what she said. Bitch lied, anyway.

Had to get out of here. So tired, so thirsty, so hot. He was dying for some coke.

He heard the man's voice again.

"Zane? Are you there?"

"Right." His own voice sounded far away.

"Zane, tell me what you want."

"I want...money." Think. "A million...no, ten million." Yeah. That should last him a while. "And you have to get me

out of here. On one of those helicopters." He fought with the
blood throbbing in his brain. Think.

You can't think any more. Stupid!

"Helicopter to Dulles. Then a flight to...somewhere where
I can disappear." A brilliant thought lit up his mind. "A country
without an extradition treaty." He was sharp, all right. He
hadn't lost it after all.

Sharp? You're an idiot! Crazy, too.

The wheels started turning, a little sluggish, as though they
needed to be oiled. "Ten million in cash, and a helicopter ride to
Dulles, where you put me on a plane to somewhere...like that."
He was so tired of thinking. Of running. Somehow it felt as
though he'd been running all his life. Running away from what
he was to what he wanted to be.

*You can't run away. You're a failure and you've always been a
failure. Only everybody knows it now.*

He heard a voice coming from the phone.

"Zane?" it said.

He shook his head to clear it. There was a man on the
phone. "Right. Money and the helicopter. And Catherine has
to come with me – she has to stand right in front of me and be
my bullet shield – until I get on the plane out of the country.
Otherwise your cowboys'll kill me." He laughed and it was really
pretty funny.

"Zane, we wouldn't – "

"Save it, motherfucker. Get the cash ready. And the
flights. I'll give you half an hour."

"But that's not enough time for me to – "

"Or you'll find Vice Presidential brains all over the wall."

Zane laughed again as he clicked the power to off.

41

CATHERINE'S HEAD POUNDED as she made her way down the stairs, Zane behind her. Something beside her mouth felt stiff, and she moved her tongue slowly until she tasted the metallic crust of dried blood.

At the second floor, her jacket and the bulletproof vest were still lying on the ground.

"Give me that," Zane said, pointing to the vest. She handed it to him, and he held the gun between his legs as he tried to pull the vest over his wide shoulders. It made it over one but not the other. It was too small to cross his broad back. He tried it on backwards, and forced his arms through, but his movement was restricted as though he was in a straitjacket.

"Fuck it," he said, and tossed the vest down. "You'll just have to be my shield."

He pulled her close to him in the familiar tight grip, and twisted her arm against her back. The pain of his grip was a welcome distraction from the fear. Fear so complete it was pain itself. Fear so intense that ending it seemed like salvation – even if that salvation meant death.

They walked slowly down the last set of stairs and through the dark hallway at the front of the building. The door was partly open, and through it Catherine could see nothing but the white glow of bright sunlight.

As they approached the door, she said a little prayer. She wasn't sure if she was praying that Zane would be hit or that he would be missed. She knew she wanted to live. Either way, a prayer couldn't hurt.

Zane had her left arm locked behind her with his own. His right hand held the gun to her temple. She could feel the cold steel of the muzzle bite her skin. He didn't want to kill her. At least, not yet. She was his ticket out. But what if he stumbled, panicked?

She took a shuddering breath and tried to concentrate on the door ahead of her.

"Push it," he said. She shoved with her free arm, and the door swung open. The glare was blinding.

For a moment, they stood still, blinking. The helicopter was right across the street, its rotors chopping. A man's voice shouted through a megaphone, "Back up. Everyone back up now." The hooves of nervous horses clattered against the hot black pavement. And the crowd surged mightily, like a great beast that would not be tamed.

"Move," Zane said. Catherine looked down, and stepped carefully onto the cement stoop in front of the building. Slowly she maneuvered down the three steps to the walkway. She could see the people, hundreds of them, held back by the horses and men. They were watching now. Silent and watching, their intense quiet punctuated only by a baby screaming.

Zane's hand on her arm was slippery from his sweat and hers. He put his fingernails into the tender flesh around her wrist to keep from losing his grip.

It hardly felt real. It felt like a dream. At the same time, it felt like the realest moment of her life.

Step.

The gun pressed against her head.

Step.

Sweat hit her left eye.

Step.

His fingernails dug into her arm.

Step.

Her mouth tasted blood.

"We're with you, brother!" A voice from the crowd broke the silence with a sudden shout. Zane pulled the gun away from her head – why? – and raised it upward, as if in salute. Some instinct told Catherine to drop. She collapsed downward with a movement so sudden that Zane lost his grip on her arm and was exposed for just an instant before he tripped over her, and in that moment bullets exploded above her head, and hot Zane blood rained down.

Catherine rolled away. Zane crumpled inches from her. The crowd roared, and out of the corner of her eye, she saw a man running at her. It was Chuka.

Oh God. The sharpshooters would only see an unknown black man running toward the Vice President. She screamed.

"No!" But she couldn't scream fast enough.

More bullets.

He fell and she struggled to get to her feet, surprised to discover that her legs worked. She reached Chuka in two heartbeats and held his head.

"Hold on," she said. "Don't leave me now. I need you." The pandemonium around her stopped. The crowd became silent.

"I love you," she said, letting the tears anoint his face. She touched his neck. The pulse of life was still there.

Shutters clicked away in the instant of quiet. A photographer took the picture of a lifetime, one that would appear around the world and win her the Pulitzer Prize.

In the background, a watchful crowd of faces looked through a line of police. And in the center, a white woman in a pink skirt cradled the head of a bloodied black man.

The Vice President of the United States and her lover, the man who ran to her side through a rain of bullets.

42

APPLAUSE BROKE OUT across the large auditorium as Catherine wrapped up her answer. She looked over the crowd, half lost in darkness because of the blinding television lights.

To her right was the Georgia Peach, Jerusha Hutchins, looking as gorgeous as ever with her beauty queen hair and Southern belle smile, wearing a tailored red suit. The pre-debate discussions had included an agreement on the height of the lecterns – Jerusha got a hidden stepstool that gave her a five inch boost so Catherine wouldn't tower over her – as well as what color each candidate would wear. For male politicians, where the uniform consisted of a dark suit and a white shirt, the only note of individualism was the tie, and no one seemed to care if they all wore the same color. But Catherine and Jerusha couldn't show up in identical suits. So they had a coin toss, and Jerusha chose red. Catherine went with a robin's egg blue that showed off her Irish coloring. She had wanted to wear green, but the stylists were appalled at the idea of a "Christmas tree debate" if the candidates wore red and green on the same stage.

Catherine found herself musing about the fact that even women running for the highest political office in the country – especially those women! – had to worry about what they wore. And that her feet, as usual, were killing her.

She pulled her attention back to Jorge Martine, the moderator, as he announced that the final question of the evening would come from Gabrielle Lao, a reporter for Fox.

"Vice President Young, Governor Hutchins, one of the most remarkable things about this election is that, after never having a major party nominate a woman as candidate for President, this year we have both the Democratic and Republican parties doing so. How do you think this has affected the race, and what, if anything, does this historic change mean about the evolution of the political process and the country as a whole? Governor Hutchins, you have three minutes to answer."

"You know, Miz Lao? I think it's just wonderful!" Jerusha gave a big smile to the audience, which cheered. Catherine smiled too. Something they could agree on.

"But I don't think my opponent and I have much else in common," Hutchins said. "Her boss, the man in the White House... for eight years, he and the Democrats ... has been growin' government. And she wants more of the same. Tonight, y'all have heard – it over and over! More programs where the folks in Washington take *your* money – *my* money – *our* money – money from the people. And... come on... don't we Americans know better than the government what we should spend our cash on? I ask y'all!"

The Hutchins crowd erupted in applause.

Catherine kept her face carefully neutral, knowing that the camera could be on her at any moment. She stole a glance into the wings, where Lily and Mike were standing, ready to join her on stage after the debate. She wished Maria could have been there too, but Maria had gone back to Brazil and her parent's home in the mountains to recuperate and get some normalcy back in her life. Catherine understood how she would need privacy after the hostage crisis, Zane's death, and the wild paparazzi carnival that followed.

Catherine held close in her heart, though, the long and careful letter Maria had written to her about all the years of wondering, her quest to find her birth mother, and her horror about what that search had unleashed. Catherine was dying to have the chance to write back and explain her end of the story – finally sharing her anguish and doubt, and her joy that Maria was safe. And found at last.

Along with the joy was the concern that she was now even in the polls with Jerusha Hutchins. Catherine's youthful pregnancy and the dramatic events of last month had made great fodder for blogs, radio, and television commentators, and for a while it had looked as though her chances of being elected were over. But slowly, as the titillating details worked their way out of the news, her numbers were improving. It was still only the beginning of October. A lot could happen before November and Election Day.

Of course, every campaign speech she made was dogged by the Georgia Peach Pickers and their signs – the latest being a nasty two-sided one that said "SAINT?" on one side with a halo over the word, and "or SINNER?" on the reverse, complete with horns. It wasn't hard to see which one Catherine was supposed to be.

She forced herself to bring her attention back to the stage, where Jerusha was finishing an answer very much like all her previous responses.

"So we need to get back… on the path… the right path… not in the left lane!" Jerusha laughed, and her supporters cheered. "Left lane ends here, right?"

The official charged with timing the answers held up a red card, and Gabrielle Lao turned to Catherine. "Madam Vice President, same question. Three minutes."

Catherine took a minute to collect herself as she faced the camera. The last question of the night. This one was easy. Her staff had been certain that it would come up. For just a moment, the memory of her campaign staff, and the glaring absence of Zane, gave her pause. Then she put on her game face, and started to speak.

"Thank you, Gabrielle, for that question." Pause. "Yes, we're going to have a woman President, aren't we? At last!" Catherine grinned, and raised both her arms to the crowd. They rose as one and cheered. Even the Hutchins supporters.

She lowered her arms and turned to the questioner. "I was wondering when we were going to talk about that issue – the elephant in the room. Or in my case, maybe I should say donkey." They laughed.

"And I think that this historical moment is exciting, and significant, and it's about time!" More cheers. "But as my opponent points out, we are two very different women, who represent different approaches to the challenges facing this country."

Catherine composed her face and her voice to convey seriousness. This is what she had come to say. She didn't know how it would play, but she had gone through too much to get to this point in the campaign and not speak the truth.

"To me, my opponent's positions, and that of her party, are not just about the size of government and what it can do – or not do. Those positions feed into our worst urges as human beings. Hoard your money. Don't trust the other guy. Keep everything you have for yourself and your family. Fear the 'others' – people who aren't like you, whether because of their nation of birth, the color of their skin, their sexual orientation, or their religion." The audience was quiet. They were listening.

"And frankly, friends, this puzzles me. Because everything my opponent stands for seems to me to be antithetical to – and the opposite of – the beliefs she purports to hold. Her nominating party, and certainly the new and vigorous Liberty Party – draws in large part from those Americans who call themselves Christians."

The crowd seemed to hold its breath. This was dangerous territory. Where was she going, their collective attention appeared to say.

Catherine raised a hand as if to reassure them. "I would never be so bold – so crass – as to question another person's religious beliefs. I just wonder – maybe you can help me – where is the Golden Rule in all this? Where is the hand reaching out to our fellow man and woman?"

Slow and then stronger applause rolled across the audience. Catherine saw the timekeeper raising a yellow card signifying one minute remaining. "We as a people are at our best – this nation is at its best – when we throw off our fear of those who are different from us. When we share what we have to offer. When we give of ourselves and our talents and follow our bravest, our most optimistic instincts – and work together to find the strength to build our wealth and grow our country together. We who are the heirs to the abundance that is the American dream must lead, not follow. We must open our minds and our hearts to new possibilities. We must trust in the promise of a better future. For everyone. Not just the ones who look like us.

"This is what I stand for. This is what my party stands for. Not closing off, but reaching out. Not keeping everything all for ourselves, but sharing what we have. Naïve? Perhaps. Sometimes you have to stay a bit naïve so you don't become bitter." Catherine laughed, and the audience did too.

"And so I ask you to vote for me as the next President of the United States… so that we can walk together into the future… on the bold and brave side of history. Thank you – and God bless the United States of America."

Catherine savored the applause as it washed over her. Somehow everything about the campaign was sweeter since it had nearly slipped away. Her chances were not gone, and her motivation was more pure. There was still a chance that she would serve the people.

She was still in the running, and she counted it a miracle.

The moderator thanked the candidates and suddenly Lily and Mike were walking across the stage to her, smiling as though they had a great secret. Just as they reached her and she opened her arms to hug them both, she heard a gasp from the audience. Her children parted so that she could see – and it was Maria, coming out on stage to join the family.

Don't cry, don't cry, don't cry! The cameras were recording everything.

Catherine reached out her arms and wrapped them around her oldest daughter. If a tear slid down a cheek, it was hidden by Maria's long curly hair, and wiped away quickly by her mother.

§

"Vice President Young!" A gaggle of voices shouted out to her. Dozens of lights flashed as cameras clicked over and over.

The press was trying to get photos and ask questions as she and the children left the auditorium after the debate. Catherine pointed at a woman in front.

"The Washington Post is planning to run a story tomorrow alleging that the husband of your opponent, Reverend Quigley Hutchins, paid Zane Zarillo ten thousand dollars for information concerning your daughter, which Hutchins then leaked to the media. Do you have any comment?"

Catherine was caught by surprise. Quigley Hutchins, paying Zane? It made sense. That's where the first rumors had started – Hutchins had contacted the President himself to ask about her "virtue" and to suggest that there was something unseemly about her past.

Catherine paused for a moment, measuring her words. "If this is true, it is a matter for the criminal justice system. I have no knowledge of Reverend Hutchins' actions regarding Mr. Zarillo."

Talking about Zane still hurt. The pain of his betrayal had not tempered her grief at losing a once trusted friend.

"Vice President Young, you're neck and neck in the polls against Jerusha Hutchins. When people learn that her husband bribed your own campaign manager – a man we now know to be guilty of blackmail and murder – in order to further his wife's campaign, do you think she'll be out of the race?"

Catherine realized that she should feel happy about such bad news for Jerusha Hutchins. But all she felt was saddened for her, for her husband, and for Zane to have concocted this mess. "That's up to the American people."

Another reporter spoke up. "Vice President Young, we understand that Mr. Obi has recuperated from the wounds he suffered at the standoff on Downey Street, and will soon be released from the hospital. Will he be remaining in this country to spend time with his daughter – and you?"

Catherine felt the quick flush of blood redden her cheeks. Stop it. They'll think you're a schoolgirl.

It was another miracle that Chuka had survived. He had been wearing a protective vest, given to him by Ralph Harwood.

The word had gone out to the sharpshooters that he was a good guy, but there was a civilian vigilante amongst the crowd who had shot at Chuka when he saw an unknown black man running toward the Vice President. A bullet had landed in his leg and one in his shoulder. The vest had saved his life.

This would be his first night out of the hospital. Chuka would come to her home and have a chance to really meet the children. Maria would be there, along with Lily and Mike.

Her whole family. The thought made Catherine glow. She realized that the reporter was still waiting for an answer. She willed her voice to become appropriately formal.

"I am not aware of Mr. Obi's travel plans. Though I am certainly happy to know that my old friend has recuperated and will be leaving the hospital."

Catherine moved away from the press scrum, letting the rest of the shouted questions go unanswered. She hugged Lily and Mike in turn, and then put her arms around the tall Maria to say goodbye. It was still a new feeling to touch her daughter. To look into her eyes.

It was wonderful to know that she would have years to get to know what was behind them.

As she made her way to the Vice Presidential limo through the crowd of well-wishers, a contingent of Secret Service agents fell in around her. "Firebird is departing the site," one of them said softly into his wrist microphone.

"Madam Vice President?" Ralph Harwood said, making his way to her from the edge of the crowd.

"Yes, Ralph?" She found herself beaming at him. It was easy to be warm these days. The shell she had let harden around herself for so many years seemed to be slipping away. Now she wondered if she had ever really needed it.

Harwood smiled at her. "I thought you might want to look at this." He handed her a folded slip of paper. She opened it as she walked down the path to the waiting car.

The DNA test results were in her hand. And they stated that Maria was unquestionably her daughter.

A long sigh escaped Catherine as something relaxed inside. The baby she had let go of so many years ago was by her side again. The child she had never forgotten.

Her memory rolled backwards down the long path that had been this summer.

The blackmail letter. The roller coaster campaign. The media carnival. The fear, the pain...and the death.

Nothing could change the past. It was gone. The drama that had been played out was permanent. And Zane was forever dead.

Catherine stepped forward as a Secret Service agent opened the door to her limousine.

"Firebird en route to the White House," he whispered into his microphone.

Dear Reader:

Thank you for taking the time to read *Running*.

For me, the best part of this book was thinking about how it would feel, as a woman, to be a serious candidate for one of the most powerful positions in the world. While at the same time having a family, a romantic history, and the occasional sore feet.

I'd love to hear what you thought about Catherine and Zane and Maria, and the situations they found themselves in. Would you do what she did, or something different? Please come visit my website at www.PatriceFitzgerald.com and tell me how you felt about my story. It's always a thrill to hear from readers!

If you could post a review of *Running* online, that would be greatly appreciated. Better yet, tell your friends. Word of mouth is the best way to connect readers to good books.

Thank you again for doing me the high honor of reading about these characters, and this world, that came straight out of my imagination.

It is the reader who makes the experience of writing complete. I couldn't do it without you.

~Patrice

Questions about *Running* for readers

1. Have you ever felt a powerful romantic attraction that you tried to resist?

2. Catherine's decision about her baby was made 30 years ago. Do you think that things have changed in terms of raising a child whose parents are of different races?

3. In Catherine's position, would you have made the same choice as she did in Paris?

4. If you knew you were adopted, would you search for your birth mother?

5. Do we treat women politicians differently than men?

6. What do you think of the radio and TV talk shows and the Internet chatter about politics – do they help inform us or simply make money for the hosts?

7. Was Zane a bad person, or did he simply make bad decisions?

8. Would you have sheltered Zane if you believed that he and Maria were in danger?

9. If the events in *Running* really happened, would the voters support Catherine once her past was revealed?

10. How do you think it would feel to run for President?

Acknowledgements

Thanks are due to so many people, including Prill Boyle, Judith Cooke, Kyra Robinov, Annie Kelleher (who was around for the genesis of this story in the beginning as well as the final editing), and to Sara Strecker for her help in formatting the print version of this book. Thanks to the Housewife Writers – you know who you are. Thanks to the amazing artist who did the cover, Christopher Steininger, and to Emily Scott for putting it into three dimensions. Thanks to Ian Leslie for the eFitzgerald Publishing colophon. And thanks to my family, who waited patiently for all that writing time to finally turn into a book I could sell.

Richard, you were indispensible, as always.

About the author

Patrice Fitzgerald is a creative person who was briefly disguised as an attorney. She has spent the last decade or so peeling away the layers and rediscovering the artist within. Her writing includes tightly plotted and fast-paced novels like this one, plus quirky, ironic short stories about sex, God, and death – not necessarily in that order – such as *Looking for Lance*, *Jungle Moon*, and *Till Death Do Us Part*. Her short stories have also appeared in several anthologies.

Patrice is the CEO of eFitzgerald, an electronic publishing company founded in the summer of 2011. Her background includes a law degree and 15 years practicing intellectual property law followed by a decade working as a freelance writer for magazines in print and online. In addition, she is a professional mezzo-soprano who sings in styles ranging from opera to jazz.

Patrice is the mother of four adult children, two by birth and two by marriage. She lives in Connecticut on the water with her wonderful programming, singing, and trumpet-playing husband. She is thrilled that *Running*, her first published novel, has become a bestseller via Amazon KDP and has been read and enjoyed by people from all over the world.

About the publisher

eFitzgerald is a fledgling publishing business that was launched on Independence Day in 2011. What makes eFitzgerald different is that it publishes primarily electronic books. Omitting the literary agent and the traditional publishing house, the company is able to keep the overhead low and use the efficiency of electronic publishing to move rapidly from the manuscript stage to digital publication.

eFitzgerald Publishing recently introduced author Frisky Dimplebuns, who shares her comic adventures about looking for love in THE FRISKY CHRONICLES. The first three installments are Dreamboat, Ugly Sexy, and Stick Shift.

The eFitzgerald independent press is also proud to be the publisher of a group of short books written from the point of view of a young man who is developmentally disabled. Multi-published author Anne Kelleher was inspired by her own brother's experiences to develop these warm and unusual stories. The first in the series, How David Met Sarah, has been endorsed by the National Down Syndrome Society, and 20% of the book's profits are to be donated to that organization. These books are written at an elementary reading level to make them accessible to everyone, including those for whom English is a second language.

Look for additional eFitzgerald titles to be released throughout 2012, including a book of poetry, four romances, a trilogy of historical fiction, a thriller by a debut author, more installments of The Frisky Chronicles, a third book in the David series, and of course, the sequel to *Running*.

Made in the USA
Charleston, SC
10 July 2016